WHAT IF?

SHARI LOW

Boldwood

This updated edition first published in Great Britain in 2020 by Boldwood Books Ltd.

Copyright © Shari Low, 2020

Cover Design by Alice Moore Design

Cover Photography: Shutterstock

A CIP catalogue record for this book is available from the British Library.

Paperback ISBN 978-1-83889-126-8

Large Print ISBN 978-1-83889-824-3

Ebook ISBN 978-1-83889-128-2

Kindle ISBN 978-1-83889-127-5

Audio CD ISBN 978-1-83889-233-3

MP3 CD ISBN 978-1-83889-821-2

Digital audio download ISBN 978-1-83889-125-1

Boldwood Books Ltd
23 Bowerdean Street
London SW6 3TN
www.boldwoodbooks.com

To my husband John Low,
Who started it all back in 1999 by pointing out that if I wanted to be an author, I should perhaps try to write something. I still hate it when you're right.
But I love you and our family more than any words on a page.
You're everything, always...
Shari x

A NOTE FROM SHARI

Before you turn the page....

Thank you so much for reading this 20th Anniversary re-release of my first ever novel.

When I wrote it back in 1999, Britney Spears had just found fame with 'Baby One More Time' and nothing much was impressing Shania Twain.

Hugh Grant was trying to seduce Julia Roberts in Notting Hill and JK Rowling had just released Harry Potter's third magical mystery.

There were only a few TV channels, DVDs were considered cutting edge technology and we'd never heard of political correctness.

Texting was relatively new and had yet to gain mass popularity and our mobile phones were mostly just used to – shock – *talk* to people. Oh, and international calls were so expensive it was cheaper to go to Benidorm for a week than to call someone there for a lengthy chat.

The internet was a novelty that made a screeching noise when you dialled it up, and you could make three cups of tea in the time it took to download a page. More importantly, given the story in this book, there was no google, no facebook, no twitter, and if you wanted to find someone you just had to hope that directory enquiries had their phone number, otherwise there was no way to track them down them other than going to their house and throwing stones at their window.

Or – like Carly Cooper – saying goodbye to your whole life and going on an international manhunt.

I really hope you enjoy this step back in time.

And I hope you fall in love with Carly, her pals and the story that started it all...

Much love,

Shari xxx

PART I

1

Oh, bollocks.

I love that word. It has a 'don't mess with me, I'm a hormonal lethal weapon' ring to it. I've been muttering it dementedly since I got out of bed this morning, because I can't think of a single thing that's right with the world today.

I reach over to refill the kettle, dropping the arm of my dressing gown in last night's dishwater and knocking over my ashtray in the process. It's not going to be one of my better days. Before you start reaching for the telephone to summon a counselling service to my kitchen, can I just say that I'm having a midlife crisis. I look and feel like Liam Gallagher after a night on the tiles and I can tell you in years, months, days and minutes how long it is since my last sexual experience. But, according to every reputable (trashy) women's magazine, this behaviour is typical of a single female of my age. One who's having a midlife crisis, that is.

Do you ever think, 'What if this is all there is to life?' Do you ever contemplate your lot and wonder why you're not a super-model in Milan? Or the director of a multinational corporation?

What about married to an international business tycoon with homes in seven countries? For the purposes of this ponderance, I'm going to ignore that I've got forty pounds on any supermodel, I have no cheekbones, zero entrepreneurial skills, I'm a hopeless commitment-phobe and I couldn't handle seven houses because I get irritated having to run the Hoover round my tiny flat.

But all that aside, look at me now. I'm sitting at my breakfast table alone, having called in sick to work with an ever more ridiculous reason ('I stubbed my toe in the garden' isn't a bad excuse, except that I live in a third floor flat), with absolutely nothing to look forward to except a chocolate croissant and a long linger over the latest edition of *Hello!* magazine. I can't help thinking, 'What if this is it?' What if this is the way my life is going to be until I'm having Zimmer races up and down the corridor of my retirement home, flirting with old men and cheating at bingo?

I suppose I owe you an explanation for this sudden outpouring of self-pity.

My name is Carly Cooper. I'm careering towards my thirties at terrifying speed, and I pay an obscene portion of my monthly salary to live in a studio-cum-cupboard in the desirable area of Richmond, near London. I arrived here from my native Glasgow via a multitude of countries, adventures and disasters (mostly due to Mr Rights who inevitably turned out to be Mr Couldn't Be More Wrongs). I'm 5'8", with long blonde hair (extensions), blue eyes (coloured contact lenses) and ample curves (in many of the non-supermodel places).

I earn a great salary doing a job I detest and therefore spend every penny of it doing things I enjoy to take my mind off work. I am officially a National Accounts Manager for one of the world's largest manufacturers of tissue-paper products. Translated, this means that I persuade buyers of large multinational companies to sign annual contracts for the supply of their toilet rolls. Don't laugh. There's a future in toilet rolls. They'll be here long after all this modern technology like CDs and carphones are on a scrap heap somewhere.

I'm officially enjoying the single life with no significant other to answer to. Believe me, to paraphrase Jerry Maguire, I absolutely know that I don't need a man to complete me. I should just be content being a single, cosmopolitan woman of the world. But unofficially, off the record, and with apologies to my fellow singletons everywhere, I'm bored, fed up and itching to be in a couple again.

I'm beginning to despair of ever finding someone to snuggle up to in front of the TV, and snog the face off when I've had one too many glasses of whatever vino is on sale in Tesco. I've started fantasising about settling down and having a family resembling one of those nauseatingly happy ones in cereal adverts. There's no denying the irony of this situation. I spent the first ten years of my adult life avoiding commitment, and now that I'm up for it there are no takers. Karma is a bitch.

My only consolation in this sad existence is my trusty group of girlfriends, who, when they can extricate themselves from their children/jobs/husbands/boyfriends, love nothing more than girlie nights out with nachos, cheap plonk and buckets of salacious gossip.

We're like family, which is just as well because my when it comes to actual blood relatives, support is thin on the ground. My parents divorced a few years ago, thank God. It's not that I'd have been opposed to them living in happily married bliss, it's just that their relationship had all the compatibility and cuddly warmth of a civil war. My mum is a teacher, very sensible, very intelligent and very proper. 'I definitely found you in a skip, darling,' she utters dryly whenever I disappoint her in any way, which is depressingly often. She's lovely really, just as long as we don't stay under the same roof for long enough for her to remember that she wholeheartedly disapproves of most of my personality traits and the way I've lived my life.

My dad, on the other hand, is a salesman. If you need a pension, ISA, zeros, gilts, stocks or shares, then he's the man. He's totally incorrigible, unbelievably irresponsible and the life and soul of every party until his friend, Jack Daniel's, possesses his body and turns him into the kind of aggressive, overbearing bore who makes you hope you got none of his traits in the gene-pool lottery.

Sometimes I wonder what they ever saw in each other. I can only suspect it was a rash decision based on a full moon and alcohol. Their marriage survived years of both shouting and stony silences before they finally threw in the towel. I'll tell you more about it later, but my brothers and I breathed a hearty sigh of relief when they finally called it a day.

Strictly speaking, us Cooper kids should have scar tissue on our souls after surviving the parent wars, but miraculously we seem to have emerged relatively unscathed. I'm the eldest, and a year later came Callum, who is 6'3", perfectly formed, with abs that look like a toast rack and a face that adorns billboards up and down the country. And no, having a model for a brother isn't as great as it sounds. I'm the 'slippers and starting the diet on Monday' kind of girl, while Callum is the aftershave guy, the sports car guy, the designer underwear guy. I once overheard a woman on a bus saying that he's the guy that she would nominate to look for her G-spot and not care if he didn't find it. Queasiness at that mental image aside, it was a proud moment and I adore the perfect bones of him.

Three years after Callum, Michael came along. Less chiselled than his Adonis of a brother, he's the sweetheart you can rely on to cheer you up when you're having a bad day, because his life trundles from one crisis to another. You could lose your job, bury your budgie and forget to tape an episode of *ER*, yet still his day will be worse. Michael is a computer genius. He spends his days locked in a world of animated psychopaths, perfecting the graphics for the nation's teenagers to fixate on as they save the world with their PlayStations.

Whereas Callum has no time or desire for a relationship that lasts longer than a weekend, Michael is more likely to crumble into a heap at the first sight of a potential girlfriend. He could write a manual on unrequited love, but his overflowing heart stops him from giving up. Every week there's a new goddess who's 'absolutely, positively and completely right for him in every way', and every week she spurns his advances and he's back to square one. He's been chucked more times than an Olympic javelin. If only they could see that he's funny, interesting, sweet, giving and he donates 10 per cent of his salary to Save the Whales.

But no, when girls look at Michael, they see a tall, almost good-looking guy, with an eccentric dress sense and 'Sucker' tattooed on his forehead. And he unfailingly chooses the ones who will chew him up without even having the decency to warn him that he's about to be spat out at the speed of a Scud missile. I adore him no matter what the rest of the female population thinks. His goddess is definitely out there, I tell him, he's just going to the wrong temples.

I speak to Callum, Michael and my closest friend, Kate, every day. Sometimes it's for two minutes, other times it's for two hours, depending on the excitement or trauma of the day. Yes, my phone bill's high, but it's cheaper than therapy and wine is allowed.

Since the onset of my official midlife crisis, they've been on the wrong end of many of my 'how did I get this life?' conversations. The thing is, I don't understand why we weren't properly prepared for reality when we were young. We were bombarded by propaganda about how girl meets gorgeous guy and they ride off into the sunset together. No one ever tells you men are like knickers – after a time, they get grey and washed out and they can have a tendency to fall down when you least expect it. Or, even worse, you find a perfect pair that you love, only to discover that your shape is changing and they don't fit any more, no matter how much you try to pull them up.

Don't get me wrong, I'm not a bitter and twisted man hater. On the contrary, I love them. Perhaps a little too often, granted. Sweeping confession coming up. I'm just going to blurt it out and get it over with. I've been engaged to be joined in the holy vows of matrimony no fewer than four times and had two further near misses, before I pulled on my Reebok high tops and did a runner. Metaphorically speaking, of course. If you ever see me jogging, you can be pretty sure it's because someone is chasing me with a weapon.

It's just come to me that I could form an ex-boyfriend five-a-side football team, complete with substitute. I realise that to some my serial chucking may seem a tad unstable, heartless, cruel or indecisive, but it was none of these. No, it was down to optimism. You see, no matter how great the guy was, no matter if he was loving, faithful, made me laugh, and set my knickers alight, there was always some incident of conflict or disaster. Whereupon, instead of persevering and trying to make it work, I ended the relationship before careering headlong into the next fiasco. I was just always sure that the next romance would be the *perfect* one – one that wouldn't require work, compromise or sacrifice on either side. Naiveté and optimism won the day, time after time. And look where that's got me.

The ringing of the phone stops me from slipping deeper into my abyss of self-reflection. I reach for the green handset with the big white buttons that hangs on my wall. The company I work for issued us all with a high-tech mobile phone a few years ago, but the accountants get twitchy if it's used for personal calls, so it usually languishes at the bottom of my briefcase, the perfect place to ignore it when it rings. My boss has started typing inspirational and nagging messages on his and sending them to us. Why, oh why, are those text thingies necessary? Whoever invented that little method of communication needs to have a serious word with themselves.

I put the green handset to my ear. 'Hello?'

'I called your office and they said you're sick, so, let me guess, you're still in your dressing gown, aren't you?'

'Maybe.'

'And there's nothing actually wrong with you.'

'Possibly.'

'Except that you're feeling sorry for yourself.'

'Definitely. It's a recognised symptom of a midlife crisis.'

Kate. My best mate. Or long-suffering mate, if we're going for accuracy. We've been pals since we sat next to each other in Primary 7, and both got detention because we wouldn't admit which one of us opened a can of Tango under our desk, causing an explosion of orange fizz that hit everyone within ten feet of us. Incidentally, it was Kate. I shared the punishment, but she's been bailing me out ever since, so I think I got the better deal.

She sighs because she's been listening to me moaning for weeks now. 'Cooper...' My pals all call me by my surname, because there were two Carlys in our Primary class and it just stuck. Now, when I hear my first name being uttered, I automatically fear that my mother is in the vicinity. 'We're going to have to make this quick, because I've got a Spice Girls tribute act due in for blow-dries any minute.'

When she's not busy being my personal relationship advisor, Kate's a hairdresser in an achingly hip Kensington salon. She came to London ten years ago, originally to be near Carol, another one of our teenage gang, who, like my brother, was hustling her way in the modelling world and looking for company. They shared a flat in Camden for a year, before Kate met a very lovely architect called Bruce, and was swept off her feet by his vaulted ceilings and elevated angles.

She lives in nearby Chiswick, with Bruce and their two amazing children: Cameron, six, and Zoe, four. Both of them have Kate's features – long chestnut hair, huge green eyes and infectious grins. I can sense that there's one on her face right now.

'You're not having a midlife crisis. You're having a millennium crisis. It's a thing. The psychological millennium bug. I read about it in *Woman's Own*, so it must be true. Or maybe it was in *Take A Break*. I really need to cut down on my magazine subscriptions. Anyway, apparently, it's not just technology that's going to implode at the dawn of the new century. It's making people reflect on their lives and relationships and make changes. They reckon the divorce rate is going to go through the roof. I keep stocking up on Bruce's favourite biscuits just to keep him on side.'

I ponder that for a moment. 'You can't beat the contentment delivered by a Wagon Wheel. Anyway, maybe you've got a point. Maybe I'm having a midlife crisis *and* a case of the millennium bug. Maybe it's both.'

Kate laughs. 'Nope, sorry. You don't get to make claims on two different crisis situations. Pick one and stick to it.'

I get the feeling she's not taking me seriously and, to be honest, I don't blame her. In my defence, as well as doing my share of navel gazing, I have made some efforts to change. For the past couple of years, I've deliberately stayed single. In my quest to understand and analyse where it all went wrong, I've been spending long nights contemplating all my past relationships, trying to understand why they didn't work out. I'm not sure it's helped, but sales of those Marks & Spencer dinners for one have rocketed.

I've just realised that I've scoffed the whole croissant and don't even remember doing it. *And* I've missed the start of *Richard & Judy*.

'Is there a cure for the millennium bug? Other than educating yourself about life from the pages of women's magazines?' I ask.

'Yes. Apparently you have to just get over yourself and take action, make changes, solve the problem. Okay, spell it out for me. Tell me exactly what's bothering you.'

'I just think...' The words catch in my throat, so I change tack. 'I just wonder if...' Nope, can't get that out either. I close my eyes, brace myself and prepare to tell her the thought that kept me awake last night. 'I can't get it out of my head that I might have made a mistake. What if one of my exes was my forever soulmate and I was just too stupid to see it? What if I trampled Mr Right in the rush to meet another Mr Wrong? Maybe I've missed my chance. How will I ever know?'

There's a pause as she considers my dilemma. I'm hoping she'll come up with something wise and insightful.

'You could always win the lottery and go and visit them all.'

Hopes dashed. Although, she's not wrong. You see, my exes are scattered all over the world. Oh yes, I did more to bring countries together than the United Nations.

I hear a bell ringing in the background at the other end of the line and Kate immediately wraps things up. 'Hot N Spicy are here, I need to go. I'll call you later and you'd better be out of your dressing gown.'

The line goes dead. I replace the handset, finish making my tea and carry it over to the sofa, Kate's words playing in my mind. Lottery win aside, maybe there's something in what she says. This is 1999. The last year of the century. How incredible would it be to have turned my life around and go into the 2000's happy, fulfilled and in love again? Let's face it, nothing is going to change unless I do something to make it happen. An idea begins to form in my mind. There's an obvious way to find out if my happy ever after lies with an ex, but where would I start? I suppose I'd do it in chronological order. That would mean going back twelve years to my first love, Nick Russo, and to a time when I still had a connection to the word 'virgin', other than the fact that I've flown on their aeroplanes...

2

The holiday was booked for the end of June, a few weeks before my eighteenth birthday, and the day after I attended the mother-ship of all that was oppressive in society, St Mary the Blessed Virgin High School in Glasgow, for the last time.

Actually, school wasn't that bad. Where else could you hang out with your mates all day, get free ciggies from the guys at lunchtime, and be involved in more daily drama than an episode of *Neighbours*? The only inconvenience was tolerating the punish-ments that were regularly meted out to me for answering back, not paying attention, and generally causing affray. But it was all innocent and done in the name of fun.

My favourite class was French, where my 'disruptive' behaviour pushed the highly strung Mr Distell too far and he made me sit behind a filing cabinet for a whole year. It was a great opportunity to catch up with lost sleep.

As for the work, much as I don't want to appear conceited, I officially possess the memory of an elephant. Even when I was staring transfixed at John Potts's thighs in biology, I could still remember every word the teacher uttered. Exams, therefore, were never a problem. Straight A student, straight zero work. Life was bliss.

I think that's why I agreed to go on holiday. I wanted to prolong the last year with my school pals for as long as possible. We knew we would all go in different directions afterwards. Sarah Moore, my friend since we were in the womb and our mothers went to antenatal classes together, was going to Edinburgh University to study mathematics. Such a rational subject for a joyfully irrational person. Carol Sweeney, Glasgow's answer to Kate Moss, was going to London to try to launch her modelling career. Jess Latham, Aberdeen University, reading politics. Politics! She said she chose it because it was sure to include lots of men and dinner parties. And Kate Wilkes, who had been butchering our coiffures for years, finally had a position as an apprentice hairdresser in a trendy Glasgow salon.

Me? I still wasn't sure what to be when I grew up, so I'd applied for university just because it seemed like the right thing to do. I didn't have the financial support to study in a different city, so I opted for Glasgow University and was accepted to study English literature. Did I really want to spend four years immersed in Keats, D.H. Lawrence and Shakespeare? I'd rather have my teeth pulled. No, I wanted to travel the world, meet interesting people and rich men who would buy me diamonds while encouraging my career as a kickass boss with a big heart and a philanthropic sideline. Years of reading Jackie Collins novels had clearly had an effect on my life aspirations. In reality, however, I was lacking the finances for an epic, global life adventure, so I applied for Uni and settled for a fortnight with my chums in the centre of the Costa Del Juvenile Delinquent, Benidorm. It was hardly St Lucia, but we were living off our parents. Or at least the other girls were. I'd saved every bloody penny for this holiday. For eighteen months, I'd spent every Saturday clearing tables and serving coffees to loud women in fur coats with diamonds the size of Gibraltar dripping from their fingers, in one of Glasgow's more 'upmarket' department stores. I hated that job. It was bad enough that I had to work on Saturdays when everyone else was hanging out and shopping at Miss Selfridge, but to make matters worse I had to wear a brown A-line overall that made me look an overcooked sausage. Not that it mattered, as I was apparently invisible as I trundled round the tables clearing away the used crockery. That was the thing with the kind of unbearably obnoxious, aloof women who frequented the store, they didn't acknowledge the presence of anyone who earned less than £100k per year. They would just carry on their conversations whilst I cleaned their tables, oblivious to the fact that I could hear every word they uttered.

'Have you *seen* her breasts lately? I didn't realise the porn star look was in this season.'

'So I said to Jeremy, Monte Carlo is *so passé*, it's St Barts this year and don't even think about flying commercial.'

'Of course I fake it, darling, otherwise we'd be at it all night and I do need my beauty sleep.'

They didn't even stop for breath, never mind to say a courteous 'Thank you' for clearing away their debris. Yet perversely, although I detested them, I vowed that one day I'd be able to drape myself in jewels and pay five pounds for a sticky bun. I would watch the way they held their cigarettes, flicked their hair and talked in exaggerated whispers, always with the self-assurance that they were above reproach. Only one thing, I decided, gives that air of confidence – money. I was determined that one day I'd be sitting there in my Janet Regers, underneath my Dior, talking about my rich husband's failure to achieve an erection. But until then, me and my sausage-shade uniform were working all the hours I could get to save up for a bit of fun in the Spanish sun.

We left for Benidorm at 10.15 p.m.. In order to thoroughly embarrass us, all our parents insisted on accompanying us to the airport. In my case it was just my mum, as my dad was in the middle of another deep debate with Jack Daniel's. I'd heard them arguing while I was packing and was relieved when it finally went quiet because that meant he'd slumped into a bourbon induced coma. I learnt when I was young not to get in the middle of them. Instead, I found a way to lock their issues in a box in my mind and escape into books, boys and pals, all the while having the same thought: I. Will. Never. Be. Like. Them.

All that fighting and staying together even though they brought no joy to each other whatsoever? No thanks. How could two people who must have loved each other enough to take their vows end up like this? If that's how marriage turned out, I'd pass, thanks. Yes, in hindsight, several engagements later, I can see the irony of that train of thought.

Anyway, back to my seventeen year old self.

By the time we got to the airport, my mum was in organisation mode, with an undertone of disapproval. 'Now, have you got the number of the British Embassy in case you have any trouble? Wouldn't surprise me in the least. Remember, don't speak to any foreign men, they might misunderstand your intentions.'

I doubted it very much.

It took us an age to get rid of the menagerie of relatives. We finally managed it by convincing them that we should go straight through to the departure lounge, lest we get trodden on in the stampede of tourists rushing through security at the last minute. We stormed into the duty-free shopping area like it was a competitive trolley dash. There wasn't a skirt longer than twelve inches or a heel under four, and we couldn't walk right next to each other because our matching perms were teased, curled and sprayed to the size of beach balls. The only thing that varied was our hair colour. Sarah was a brunette, Kate was chestnut, I was light ash blonde (straight out of a box of dye from the chemist), Jess's mane was fiery red and Carol was the one who put us all in the shade because aside from her natural dark tresses, she was 5' 10" tall, and made Cindy Crawford look average. Right now, her perfect white teeth were glinting as she adopted the same gleeful expression as the rest of us. We were ecstatic. Two weeks of fun and freedom with not a responsible adult in sight.

We made straight for the ciggies and alcohol section of the duty-free. Five bottles of vodka, 1,600 Benson & Hedges, and five bars of Toblerone later, we settled down in the bar to await our departure to Alicante.

Sarah and I were doing our best rendition of Whitney's 'I Wanna Dance With Somebody', when we were rudely interrupted.

'Right,' bellowed Jess, doing her best Margaret Thatcher impersonation. Not that we were fans. Thatcher had just been voted in for a third term and in our working-class area of the West of Scotland that result was about as popular as sexually transmitted warts. 'If we're going to get through the next two weeks without getting arrested or killing each other, we need to set some ground rules.'

The rest of us groaned in horror.

'Jess,' countered Sarah, 'we just got rid of the wrinklies and now you're going all maternal on us. Calm down and have another vodka.'

'But we've got to have some rules,' persisted Jess, 'or we could end up spoiling the whole holiday.'

'What are you on about?' Kate interjected.

'Well, for example, I think we should agree that no men are allowed back to the apartment.'

This was greeted with total silence, save for the clinking of ice cubes as we all felt a sudden need for a large slug of alcohol. It's not that we were promiscuous. In fact, unbelievably for five seventeen year olds, not one of us had done the whole deed, but we weren't angels in the penis department. I'd had the same boyfriend, Mark Barwick, on and off all the way through high school (we were currently very much off), and we'd crossed a few lines, but nothing that could risk pregnancy. I had no intention of going any further than that with some stranger in Benidorm, but the whole point of the holiday was to have some uninhibited, unconstrained-by-parental-sensibilities, memorable fun.

Carol spoke up. 'I'm not sure I agree with Jess on that one, but I do think we should have some ground rules so that any dodgy stuff gets nipped in the bum.'

My pal was gorgeous, but she was hopeless with her sayings and regularly had us in stitches when they came out wrong, back to front, or upside down. Or upside backwards, as she would say.

I nearly fell off my chair. In all the years I had known Carol, she had never demonstrated any sign of having one responsible brain cell, never mind a whole grey matter of them.

She continued, 'I propose the rules are as follows: a. We must snog at least one new man every night; b. We must go home only when we can no longer walk due to overindulgence in the falling-down juice, and; c. No full sex, blow jobs only. How does that sound?'

I don't think the lady at the next table needed to hear all that, because she suddenly started to choke on her cuppa.

The rest of us dissolved into hysteria.

'I've got another one,' piped Kate when she regained her

power of speech. 'No cooking, tidying up or washing dishes of any kind.'

By this time, Jess was a mild shade of puce.

It was my turn. 'And remember, girls, if you do get swept off your platforms by an exotic lover, reinforced condoms must be used at all times.'

The woman at the next table was now requiring resuscitation.

Jess mumbled, 'Okay, okay, but no men in the apartment, please.'

We all nodded furiously, tears rolling down our cheeks.

'Whatever you say, Jess, we'll do our best,' I reassured her. And I meant it. Kind of.

* * *

We arrived at the apartment in the middle of the night. This was a blessing, as due to fatigue and too much vodka, we didn't register the full extent of the dump. Whoever had written in the brochure that it slept six, must have presumed that the six were highly intimate and would sleep on top of each other.

The main room contained an old sofa and two camp beds. Another three camp beds were behind a curtain in what was obviously a large cupboard in a previous life. In the kitchen, there was a one-ring cooker, a mini-fridge, a cracked sink and a colony of ants. As for the bathroom, let's just say that I was hopeful that there would be showers at the pool and public toilets nearby.

But we didn't care. We slumped on to our beds, fully clothed, and were sleeping within thirty seconds.

We woke the next morning to the sound of trains thundering over our heads, then we realised there were no trains and the noise was our hangovers systematically crushing our brain cells. God, it hurt. Ever sensible, Jess came to the rescue with paracetamols all round and we decided the only cure was a day at the beach.

In order to deny the ants time to nest on our body parts, we were out of the door in five minutes, looking like we'd slept under a bush.

We made our way to the beach and parked ourselves in the first available clearing.

'Who needs Glasgow?' Kate murmured happily, as she slapped on enough oil to lubricate a Ferrari.

We spent the rest of the day in a semi-conscious state, waking only when one of us yelled 'Pec alert, pec alert' as a gorgeous specimen of the male variety passed by.

It was all very civilised, like an episode of *Wish You Were Here*. Until later that evening...

Kate and I retreated to the balcony – in Glasgow it would have been called a window ledge – with two large drinks, to give the others space to get dressed. When they were done, we told them to go on ahead. 'We'll meet you in the Scotsman later,' Kate yelled through the window, naming a pub that we'd passed earlier in the day. We were rubbish tourists. Travel to a completely different country, and head for a bar that was connected to the homeland we'd left less than twenty-four hours earlier. But in our defence, it was playing Simple Minds hits at full volume, and Jim Kerr's dulcet tones were like some kind of sci-fi mind-warp that we were unable to resist.

Kate and I took an age getting ready. By the time we were done, we'd tried on twelve different outfits each, reapplied our make-up twice and experimented with more hairstyles than Madonna. We'd also consumed half a bottle of vodka and a gallon of fresh orange. It wouldn't have mattered what we looked like, we were seeing double anyway.

We staggered to the Scotsman, stopping at every pub on the

way there for a light refreshment. By the time we finally arrived, it was almost midnight. Carol and Sarah were in deep conversation with two of a gang of six lads from Edinburgh.

I glanced around. 'Where's Jess?'

'She's here somewhere', replied Carol, gesticulating towards the crowded bar. 'She must have gone to the loo.'

Within minutes, Kate and I had succumbed to the general revelry and loud music that blared from the speakers. I found myself dancing with a chiselled Dutchman called Henk. I eventually got bored with the repetitiveness of hip grinding to 'Boom Boom Boom Let's Go Back To My Room', made the infamous toilet excuse and staggered off to round up the others.

I had to surgically remove Kate from a perma-bronzed Frenchman, before rounding up Carol (singing 'Hey Big Spender' on a bar stool), and then Sarah (slumped under a sink in the toilets). Where was Jess?

Panic set in briefly before total hysteria sobered me up immediately. We searched everywhere. At one point, we even conducted a desperate rummage in the huge bins outside, but she was nowhere to be seen.

We were getting frantic and maniacally scanning every man in sight to see if he showed any sign of being a homicidal, psychotic kidnapper. We thundered back to the apartment, searching every doorway and dingy alley on the way. All the while, I had a picture of my mother in my head, a knowing, smug look on her face saying, 'I told you that you'd need the number of the British Embassy, dear.'

I fumbled for a key as I neared our door, only to be stopped in my tracks. What the hell was that racket? All I could hear was a resounding chorus of 'Livin On A Prayer', and it was coming from inside our apartment.

With still-shaking hands, I opened the door and was

confronted by the most ludicrous sight. Three men in sombreros were singing at the top of their voices, another was playing an ancient guitar and yet another was fast asleep with a pyramid of beer cans on his belly and his socks hanging out of his ears. In the middle of this melee was Jess, red curls now expanded by the humidity to the size of a sun lounger, beer can in hand, shouting, 'Girls, I was starting to get worried about you. Come in and meet the lads.'

I was struck dumb and rooted to the spot. I struggled to construct a sentence, but somehow nothing seemed to articulate the forty-seven different emotions that were coursing through my brain. Carol stepped in.

'What the fuck is going on, Jess?' Succinct, but it was better than I could manage.

Four men looked at us in anticipation. The sleeping beer holder never stirred.

'I met them outside the Scotsman,' she gushed, having the decency to look mildly ashamed. 'They're from Barnsley, and they've got nowhere to stay because they got kicked off their campsite. I felt sorry for them and brought them back here. I said they could stay with us. It's okay, isn't it?' she pleaded.

I was still struggling to regain my power of speech.

Kate sighed loudly. 'Sorry, Jess, but we've got rules in this apartment,' she said forcibly. 'No men allowed.'

Jess's face had a look of sheer horror and she was just about to embark on her full Petrocelli mitigation speech when she noticed a smile flickering across Kate's lips. Carol's shoulders started to shake and within seconds we were collapsed in a cacophony of laughter and relief. We even woke up Sock Man.

We stayed up until dawn, drinking and exhausting our repertoire of chart hits from the previous decade. At 6 a.m., we concluded with a rousing rendition of 'A Kind Of Magic', before slumping to sleep where we sat. We'd already given up on the idea of allocating beds (ten people in a flat designed for two just doesn't work) and decided that wherever we could clear a floor space, that's where we would sleep. I can't remember who, but at some point, someone butchered Paul Young's hit and the song of the night became Wherever I Lay My Arse, That's My Home.

The Barnsley guys, we surmised in our drunken state, were both harmless and entertaining. Dave was the guitar player, 5'8", with a cute grin and a wicked line in jokes. Brian and Barry were brothers, who spoke in synchronisation – one brain with extra arms and legs. Ritchie was the heart-throb – tall, dark and devilishly handsome, with a body that had seen one or two dumbbells in its time. And as for Sock Man, he didn't so much as open his eyes all night so we decided that from then on he would officially be called, well, Sock Man.

The first three days were pretty much a repetition of the first, only with more participants. The guys assumed brotherly roles, getting us drinks at the beach and warding off any unwanted advances by claiming to be brothers/boyfriends/husbands depending on the situation. Carol, however, decided that she wanted to get intimate with Ritchie's abdominals, so they alone embarked on a bit of incest, but that apart it was all very platonic. On day four, everything changed.

It started fairly inauspiciously with a long lazy day at the beach, lots of Ambre Solaire, and the odd game of beach volleyball between visits to the bar for cocktails. We returned to the apartment at six, to prepare for yet another night in Benidorm's high spots. And when I say high spots, I mean anywhere that sold alcohol and had music that was louder than Concorde. We had developed a very efficient rota system for the bathroom. The boys would go first, and while they were showering, we would have a happy hour on the balcony. When they were done, they would clear out to the pub, leaving us to get ready and meet them later. All very civilised, if it were not for the inevitable clutter, water fights and general mayhem which inevitably ensued.

Unusually, I showered, dressed and made-up fairly quickly that night, having come to the conclusion that it was too hot to fart around and it wouldn't matter if you had a face like a sunburned arse, in this town you were still guaranteed male attention.

By the time we reached the Scotsman, the guys were on a table singing 'High Ho Silver Lining', so we took the opportunity to steal their seats. A bad move as they proceeded to sit on our knees until cramp forced us to dump them unceremoniously on the floor.

At around eleven o'clock, I was feeling decidedly shaky on my stilettos when a tall blond guy walked in, followed by a dark-haired bloke. The blond shouted a greeting to Sarah. I vaguely remembered him as Graham, the guy that she'd been fraternising with the night before, after his great line in chat won over both Sarah and the approval of our self-appointed Barnsley body-guards. He made his way over to our table, while his friend fought his way to the bar. Through the crowd, I could just make out the top of his head as he waited to be served.

Graham took up position on Sarah's knees just as his mate turned round and started to make his way towards us. My heart stopped. Within seconds, I required oxygen. I was just about to search for a brown paper bag to hyperventilate into, when his eyes caught mine. They were so blue that, had this been in the nineties, I would have sworn they were coloured contact lenses, and they were framed with eyelashes that Max Factor would have killed for.

He was about twenty-one, had jet-black hair, dark skin and the jawline of an American soap actor. He was stunning. His eyes held mine while he covered what seemed like the mile and a half to our table. He put the drinks down, still staring. A smile crossed his lips, revealing teeth that I wanted to tap to make sure they were real. My heart thundered so loudly that I was sure it was drowning out the ridiculous 'Shudupa Ya Face', that was blaring from the speakers. He stared a bit longer, then slowly, in a soft Scottish accent said, 'Are we leaving?'

My brain screamed, searching for a witty reply that would have the others clutching their sides, but my power of thought had deserted me.

'Yes.' Yes? Was that it? Was that all an educated, smart-mouthed female could come up with? My first encounter with love at first sight had rendered me witless.

He put his hand out and I took it, still lost in his gaze. I followed him outside, where he turned right and started walking, saying nothing. After about a hundred yards, he stopped, put his hands on my face and kissed me slowly. I felt my legs buckle underneath me. God, what was happening?

We kept walking, turning left, then right, until we were entering one of the big posh hotels on the seafront. We passed it every day on the way to the beach and it definitely wasn't the kind of place that would have ten people to a suite, with a bloke in a sombrero playing guitar and a comatose drunk called Sock Man. We took the lift up to the sixth floor, then entered his room, where he turned and kissed me again. Only this time it didn't stop.

He unbuttoned my top, dropping it to the floor, then slid my skirt over my hips to join it.

Meanwhile, my enthusiasm for the situation was made clear by the fact that I had somehow managed to remove his shirt and trousers. I should probably have stopped and considered whether I wanted to lose my virginity to a complete stranger, but it felt so good that nothing short of a tranquiliser dart could have stopped me. We tumbled onto the bed, kissing, groping. Before I knew what was happening, a condom appeared and then it was on and his naked body was pressed against mine.

'Lift your hips,' he whispered, nuzzling my ear.

What did he mean? How high? Somehow this just wasn't the time to say, 'Excuse me, but I haven't done this before so do you think you could possibly draw me a diagram of the exact angle of elevation which you require?' I knew I should have paid more attention in biology when they were giving 'The Talk'. Or maybe rewound the steamy bits in 9 ½ Weeks.

I tilted my pelvis and he slid slowly and gradually inside. My body welcomed him eagerly. He continued to move out and in, sending glorious waves of ecstasy coursing to previously unstimulated areas of my anatomy, until eventually he came shuddering to a halt, just as a new feeling deep in my pelvic area caused an explosion I'd never felt before. So that was what all those orgasm articles in Cosmo were raving about then.

He collapsed beside me, then turned and touched my face.

'You're beautiful,' he whispered.

I smiled. 'Thank you,' I gasped, breathless. I didn't know what else to say. My mother had always taught me that if someone gave you a compliment you should smile and thank them. I don't think she meant that to apply after a stranger had just been intimate with your tickly bits, but then I wasn't sure of the rules of this new game. What exactly are you supposed to say after a guy has met you, said 'Are we leaving,' followed by 'Lift your hips' and your only utterance has been a feeble 'Yes'?

I searched my brain for points of reference. I was sure this was when the guy rolled over and was snoring within ten seconds. Why then was his finger tracing the outline of my nipple? Now my stomach. Now my thighs. Good God, he wanted to do it again! Was this normal?

He pulled me on top of him and without thinking I was suddenly moving, using muscles I didn't even know I possessed.

We made love twice more, once in the bath, and it was starting to get light when we fell asleep, me still with an inane grin on my face. So this was it. Virginity gone. After years of fumbling with my on-off ex, Mark Barwick, resisting the temptation to cross the last line, I'd had my first sexual experience with a man I couldn't have picked out in a line up only a few hours ago. It should feel so wrong, and yet it just felt perfect.

The sun streaming in through the window woke me at ten o'clock. For a moment I didn't know where I was, then I remembered. I started to get up when pain forced me to slump back down. My legs felt like they'd run a marathon. I stumbled to the bathroom, gathering my hastily discarded clothing as I went. I looked in the mirror. Big mistake. My face was red, my eyes looked like a road map and my hair had clearly exploded during the night. I couldn't let him see me like this – the shock would scar him for life.

I dressed and did the best repair job possible before surreptitiously making for the door. I had just pulled it open when he sleepily mumbled, 'Can I see you tonight?'

'Sure,' I replied without turning round, 'I'll be in the Scotsman.'

I staggered back to the apartment, praying that nobody would be awake. I quietly opened the door and was just about to breathe a sigh of relief when I saw a sea of expectant faces. The gang were indeed up and broke into a standing ovation.

Laughing, Kate gave me a drink.

'What's this?' I stammered.

'It's a new cocktail we invented for you. It's called an Invaded Vagina.'

Oh, the embarrassment. Was nothing private in this world?

'But how did you know?'

Sarah butted in. 'Graham here,' she said, gesticulating to my night of passion's friend, who was sitting in the corner, 'went back to the hotel last night, but he heard you inside, so he hotfooted it over here with a full report.'

I was mortified. Ground open up now and swallow me please.

'Well, aren't you going to say anything?' Jess asked.

I paused. 'Graham,' I said ashamedly, 'what is your friend's name?'

It was difficult to hear his reply over screams of amusement and mock outrage from the others. 'Nick,' he said, joining the laughter. 'Nick Russo.'

* * *

That evening, unlike the night before, I took hours getting ready. Every outfit made me look too fat, too small, too flat chested. Every hairstyle made me look like my mum or my gran. So this was what happened then. You spent one night with a man and suddenly you morphed into an indecisive, neurotic nightmare. I kept waiting for the seeds of regret to set in, but they never did. I just couldn't wait to see him again.

When we got to the pub, there was no sign of him. I was glad of the crowd and the noise because at least it stopped the girls' endless interrogation about the night before.

It's not that I didn't want to tell them, I just couldn't talk about something that I didn't understand.

How should I act? Should I be coy, distant, friendly, forward? Where was the bloody rulebook? In the end, I settled for terrified and anxious.

All night I kept staring at the door. Eventually, at about ten o'clock, Graham entered. My heart leapt, then sank faster than a stone as I realised that he was alone.

'Where's Nick?' I asked, scared of the answer.

He shrugged and there was something uneasy in his posture that sent my alarm bells straight to screech levels. 'I don't know, Carly, I'm not sure if he's coming down tonight.'

The others looked uncomfortable now too, all the guys' eyes immediately drawn to their feet. They must teach that in Men School – 'When one of your fellow males is ceremoniously dumping a member of the female sex, you must immediately stare at the floor, or you'll be stricken down by the Testosterone God.'

I couldn't speak. I stood up, grabbed my bag and fled, not stopping for a second lest they saw the tears that were threatening to blind me.

After running for what seemed like miles, my brain locked in a mantra of 'Bastard, Bastard, Bastard', I found myself at the beach.

This had never happened to me before. Never had any guy let me down or upset me, never mind make me cry. I had always thought that I was indestructible.

I found an overturned dinghy on the sands and collapsed against it, facing out to sea. Why is it that at times of crisis I always see a vision of my mum lecturing me?

'They're only after one thing, you know.'

'Never give in to sex because they'll just cast you aside like yesterday's newspaper afterwards.'

I felt like banging my head on the dinghy, just to get rid of the sound of her voice. A coma would definitely be preferable.

That was where he found me hours later, eyes swollen from crying, mascara ingrained into my cheeks, hair so flat that it resembled a balaclava.

I felt a movement beside me and he sat down, put his arms around me and squeezed tight. I stared at him in dumbstruck shock.

'How did you find me?'

'We were all looking for you, and Kate figured you'd be here. The others headed back to the bar when we spotted you. I promised the girls I'd bring you back later. Carol said if I didn't, she'd remove my nuts.'

That made me smile, but I couldn't get any words past the massive lump that had formed in my throat.

'Why did you run off?' he went on.

'I thought I'd made a horrible mistake. I thought you weren't coming,' I spluttered through the tears that had started again.

'Don't be daft,' he smiled. 'I just fell asleep while I was getting ready. I was a bit late, that's all.'

'Oh.' Conversational skills were on annual leave again.

'But I do think we have to talk.'

Here it comes, I thought. *The whole 'holiday romance, it was just a bit of fun' thing.*

'Why didn't you tell me that you'd never had sex before?'

Hello again, mortification. My cheeks burned. 'How did you find out?' Was it that obvious? Oh, the indignity of it all.

'Kate told me,' he replied. 'She was explaining why you did the hundred metre sprint when Graham appeared without me.'

Oh. Relief.

'I don't know,' I answered honestly. 'There didn't seem to be the right moment.'

'So why did you do it then?' he persisted.

'I don't know that either. It just felt right.'

He laughed. Laughed! I was sitting there feeling like my heart had been shredded and he was laughing. He kissed the end of my nose, then drew me in close to him, dispelling my indignation in a heartbeat.

'I think I'm going to like you, Carly Cooper. Now, come on, we've got some catching up to do.'

* * *

The rest of the holiday passed in uninterrupted bliss. The next morning, we went back to our apartment with all Graham's clothes and swapped them for mine. Graham and Sarah were delighted – they were fast becoming a permanent feature.

Nick and I were the same. We woke up together, sunbathed together, went to the pub in the evening with the rest of the gang, but still never leaving each other's side. And we laughed. We laughed about silly, stupid things. I had fallen sombrero over espadrilles, totally and completely in love. And so had he. It was amazing. His face lit up when he saw me, we talked constantly about everything on the planet and then he made long, gorgeous love to me every night.

If I'd stopped to think about it in any depth, I'd have acknowledged how lucky I felt. Nick Russo was the first guy I'd ever slept with and he was sweet and kind and funny, and showed no dickhead tendencies whatsoever.

The last night finally came. My stomach had been in knots all day and I was alternating between a longing to handcuff Nick to the bed and savour every moment, and wanting to curl up in a corner and cry.

We went out to dinner, for once without our merry band of friends.

'We can't let this end here, Cooper,' he said as he held my hand so tightly that it felt as if he was dislocating my knuckles.

'How can it not?' I implored. 'We live on opposite sides of the country, we can't drive and we're skint students.'

The truth was, I could probably make the trip to his home in St Andrews by bus and train, and he could travel to see me too. The distance wasn't insurmountable, but geography and logistics weren't the real issue here.

You see, I adored him. This had been the most perfect two weeks of my life, I had lost my virginity to the most amazing man and I could see the future. If we tried to continue this at home, it would get lost amongst protracted separations, late night phone calls and living in different towns. Even in my sun-damaged, alcohol-poisoned, euphoric state, I knew that we were much too young for this. Eventually, we would both meet other people and it would end horribly, with tears and tantrums, recriminations and regret. I didn't want that. I wanted to remember this forever for what it was – the best episode in my life ever.

I tried to explain this and, eventually, his sad eyes told me that he got it.

'Tell you what, Cooper, one day I'm going to come and find you. Then, we'll get married and live in happily shagging bliss for the rest of our lives.'

'You promise?' I asked, smiling.

'I promise,' he replied, as he squeezed me tightly, then kissed me goodbye.

I never saw Nick Russo again.

3

BELIEVE – CHER

I pour another coffee and attack a box of Marks & Spencer's chocolate eclairs. I'm having trouble eating them because of the huge smile that's still on my face. Nick Russo. I haven't thought about him for years.

It's strange too, to think about the person that I was then: fearless, full of energy, embarking on every day like it was a great new adventure. But then, everyone is indestructible when they're seventeen, aren't they?

Sure, I was sad when I returned from holiday. I spent two weeks mooning around, listening to Commodores records and crying on the shoulders of anyone who would listen. Thank God for the eighties shoulder pads.

Then I decided that I was bored of being boring and set off in pursuit of another drama. Over the next couple of years, I would think about Nick periodically, but that soon faded as he was replaced by the next love. And the next. And the next.

I think about calling Kate back, but I doubt she'll have finished with Hot N Spicy yet. I briefly consider phoning Carol instead, but she's a nightmare to get hold of and never answers her phone.

These days, Carol is still single, still beautiful and is the figurehead of the Elegante fashion house, spearheading all their advertising campaigns: 'Elegante – The Nineties label for the Thirties Woman!' Despite the more than healthy financial rewards, she's pissed off because now everyone knows she's circling thirty and she reckons that her appeal to rich, shallow men seeking a trophy girlfriend to lavish with copious amounts of expensive gifts, has decreased by 25 per cent.

In saying that, it doesn't seem to have deterred her current beau, who does something in finance and has just awarded her a Harrods charge card. She's probably there now, sipping champagne in Chanel, while I'm drinking tea and dipping my dressing gown sleeve in dishwater. It would be so easy to be bitter.

I decide to call Jess instead, but I get someone else in her office and I don't want to admit that I'm just a pal calling for a chat, so I blatantly lie.

'Could you please give her a message for me? This is her mother here. Could you tell her that my new hip replacement has fallen off and I need her to call me back immediately?'

'Oh, you poor dear,' she coos. 'I'll pass it on immediately.'

Ten minutes later, Jess calls back. Her job as researcher for the Right Honourable Basil Asquith, MP, keeps her really busy, especially as it involves extracurricular activities that go WAY above the normal duties involved in serving your country. More of that later.

'How's your hip, Mum?' she chortles.

'It's facing the wrong way, dear, I just keep going around in circles,' I reply.

She laughs. 'Are you phoning about tonight?'

God, I'd forgotten all about it – our monthly night out. Kate normally reminds me, but I clearly distracted her with my woes earlier. 'What's the plan? Can Carol and Kate make it?'

'Eight o'clock at Paco's and, yes, they're both coming.'

Fantastic! I haven't seen Carol for weeks. 'I'll be there, but that's not why I called. I've just been thinking...'

'Don't do that, you know it gives you a migraine.'

'Sad but true. But anyway – guess who I was thinking about, and it involves sex.'

'Brad Pitt. Patrick Swayze. Tony Blair.' A pause. 'Actually, that last one might have been me,' she admits.

'I thought you came down on the other side of the political divide?' I tease her.

'I do, but it doesn't mean I'm not human.'

'Nope, you just have really disturbing taste in men. Anyway, back to me,' I chuckle. 'I was thinking about Nick Russo.'

'Nick who?'

Typical. One of the most important events in my life and one of my best mates has no recollection of it.

'Nick Bloody Russo,' I reply. 'Remember, Benidorm, the Invaded Vagina?'

'Good God, Cooper, you need to get out more. What made you think of him after all this time?'

'I'm having a midlife millennium crisis and it's making me reminisce about past glories.'

'You *really do* need to get out more. Listen, I'm just heading into a meeting but you can tell us all about it tonight, presuming that your phantom hip loss hasn't affected your ability to get to Paco's.'

My reply was half words, half giggle. 'It'll be a struggle, but I'm sure I'll manage.'

'Excellent. And, mother, remember to wrap up warm – a chill at your age could be life-threatening.'

I hang up and make another coffee, suddenly cheered by the prospect of a night out where the conversation will revolve as always around men, sex and gossip, with the latest tale of premenstrual trauma thrown in for good measure.

It's amazing that we've stayed so close all these years, even though we're all so different. Even more amazing is that we all ended up living in London, a few hundred miles from where we grew up. Our friendships have lasted longer than most marriages. From stilettos in Benidorm to facials in Belgravia (courtesy of one of Carol's boyfriends, who was richer than most oil states), we somehow manage to alternate our dramas and disasters, so that the other three are always there to pick up the pieces. And, of course, every small cause for a celebration gets treated like it's the best thing that's ever happened on the face of the earth – new jobs (all), salary increases (mostly Jess), new men (mostly Carol and me), negative pregnancy tests (Carol), marriage and births (Kate).

That thought rewinds in my head as something jars with me. 'The other three.' There used to be five of us in our teenage gang. It suddenly strikes me that the difference between then and now, apart from a few wrinkles and the need for Wonderbras, is Sarah. We lost touch just a couple of years after that Benidorm holiday. I must remember to ask the others about her tonight. Maybe one of them has heard something through the Glasgow – London grapevine.

I put my feet up and flick through the copy of *Metro* I picked up on the tube the other night. I stop at page sixteen where there's a poignant article about a guy called Joe Brown from Maidenhead. Joe, it seems, discovered he only had a year to live. He embarked on a kamikaze mission and in those twelve months ran up £20,000 worth of debt, doing everything he'd always wanted to do. The Monte Carlo Grand Prix. The carnival in

Brazil. Jazz cafés in New Orleans. He did it all. The poor guy died in the end, but despite the sad ending, I know he's a man after my own heart. It starts the brain cells ticking again. Life really is too short. What if I died tomorrow? There's so much I still want to do. I want to travel. To meet my soulmate. To find a job I don't hate and a home that I love.

A realisation hits me. To achieve any of that, I need a cunning and devious plan to change my life. I'm never going to love my job. And Mr Wonderful, successful but not a workaholic, sensitive but strong, gorgeous but not vain, rich but not flash, is not going to find me sitting in my kitchen eating her second stale croissant of the morning.

A smile overtakes my lips as an idea starts to form. Joe Brown did it the right way. He lived on his own terms and it's time I started doing the same. There is less than a year until the new millennium and if I want to get my life sorted out by then, I have to get a move on.

Within moments, I've made my mind up. Sod it. What have I got to lose? I frantically search for my bills box, source of many a tear, and empty it out, searching for my bank statements.

I know what I'm going to do. I just need the nerve to see it through.

But first, I need to tell the girls.

4

RESPECTABLE – MEL & KIM

I never did go to university. The thought of having to dress constantly in black, wear eyeliner out to my ears and spend my life in the Student Union discussing the scourge of capitalism was too awful to contemplate. Incidentally, I've no idea if that's what University is really like, but I can see now that I painted that picture in my mind because four years at university meant four more years staying at home, and that was the part of the equation that really did fill me with horror. I loved Callum. I loved Michael. But a drunk dad and a highly strung mother who could barely stand the sight of each other didn't make for a fairy tale existence for the rest of us.

More importantly, I was desperate for excitement, fun and adventure but didn't have a clue where to start.

'What should I do, Callum?' I implored of my sixteen year old brother, as we sat huddled on my bed with four packets of Golden Wonder pickled onion crisps and two Yorkies to sustain us. My younger sibling, Michael, thirteen now and all gangly limbs and freckle-faced cuteness, was lying at the foot of the bed, his head on my shins, but he was wearing headphones, eyes closed as he listened to his favourite Guns and Roses tape on Callum's old Walkman.

Callum's reply came with an eye roll and a shoulder nudge. 'Give it up, Carly. You've been asking me the same thing for weeks and I still don't know. Just make a decision and go with it.' Insightful, emotional chats weren't his strong point. He made up for it with killer bone structure and brooding good looks.

His argument had merit though. I had been in the same room, having the same conversation, eating the same junk food ever since my mum had grounded me because I wouldn't go to university. I didn't even have pals on hand to break me out of domestic jail, because, as planned, Jess and Sarah had both left for their respective universities in Aberdeen and Edinburgh, Carol had gone to London to try to get some modelling work, and Kate was working fourteen hours a day as a junior hairdresser. Callum was the only one brave enough to risk my mother's wrath, not to mention the barbed wire around my bedroom door and the threat of land mines in the hallway, to sneak in to talk to me.

All I had was a fourteen inch portable TV for company, the only channels were BBC1, BBC 2, ITV and, if the wind was blowing in the right direction, the stars were aligned and I managed to bend the aerial to some kind of angular perfection, I'd get Channel 4 for about ten minutes at a time, before the screen would go fuzzy again. There were only so many times I could listen to my limited album collection and I'd read every Jackie Collins, Judith Krantz, Shirley Conran and Jilly Cooper novel in the library. It was as close to house arrest as possible without turrets and an armed guard, and I was bored rigid.

'Mum and Dad won't let you stay here unless you go to uni, sis.'

'You're right, I need to move out, but where? I want to travel, to do something different.'

'How much money do you have?'

'About two hundred pounds.'

That was a fortune to me, the result of working overtime at the posh café and the fact that my family had all given me money for my birthday a couple of months ago. Well, there was no point buying me clothes, they'd be out of fashion by the time my parents released me from my bedroom. Besides, unless Miss Selfridge started doing a natty line of prison pyjamas, I didn't have much call for new togs.

'I want to be sensible about this though. I don't want to blow it and have to come back begging to Maw and Paw Walton downstairs.' The Waltons was one of my favourite TV shows. Set in the Blue Ridge Mountains in Virginia during the Great Depression, the Walton family consisted of a Maw, a Paw, grandparents, about sixteen kids, and every episode had some kind of tragedy that made my gran and me sob into our chocolate digestives.

'Sensible? None of this is sensible, Carly. Sensible would be uni and a boyfriend called Jeremy who collects stamps. It's just not you.'

Callum was right. It was time to be assertive.

Next morning, I dressed, waited for my parents to leave for work and then charged down to our local travel agent.

'I want to go away,' I blustered to the insipid looking woman behind the desk.

Her default customer service setting was clearly 'patronising and wholeheartedly indifferent'. 'Yes, dear,' she said, with treacly condescension, 'and where would you be wanting to go?'

'I'm not really sure. I want to leave tonight, I want to go abroad, one way, and it's got to cost less than sixty pounds.' A travel agent's nightmare. I could see her visibly inhale, straighten up and sneer all at the same time.

'Well, dear, the only options I can suggest would be by coach and ferry, and there are two leaving from Glasgow today. One is to Paris and one to Amsterdam.'

I contemplated. Paris sounded great, but wouldn't it be crowded with couples being nauseatingly romantic and tourists with huge video cameras that make you feel like you're in the middle of a BBC outside broadcast?

'I'll have a one way ticket to Amsterdam, please.' If all else failed, I could always buy a feather boa and get a job as a go-go dancer.

I'm ashamed to say, I took the coward's way out. Maw and Paw Walton were informed of Mary Ellen's defection by a shamefaced John Boy later that night, when I was safely mid-Channel. Callum was a star and persuaded them not to immediately round up a posse and track down their prodigal daughter. I'd left Michael my entire stash of Wham bars, so he was nonplussed by the whole situation.

I arrived in Amsterdam the following afternoon, exhausted, bedraggled and feeling like I hadn't washed for a month. I made for the tourist information office and enquired after the cheapest hotel in the city. And cheap it was. Nestled behind the Grand Hotel Krasnapolski on the Damstraat, the gateway to the Red Light district, was the Dam Central Hotel. Or the 'You've got to be damn well joking to call this a hotel', as it's better known.

I humped my bag up four flights of stairs, dodging the holes and empty beer bottles to a room that made the tatty apartment in Benidorm look like the Hilton.

After unpacking my clothes, I flopped on to the bed, ignoring the puff of dust that rose around me. I kept thinking I should be terrified, but I wasn't. I was smiling like a Cheshire cat and feeling, well, exhilarated. I felt like the world was at my feet, alongside the ancient carpet that had more holes than a colander and some extremely questionable stains.

That afternoon, I trawled the streets of Amsterdam, stopping in every café and bar to enquire after work. By early evening, reality had begun to dawn as I absorbed a few unassailable truths. I knew no one in this city who could help me. I had no work permit, so I was officially unemployable. And I wasn't desperate enough yet to get my kit off and sit in a window.

I was starting to feel despondent. What if this was a gargantuan mistake? What was I doing in Amsterdam with no job, no friends and only enough money to buy baked beans for a week? How insane was I? The only experiences I'd had of Holland, prior to giving up my whole life to come here, were clogs and bloody tulips. Not a firm foundation for a life altering decision.

I trudged back to the hotel and had just turned the corner in to the Damstraat when a large gold sign illuminated above an impressive carved door caught my eye. 'The Premier Club', it said. It must have been closed when I passed earlier because I hadn't noticed it. I checked it out. No women in windows trying to tempt business inside. No tacky lights. Just an expensive looking black stone façade and white spotlights that gave it an edge of glamour.

I was about to walk on by when I summoned one last burst of energy. I marched up to the door, only to be stopped by a bouncer who made Lennox Lewis look undernourished.

'Can I help you, mam?' he enquired in an American drawl.

'I'm here to see the owner of the club,' I replied boldly.

'Is he expecting you?'

'Yes, he told me to come here tonight,' I retorted indignantly.

'Just one second, mam.' He disappeared inside to return five minutes later. 'Go right ahead, he's in the office upstairs.'

I couldn't believe the bluff had worked, and I was suddenly wary. That was too easy. What was I doing? I was in the middle of a strange city, no one knew where I was, and I was about to go into the depths of some club that may or may not be entirely shady. If I had any sense, I would run. Flee the scene. Bolt to safety. But, of course, I had none, so I made my way upstairs and knocked tentatively on the first door I saw.

'Come in,' answered another American voice.

I entered, trepidation echoing in every step. This guy could be a mass murderer for all I knew. He could be a pimp, a drug dealer or Holland's biggest trader in white slavery.

Sitting behind a large black glass desk, the man looked up and I could see the hint of a smile in his expression. He was about thirty-fiveish, broad chested, with hair that was thinning on top, wearing what could only be a designer suit. He was handsome in a rugged kind of way and I instinctively trusted him. Hopelessly naive, eternally optimistic. There was a pattern forming there already.

'I'm Joe Cain.' His eyes crinkled up at the sides as his smile widened a little. 'And I may be losing my memory, but I don't remember asking you to come here.'

'I'm sorry I lied, but I just wanted to talk to you. I need a job.'

And then, to my eternal embarrassment, I burst into tears. The full waterworks. There were fluids flowing from every facial orifice.

'I'm sorry,' I gurgled, 'I'm not normally like this, but I've had a really bad day.'

He jumped up, obviously terrified of this apparition in front of him, a cross between a burst pipe and a Cabbage Patch doll. I'm so not attractive when I cry.

He came round to my side of the desk and handed me a tissue. 'Why don't you tell me why you're here. What did you run away from? Are you in trouble?'

'I didn't run away,' I snottered.

I told him the whole story. It sounded so trite, so pathetic. The gist of it was that my parents are a nightmare, I didn't want to stay at home, I was stupid enough to think I could come here and have an epic adventure and I was a complete tit for doing it with no money and no back up plan.

'So I came here and now I really, really need a job. I worked in a restaurant for years and I'm a really good waitress. I just need a chance.' Ok, so calling the bistro full of snotty snobs a 'restaurant' was a stretch, but he had no way of knowing that.

When I'd finished, he looked at me earnestly. 'What age are you?'

'Eighteen,' I replied.

'Do you have permits to work here?'

'No.'

'Do you do drugs?'

'God, no. The strongest drug I use is paracetamol.'

He laughed. 'This is a very upmarket club. No drugs, no sex, no gambling. There's live entertainment and dancing every night and it's strictly respectable. It's one of the few places in Amsterdam where professionals can relax and entertain clients or bring their wives without masses of tourists or all the sleazy stuff. Do you think you could handle that kind of clientele?'

It was a valid question – I was sitting there looking like a groupie for the Grateful Dead. I thought back to the unbearably arrogant women from the café. I hadn't murdered any of them, so clearly I was cut out for this environment. And as an extra bonus, this was a classy venue so my previous fears of resorting to go-go dancing were fading fast.

'Of course I can.'

'Well, I tell you what. Something says to me that you're not trouble. Three of our waitresses haven't shown up tonight. If you can start right now, I'll give you a trial. I'll pay you cash, that way the permits won't be a problem.'

I wanted to hug him, but I tried to show a modicum of

restraint. I'd already had one emotional breakdown in front of the poor guy, so I didn't want to completely terrify him by invading his personal space and going for a full blown cuddle.

'Go downstairs and ask for Jackie – she'll find you a uniform.'

Please God, don't let the uniform be a rabbit's tail and a pair of ears.

'Thank you,' I stammered. 'I'll work really hard.'

And I did. For six months, I worked six nights a week in the club – no rabbit's tail, no ears, and the place was as classy as Joe had promised. I made friends easily with the other girls and would often arrange to meet them before work for coffee. We'd sit in a little café on the edge of a canal and drink coffee and people watch all afternoon. Transsexuals, transvestites, drag queens, drag kings, dominatrix, gay couples, straight couples – it seemed like every section of society was represented on the streets of Amsterdam, without judgement or prejudice. It was a world away from my working class, close knit upbringing and I adored it. The only downside was that I missed Kate, Sarah, Jess and Carol desperately and wished I could share this with them, but as a first year apprentice in a hair salon, struggling students, and a fledgling model, none of them had the money to come over, even for a weekend. I had to settle for quick notes dashed off on postcards, letting them know I was still alive.

In some ways, I'd transitioned to a new life, a new world, and most of the time it felt like my previous life didn't exist. There was a lot of that in this city. Maybe that's why I continued to live in the Dam Central Hotel, even though the girls from the club thought I was insane, because in a funny way I'd grown to love it. The owner was an eccentric Frenchman called René, who, after he had established that I wasn't a drug dealing hooker, became almost fatherly in his affection for me. Or at least, what I thought fatherly affection would be like if it wasn't drowning in bourbon. He would wait up for me in the evenings and bring me coffee each morning whilst I regaled him with stories about the previous night's customers. The businessmen who dropped more money than I earned in a month on their bar bills. The models who looked like they could do with a pie. The fashionistas, the glitterati, the celebrities, the bizarre characters in their outlandish costumes. The pimps and dealers that made the mistake of trying to do business and were rapidly ejected by the security guys.

As for Joe, he always made time to have a quick chat in the evenings and he'd often join us for a dawn breakfast at the end of a shift, or for coffee in the afternoons. Watching him work had been an education. He ran the club like clockwork, with a fine balance of toughness and decency, and despite our age difference, we always seemed to have loads to talk about. He made me feel safe, protected, but it was more than that. We were friends. Not close enough that I could give him my opinion of the stunning women he occasionally dated – all gorgeous, glamorous socialites on the Amsterdam scene, and all of them brief flings that he never seemed to take too seriously – but close enough that we would watch an afternoon movie at the cinema and spend hours debating the merits of Miami Vice versus Hill Street Blues.

I was settled. I was happy. Until the universe decided to toss a grenade in my direction.

On a chilly afternoon in March, I was sitting in the coffee bar on the ground floor of the hotel, watching the world go by through the large window that faced on to the street, when suddenly my mother passed before my eyes. I closed them quickly, thinking that someone must have slipped a hallucinogen into my croissant, but when I reopened them, she was still there. And so was my dad. And my gran. My GRAN, for God's sake! She'd never been further than Skegness in her life. This might only be a sea away from Scotland but I lived on the cusp of a different world and not one that my granny should ever have to see.

My heart started racing and I didn't know whether to make a dash for the back door or hide under a table. I opted for the nearest table. Shit, shit, shit. Maybe they would pass by. Maybe they were just on a weekend break and it was just coincidence that they were here. Or maybe Callum had told them where I was and they'd come to drag me back, kicking and screaming. I'd written to them when I got a job and told them I was living in Amsterdam, but I hadn't said where exactly, just that I was safe and well, and having an adventure. I'm fairly sure my mother's head would have exploded on reading it. Only Callum knew my actual address, courtesy of weekly letters I sent to his best friend's house, and I'd sworn him to secrecy.

Shit, shit, shit. I felt a draught as the door opened and then the footsteps of people entering. *Don't let it be them. Don't let it be them. Don't let it be them.*

'Excuse me,' said the unmistakable voice of my mother to a stunned René, who was still reeling from the fact that one minute I'd been chatting to him and the next I was camouflaged as a table leg. 'I'm looking for my daughter. Her name is Carly Cooper.'

Silence.

'Does she live here?' my mother persisted in her posh 'telephone or talking to the priest' voice. I knew what she was doing. She was looking around thinking that the hotel was a dosshouse and all the people in it were obviously fugitives who'd broken their bail conditions.

More silence. Now I knew how criminals feel when they're cornered by the police. There was nowhere to go, nothing to do except surrender with my hands in the air.

I slowly rose from under the table, banging my head on the way up. I smiled ruefully.

'Hi, Mum,' I stammered. 'What brings you here?'

As reunions go, it wasn't the warmest. My mum had come on a mission to take me home and had brought my dad and gran in the hope that they'd back her up. That was the first flaw in the plan. My dad was already eyeing the bar and my granny had plonked herself down at a table with two punks sporting blue Mohicans and was telling them about the terrible time she'd had last time she went to the hairdressers for a perm and a silver rinse. Her curls were still a shade of pale purple. She was a giggle, my gran, and I adored her, but that wasn't enough to get me on a plane home.

I was outnumbered but defiant. I had no intention of leaving. After all, couldn't they see that I was still in one piece after six months? When I put this point to a foaming-at-the-mouth mother, it was swiftly rebuffed.

'Look, madam...' She always called me 'madam' when she was severely pissed off. 'We left you here for six months, thinking that the novelty would wear off and you'd eventually come home, but you obviously prefer living in squalor!'

René looked mortally offended.

'But this has gone on long enough, so you're coming with us, young lady, this minute!'

Eventually, after much shouting and arguing, I brokered a deal using powers of political diplomacy that would have made Jess proud.

'Tell you what, Mum,' I conceded. 'Stay for two days and you can meet my friends and see where I work and if you still disapprove, then I'll come back.' I wasn't sure what that would accomplish, but I was desperately trying to buy time.

She hummed, hawed, pursed and unpursed her lips, before

realising that, short of dragging me out by the hair, it was as close as she was going to get to victory in round one. She reluctantly agreed.

My dad finally found his voice. 'Do you have to work today?'

'No, Dad. It's my night off tonight.'

'Well then, I'll tell you what. Why don't we go back to our hotel and change, then we'll meet you back here at eight and you can show us the Amsterdam night life.'

I knew what he was doing. He wanted to go out on the town to see if his closest friend also vacationed in Amsterdam, but I didn't care. He was offering me a reprieve from my mum's disapproval. God bless Jack Daniel's.

They arrived back at eight o'clock on the dot. My mum always was a stickler for punctuality. It was a warm spring evening and in a world of tourists and jaw dropping characters, she stuck out like a sore thumb in her flowery dress and sensible pumps. My granny was wearing her trusty faves – crimplene slacks and her best bingo cardigan – and my dad, in his seamed chinos and polo shirt, looked like he was en route to the nineteenth hole.

'What do you want to see, Dad?'

'Why don't we just have a wander around this area and we'll see where it takes us?' He was already slurring slightly.

'But, Dad, this is the Red Light district.'

'We'll see something new then, won't we?' he replied with a wink.

My mother snorted her disapproval and I grinned. My dad really was the oldest swinger in town.

We set off down the adjacent streets. It was fairly quiet, the crowds not usually building up until after nine, but already there were some girls sitting in their windows, hoping for early trade. This wasn't helping my case to stay here at all. My mother wouldn't last two hours here, never mind two days.

I was on the lookout for a sling to keep her chin off the ground when we suddenly realised that my gran was no longer with us. We searched around frantically and finally saw her about a hundred yards back, staring in a window with a red light above it and a buxom brunette, wearing a leopard-skin bra and G-string, sitting in it. My gran looked like a senior citizen lesbian voyeur.

'Gran,' I shouted. 'Come on. What are you doing?'

She bustled up to us. 'I was just looking in the window of that lingerie shop, dear. I may be too old to wear it, but I can still admire it,' she added with a twinkle in her eye.

The rest of us collapsed in hysterics. Even my mum managed a giggle. Thank God Gran hadn't had her specs checked in ten years. She honestly thought she was looking at a mannequin modelling the latest line in undies.

We wandered on until Gran demanded we stop for liquid refreshment. Needless to say, Dad wasn't arguing. In the first pub we came to, there was an eclectic mixture of pimps, pushers and tourists sampling the seedier side of the city.

We got drinks at the bar and found a free table. After a few moments of my mother's silent disapproval, I was relieved when my gran broke the tension by announcing she was going to the loo. Standing up, she was scanning the place for a LADIES sign when a giant of a man wearing a gold rope the size of a tow chain passed her.

'My, that must have cost a fortune, son,' she remarked, invoking that Glaswegian theory of life that says it's perfectly acceptable to speak to everyone you meet and verbalise every thought with no offence intended.

He looked at her like she was insane and thankfully kept walking.

'He must have some job to be able to afford jewellery like that,' she whistled.

'I, erm, think he's in sales, Gran.'

A frown of puzzlement creased her pan stick foundation. 'What kind of sales?'

'I really don't know. Maybe coke?' It was one of the most popular drugs of choice among the clubbers around here.

'Oh, I wouldn't be having any of that,' she wittered. 'Those fizzy drinks give me terrible indigestion.'

I put my head in my hands as she spotted the toilets and beetled off. Tears of laughter coursed down my face. She really was priceless. She was also going to land us in serious trouble unless I got her away from this madness. I decided to take them to the Premier Club. At least there we would be safe from my gran's naive utterings and there would be a better class of reveller for my mother to disapprove of.

As we approached, Chad, the doorman, grinned widely.

'Hey, Cooper, what you doin' here, babe? I thought this was your night off.'

'It is, Chad, but my family have arrived from Scotland and I just wanted to let them see where I work. Can you let Joe know we're here?'

We went inside and found a table. The act tonight was a Harry Connick Jnr lookalike, who was belting out 'I've got you under my skin'.

'Oh, I love this song,' exclaimed Gran as she dragged my dad on to the dance floor, an easy task now that his limbs were lubricated to the consistency of rubber. She was soon quickstepping her heart away, looking like a star performer from *Footloose – the Senior Years.*

Joe joined my mum and I at the table. He immediately registered the general displeasure radiating from my mum and had the whole situation sussed in ten seconds.

'Mrs Cooper, I'm Joe Cain. It's a pleasure to meet you.'

Mum gave him a look that would freeze hell, but Joe just kept on going, at his charming best.

'You must be really proud of your daughter.'

Proud? What was he up to? My mum looked like she was about to develop an ulcer the size of Orkney and he was saying she should be proud.

'And what exactly should I be proud of, Mr Cain?'

'Of Carly. She's done great since she got here. I think it's so commendable that she's over here, working hard whilst developing her language skills and cultural education.'

'Really?' I couldn't tell if her tone was sarcastic, disbelieving or mellowing.

'Why yes, Mrs Cooper. Her Dutch and French are coming along great and she spends her whole life in the museums and galleries here. It's invaluable experience for a girl of her age.' He grinned at me.

What in God's name was he on about? The only French and Dutch I spoke was 'good evening' and 'goodbye'. And the only time I went near a museum was to sit on the steps outside on a sunny day to top up my tan.

Stop, Joe, stop, I silently willed him.

But my mum was definitely softening. She had relaxed her shoulders and was almost smiling.

He continued. 'And as for her work here, well, you can see that this is a very respectable club and Carly has worked so hard that we've decided to promote her to assistant manager.'

WHAT? Had he been taking the kind of drugs that were strictly banned from the premises? This was all news to me. I mean, sure, I loved my job and was always ready to work extra hours and stay late. And yes, I'd taken to organising the staff and doing the weekly orders. But promotion? I wanted to kiss him.

When Fred and Ginger returned from the dance floor, Mum introduced them to Joe. Within ten minutes, he'd won them over, using charm on my gran and a free bar tab on my dad.

He sat with us for the rest of the evening, even persuading my mum to dance a couple of times. He was outstanding and at some point my heart did a somersault and I started to see him in a whole new light.

We finally left at 3 a.m., everyone a little drunk (or a lot, in my dad's case) and very happy. Joe walked us to the door and insisted that we let him take us to lunch the following day.

'That would be just lovely, Joe,' my mum agreed amiably. 'I'm looking forward to it already.' It was my turn now to scrape my jaw off the floor. I'd never seen her look so... I struggled to pinpoint it, before realising with shock that she was *relaxed.*

Joe winked at me and I blew him a kiss. He was spectacular.

The next day, lunch in the conservatory of the American Hotel was followed by a tour of the Van Gogh Gallery, where I pretended I'd been there many times before, and then dinner in the Krasnapolski. Joe gave me another night off and for once he didn't go to work either. He couldn't have been more attentive to my family or to me for that matter. What was going on? And why had my heart started thundering the minute he walked into a room?

My mum and gran sat down to breakfast with me on their final day. Dad was upstairs nursing his daily hangover.

'Carly, your dad and I have been talking and it seems that you've done well for yourself here. We would have no right to force you to come home and I'm sorry I underestimated you. I was only concerned because we want you to be safe. I hope you know that.'

'I do, Mum,' I said, not sure I could believe what I was hearing. Sweet Jesus, it was a miracle. 'But I'm happy here and I don't want to leave.'

Gran spoke up. 'That's okay, Carly, ma darling. We understand. If I had a friend like your Mr Cain, I wouldn't want to leave either, pet. He certainly loves you.'

He does? Whoa. Since when? How come I didn't know this? Surely it was all a big act to save me from the wrath of the mighty Cooper clan?

I was still dazed as I saw them off in a cab to the airport. My parents weren't big on displays of affection, but my granny wrapped me in a bear hug. 'Have a ball, pet,' she whispered. 'Don't do anything I wouldn't do. Right enough, that doesn't leave much.' With a cheeky cackle, and pursed lips from my mother, they were off and strangely, I was sad to see them go.

* * *

'Get yourself together, Cooper,' I told myself as I got ready for work that evening. I couldn't believe it, I was nervous. Or excited. Or something that was definitely making me shake as I applied my mascara.

I went to the club early, hoping Joe would be there. He was. I tentatively knocked on his office door.

'Come in,' he shouted.

I entered slowly, trying my best to smile but only managing a demented grimace.

'Hi. I just wanted to thank you for being so great with my parents. You didn't have to do that and it was really nice of you. Don't worry, I know you just said all that stuff about a promotion to get my mum off my case, so I'm not expecting anything. I want to pay you back for all the money you spent on us and I'll make up the extra night off this week.' My brain was screaming at me to stop talking, but my mouth was on Mission Babble.

He sat back in his big leather chair, a languid grin on his face.

'Number one, it was no problem – your folks are nice people. Number two, the promotion is genuine – I was going to tell you later in the week. Number three, I don't want you to pay me back – I enjoyed myself. Number four, you don't have to make up any time – you do so many extra hours that you're owed a few days off.'

I was stunned. Even more surprising, I was experiencing something other than just a thudding heart now.

'Joe, can I ask you something?' Oh no. My gob was running away with itself and my brain was desperately trying to apply the brakes.

'Sure.'

'Can I kiss you?' Brake fail. Screech. Crash.

'Sure.' He laughed as he stood up and leaned over the desk, turning his head to one side and proffering his cheek.

I reached up slowly and touched his chin, turning his face as I did, so that his eyes met mine. I brushed my lips against his once, then again, then I launched an all-out assault, stopping only for breath when I began to turn a mild shade of pink. This was shocking. Crazy. And absolutely bloody wonderful. But what was wrong with me that my attraction to men seemed to come out of nowhere and ambush me? It had been the same with Nick Russo in that Benidorm bar, and now Joe had gone from my lovely boss to intoxicatingly attractive in the space of a couple of days.

'I think we need to talk,' he whispered, panic in his voice. 'Let's get out of here.'

'But what about the club?'

'It's quiet out there. Chad can look after it tonight,' he insisted.

He grabbed his jacket and my hand and pulled me outside. We walked silently for what seemed like miles, before stopping at an ancient wooden bench on the edge of one of the canals. I waited for him to say something, too terrified to speak in case I had this all wrong. Was he going to give me a lecture about how he was the boss and couldn't fraternise with the staff? Was he going to fire me? Did snogging the boss constitute gross misconduct? Or was he just going to say that I was incredibly stupid, pat me on the head and tell me to keep my tongue well away from his tonsils in future?

Eventually he spoke. 'I've wanted to kiss you for such a long time.'

Phew!

He continued, 'You see, I'm in love with you.'

'I know.' It came out with a matter of fact nod and shrug.

'You do? How?'

I giggled. 'My gran told me.'

His eyes crinkled up in that gorgeous way as he laughed too, then leaned over and did that kissing thing again for a long, long time.

* * *

We were still smiling when the sun came up the following morning and we were still sitting on the same bench planning our future. I'd gone from zero to love in two point five seconds and it felt oh so right.

We'd decided that I would leave the hotel and move into his flat. He told me that he was going to open a new restaurant across town and he would split his time between both outlets, leaving the day-to-day running of the Premier Club to me. I argued that I was too young, and an illegal alien to boot, but he disagreed and said that I was more than capable and that my permits would be through any day now. It was the most warm and bubbly feeling. This amazing guy believed in me. And he loved me!

He took me back to his flat that morning and slowly undressed me, his hands tenderly drifting over my body, touching and probing everywhere. Thank God I'd worn my best underwear.

We stayed in bed all day – making love, talking. At one point we were discussing music and I confessed my hidden love of Elvis. Joe broke into an impromptu and really terrible rendition of 'Burning Love'. I hoped he would never suggest the rhythm method of contraception because he obviously had none. But I didn't care. Every fibre of my being told me I was on to something special with Joe Cain, and the next six months proved me right.

We worked in the evenings and slept late in the mornings, waking to make love before having a long lunch. The afternoons were filled with long walks and I finally did venture inside Amsterdam's many museums and galleries. We would lie in the park, my head on his chest as he read to me or simply stroked my hair while I snoozed. Every day I fell more in love with him and I just knew, without a doubt, that we were meant to be together.

On the anniversary of my arrival in Holland, we went to our favourite Italian restaurant. Joe had been edgy all week and I was beginning to panic. What was wrong with him? Was he bored with us? I thought we'd been so happy, but maybe I'd missed something? He hardly spoke throughout the meal. I tried to be windswept and interesting, tried to draw him into conversation, but he wouldn't have it. He was completely distracted.

Panic turned to sheer terror as he jumped up and asked for the bill the minute we'd finished our coffee.

We made our way outside and instead of looking for a taxi,

Joe turned right and started walking, dragging me behind him. Bugger, I was going to break my neck – my shoes were definitely not made for walking. I could feel the blisters rising when he finally came to a stop at the bench where we'd spent our first night together.

'What are we doing here, Joe? Tell me what's wrong,' I begged.

He sat me down and looked at his watch. What the hell was going on? What was he waiting for?

He said nothing.

I turned to face the canal, contemplating jumping in if the night got any worse, when suddenly I saw it. Approaching slowly from the west was a canal boat, lit up like a Christmas tree. As it neared us, I could see that it had a massive banner on the side, words emblazoned on it. I squinted to read it, only managing when it was directly in front of us.

COOPER, I LOVE YOU. MARRY ME.

I squealed, my hand flying to my mouth. It was only when I caught the questioning glint in his eyes that I realised he was waiting for an answer.

I threw my arms around him. 'Yes, yes, yes,' I screamed between kisses, until he disentangled himself and pulled a box from his pocket. When he opened it, there was the most beautiful diamond solitaire I had ever seen.

'I thought I'd better wait until you said yes before showing you this,' he laughed. 'I know how shallow you are and I didn't want you saying yes just so you could get the diamond.'

'You know me far too well, Mr Cain,' I answered, heart swollen to bursting point. 'Do I get matching earrings if we last a year?'

As always, his eyes crinkled as he laughed, and if it was possible, I loved him even more. In fact, I was so besotted that I managed to get over the twinge of sadness that I wasn't sharing tonight with anyone from home. Callum would interrogate Joe to make sure he was good enough. Michael would love the thought of having another brother. Kate would hug me, Sarah would shriek with happiness, Carol would try to work out the value of the ring and Jess would give me a full run down on the legal implications of marriage and divorce. I pushed the longing away. I missed my girls and my brothers madly, but the excitement of working in the club and living with Joe seemed a million miles from my old life.

My pals would love him, though. I was sure of it.

Joe. My fiancé. The girl who had spent years watching her parents' marriage and vowing she'd never walk into that trap, was engaged. And crazy as it was, it felt great to have someone who loved me so much he wanted to spend a lifetime with me.

That night, we went home and had the most passionate sex I'd ever known. It was ferocious: licking, biting, swinging from the lights... I'm sure most of it would have been illegal in several countries. But thankfully, not Holland. When we were finally satisfied, I felt like I required oxygen and a pacemaker.

Joe rolled over. 'Cooper, tell me your ultimate sexual fantasy.' This was a game we often played before, during or after sex – there was a prize for the most original composition. Our fantasies were like cocktails. We had a fantasy of the week, a daily special fantasy and a monthly themed fantasy. It was all harmless humour and most of them were so ridiculous that we usually ended up in fits of giggles.

'The ultimate one?' I enquired.

'The ultimate one,' he responded. 'The one that you definitely want to do in this lifetime.'

I racked my brains, trying to think of the most interesting one. There were loads to choose from, but, to tell you the truth, although I had fun thinking about them, I wasn't sure that I actually wanted to physically act on them.

Come on, Cooper, play the game.

'I guess it would be the one where we have sex in a room full of strangers – that would be a turn on.'

Mistake. Big mistake.

A week later it was our night off and Joe and I went to our usual bar on the edge of the Red Light area. After six-too-many cocktails we left and Joe steered me to a concealed doorway in an alley off the Leidseplein. I didn't give it a second thought. Joe knew the city's nightlife inside out and had taken me to loads of gems that were off the beaten track.

He rapped on the door. After a few minutes, it was answered by a burly chap with an English accent and a bad wig.

He beckoned us inside. I was ten feet inside the door when I froze to the spot. Everyone was naked. The bar was full of people sipping cocktails and chatting like it was the most natural thing in the world (which, I suppose, it was, really). Mother of God, you didn't find bars like this in Glasgow. It was too bloody cold there, for a start.

The shock sobered me immediately. I scanned the room. Good grief, there was a couple having sex in the corner and nobody was batting an eyelid.

Joe put his arm around me. 'It's your fantasy, Carly. We can do whatever you want.'

How about a dash to the door?

I took a deep breath. I could handle this, I thought. I was a cosmopolitan woman of the world. Anyway, hadn't I come to Amsterdam looking for adventure and new experiences?

As usual in times of crisis, I got a mental image of my mum. She didn't have to say a word – she just pursed her lips and frowned, shaking her head.

I forced the image from my mind. Come on, Cooper, get a grip. No-one else here was in the least bit flustered, so why was I the same colour as the red lights spinning on the ceiling? I could do this. I could.

Time to put on my party pants. Or rather, to take them off.

We checked in our clothes at the cloakroom and made our way to the bar. It was bizarre. From the necks up, it looked like a room of lawyers, teachers and doctors, but from the necks down, it was a party in a nudist colony. And there was I, in the middle of it all, wearing high heels and a smile. Why hadn't I stuck to that last diet? My wobbly bits were trembling. More deep breaths. I sucked in my stomach until my abdominal muscles threatened to snap. Then I realised something. Nobody was looking at me. Nobody was inspecting my thighs for cellulite or pointing in horror at the size of my bum. I started to giggle.

'What?' Joe asked. 'What are you laughing at?'

By this time, I was splitting my naked sides. 'I can't believe I'm doing this. If the girls at home could see me now, they'd think I'd lost it and ambush me with a packet of pants!'

I tried to see the whole thing as a turn-on, but it was too ridiculous, so we settled for a game of pornographic 'I Spy' and a quick grope behind a pillar when I was positive that nobody could see us.

Eventually, we went home and slumped into bed, still giggling like kids during their first sex education lesson.

Joe pulled me on top of him. 'Tell me another fantasy, Cooper.'

I'd learned my lesson. 'No way, Mr Cain. You take things entirely too literally.'

* * *

Over the following months, our roller-coaster fired along without any major derailments. Thankfully, our sojourn to the 'bare bum bar' was never repeated and we continued to have long nights and mornings of love with lots of fantasies thrown in to keep things interesting.

In fact, that had started to niggle somewhere in the deep recesses of my brain. It seemed like our sex life revolved more and more around talking dirty than it did around love. I chided myself that I was just moaning about too much of a good thing. After all, I enjoyed the fantasies. But every night...?

It was a small price to pay. During the days, Joe was his usual funny, kind, caring, protective, interesting, gorgeous self. We spent endless hours talking about our wedding, a knees-up back in Scotland with my girl gang as bridesmaids. One Christmas Eve, I'd called everyone with the news. My granny had whooped with glee, my mother had said she hoped I knew what I was doing and my brothers demanded to meet him and asked if he was any good at football. My dad asked if he got a discount at the club now. I told him he was barred.

Next I called Kate's house, hoping all my pals would be there, and they were. They'd all huddled around the phone, and when I'd told them I was engaged they'd shrieked with excitement for me. I promised I'd bring Joe back to meet them soon, but it hadn't happened. The problem with owning and running clubs pretty much single-handedly is that there's no one to take over when the boss wants a break. Chad could cover for a few hours, but he had his hands full on the door. All our staff were part-time, so – other than me – Joe didn't have anyone he could trust with managing things in his absence. Add to that his workaholic nature, and I was beginning to wonder if we'd ever get a break. Every time I mentioned it, Joe would promise me we'd get a holiday soon and my hopes would rise, then fall again as more time passed and it still didn't happen.

On a freezing cold night in January, as I made my way to work, I knew it was going to be a quiet night. I was on my own, because Joe was out scouting other clubs, searching for his next investment. There were few tourists at this time of year and the six inches of snow on the ground would stop most of the locals coming out. By midnight, only a few tables were busy as I worked the room, chatting to all the regulars. At a corner table was a couple I'd never seen before, so I introduced myself as I passed them.

'Pleased to meet you,' the guy replied. 'It's a great club you've got here.'

I stopped in my tracks. It was the broadest Glasgow accent. I turned and smiled.

'You're from Glasgow!' Why did my stomach just do a somersault in glee? And why did I want to hug them? 'Let me buy you a drink,' I offered, suddenly excited. Maybe it wasn't going to be such a dull night after all.

When I took over their drinks and joined them, they introduced themselves as Fraser and Wendy. They were over on a weekend break and as we chatted, it transpired that not only were they from Glasgow, but they were from the same area as me. In fact, Fraser played in the same football team as my brother, Callum.

I interrogated them for stories of home. How was Callum? Did they know Michael? What about Kate, Carol, Sarah and Jess? Fraser told me that my brother had broken his leg the week before. I was stunned. Callum had broken his leg and I didn't know about it. What kind of a sister was I? I felt like I'd been overtaken by a variety pack of emotions. On the one hand, it was great to talk to people from home. But on the other... well, it was strange – I had never been homesick before and now waves of it were sweeping over me.

At closing time, they staggered out, drunk on the drinks that I had been plying them with as thanks for answering my relentless questions all night. I let all the staff go and as I waited for Joe to collect me, gloom descended. I tried to pinpoint what was wrong, but I couldn't understand it. Suddenly, I just wanted to get on the first plane available and go home.

I sat silently in the car all the way back to our apartment, then listlessly undressed and climbed into bed. Joe put his arms around me.

'Make love to me, Joe,' I asked.

'Sure, babe. Why don't you tell me a story first?'

He didn't get it. I didn't want acrobatic sex and horny fantasies. I wanted him to make slow tender love to me. To make me feel better. To make me feel like I belonged here.

I rolled over and stared at the photo on my bedside table. It was of all the girls on our last day in Benidorm. We were literally falling over each other as we made daft gestures into the camera, faces the colour of tomatoes from too much sun. We looked like we didn't have a care in the world. What were they doing right now? Our friendships were still there, but we'd all gone our separate ways and our contact was limited to the occasional letter or infrequent phone call, always instigated by me because Sarah and Jess were skint students, Carol was working in a bar between modelling gigs to make ends meet and Kate was living on just over thirty quid a week as a junior in a salon.

I reached for the phone to call Kate, but stopped myself; it would only make me feel worse.

Instead, I turned to look at Joe, who unfortunately was in an extremely unattractive, open mouthed mid-snore. Did he ever feel like this? Did he ever want to be somewhere else (I mean, other than a nudist bar in Barbados – fantasy number forty-six)?

Maybe it was an age thing, I mused. Joe was thirty-seven, I was nearly twenty years younger. He was only the second man I'd ever slept with, for God's sake. And if I married him, then he'd be the last. Panic began to rise. Did I really want to look at the same penis for the rest of my life? What if this was a huge mistake? What would life be like in ten years' time – would I be married with six kids by then, covered in food, tears and snot, trapped in domesticated hell? I wasn't ready for this. I wasn't ready to promise the rest of my life to this man, no matter how bloody spectacular he was.

And spectacular, he definitely was. I touched his cheek. He was everything I'd ever wanted. He was funny, sexy, smart...

I was so confused. I mean, this wasn't a mild dilemma, like would I take the holiday or the car if I won on *Family Fortunes*. This was a full-blown life-changing crossroads and I had no idea which way to turn.

When I got out of bed at 5 a.m., the world seemed different. Joe still lay sleeping beside me, the snoring now ceased, the mouth closed and looking unbearably gorgeous and touchable. But it didn't matter. I knew what I was going to do and I hated myself for it.

I leaned over and kissed him, feeling traitorous but unable to stop myself from betraying him.

You see, I knew I wasn't staying. I knew I had to go home for a while. Back to Callum and Michael and my gran and the girls. Back to Maw and Paw Walton. Just home. But I knew that if I told Joe, he would insist on coming with me and that wasn't the answer. I wanted to go alone, to see my mates and my family. To think about us and what we were doing. He would never understand. After all, hadn't we vowed never to spend a night apart?

I took the coward's way out. I took off my engagement ring and placed it on top of my signature.

Dear Joe,

the note read,

I'm so sorry. I need to go home for a while to do some thinking. I'll be in touch soon. Love you – always,
   Cooper x.
   PS I'm leaving the ring, so you know I'll be back.

I rushed to Schiphol Airport and caught the 7 a.m. flight to Glasgow.

I never saw Joe Cain again.

5

HIGH – THE LIGHTHOUSE FAMILY

I arrive at Paco's on Chiswick High Road fifteen minutes late due to a wardrobe crisis – pink pedal pushers are NOT for a woman of my curvatures and complexion – and the Number 57 bus driver refusing to go over twenty miles an hour. Chiswick is the most convenient meeting place, given that Kate lives around the corner, I'm only a few miles away, Jess can hop on a direct train from Westminster and Carol is dating a minted bloke who provides a car and driver to take her wherever she wants to go. As I charge into the packed restaurant, it crosses my mind again that I need to ask the others if they know what happened to Sarah, but I get sidetracked by their cheers.

Kate and Jess have obviously filled Carol in on my day's deliberations, because in front of them all are glasses full of red liquid – the unmistakable murky hues of the Invaded Vagina. I've never asked what's in it and I'm pretty sure now isn't the time to find out.

'Cooper,' Jess greets me, her Glaswegian accent softened by an overtone of posh London. 'We were just about to call in a search party.'

There are kisses and hugs all round, before I eventually park myself, desperate to fill them in on my latest episode.

Jess, dressed in a classic navy power suit, takes charge as usual. As a political researcher and (secret) girlfriend of Basil Asquith, MP, she's used to participating in important meetings and keeping things in order.

'Right then, who's got anything major to report this week?' she asks, her red, chin-length bob not even budging as she scans her audience.

Three hands shoot up, including mine, one almost decapitating a passing waiter. Bloody hell, THREE major news items. Normally we're lucky if there's one and we just fill the rest of the time with essential tasks like swapping salacious celebrity gossip. Most of that comes from Carol and Jess, with occasional top-ups from Kate. I wouldn't come into contact with a celebrity unless I tripped over one when I was putting my bins out. I definitely have the least glamorous life in my circle.

'Marks out of ten for importance, juiciness and trauma value?' Jess requests.

'Four,' Carol replies, through a perfect, rose pink pout. It would be easy to hate her. She hasn't gained a pound since we were fourteen, and she still has Cindy Crawford's easy elegance and killer cheekbones. Even more irritating, she can throw on any old thing and achieve the kind of look that would take me a week and a half to put together.

'Nine,' adds Kate.

'Ten,' I smile gleefully.

There's a round of surprised faces. We haven't had a ten since Jess caught her boyfriend in bed with his allegedly erstwhile wife and proceeded to assault him with a table lamp, causing him to flee his home with only his ministerial red box covering his dignity. It is a complicated relationship. Jess definitely isn't the kind of woman who would entertain an affair, but Basil's marriage has been over for years, and he and his wife keep up the façade for the sake of his political career and her social standing. Personally, I think Jess should run a mile from the pair of them, but she loves him, so I try not to judge.

We decide to spill in reverse order, leaving the biggest until last. I can barely contain myself so I sip my cocktail to keep my gob otherwise occupied.

Carol starts with a sigh. 'Clive wants to take me to Antigua for two weeks.' Clive is Carol's latest boyfriend. Private-school educated, great connections, family money and he's invested well in all sorts of technology that I don't understand, so two weeks in a luxury resort wouldn't even make a dent in his petty cash.

I almost splurt my drink across the table. 'And that's a problem?'

'Two weeks! Fourteen whole days and nights of Clive. I mean, he's very nice and all that, but normally I don't even hang around long enough to brush my teeth in the mornings. It's usually meet, expensive dinner somewhere fabulous, his place, orgasm, and then I'm out of there.'

And she's not kidding. Carol treats her boyfriends like a session at the gym – a bit of a chore, a few grunts and groans, but the rewards are worth it.

We deliberate her dilemma over our starters. It would be easy to look at Carol's gorgeous, luxury life and think she has it all. Or that she's aloof and shallow. Actually, she *is* pretty shallow, but that's not a surprise in her world. Underneath, though, she's just the working-class girl from Glasgow, who grew up on a council estate with a mum who worked three jobs to support her family, and who knows that she has a time limit to capitalise on her exquisite appearance. For all her stunning looks, rich boyfriends, flash cars and first-class flights, she's just like the rest of us –

flawed, complicated and still figuring life out. We decide that she should go. After all, how bad could it be? As long as she takes the latest Jilly Cooper, an empty suitcase for shopping trips and calls us on Clive's phone bill if boredom sets in, she'll be fine.

We move on to Kate before Carol gets the brochures out and makes us all sick with jealousy.

To my surprise, Kate looks flushed. This is the woman who copes with two kids, a full-time job, a house and husband and all without breaking into a sweat. A minor earthquake couldn't break Kate's stride, so if she's perturbed in any way, then I've got a feeling that it's something huge. I'm not wrong.

'My cocktail doesn't have any alcohol in it because I'm, er, well, might be pregnant again.'

There is a stunned silence.

I look to the heavens for inspiration on what to say. Instead, all I see are wooden beams with what looks like dry rot.

I tentatively ask, 'Is this good?'

She bursts into tears.

My God, Kate never cries. She's the emotional equivalent of Gibraltar.

'It's just so unexpected,' she blurts. 'I thought my days of booties and nappy rash were over. But I am happy, honest. Just a bit shell-shocked. It's really early, just a couple of weeks but my period hasn't come and I recognise the signs. I'm hormonal. And emotional. One minute I'm over the moon and the next I want to punch everyone I meet. One of Hot N Spicy nearly got a roller brush surgically inserted today.'

'What does Bruce think about it?' Carol probes, Antigua now firmly shoved to the back of her mind.

'Oh, you know Bruce, he's delighted. He's already designing an extension and a hydraulic cot. Poor bloody baby will spend half its life with motion sickness.'

We all laugh, including Kate.

She dries her eyes and raises her glass. 'Here's to maternity bras and piles.'

We all join in the toast before descending on her with congratulatory cuddles and kisses, much to the bemusement of the surrounding diners.

Our main courses arrive and everyone ignores them, too busy discussing names for the baby and the pros and cons of having another child.

Cons: less money to go round, lack of sleep, more stretch marks and, statistically, more probability that one of the kids will end up with a criminal record (this is Jess's little chestnut – she's obviously been researching crime today).

Pros: more presents at Christmas, someone else to visit you when you're in a care home and, statistically, more probability that one of them will end up running the country (also Jess's contribution).

I catch Jess's expression out of the corner of my eye. She's doing that thing again where she looks happy on the outside, but her eyes tell me she's miserable on the inside.

'What's up?' I ask her gently. 'You okay?'

'Sure. I was just thinking that in my present situation, the chances of me having children are up there with winning the lottery and shagging Jeremy Paxman.'

Jess is in that age-old crap situation which, considering she's the smartest of us all, is quite difficult to fathom – the unhappily unmarried mistress. If Basil Asquith's constituents only knew what he is thinking when he advocates corporal punishment (being attached to his antique king-size bed with handcuffs), they may take their vote elsewhere. But Jess is inexplicably attracted to him.

Their affair started four years ago, when she took a post as his researcher, and has motored along, fuelled by endless promises to 're-evaluate his marital situation'. Meanwhile, Mrs Asquith poses quite happily with him at their country estate in endless editions of *House and Garden*. The irony is that Jess is gorgeous (she always reminds me of Julianne Moore), successful and fiercely intelligent. She's also second only to Kate in being grounded and innately sensible. The whole Basil thing is obviously an episode of diminished responsibility from which she'll recover at any time.

She visibly shrugs off her melancholy and turns the over-table light so that it shines in my face. 'Anyway, Cooper, it's your turn. Spill the story.'

I'd almost forgotten I had something to share.

The others are staring at me in anticipation.

I pause for effect, then reach into my bag and pull out two letters and my purse.

'This,' I say placing the first letter down on the table, 'is my letter of resignation. Goodbye bog rolls.'

I place down the next letter, amused at the three confused faces around the table.

'And this is a note to my landlord, terminating the lease on my flat.'

Confusion is now approaching astonishment.

'I've decided that by the turn of the century, I'm going to have found the love of my life and the first place I'm going to look is in my past. So these...' I hold up my credit cards, '... are going to take me around the world to find every poor bugger who has ever had the misfortune to have exchanged bodily fluids with me. Ladies, we have a mission. We're going in and we're taking no prisoners...'

6

THE ONLY WAY IS UP – YAZZ AND THE PLASTIC POPULATION

I arrived back in Glasgow on a cold January morning, having spent the whole flight in a catatonic state of misery. It must have been obvious because the air hostesses removed all sharp objects from my dinner tray.

I had no idea what I was doing there, where I would go, or what alien life-force had possessed me and transported me back to the very place I had fled only eighteen months before. And I missed Joe already. I wanted to phone him and tell him to come and rescue me, that it had all been a mental aberration caused by bad seafood, or the ozone layer, or something, anything that would excuse the fact that I'd deserted him. I commandeered a taxi and gave the driver my parents' address. On the way there, we passed my old school and my spirits lifted as I thought of the girls and wondered what they were doing.

I was beginning to relax when we stopped at a junction and I was confronted by a huge billboard with a gorgeous dark-haired female with blue eyes the size of billiard balls lounging on a sofa. A slogan underneath said, 'Lie on something soft and warm tonight.' As I pondered it, I looked closer and shrieked so loudly that the driver swerved and narrowly missed a rather well-dressed lady with a poodle.

'That's Carol,' I screamed. 'She did it, she really did it!'

I could see that the driver was wondering whether to take me to the address I'd given him, or just drop the shrieking girl here and write off the fare.

'You don't understand,' I explained hurriedly. 'That's one of my best mates up there.'

'Of course it is, and my day job is commander of the space shuttle,' he added dryly.

I didn't care. I suddenly felt that I was back where I belonged, and excitement was washing away all the doubt and regret.

We arrived at my parents' and I jumped out, giving the driver a huge tip in case the poodle sued for emotional distress. I rummaged in the back porch for the house key and let myself in. Security isn't exactly watertight in our street.

My mum was cremating bacon in the kitchen and lost control of her spatula when she set eyes on me. To her credit, she looked pleased to see me and didn't launch into an immediate interrogation as to why I was there and how had I messed up this time. I had a feeling that would come later.

'Where is everyone?' I asked.

'Callum and Michael are still in bed and your dad was last seen comatose on the lounge sofa. He's probably still there unless he's discovered a pub that opens at 8 a.m.,' she added, with an automatic tut of disapproval. No change there, then. These two needed a United Nations peacekeeping force.

I bounced up the stairs and through the first door, where Callum lay sleeping in the middle of a room that looked like it had been ransacked. I launched myself at him, doing a belly flop of a landing that ended with a thud that sounded like plaster cracking. Shit, I'd forgotten about the broken leg.

He yelled, 'What the f—' before stopping mid sentence, his face lighting up. 'Carly, babe, you're back!!!' He'll make a great detective.

I smothered him with kisses, then went next door to Michael's room. At fourteen, he had well and truly embraced the teenage life and he was sleeping soundly in his Rambo T-shirt and boxer shorts, with one leg hanging out of the bed. I ruffled his hair and tickled the end of his nose. He thwacked my hand away, still sleeping. I stuck my fingers in his ears. That did it. He opened his eyes and squinted, desperately trying to focus on his attacker. Then recognition dawned and he jumped up, tripped on the duvet and landed spread-eagled on the floor. You'd think I'd been gone for decades, as he climbed up and hugged me so tightly he cut off circulation to my lower extremities. I extricated myself before my toes turned blue. It was the best welcome ever. 'I missed you, shorty,' I told him, clinging on, realising I was fighting back uncharacteristic tears.

At which point, he remembered he was fourteen and a teenage boy.

'Yeah. Eh, me too. Did you bring me a Toblerone from the Duty Free shop?'

* * *

I spent all afternoon on the phone to the girls, announcing my return. Thankfully, Jess was already home from Aberdeen Uni for the weekend, Sarah said she'd jump on a train from Edinburgh, Carol had come back for a photo shoot in Glasgow, and Kate was working in the salon but she finished at 6 p.m.. All of which made for the hasty organisation of a full-blown homecoming celebration that evening. It was ridiculous. I kept thinking that only the night before I had been lying beside the man I thought I was going to spend the rest of my life with and now, after abandoning him without explanation, I was planning a night out on the town.

What kind of terrible person was I? *It's just for a couple of weeks*, I told myself. *You just need some breathing space. He'll understand.* And if I was only going to be home for such a short time then I really should make the most of it.

The guilt lasted about ten more minutes before I immersed myself in the dilemma of what to wear. I wanted to look as stunning as I could manage without liposuction and a breast reduction.

I settled on black skintight trousers (I'd seen *Grease* twelve times) and a black vest. I pulled my hair up and secured it in a band on top of my head. Four inch stilettos which threatened to disfigure my feet for life completed the outfit and I was ready to go.

* * *

The girls had suggested meeting in Winston Blues, a new pub/club that had opened locally whilst I was away.

As I entered, the butterflies in my stomach were doing the twist. I looked around for a familiar face and saw one at every corner. My God, it was like a St Mary's reunion. It seemed like everyone from my year at school was there and there wasn't a stranger in sight.

Callum and his mates were sitting in one corner and beckoned me over, but before I could move, I heard the roar of multiple hands doing a drum roll on a tabletop. Spandau Ballet's 'Gold' blared from the speakers as I turned to see the source of the racket. It had to be them. The 'We did Benidorm and survived' team were dressed to the nines. It was so good to be back.

A gallon of cocktails later, we were on the tables, on bar stools and, for the more sensible amongst us, on the dance floor. Who needed aerobics when we had Slippery Nipples and Duran Duran?

Much later, I made my way to the ladies' to repair the inevitable damage caused by heat, sweat and drinking multi-coloured cocktails. The crowd was dense and as I battled my way through it, I felt like I was storming a picket line. Someone pushed me from behind, obviously in a rush and having a toilet emergency. It was too much for the four inch stilettos. They teetered for a second before collapsing and taking me with them. I was halfway to the ground, trying frantically to land on my bum with some semblance of dignity when a hand reached out and grabbed me, pulling me back up. I looked up into the laughing face of Mark Barwick.

Mark Barwick. The first, second and third love of my life. Actually, we split and got back together so many times we probably made it to double figures. I'd been besotted by his floppy brown hair and huge hazel eyes. I had started seeing him when I was twelve because he reminded me of David Cassidy, but he was more than just a pretty face. He was funny and crazy and full of surprises. Every girl in my class had a crush on him and he loved it. It was a relationship of 'firsts'. He was the first guy who ever kissed me – a real kiss, with tongues. He was the first guy who ever felt my breasts. He was the first guy who ever told me he loved me. Not that we had full sex – that came later with Nick Russo – but he was the first guy I wanted to marry. Granted, I was fourteen when I decided that, and I'd changed my mind by the following weekend because he refused to come and see *Flashdance* with me at the cinema.

That was the problem with us. We were way too young, he

was way too stubborn and strong willed and so was I, and the result was five years of brilliant highs and huffy lows.

'Falling at my feet again, Cooper? That's nothing new,' he laughed.

Did I mention that he could also be arrogant, overconfident and witty?

'Just as long as you don't expect me to do anything to your anatomy while I'm down there,' I replied tartly, hoping my face wasn't making it obvious that I was delighted to see him.

Fate intervened and the lights in the club came on. Shit, why hadn't I made it to the toilets before this happened? I knew my make-up was landsliding down my face and shining like it had been turtle-waxed.

'How are you getting home?' he asked.

'Walking.'

'In those heels? You'll end up in Casualty. Tell you what, I'll come with you – for protection purposes only, of course.'

I should have said no. I should have fled the scene, but there was no way I could move at speed in those shoes. Instead, I just nodded.

I said goodbye to the girls, who had all paired up with their latest boyfriends.

Mark took my hand and led me out, both of us automatically slipping back into comfortable familiarity. We talked all the way home about everything but us. He told me how he was studying law at Glasgow University. How he had a girlfriend from Edinburgh called Sally. How he still socialised with the guys from school.

I told him about Amsterdam. About Joe and the club. About René and the Dam Central Hotel. About all the people I'd met and all the strange characters that littered the streets. Twice I stumbled in my skyscraper heels and twice he reached out to catch me, saving me from fractures and dislocations. When we reached my house, he stopped and turned.

'Why did you leave, Carly? You didn't even tell me you were going. There was Benidorm, then you were grounded, and the next thing I heard was that you'd gone. Why didn't you tell me?'

'Mark, we'd broken up. In fact, if I remember correctly, *you'd* chucked *me*.'

'We were always breaking up, but we always got back together.' It was true. We'd had more comebacks than Elvis.

'It wouldn't have changed anything, Mark. I just wanted to go away and find something new.'

'You mean *someone* new.'

I started to get annoyed. What right did he have to castigate me? After all, he was hardly drowning his sorrows with Sally from Edinburgh. He hadn't exactly condemned himself to a religious order of celibacy whilst pining desperately for me. How was it that he could instantly press the buttons that made my temper boil?

I was about to unleash a tirade of recriminations (you know the ones: 'You did this, you did that, three years ago last Tuesday you hurt my feelings and by the way I've always hated your aftershave...'), when his eyes met mine and his face moved closer... and closer... and I didn't move away, not even when he began to kiss me so softly, so gently, my lungs forgot to breathe.

He finally stopped. He looked at me, sadness all over his face.

'I know you've moved on now, Carly, but I'll always be here for you. Friends?'

Was this what friends did? I didn't think Joe would have agreed. Shit, Joe. What was I doing? How could I kiss someone else? This was a breather. A break. Why was I puckering up with the first, second and third love of my life?

'Friends,' I heard myself saying. 'Always.'

* * *

A few weeks later, I knew I was going to have to make a decision. I had been in total denial about Joe, about why I was home and about what I was going to do with my life. This wasn't just a breathing space; it was a full-scale surgical removal. I couldn't talk to my parents about it. My dad was only interested in where his next drink was coming from, and my mother was so uptight she wouldn't understand. Now that I was home again, I'd come to realise a few things about our relationship. I was beginning to understand that we'd never been close because she just couldn't relate to this daughter who was nothing like her at all. She still lived in the town she grew up in, and she'd married my dad at sixteen and stuck with him because that's what you did in her world. The concept of having multiple relationships and getting out there and seeing what the world had to offer was alien to her, so I knew she'd tell me to take the safe bet, stay at home, get a job, and live a life similar to hers and that was the last thing I wanted. Being home had only made me see that even clearer.

I went to see Kate, who was working in a nightclub called Chandeliers, to subsidise her meagre hairdressing salary. At the door of the club was Ray, the owner, whom I'd become friendly with over the previous month, as I spent almost every night in the familiar surroundings of mayhem and blaring music. I had regaled him with stories about the club in Amsterdam and we'd spent a few nights swapping tales of the drunken debauchery and decadence of the entertainment industry.

'You still here, Cooper?' he greeted me. 'I thought you were heading back to Mr Wonderful for a spot of clog dancing?'

I laughed. 'I'm having a bit of a dilemma on the clog front, Ray. Don't know if my bunions can stand the pressure.'

It was his turn to be amused. He beckoned me inside and we

went into his office. Two coffees later and I'd explained what was going on.

'Has he tried to contact you?' he asked.

'He doesn't have my mum's address or phone number, so he doesn't have any way of reaching me. When I started working for him, I just gave him the address of the hotel I was living in at the time. And anyway, that's not his style. Joe trusts me. If I say that I just need a bit of space, then he'll trust me to go back. The thing is, I don't think I want to. I've kind of realised that I'm not ready for the whole marriage thing and if I tell Joe that he'll never forgive me.' Not that I was even sure he would forgive me for disappearing on him. In my almost twenty year old brain, it was a no-win situation. 'I think I want to stay here.' There, I'd finally admitted it. I had goosebumps from head to toe.

'So, stay. What's the problem?' he shrugged.

'Ray, it's not that easy. If I stay here, then I need to find somewhere to live and a job and I have to find them quickly. I'm running out of money and there's no way I'm asking my parents for help.' I'd told him all about the set-up at home on a previous visit.

'Tell you what, Cooper, there's a job for you here. This place is getting so busy and my other three clubs are the same. I could do with someone I trust in here to look after things when I'm not around.'

It took a moment for me to take that in. 'How do you know I'm trustworthy? For all you know, I could have embezzled thousands and right now I could be on Interpol's most-wanted posters.' I was stunned but over the moon at his offer.

'You're right, Cooper, you could be, but you're Kate's mate and she's a good girl, so I'll take a chance. You've got a great way with people and I think you'll make money for me here.' I was starting to feel warm and bubbly when he laughed and added, 'And if one penny goes missing, I'll break your legs.' Well, at least we both knew where we stood – me on legs that I might one day have to pick up and carry around in a shopping bag.

I took the offer and started the following evening. Problem number one solved.

By the end of the week, I'd hijacked the lounge in Kate's flat and turned it into a bedroom, with a little help from a clothes rail and a futon. Problem number two solved.

And problem number three? Well, I just put Joe to the back of my mind, blocked out the whole chapter and never did contact him. I knew it was wrong and I was mortified, but putting Joe Cain in a box and sealing it was the only way I could deal with it. I also swore off men for the foreseeable future.

Unfortunately, the foreseeable future turned out to be shorter than I'd anticipated.

* * *

I was standing on the door of the club a few weeks later, trying desperately to get the bouncers to focus on checking the ages of the females who were attempting to enter, rather than their breast size, when a crowd approached and I spotted a familiar face: Doug Cook.

Doug was a year younger than me in school and a friend of Callum. He had been in and out of our house since we were kids and was always the life and soul of every party. I gave him a hug, surprised at how much he'd changed in the two years since I'd last seen him.

He must have grown about six inches and he towered over me. His short blond hair was falling just over his green eyes. I could see every muscle in his chest and abdomen clearly defined through his tight white T-shirt and his beautifully developed thighs stretched his black jeans. Either he'd had a body transplant or taken up permanent residence in a gym, and I would have to have been wearing a balaclava backwards not to notice that he was seriously attractive. I tried to dampen down the physical reaction that was stirring my libido.

This was Callum's best friend. Did that constitute incest? Was I becoming completely depraved and controlled by my oversexed hormones? And anyway, wasn't I still in mourning for Joe? That did it – the thought of Joe made my heart plummet to the pit of my stomach. My conscience had finally kicked in.

Doug and I chatted for twenty minutes, catching up on old gossip. That's when I suddenly realised that I was sitting on my hands lest they develop a mind of their own and wander to the vicinity of his biceps. Every time he smiled, I wanted to stroke his face. So much for conscience. I needed to have a serious chat with myself. Eventually, he went inside to join his friends and two minutes later Callum arrived.

'Callum, inside, now,' I ordered, motioning to my office. I sat him down and interrogated him for information on Doug.

Callum was stunned.

'Christ, Carly, he's like family.' I was right about the incest bit.

'So shoot me, Callum. I can't help it – he's adorable. I nearly jumped his bones the minute I saw him.'

'Eeeew, too much information,' he groaned. 'Just promise me something, sis.'

'Anything.'

'Don't let me see anything involving tongues.'

With a shudder, he gave me a quick hug and retreated to the bar.

At the end of the night, Doug knocked on my office door.

'Carly, I was just wondering if you wanted a lift home.' He looked nervous, but not half as nervous as I felt. I was pretty positive Callum wouldn't have told him I was interested so maybe that meant Doug had sensed something between us too.

'No thanks, Doug. There's a crowd of us going down to Largs. Unless, of course, you want to come.' *Say yes. Say yes. Please, say yes.*

Working in nightclubs reduces your social life to that of an agoraphobic, so we tended to go out after work. There were only two options at 3 a.m.. Option one was Glasgow Airport, where the café was open all night. Option two was Largs, a seaside town about forty minutes away, where we'd make a bonfire on the beach and spend a couple of hours drinking beers and singing along with Mad Mitch, the worst bouncer and guitar player on the planet.

'Eh... sure. Sounds good. I'll wait in the car,' he nodded and I sat on my hands again so I wouldn't punch the air.

At Largs, it was freezing cold and we snuggled up as Mitch tortured 'Let it Be'.

Every time I looked up at Doug, I waited for him to kiss me. My lips were permanently puckered, but there were no takers. At 6 a.m., he dropped me at my house.

When he pulled on the handbrake, he turned his gorgeous face to me. 'You know, for years I had a huge crush on you.'

What did he mean, 'had'?

'And now?' I tried to act cool and keep the hope out of my voice.

'Let's just wait and see.' With that, he leant over and kissed me on the cheek.

I got out of the car and went inside. What the hell was all that about? Wait and see? What exactly was he waiting for?

The following evening, he appeared at the club and again we went out afterwards. We cuddled and talked, but still no smooching. This went on for two months. Most nights, Doug would take me home, we'd talk for a couple of hours and then he'd kiss me on the cheek and leave.

Thankfully his job as a salesman in a local garage meant that he didn't start work until eleven o'clock, otherwise sleep deprivation would have killed him.

My confidence was plummeting to an all-time low. Was I completely unattractive? Had his crush well and truly worn off?

I discussed the situation with the girls, and then ignored their suggestions of 'Forget him' or 'Just tell him straight out that you 're a sure thing!' I knew I had to leave it up to him.

Puzzled but persistent, I invited Doug round to the flat I shared with Kate for dinner one Wednesday night, the only night of the week that I didn't work and Kate did. I promised him a great meal, so it was action stations as my culinary skills extended to Pot Noodles and banana sandwiches. I phoned Roberto, the owner of a nearby Italian restaurant and explained the problem. He came up trumps. In exchange for free tickets to the nightclub for the next month, one of his guys arrived at my door half an hour before Doug with a veritable feast. I bunged it in the oven.

As I opened the door to him, my hormones surged. He was so beautiful that I just wanted to take his hand and drag him to bed.

Instead, I served dinner, accepting his compliments on my cooking with grace and humility, knowing that my chances of going to heaven were diminishing by the minute.

We cuddled up on the couch afterwards and it finally happened. He kissed me. It was tentative and tender as he stroked my face and ran his fingers through my hair. When I eventually came up for air, I gave in to weeks of curiosity.

'Doug, can I ask you something? Why did you wait so long?'

He shrugged, flushed a little. 'I just think this is going to be really big and I want to take it slow. I don't want to rush things and fuck it up.'

'How big?' I asked, stunned at his sincerity and thought-fulness.

'Forever big. Huge. Massive. Weddings and babies big.'

Oh, God. In my head, I hadn't got past multiple orgasm big. I was still on wild passionate affair and he was already on mort-gages and lifelong commitments. Next, he'd be washing my car on a Sunday and I'd be checking his pockets before taking his suits to the dry-cleaners. Panic set in. Hadn't I just left this situa-tion six months before? I lapsed into a pensive silence. Why did everyone suddenly want to talk about bloody weddings? I thought that all men were supposed to be complete commitment-phobes who avoided the 'm' word like it was contagious?

'Don't worry, babe,' he whispered, holding me close. 'Like I said, we'll take it slow.'

I should have realised then that I was doomed, but I had more pressing matters to worry about – we kissed and cuddled for the rest of the night, but *still* not a breast was fondled.

I called an emergency meeting of the girls the next morning. Jess was in Aberdeen, but Sarah was home and Kate and Carol could make it too. They met me at Roberto's and as I relayed the previous night's events, their hilarity was deafening.

'Talk about out of the frying pan and into the sauna,' Carol exclaimed. Her command of common sayings hadn't improved, but with the money she was starting to make from modelling, she didn't care. Nor did she notice that every waiter in the restaurant was staring at her in a catatonic trance whilst sucking in his stomach and puffing out his pecs.

'I think it's sweet that he's already thinking about that kind of stuff,' Sarah offered. She'd always been a hopeless romantic, so I discounted that opinion immediately.

Only Kate had a modicum of balanced sensibility. 'Are you in love with him?' she asked quietly.

All joviality ceased and four pairs of eyes focused on me, waiting for the reply.

'No, no, no. Well, maybe, potentially. Oh, God, I don't know. It's so soon after Joe. But yes, I think about Doug constantly and just want to be with him all of the time. I'm pathetic, pathetic, pathetic.'

Their silence offered no contradiction of my self-flagellation.

'Well, just do as he says and take it slowly.'

Fair point. But in the sex and fondling department, my version of taking it slowly was positively meteoric compared to Doug's.

Over the next few nights, he alternated between kissing me passionately, nibbling my ears and nuzzling my neck. Occasionally, his hand would creep up my back under my jumper, but no more than that. I'm ashamed to admit I resorted to guerrilla tactics. I even tried going braless and when his hand crept up my back, I swung around quickly, hoping he'd inadvertently stumble upon a breast. But nothing worked. Nothing.

Until one night, a few Wednesdays later, after another of Roberto's masterpieces was fraudulently disguised as my own creation. We sat on the floor, food on the coffee table, when Doug looked up and took my hand.

'Cooper,' he said solemnly, 'this has got to stop.'

My heart skipped a beat. What did he mean, stop? We couldn't stop now. I was falling more in lust with him by the minute and, barring the fact that he obviously had the sex drive of a monastic celibate, I had come to realise that we were actually really good together.

'What's got to stop?' I ventured tentatively.

'The fact that we've eaten our way through all of Roberto's menu.'

Shit! He knew.

I collapsed in a fit of giggles.

'How did you know?'

'The garnish was a giveaway. Nobody heats up a garnish.'

Caught red-handed. How was I to know that I should have taken the decoration off the plates before putting them in the oven?

He stood up and pulled me to join him. What was this? Action stations. Incoming fondles. Without saying a word, he unbuttoned my blouse and took off his shirt. He led me to bed and lay me down, silently removing first my jeans, then his. I reached up for him, pulling him on top of me. He slowly traced an invisible line around my nipples and then down to my stomach. He rose above me, then entered me, all the while staring into my eyes with the most beautiful smile on his face. He didn't utter a sound as he started to move back and forwards, surging inside me.

I'd just adjusted my hips and wrapped my legs around his back, starting to match his rhythm when suddenly he juddered and then stopped. My God, he'd come. It was the quickest ejaculation in history and he still hadn't made a sound. I looked up questioningly, wondering what he would say, but he said nothing. He just smiled and rolled off, satisfaction all over his face.

Had I missed something? Had I had some weird blackout and missed twenty minutes of time, coming round just at the crucial moment? Or had I just had a sexual encounter that was quicker than boiling an egg?

'I love you, Carly,' he whispered.

'I love you too, Doug,' I replied automatically. And it was true, I did. I think. Okay, maybe it was a teeny bit confused with lust. And yes, so the first sexual encounter was like making love to a silent man in a hurry, but it was only sex. In every other way, he was perfect.

I couldn't help comparing him to Joe, who turned me on so much with his whispers during lovemaking, but then that had driven me crazy in the end, too. I was just being bloody fickle, I told myself. The sex would get better, I knew it would.

As for taking things slowly, well, I suppose we did – compared to, say, a Formula One Ferrari.

* * *

Things took on a terrifying momentum. Soon Doug was talking about joint bank accounts and property prices.

A few months later, Jess and Sarah came home on leave from uni and we had a girls' night at Kate's. It was like Benidorm, without the sun and sand. We each brought the group up to date with the latest news: Carol's new contract, modelling lingerie for an upmarket department store, Kate's promotion to 'trainee stylist', Sarah's attempt to seduce her maths tutor, and my romance. Jess was gobsmacked at that development.

'What's happened to you, Cooper? So much for travelling the world and meeting interesting people. You were the last person I expected to marry a guy from their home town and settle down before they reached twenty-one.'

'I know, Jess, but I got my fingers burnt up to the elbows with that one. I'm sure Joe will have a contract out on my head by now. And anyway, what more do I want?'

'Sex that lasts longer than it takes to make a Pot Noodle?' Carol volunteered.

I ignored her, even though she was right. We were up to about three minutes now so it still wasn't rocking my world. It would get better. I just had to give it time. Meanwhile, my indignation was in full flow. 'Doug's gorgeous and smart and we've known each other since we were kids. I love him to bites.' I meant 'bits', but my Malibu and pineapple had kicked in.

'Exactly!' Jess's eyes narrowed. 'You've known him for ever. Do you really want to go through life with no surprises?'

'For God's sake, you lot, back off. It's not as if I'm marrying the guy next week. I mean, we're only going out together. I'm not getting married until I'm at least thirty.'

They all looked at me knowingly. Or maybe they just had glazed expressions caused by too many Malibus.

* * *

When Doug arrived the following evening, I was unusually quiet. After at least twenty 'what's wrong?'s (him) and the same number of 'nothing, I'm fine's (me), I eventually spilled.

'Doug, do you think maybe we're too serious? Do you ever wish that you were still going clubbing with your mates and meeting new girls every night?'

He looked at me with a horrified expression. 'Why would I want to do that? I've already found everything I could ever want.'

He looked like he was about to faint, so I backpedalled furiously. What was I thinking? How could I even contemplate hurting Doug? I loved him like he was already one of the family.

He practically was.

Six months later, we were planning our engagement party and putting an offer in on a semi-detached in the next street to my parents. My mother was suggesting having meetings with Doug's mum to discuss guest lists and the co-ordination of the table covers with the bridesmaids' dresses.

And I went along with all of it, somehow unable to press the brakes. I felt like I'd created a monster. My life was no longer my own as I was dragged round wedding shop after wedding shop, trying on dresses that made me look like a cross between a Christmas cake and a toilet roll holder.

Yet, it was worth it all to be marrying Doug. Somewhere along the way, I started to miss him if he left the room for more than five minutes. I wasn't content unless he was beside me, wasn't complete unless he was holding me tight and telling me how he loved me.

Anyway, it was time I gave up on my wild fantasies and accepted that this was the way life was – you went to school, got a job, settled down and had babies. And no, I wasn't settling for the easy option (as Jess claimed), I was recognising Mr Right when he was standing in front of me and grabbing him with both hands.

We set the wedding date for February of the following year, two years after we'd met again in the club. Plenty of time to get used to the idea of being Mrs Cook. It was an ironic name, considering I still couldn't boil a kettle. Not that Doug minded. He did most of the cooking now and he swore he enjoyed it. Sicko.

The only nagging worry I had was about our sex life. I kept telling myself to look on the bright side – we could go to bed at 9.55, make love and I'd still catch the start of *News At Ten*. At least I'd never have to plead a headache to get out of having sex, because most times it was over before I realised it had started. And I'd never get cystitis.

I know I should have tried to talk to him about it, but any time I raised it, he just told me how wonderful I made him feel and how much I turned him on. Who was I to rain on his parade? I couldn't bring myself to hurt him, to question one of the aspects of our lives that made him so happy. Sex isn't everything, I rebuked myself. I could change it over time. It would get better as we grew together. It was just the honeymoon phase that was causing the, erm, swift conclusions.

The months flew by. The seasons changed but how we felt about each other didn't – until the last minute.

It was all Danielle Steel's fault.

I was lying in bed reading yet another of her novels, rapt in the story of the hero who had just whisked the heroine off to New York, presented her with diamonds and asked her to marry him, when I had a sudden realisation. That would never happen to me. I would never be 'whisked off' – we had to save for six months for a week in Lanzarote. Doug insisted on investing all extra cash in our pensions. And I couldn't even remember how he had proposed. We'd just kind of fallen into it. Holy crap, was I never going to have any excitement in my life again, ever?

But, once again, knee-deep in denial, I shrugged it off. Who needed excitement when I had Doug?

* * *

The girls had planned my hen night meticulously. They were so happy for me. Jess, Sarah, Kate and Carol were to be my bridesmaids and would look stunning in dresses designed by Carol and made by a dressmaker friend whom she'd met in a fashion house in London.

We began the night in a trendy Glasgow restaurant, before moving on to an even trendier pub, full of Glasgow's beautiful people. God, I'd forgotten what it was like to be out on the town. For the last year, I'd either been working in the club or sitting in my bedroom or Doug's watching a video. I'd wanted to move in together first, but he didn't see the point of wasting money on rent when we were saving furiously for our big day.

The hen night was a riot of laughter and we had no intention of slowing down when we ended the evening in our old favourite, Winston Blues. As we entered, I saw the owner, Richie (or rather I saw two of him), rolling his four eyes as he contemplated the mess our high heels would make on his furniture. He wasn't wrong. Within minutes, we were on top of the tables belting out 'Mustang Sally'. At one point, I moved too close to the edge and concussion loomed as I toppled over, only to be caught at the last minute. Mark Barwick saved the day again. How was it possible that he was always in the right place at the right time?

'Cooper, we have to stop meeting like this.'

I laughed as he set me down in an upright position. 'We definitely do.'

'I hear you're marrying Doug. Congratulations.'

I looked up to see if his smile extended to his eyes, but I couldn't focus. Too many Legal Intercourses. I managed a lopsided grin.

'I am.'

He nodded thoughtfully. 'Take care of yourself, Coop. Be happy.'

'I will, Mark,' I may have slurred slightly. 'You too.'

He was lost in the crowd within seconds and I clambered back up for an encore. Ten minutes of wanton gyrations later, the DJ suddenly switched from Kylie's 'I Should Be So Lucky', to Roxette's 'It Must Have Been Love'.

I frantically looked around my feet, hoping that someone had installed a plastic slide at the side of the table, because in my condition I couldn't see any other way of getting down without a parachute. No slide. I was about to shout for someone to call out a rescue helicopter when two arms reached around my waist and gently lowered me to the floor. I didn't even have to look. Mark had rescued me so many times he should be wearing his underpants over his trousers. The thought made me giggle.

He swung me round and suddenly we were dancing. Or rather, he was dancing and I was swaying as I concentrated on remaining upright. My arms were round his neck and I was holding him tight.

Mark laughed. 'Did you request this song just for me?'

'Just a freak coincidence.'

We both knew he'd been my first love and I'd been his. Mark had always been there. When I wore my first bra, Mark tried to take it off. The first time I got suspended from school, Mark went to see my parents and took the blame. The first time I ever got drunk, he picked me up and took me home. I'd spent years writing 'Carly Barwick' on my school jotters and taking detours around school between classes just so that I'd inadvertently bump into him. Years later, we were still bumping into each other, but the only difference now was that I was about to be Mrs Carly Cook.

Kate found us as the lights went up.

'C'mon, children, time to get the blushing bride home to bed.'

I stared at Mark. Oh bollocks. I felt familiar feelings rising up to my throat. It was attraction. Excitement. Danger. I felt like I was on the edge of a ski slope and just about to jump. I just couldn't remember whether or not I'd put my skis on.

'Mark's coming home with us,' I said, still staring at him. 'Aren't you?'

He paused. Shit, the skis were still in the cupboard.

He stared back, then slowly, almost imperceptibly at first, began to nod his head.

'Oh, no,' Kate groaned, as she slapped her hand to her forehead, 'another crisis coming up.'

When we entered the flat, Kate went straight to her room. She never could bear to watch drama unfolding. I turned on the stereo to compensate for the paper-thin walls. She didn't like to hear dramas either.

'Angel Eyes', by Wet Wet Wet, crooned from the speakers. In

minutes, our clothes were off and, oh, it felt good. No, it felt amazing. As he rose above me, hips moving, it didn't even cross my mind that I was being unfaithful. This was Mark. Carly and Mark. It was like Richard and Judy, without the sofas.

He didn't whisper sweet nothings, make false promises, make me swear undying love. I didn't worry about him respecting me in the morning, or hold my stomach in, or hide my unshaven legs. And I didn't fake my orgasm. More than seven years after I first kissed Mark Barwick, I finally felt what it was like to make love to him. If I'd known he would feel that good, I'd have done it years ago.

I fell asleep grinning, wrapped around him like cling film.

* * *

A banging noise woke me the next morning. I tried to open my eyes, but someone had superglued them in the night. My head hurt and a carpet had been fitted to my tongue. I felt an arm across my chest.

'Doug, I think I'm paralysed,' I groaned.

No reply.

'Doug, call the paramedics. I need a body transplant.'

Still no reply. Had I suffocated him in the night?

I forced an eye open. I opened my mouth to scream, but my tonsils were on strike. If I wasn't in need of medical attention before then I was now. I was about to have a heart attack. Not Doug. Definitely not Doug. Mark Barwick's face was only inches from mine.

He was sleeping soundly, his fingers intertwined in my hair. At least that explained why I couldn't move my head.

I winced inside. What had I done? I was a total fuck-up!

There was more banging, coming from the direction of the

hall. I fought the pain barrier and the paralysis and jumped out of bed. A chain of disjointed thoughts had suddenly flashed through my head. Bed – sex – Mark – morning – banging – door... Doug!

I rushed to see if my worst nightmare had just come true. I peered through the peephole, praying that it was the postman, the milkman, the bailiffs, even my mother. But no, as my eyeball focused, I saw the gorgeous blond hair and the concerned furrow of those familiar brows.

I panicked and burst back into my bedroom, launching myself on Mark.

'Mark, wake up, wake up!' I hissed. 'Doug's at the door.'

He was instantly awake. 'Oh, shit, Carly,' he moaned.

'Is that it? Mark, do something! Get dressed. Quickly. Go out the window.'

'Carly, we're on the third floor.'

'Okay, good point.'

I was verging on hysteria.

I thought frantically, forcing myself not to hyperventilate.

'Right, I've got it. Get up, quick, come with me.'

I dragged him out of bed, grabbed his worldly belongings into a bundle and thrust him into the hallway and towards Kate's door.

'Kate, Kate, incoming traffic. Don't even ask, just go with this, please,' I begged.

I pushed Mark into Kate's bed and ran back to the door. I opened it, yawning, rubbing my eyes and doing a feeble impersonation of someone who'd just woken up.

'Shit, Carly, I was just about to call the police. I thought you'd been murdered in your sleep.'

I shuddered, thinking that if I'd given Doug a key to the flat, then that would have been a real possibility.

Mark staggered out of Kate's room, heading for the bathroom. Doug looked shocked as he said hello.

He pulled me in to the bedroom. *He knows*, I thought, *he knows.*

'Carly, why didn't you tell me?'

Because it would have been like ripping your heart out and stamping on it?

I was still silent as my heart stopped and I braced myself for the explosion.

It didn't come. Instead, I got a large helping of concern. 'Why didn't you tell me about Kate and Mark? Oh, sweetheart, I know you and him were an item a long time ago, but even so, it must still be hard for you to have them sleeping together next door.'

I shrugged my shoulders. I couldn't bear this. I had just committed the equivalent of mass murder to this guy's heart and here he was worrying about *me*. I didn't deserve him. I really didn't. I almost wished he would shout and scream at me instead.

'Baby, you look knackered. C'mon, let's go to bed.' I followed aimlessly. I'd lost the will to live.

We climbed into bed and as he cuddled me tightly, a look of discomfort crossed his face. He pulled one arm away and it disappeared under the covers. When it resurfaced, it was holding a...

Oh I couldn't bear it.

It was holding a condom wrapper.

Doug studied it like he expected it to morph into something else, then he looked at me disbelievingly as realisation dawned. He didn't even speak. He didn't have to – the expression on his face said everything.

'Doug,' I began, but he cut me dead.

'Don't say a word. Just don't.'

Instead, I closed my eyes and kept them shut as he got up, dressed and left. Only the slamming door broke the total silence.

I stared at the ceiling, too numb even to cry. I was waiting to wake up and discover that this was all a horrible dream when Mark appeared in the doorway.

'I heard him go. Does he know?'

I nodded mournfully. 'I thought condoms made sex safe,' I sighed, the irony seemingly ludicrous.

Mark stared at his feet for a long time.

'I'm so sorry, Cooper. I guess for once I didn't save your ass.'

I thought about Doug and our relationship. Would I truly have been happy for the rest of my life? Would what we had honestly have been enough? Would I really have slept with Mark if I'd truly been in love with my fiancé? Or was this my way of sabotaging something because I didn't have the courage to face the fact that it wasn't right?

'I don't know, Mark,' I replied, sadness crushing me. 'Maybe, you did.'

And no, I never saw Doug Cook again.

7

STOP – THE SPICE GIRLS

'You're going to do what?' Kate bellows, clutching her sides and stomach like she is afraid that the shock will force the immediate birth of the baby. I can't decide if she is yelling out of outrage or excitement. Outrage wins.

In the restaurant, all conversation ceases as a hundred diners strain their ears to hear what is causing the commotion. Judging by the incredulous faces of my dinner companions the audience probably thinks I've just confessed to some kind of heinous crime or sexual deviance.

'I'm going to find my ex-boyfriends. Track them down. Hunt them out. I'm going to see if I made a mistake in letting them go.' I'm grinning, but, strangely enough, nobody else is. 'You know what I was like back then – I was a relationship disaster and bailed on every one of them.'

I notice no one contradicts me, but neither do they point out the reality that I'm still a relationship disaster, so, on balance, I take the win.

Jess comes to my rescue. 'Okay, I'm quite sure you've thought long and hard about this—'

I interrupt her. 'I just thought of it today.'

She persists, ever hopeful. 'And that you've got the finances to carry it off.'

'I don't have a bean. It's all going on my credit cards.'

Jess winces. Her rescue attempt is running aground. 'At least tell us you've got a plan.'

I pause, carefully considering what I'm about to say. I know that one wrong word and they'll have me chained to the table leg until they can talk sense into me.

I take a deep breath. 'Look, I know it's crazy. I know I'll probably fall flat on my face, but I have to try. I feel like this is a watershed year. We're careering towards a new century and I want my life to be as happy as it can be. I'm a grown woman and for the last year my sex life has been battery operated, for God's sake.' There are a few splutters from nearby tables. I probably shouldn't have said that out loud. Still, I persist, 'A voice inside me just tells me that this is the right thing to do.'

Kate sighs. 'I've warned you before about those voices. You're far too old to have an invisible friend.'

They're warming. The edges of their lips are beginning to quiver. In a minute, Jess might even smile.

I press on. 'I haven't met anyone I felt strongly about for a long time and maybe that's because no one matches up to the guys I've been in love with. I just need to be sure that I haven't made a huge mistake by chucking away someone who would have made me really happy if I'd had the sense and maturity to see it.'

'But every one of them ended badly,' Carol points out. That's Carol. She only comes out with a dose of reality once in a blue moon and it's always when you least expect or need it.

'I know they did, but it was always my fault. Every one of them bit the dust for the sole reason that I bailed or self-destructed the minute I had doubts. In their own different ways, they were all great guys. Maybe I just gave up too soon. And I want to find out if that's the case.'

Kate regains her composure and asks again for the plan.

'I'm going to start from the beginning and trace them in order of meeting them. Don't know why, it just seems logical.'

Carol goes for pragmatic sarcasm. 'Oh, yes, we've got to keep this logical.'

I roll my eyes in mock affront.

Jess intervenes. 'But how are you going to find them? You haven't seen some of them for years.'

Carol jumps back in. 'Clive says one day we'll be able to find absolutely anyone and anything just by searching on the internet. One of the companies he invests in is working on it already. I don't have the heart to tell him it's a mad idea and he's wasting his money.'

I brush past her technology update by explaining that I'm going to go to the last place I saw them and take it from there. Not an exact science, but it's all I've got. Actually, going back to where I met them is part of the adventure. I can't wait to travel again.

'Jesus,' Kate groans, 'Cooper, this is real life, not an episode of *Cagney & Lacey*.'

I thought she was coming round to the idea. Obviously not.

'What's the alternative, Kate? Stay here and stay miserable? Okay, talk the pros and cons through with me then. Let's start with the cons.'

Kate starts. 'Con Number One. You're giving up your career.'

'I bloody hate my job, Kate. When I was a kid, I never dreamt of growing up and riding off to sell toilet rolls. What am I going to say when I get to heaven? "Hello God, what can I get you? Padded, quilted, one-ply, two-ply, white or pink?"'

'Point taken, but you're successful, Cooper. You've climbed up the ladder and now you're going to slide back down it and land at the bottom.'

'Well, at least I'll bounce,' I say petulantly. 'Have you seen the size of my arse lately?'

The smiles turn to chuckles and I hope that's a sign that I'm beginning to win them over.

It's Carol's turn. 'Con number two. They're probably all married with kids by now. You could have some extremely irate wives on your hands here.'

'If they're married, I'll back off straight away. I'm not doing this to upset anyone, Carol. First sign of a wedding ring and I'll be out of there.'

'Think that's what got you into this mess in the first place,' Kate quips. I ignore her. This is no time for accuracy and perceptive insight.

Back to Jess. 'Con number three. You could end up with nothing, Carly,' she says softly, her eyes beseeching me to change my mind.

I smile ruefully. 'I haven't got anything now. At least not anything that matters.'

They collectively howl in indignation.

'Except you guys,' I add quickly, before they reach for sharp objects. 'And my family. But I'll always have you lot, no matter what happens. Everything else is just "things" and they mean nothing to me. Does my obscenely expensive lava lamp keep me warm in bed at night?'

'Not without the risk of electrocution,' Kate smiles.

I sit back. What would I do without my friends? We've been together since flares were in fashion the *first* time. And we'll still be doing monthly dinners with a crisis before every course when we're fifty. God knows what our dramas will be then. Judging by the way this is going, I'll still be single and wailing about my tragic romantic life.

The desserts come, the waiters concentrating furiously to avoid being so distracted by Carol's gorgeousness that our selection of sundaes bite the dust.

Kate looks at the others for psychic consensus and obviously gets it. 'Okay, babe, we're behind you.'

The others nod reluctantly.

'Just think, Cooper, this is worse than the time you decided to convert to Buddhism and sent a letter to the Dalai Lama requesting a personal audience,' Carol laughs.

'I only did that so that I could meet Richard Gere,' I retort huffily, still narked by the fact that I didn't actually get a Pretty Woman moment.

'Or the time that you found out where Liam Neeson was filming and stalked the set hoping he'd notice you,' Jess adds.

What are they suggesting? That, in the past, my schemes and plans have been somewhat misguided?

'No, no, no,' Carol protests. 'The best one was when you sent that poem to Madonna. You waited months for her to release it as her next single. You even spent the expected royalties.' Another cacophony of shrieks and giggles.

'How did it go again?' Carol splutters. *'I'll stick with you in the sun and the rain...'* she croons. *'If you bring the whip and I'll bring the chains...'*

People are staring at the hysterical women now and Kate is crossing her legs to avert any potential accidents.

'I still can't believe she didn't release that,' I murmur, feigning outrage.

I get the point though. In the past I've been somewhat over-optimistic in my hopes and dreams. But that doesn't mean I should give up trying.

Somewhere there's another life just waiting for me. And before we get to the year 2000, I'm going to find it.

8

I threw myself into work after the Doug fiasco, feeling second only to Third World dictators in the villain stakes.

The consequences of my actions measured eight on the Richter scale of devastation. Every time my mother cast eyes on me, she clasped a damp cloth to her brow and muttered that I had obviously inherited my lack of scruples from my dad's side of the family. She even took to praying for me at mass. I tried to console her with the thought that Mary Magdalene had been a bit of a tart and God forgave her, but it fell on deaf ears.

A few weeks after Doug called off the wedding, Callum broke his vow of silence to me only to tell me that his friend had transferred to the Manchester branch of his national car sales chain. I decided the universe was twisting the knife. Not only had I desperately hurt and humiliated Doug, but now I'd caused my brother to lose his mate.

Callum was not happy. I racked my brain to think of a time when he'd been more pissed off with me than this. The only thing that came close was when we were kids and I glued two peanut breasts on to his Ken Doll so that he'd look stunning in a silver lamé frock that I'd made from Bacofoil. It resulted in me being battered over the head with a busty Ken. Somehow that paled into insignificance compared to this.

As for Mark, well, I didn't want to be seen within a hundred yards of him so I ignored his calls until they stopped coming. He fell into the 'men' bracket and I resolved that I'd rather don an anorak and take up trainspotting than go near another member of the male species. I just hoped that 'Sally from Edinburgh' was far enough away that the jungle drums wouldn't reach her. One devastated relationship was bad enough.

I worked day and night for ten months, enduring the stares, finger pointing and gossip of the club-goers. My exploits had become legendary. I was mortified and I knew I deserved every bit of the toe-curling embarrassment.

The only good aspect of having the social life of a hermit was that I saved enough money to move into my own flat, allowing Kate to reclaim her lounge.

April came and I started thinking about my impending twenty-third birthday. A joyous event, was it not? An excuse for rapturous celebration and copious amounts of good wishes from my fellow human beings? At this rate, I'd be having the party in the phone box at the end of the road.

I decided that I had to get away to somewhere nobody knew me. Somewhere they didn't ring bells and cry 'Plague' when they saw me coming.

I approached Ray and begged for a month off. He was going to be the only other poor sod in the telephone box with me, as, unlike the rest of the planet, Ray was actually quite pleased with me. Takings in the club were up by 20 per cent, fights were down to a manageable level (average of two black eyes and a concussion per night) and the roaring trade in illegal substances was now, if not completely wiped out, then at least forced outside the club rather than inside.

I'd done my job, so after an impressive amount of grovelling, he finally agreed to give me three weeks off. I didn't want a package tour surrounded by loved-up couples, so I decided that America was beckoning me. I knew no one there, I had no American baggage, so I could just go, mind my own business and stay out of trouble.

A few days before I was due to leave, we were having a 'Psychic Night' in the club. It was my new idea for a Wednesday evening, the only night of the week that we'd previously been closed. Now, nearly two hundred people, 90 per cent of them women, scrambled for tickets every week to see the floor show. It was completely manufactured and more theatrical than spiritual, but everyone loved it.

First up every night was The Mighty Romano, who would summon spirits from the other side and would pass on messages to the audience. 'Dave says the money is under the floorboards' (obviously a drug dealer when he was alive) or 'Edward says he still loves you and is waiting for you' (despite the fact that he died of a heart attack whilst shagging his secretary).

It was all nonsense to me. The only spirits I believed in were gin, vodka and Bacardi and we sold those to the mystic followers by the bucket.

On this particular night, I was standing at the back of the audience, picking off my nail varnish to relieve the boredom of Mighty's performance, when a comment triggered my attention.

Mighty repeated it. 'I have an old lady called Catherine here. She's looking for her great-granddaughter.'

My great-grandmother was called Catherine. Coincidence, I told myself, so were half of the Irish Catholic great-grandmothers in Scotland.

Mighty Ridiculous continued, 'She says her great-grand-daughter is about to take a trip.'

I looked around the entranced sea of faces to see if anyone was claiming the message.

'She says to tell you that you've lost your way recently, but not to worry. The reason for everything that's happened will become clear on the trip. It concerns a man, a tall, dark man. She says that he's the one you've been looking for.'

I was rooted to the spot. Why didn't I get one of the ones concerning oodles of cash hidden in the rafters? No, I had to get a prophecy that I was about to have an altercation with an age old fictional cliché.

It's a load of bollocks, I told myself. Mighty Full of Crap was probably Joe Bloggs, a plumber from Bradford, during the day.

I saved the whole evening on a mental floppy disc labelled 'Bullshit' and stored it at the back of my mind with the other assorted junk. I didn't have time to dwell on it anyway. The next psychic sent messages from a man on the other side to 'his Maggie', and two Margarets in the audience came to blows over who it was meant for. The next medium predicted a woman would meet Tom Jones and she promptly fainted. Ten minutes later, we had a fire alarm and had to clear the room. My point was proven. It was obviously all a load of old tosh, because not one of the psychic stars had seen that coming.

* * *

New York was everything I'd dreamt of and more. I'd seen `When Harry Met Sally' at least a dozen times and now I was here, in their world, although absolutely resolute that there would be no orgasms, either real or fake. The hotel was opposite Madison Square Garden and had definitely seen better days, but the peeling paint and the dusty rooms gave it a comfortable lived-in feeling, like ten year old slippers.

I soon settled into a routine, rising at seven every morning and wandering up to Central Park. I'd spend an hour walking briskly round the park, watching the early-morning masochists jogging, cycling and roller-skating, before heading to a coffee house on 57th Street for a coffee, a croissant and a gab with the French owner, Pierre. He reminded me of René and caused frequent pangs of longing for Amsterdam and Joe. It was hard to believe that it was almost three years since I'd left there. After breakfast, I'd return to the hotel and change before continuing my on-foot exploration of the city. I systematically worked my way up and down every area – SoHo, Little Italy, Chinatown, Tribeca, Greenwich Village, taking in the sights, the sounds and trying not to look like a tourist who had everything she owned in the bum bag that was strapped around her waist. I'd read a newspaper story about thefts from hotel safes and I wasn't taking chances with my travellers cheques.

At six o'clock every evening, I queued at the discount theatre ticket booth in Times Square to buy a cheap ticket for one of the performances that evening. *The Phantom Of The Opera, Miss Saigon, Les Misérables, Cats* – I saw them all with just a Diet Coke and a hot-dog for company. Scotland, work, Doug and Mark could have been a million miles away as I slurped the ketchup from my bread roll, but I realised, with a sinking feeling, they were getting closer every day.

One evening, gloomed by the fact that it was only two days until I went home, I took the latest Sydney Sheldon down to the bar and proceeded to launch an all-out assault on the hotel vodka stocks. After an hour or so, the novel was abandoned as the Smirnoff struck up a conversation with the other sad characters sitting alone at the bar. Sometimes my dad's genes kicked in with a vengeance.

By midnight, I was leading a rousing chorus of 'Flower of Scotland', shouting the words before each line so that the multitude of nationalities could join in. I sounded like a Scottish Television Hogmanay broadcast. I moved on to 'Scotland The Brave', 'The Skye Boat Song', and was preparing to burst into 'I Belong to Glasgow' when the quick reflexes of a passing waiter saved me from certain concussion as I wobbled on my bar stool. The kind soul escorted me to my room and ceremoniously dumped me on the duvet, before returning to the bar, his good deed done for the day.

Next morning, I woke with a head that felt like the Yankees had been using it for baseball practice. I groggily looked at my watch, surprised to see that it hadn't been lost or stolen in my stupor of the previous night. Nine o'clock. Well, so much for my early-morning jaunt to the park. Coffee and bacon sandwiches, I thought, and don't spare the calories.

I dressed slowly, each movement threatening to relieve me of my stomach. I descended in the lift, face pressed against the cold steel doors for comfort, removing it just in time to avoid falling flat on my face as they flew open at the ground floor. I staggered out and looked around for the exit, having left my sense of direction and memory at the bottom of a vodka glass.

I stopped in my tracks. Holy shit! I clasped my hands to my head. I was hallucinating. All around me were grotesque figures – men with huge deformed ears, others who were half-human, half-beast, children with two heads dragging mangled limbs. I'd died and gone to hell.

I looked around frantically, bile rising in my throat. I could see hotel staff behind reception, going about their normal business, not batting an eyelid at this horror in front of them.

Deep breath, deep breath, stay calm. This was obviously a figment of my imagination. What the hell did I drink last night?

I edged my way around the foyer, head down, lest I make eye contact with one of the beasts and be beamed up to their planet where I'd be impregnated by a predatory creature. Watching Alien 2 in my room a few nights before had clearly left scars and I was no Sigourney Weaver.

I occasionally peeked up to see if the monsters had gone, but no, they were getting closer: chatting, milling around, interacting with each other like they were normal beings.

I finally reached the door, but a huge board blocked it. Standing in front of it, I was deafened by the roar of my beating heart. Panic was rising. I squeezed past the obstacle. I was almost there. The automatic doors gradually opened. Free! I burst out into the morning sun. Holy Sigourney, the relief! I was never drinking alcohol again.

I turned around to check that I hadn't imagined it all, but I couldn't see past the board. The board. What did it say? I squinted, trying desperately to focus, before emitting a cackle so loud that passers-by crossed the street to avoid me. In huge letters it read:

HERE TODAY – NATIONAL STAR TREK CONVENTION.

I smiled all the way to Pierre's and stumbled in the doorway.

'Ma chère,' he chided gently, 'you look, how you say, like sheet.'

* * *

That evening, I called Kate.

'Just wanted to check that armed guards haven't been posted at the airport to prevent me re-entering the country,' I explained.

'They have,' she quipped, 'but we've formed an underground resistance and we plan to create a diversion while you commando crawl through Arrivals.'

My head still hurt when I laughed.

'Anyway, down to the important stuff. Did you meet Mr Tall, Dark and Handsome?' she asked.

It took me a moment to suss what she was talking about. I'd completely forgotten about Mighty Romano's prediction. Kate, however, was obviously still clutching on to the prospect of a fairy tale ending.

'No,' I replied, 'but I did have a run in with Dr Spock and a Klingon. It's a long story.'

Bewildered silence.

'I'll explain when I get home,' I promised. 'Can you collect me at the airport, please?

'Of course. I'll bring a banner saying, "Congratulations, you managed to stay out of trouble for a whole three weeks" I'm proud of you,' she teased. 'No men, no disasters, and you haven't been arrested.'

She was clearly forgetting that I still had a whole day left to go.

* * *

I checked in at the British Airways desk with a heavy heart, then trudged through security and on to the departure lounge. I consulted the screens and saw my reprieve – the flight was delayed for six hours. Yes!

I made for the bar. As I waited to be served, my eyes fell on a sight of unrivalled gorgeousness. At the other side of the Lshaped marble counter was a real, live Ken doll (without the peanut bosoms), crossed with the Marlboro man. I looked him up and down, feeling the old twinges of attraction that had got me into so much trouble before.

I looked away quickly, remembering that I was to men what the Colorado beetle was to potato crops. I would NOT be tempted again, EVER.

Okay, just one more peek...

He was about twenty-five, over six foot tall, with black hair, piercing green eyes, eyelashes that you could dust furniture with and a burnt wood tan. He was broad, with hands like shovels and biceps bigger than rugby balls. And the whole package fitted perfectly into a black T-shirt and jeans. I stared, mouth open. Was he Mighty Romano's tall, dark guy?

He spoke to the barman, asking for change for the telephone, then disappeared out the door.

No, no, come back, I silently pleaded.

But he didn't return.

'Bollocks,' I fumed, making a mental note to give Mighty Romano a swift kick in the nuts when I got home.

I passed the six hours with four lads from Birmingham and an old lady from Hull who proceeded to Tequila slam us under the table.

As I boarded the plane, I realised that I had acquired a Stetson and double vision. I squinted, as again I tried to focus. I definitely need my eyes checked, I thought. 52C. 52C. I struggled to spot the position of my seat. My head swivelled, before jarring to a halt.

It was him. Tall, dark and handsome. I drew closer, maniacally counting off the row numbers until I was standing at the empty seat next to him – 52C. He turned, looked up at me and smiled.

'Hi,' he drawled. He proffered his hand. 'I'm Tom.' That explains great-granny's intervention – he had a beautiful Irish accent.

'Carly Cooper,' I smiled, hoping that I had no foodstuffs stuck in between my teeth. 'Pleased to meet you.'

I don't know how it happened. It was fate, destiny, kismet, Tequila. I stuck to coffee and water from the drinks trolley, gradually working my way back to semi-sobriety as we spent the first four hours talking, laughing and swapping stories of our lives and our trip. He had just spent a month in Canada before travelling to New York for a few days. Spookily, he was detouring via Scotland because he'd missed his flight to Dublin that morning due to a traffic jam on the Verrazano Bridge. Thank you, traffic gods.

My mind was working overtime. I was sitting so close to him that I could hear his heartbeat. Or was that mine? Our shoulders were touching, our legs were touching, our hands occasionally brushed against each other's. It had been a year since Doug and I split up. Surely I was up for parole by now?

Feigning tiredness with big yawns and rubbing of the eyes, I supposedly closed my eyes for forty winks. After a respectable time lag, I slowly let my head fall on to his shoulders. He didn't move it. Progress! I then turned a few degrees, throwing my arm across his toast rack stomach and snuggled into his chest. I made what I hoped were gentle sleep noises.

Still no defensive moves from the target.

Hold on, a counter-attack coming up.

He moved his arm.

Don't push me the other way, I thought, having a vision of me landing sprawled in the aisle.

He lifted his arm higher. I waited for an all-out assault, but his arm came slowly around my shoulders and cuddled me close.

I waited another ten minutes or so before making a gradual

awakening. Through half-shut eyes, I looked up at his face and grinned apologetically.

'Sorry,' I murmured, 'I seem to have got caught up in you somehow.'

He returned my smile. His lips were inches away from mine. He stared into my bloodshot eyes, and slowly, slowly leaned down and kissed me. The surrounding passengers had stopped watching the in-flight movie and were now openly staring at the romance unfolding in front of them.

We remained suctioned at the mouth until the seat-belt sign came on to signal our descent.

'Where are you going from here?' I asked.

He explained that he had to transfer from Prestwick Airport to Glasgow Airport, an hour away, for his flight to Dublin three hours later.

'I live not far from there.' I offered, 'You're welcome to stop at my house for a shower and a bite of lunch.' I was just being hospitable. We Scots are renowned for our friendliness to foreigners. He agreed, thanking me for being so thoughtful.

If only he'd known what was ahead of him. Tom McCallum came to my house for a shower... and stayed for a month.

Kate was waiting to collect us and her reaction when I alighted from the arrivals hall went something like joy (she saw me), to excitement (she waved frantically), to confusion (hang on, who was the guy beside me), to shock (and why did he have his arm slung over my shoulder) to crap, what's she done? We almost crashed at least four times on the way back from the airport, as she got distracted by staring, open mouthed at Tom in the rear view mirror. We stopped at the local deli on the way home and picked up French bread, pâté, cheeses and fruit, before miraculously making it home in one piece. We invited her to join us for lunch, but she refused. Instead, she politely shook Tom's hand and then hugged me for just long enough to hiss in my ear, 'If you don't call me with details by dinner time, I'm calling the police and telling them it's a hostage situation.'

I made lunch, feeling proud that I had been shrewd enough to buy foods that required no contact with a cooker. No point in terrifying the poor man with a hot plate disaster. I poured two glasses of wine and we sat at the dining table, feeling like we'd known each other for years. Plates cleared and glasses empty, I looked at the clock.

'Tom, it's time for you to go or you'll miss your flight,' I sighed.

He stood up, came round to my side of the table and pulled me to my feet. He kissed my mouth, my neck, the tip of my nose.

'I don't think I'm going anywhere,' he murmured.

Now, common sense should have kicked in at any point around that time. I had only met this guy twelve hours ago. He could have been a psychopath on the run from the FBI, a con man or a thief. So, did I ask him for proof of identity and a CV? Did I grill him for evidence of a criminal past? Did I push him up against a wall and frisk him? (Well, actually I did, but not in a searching way). No, I whisked him to my bedroom quicker than you could say 'Have you got more skeletons in your closet than the nearest morgue?'

Hours later, it was getting dark outside as we sank back on to the pillows, exhausted. I was covered in sweat, hair stuck to my scalp, mascara streaking my cheeks. Thank God for the louvre blinds which threw the room into a state of semi-darkness. We cuddled for hours, reflecting on the day.

'This has been the craziest day of my life,' he whispered.

I was going to agree with him, but I hate to tell lies. I'd dinged much higher bells on the crazy day scale.

'Do you believe in love at first sight?' he asked, his eyes searching mine in the dim light.

'I'm not sure,' I replied, fudging the truth. No point in letting past experiences get in the way of a romantic moment.

'I wasn't either, but I think I'm beginning to be convinced,' and he started again, kissing me from top to bottom until we drifted off into a long, contented sleep.

* * *

'Tap-tap-tap-tap, tap-tap.'

The familiar sound woke me with a start.

Mother! It was her usual knock on the window before she let herself in with her spare key.

I pushed Tom out of the bed and he landed with a thud on the floor. He looked up quizzically.

'It's my mum,' I hissed. 'Quick, hide in the bathroom.'

But there was no time. She came bounding up the stairs, her speed taking me by surprise. Since when was she ever in a hurry to see me?

Tom dived into the walk-in wardrobes.

Mum blew in the door like a tornado and perched on the end of the bed. The concept of privacy and personal boundaries had yet to reach her world.

'Darling, just a quick visit to make sure you arrived back in one piece. I'm off to the Women's Institute for my new wine tasting class. Will you nip over and check on your father later? Actually, call him first to make sure he's there. He's off work today so the chances of him making it out of the pub are slim.' Now that Michael was making plans to move out and go to college, they weren't even making a pretence of being happy together any more. Michael, Callum and I had a sweepstake running on when their divorce proceedings would kick in. If they called the lawyers anytime in the next six months, I was on to a mega pack of Wotsits and a family sized Whole Nut.

Mum was just about to turn on her heel and bolt out, safe in the knowledge that her firstborn was intact, when she froze.

'What was that?' she gasped.

What? Did she have radar instead of ears? I hadn't heard a sound.

'There it is again,' she whispered.

I still hadn't heard a sound. She tiptoed over to the wardrobes, whilst I could only look on, astounded. In one movement, she reached the doors and threw them back. There stood Tom, tall, handsome, bright red and with only the ostrich feather hat that I'd bought for my cousin Dee's wedding covering his dignity.

Mum rounded on me in horror, for once utterly speechless.

'Mum,' I began weakly, but it was no use. She backed out of the door in a stunned trance, before sprinting down the stairs and out of the front door, a resounding slam marking her exit.

I looked up at Tom's bemused, mortified face.

'If it's any consolation, I introduce all my boyfriends that way,' I deadpanned.

'Really?' he said, laughing now as he climbed back on to the bed. 'In Ireland, we tend to find a cup of tea and clothing works better at the first meeting.'

* * *

I went back to work the following night, taking two cartons of cigarettes for Ray.

'Cooper, you shouldn't have! Did you treat yourself to anything nice?'

'Funny you should ask that, Ray. I'd like you to meet Tom...'

For the next four weeks, Tom adopted my habits of staying up most of the night and sleeping late.

Every day was a revelation that saw us fall more and more into love, lust and healthy obsession.

But this time it felt amazing. For once, there were no niggling doubts. None! We fitted together perfectly in every way, both physically and mentally. He was a gorgeous man, sensitive but strong, protective but encouraging. He adapted completely to my world, no mean feat for a well balanced individual, and to the people in it.

Even Callum warmed to him after he got over his feelings of disloyalty to Doug. Michael thought he was great, and a couple of nights a week they'd hang out together, playing pool or renting a video when I was working. And, as for my gran, if she ever wanted a toy boy, then Tom was the number one candidate. She swore he was the double of my Irish grandfather when he was alive, a thought that put a smile on her face.

The only cloud on the horizon was Tom's family. He worked on his parents' dairy farm about fifty miles from Dublin and they were becoming ever more demanding of his return. Eventually he could stall it no longer.

'I need to go back,' he told me, one morning, as we lay in bed watching the sun come up.

'Don't...' I stopped him, by putting my finger on his lips. I didn't want him to go, couldn't bear the thought of waking up and not hearing his gorgeous voice in my ear, whispering good morning. We had gone from zero to love and bypassed everything in between. Sure, it was quick, but – stop me if you've heard this before – this time I knew it was right. We were perfect for each other. He kissed my fingers one by one, before his eyes locked on mine.

'Come with me,' he said.

I swallowed back my sadness. 'I can't. I don't have any more holidays and if I up and leave Ray will sack me and...'

'Come forever,' Tom pressed, cutting me off.

'But... but...' It wasn't clear what he was saying and I didn't want to presume. 'You said your parents would never accept us living together.'

His gorgeous grin was infectious. 'They will when we're married.'

And of course – again, stop me if you've heard this before – right there, right then, that felt like the best idea I'd ever heard.

We spent the next couple of days working everything out. He had to go back soon, so I switched my shifts around so I could take two nights off together. The plan was that I'd go with him, meet his family, and then return to Scotland while he stayed there and went back to work on the farm. For logistical reasons, we agreed to do the long distance relationship thing for six months before we married and I moved there – it was the best way to get some cash together for the wedding as we'd both blown all our savings on our respective trips. I had to sell my house and resign from work without letting Ray down. Most of all, it would take at least six months to persuade my mother to speak to me again, let alone help me organise a wedding. At least we still had the dresses from last time.

Thrilled, excited, high on love, we flew to Ireland, me with visions of *Little House on the Prairie* at the forefront of my mind. I knew nothing about farming. The closest I'd come to pasteurisation was putting milk in my tea.

Tom explained that the farm had been passed down through the generations and when his parents retired it would become his. I resolved to adapt to country life. I've seen *Emmerdale* and I had visions of Land Rovers, Barbour jackets and naming the cows Daisy and Ermentrude.

My first impressions backed up my picture-perfect expectations. The scenery was stunning as we left the beautiful city of Dublin for the homestead. Every corner we turned revealed more landscapes of breathtaking splendour. Bubbles were rising in my stomach. I was going to love it here.

We arrived at Tom's house in a muddle of activity – chickens, geese and dogs were all flapping around as his mum and dad came out of the door to greet us.

Tom's father was the image of him. Tall, grey-haired, with the same twinkling green eyes, I adored him on sight. He took my hand and bowed, smiling as he kissed my knuckles.

'Well, if it isn't just the dog's bollocks to be meeting the lass who's won the heart of our Thomas,' he announced and swiftly received a slap across the back of the head from an irate Mrs McCallum.

'Joseph, what kind of language is that to be using in front of a young lady?' she exclaimed.

I looked behind me to see what 'young lady' had entered, but there was nobody there but me. I winked at Tom's dad.

'It's the dog's bollocks to meet you too, Mr McCallum,' I laughed.

A grin overtook his face.

Mrs McCallum tutted disapprovingly and bustled me up to my room. As she opened the door, I realised that this was most definitely not going to be an intimate weekend. The room looked like it hadn't been used in years, but it was perfectly preserved and spotlessly clean. The floral wallpaper was pink and blue, matching the antique rose carpet and curtains. There was a pine dressing table and wardrobe, which matched the bedside tables guarding the single bed.

Well, I reasoned, what was I expecting? They were obviously a traditional Irish family who believed in morals, standards and respectability. I could understand that. Almost. And anyway, it was only for a couple of days on this trip. Hopefully, by the next time I came over, they'd realise that Tom and I were going to be a permanent thing.

We sat down to dinner at six o'clock on the dot. Tom and his dad stayed at the table as his mum beetled back and forth to the Aga. I offered to help but was shooed away with barely concealed irritation. It was probably just as well. My cooking skills weren't going to impress anyone.

She dished up huge bowls of mashed potato, vegetables and a thick meat stew. As we ate, Mrs M continued to go to and fro. She didn't sit down until we were almost finished and only then because Tom asked her to.

'Mum, Dad, I've got something to tell you,' he announced.

Call it intuition, but I knew what was coming. And from the appalled look on his mother's face, so did she.

I held my breath.

'Carly and I are going to be married,' he revealed, beaming.

I almost choked on my turnip. I had expected him to share the news when they'd got to know me a little, not before we'd even got to pudding on his first night back.

Two things happened at once. Tom's dad jumped up to congratulate us, leaned over the table to give me a hug and somehow managed to put his elbows in what was left of the mashed potatoes, whilst his mum turned purple and keeled over. We picked her up and put her head between her knees.

Tom looked at me for reassurance that he'd done the right thing. I smiled at him reassuringly, hoping that he couldn't see I was bluffing. Surely Mrs McCallum would see how in love we were, and then get used to the idea and be happy for her son?

The fact that she picked up her rosary beads and took off for a lie down made me wonder if I was being too optimistic again.

His dad, however, was more enthusiastic about the impending nuptials, and later that evening, Joseph insisted on breaking open his best bottle of Bushmills in celebration. We toasted our future, our children's future, our future crops. It went on all night until we were very drunk and – mother in law aside – I was on a lovely little cloud of happiness and contentment.

All too soon it was time for me to go home. I cried so much at the airport, the thought that I wouldn't see Tom every day was too much to bear.

'It won't be long, ma darlin',' he tried to cheer me up. 'I'll send you a cardboard cut-out of me to talk to. Anyway, it's only for six months.'

I couldn't even raise a smile. Six months seemed like a lifetime away and not even the prospect of seeing each other two weekends a month, one in Scotland and one in Ireland, could console me. I looked around for a manacle to attach myself to his ankle, but all I saw was a huge board announcing the final call for my flight back to an empty bed. I kissed him, I said another goodbye, then I trudged through the gate, my heart aching.

That evening, I dragged myself into work.

'Cooper, office, I need to talk to you,' Ray bellowed the minute I walked in the door.

My spirits rose. Maybe he was going to fire me and I could be on the first flight back to Dublin the next morning. I've always been very rational when in love.

I lurched expectantly into the office.

'Cooper, we signed final contracts today on Tiger Alley. We take over on Monday.'

My jaw hit the floor. Tiger Alley was an iconic Glasgow nightclub, the biggest in Scotland, with 4,000 clubbers on a busy night. It also had a ferocious reputation for prostitution, more drugs than a high street chemist chain, and a criminal record that would fill a library. It definitely wasn't for the faint-hearted and I'd had no idea Ray was planning to acquire it.

'I'm putting Carter in to manage it,' he added, naming Paul Carter, the manager of one of his other clubs.

I exhaled in relief.

Too soon.

'And you, my little darling. I want you to manage it with him and control the door.'

The voice of sarcasm in my head went into overdrive. Brilliant. Beam me up, Scottie. My life just got better and better.

I had to cancel my trip to Dublin two weeks later as Ray had blocked all holidays for the next decade to get Tiger Alley sorted out. The problems were endless: staff stealing from the tills, booze being delivered then going straight out the back doors into unmarked vans, rampant prostitution levels and, worst of all, two drugs families feuding over the territory. I had fourteen stewards working on the door with me, another thirty-two inside, and it still wasn't enough. Every night was a battle from start to finish, with us on the losing side, but we weren't giving in.

First things first. We identified the main culprits in the petty crime department. To the threats of law suits, violence and the removal of our internal organs, we fired the assistant manager, twenty-two bar staff, eleven bouncers and the cellarman. Another dozen bar staff walked out in protest – no bad thing given the circumstances.

We drafted in trusted staff from the other outlets in the chain to man the pumps. It was frantic, fretful and full of mishaps, but I loved every adrenalin-fuelled minute of it. I called in every favour I was ever owed and a few that I made up besides. At one point I had Kate, Carol, Sarah, Jess, Callum and Michael serving behind bars.

Paul and I worked eighteen hours a day. Some nights we

didn't even go home, collapsing instead on the overstuffed sofas in the lounge. The club had become an obsession with both of us. We were determined to turn it around and make it work. And anyway, it kept my mind off the fact that my gorgeous Tom was hundreds of miles away.

Eventually, the numbers through the door dropped every night as undesirables got the message that they were no longer welcome.

Phase two of our plan swung in to action. We brought in decorators, interior designers, publicists and an advertising agency that came up with a media promo campaign.

We booked the most popular bands for week nights and the trendiest DJs for the weekends. The numbers started to rise, but it wasn't enough for Ray, who wanted a fast return on his investment. We needed a capacity crowd nightly and quickly to satisfy him.

We decided to host a 'relaunch' party on the first Friday of the following month. But it wasn't entirely straightforward. We had a plan. Or rather, I had a plan and if I had bollocks they'd be well and truly on the line. We advertised it in the press for ten days beforehand, and, telling the staff that we expected only a small, select crowd, we gave most of them the night off and retained only a trusted few bar staff and our eight most discreet bouncers.

The club usually opened its doors at ten o'clock to catch any early trade, although the masses wouldn't start arriving until after eleven. 'We've Got The Power' by Snap blared from the external speakers as the first of our adoring public poured out of taxis just after ten.

Baz, our head steward, looked at me questioningly.

I shook my head.

'Sorry, folks,' he apologised, 'we're already full.'

'But it's only ten thirty,' argued a petite female in white PVC hot pants with stilettos to match. In that outfit she wasn't getting in anyway, she looked like a Q-tip.

'Well, darling, you'll just have to get here earlier next time,' Baz chided, giving them the story we'd asked the door staff to deliver.

This set the pattern for the rest of the night. Not one person got through the doors. We knocked back everyone, regardless of age, status or bribes. Inside, the few bar staff that remained spent the time training on the new cocktail menu.

Next day, the phones were relentless with enquiries about opening times and dress codes.

I gave Paul a playful dig in the ribs.

'People always want what they can't have.'

He'd been cynical about the plan, so I admit to gloating.

That night, they came in droves. Word of mouth had spread around the city.

Ray chuckled as he congratulated us. 'All these lies. You'll never go to heaven, Cooper.'

I think my track record in the romance department had already established that fact.

This time, however, things were still looking good.

I still couldn't take time off to go to see Tom, so instead he continued to come over for a few days every month. We'd spend every spare moment of our time walking at the beach or lying in bed planning our future. As Tom talked of harvests and agriculture laws, I hung on his every word. It wouldn't have mattered if he were reading out the Yellow Pages, I'd still be hypnotised by those piercing green eyes and soft Irish voice. This man was so going to be the father of my children. My ovaries danced every time he came near me.

Sometimes he would get annoyed that I couldn't spend more time with him, as I had to work nights when he was over, but what could I do? I couldn't let the guys at the club down and if Tom loved me, then he should understand that. Anyway, I was doing this for him too. Ray had promised me a huge bonus if the club hit the astronomical targets that he'd set and every penny of that was going to the wedding fund. And the phone bill! When Tom was in Ireland, we still had our long, lingering phone calls every night, even if they were sometimes punctuated by my snores as I fell asleep after another eighteen hour shift.

Inevitably, Christmas loomed and so did the end of Tom's patience. I knew that he was anxious for me to stop work and move to Ireland as soon as possible. I was too, although I must confess to one or twenty moments of trepidation when I realised that I'd be expected to cook, clean and share a house with his parents. I'd never been a fan of communal living and I came out in a rash if I even saw a vacuum cleaner. I could sense his mother's disapproval from over three hundred miles away.

Still, it would be worth it to snuggle down at night with the most gorgeous, loving, kind and funny man on the planet.

Looking back, I should have seen that this was a disaster just waiting to happen.

Tom wanted us to spend the festive season in Ireland, but the last two weeks of December are the busiest of the year for any club, so we reached a compromise – he would spend Christmas with his family and then New Year in Scotland with me.

I'd be working Christmas Day anyway, but I planned to nip round to my parent's house to see them for a quick dinner, until I got a call from my mother that derailed that idea.

'Just to let you know, Carly, we're not doing Christmas dinner this year.'

I'm ashamed to say my first reaction was relief that I didn't have to spend my only two hours off on Christmas Day listening to my dad rambling and my mum moaning about the state of him. I already knew that my gran was off on a cruise with her line dancing pals, Callum was in New York, and Michael was going to an all-night rave.

'No worries, Mum. Are you and Dad going out instead?' I asked, trying to make conversation.

'No, darling, we're divorcing. I know we should have told you face to face but you're always so busy.'

I was stunned into silence. They were actually doing it. I did a quick self-scan to check for twinges of hurt or sadness, but there were none. They should have done it years ago. Neither of them were bad people, but they didn't belong together and they truly made each other miserable. Maybe this would spur my dad to do something about his drinking and perhaps my mum could finally find some happiness. It could only be a good thing.

'Are you ok, Mum?' I asked her, feeling a bit weird. She'd never been the type of woman to talk about her feelings or to show emotion or sentimentality. I'm sure a psychologist would have a field day linking up my parents' dysfunction to my commitment woes, Callum's flippant disregard for relationships and Michael's insecurities, but we weren't the kind of family that delved into any kind of self-reflection.

Case in point...

'Absolutely,' my mum replied curtly. 'Bloody relieved to tell you the truth. Anyway, must go. I've a step class at one o'clock.'

The line went dead. Holy crap. I immediately dialled the number of the student flat that Michael had moved into in September.

'Hey, just checking in,' I told him, with as much cheeriness as I could manage. 'How're you doing?'

'Not bad...' he said. Oh God, did he not know? '... for a child from a broken home,' he added. So he knew. Relief.

'I just heard,' I told him. 'How are you feeling about it all? You know that if you need me I'm always here. You can stay with me over Christmas if you want to.'

'Eh, thanks, sis, but I'm good. Honestly.'

I heard another voice in the background at his end. 'Mikey, baby, come on...' a female purred, giving me the giggles. No wonder he was fine.

'Mikey baby?' I asked him, my amusement obvious.

'It's... erm... need to go. Love you, sis.'

A swell of happiness drowned out the worry. Mikey baby was happy and was going to be ok. I left a message on Callum's answering machine, but I knew he'd be fine too.

And me?

I really had no idea how to feel, so I went with my usual approach to anything deeper than the fluid in my contact lens case – I compartmentalised it into a box in my mind, shoved on a padlock and consoled myself with the thought that my Christmas dinner would now consist of a mega pack of Wotsits and a family size Whole Nut.

And at least I still had New Year with Tom to look forward to.

I was missing him, but I was way too busy to dwell on it. Christmas passed in a blur, as we worked round the clock to accommodate a full house every night, and spent the days getting the club ready to do it all again. No time off, no cosy yuletide moments, just hard graft creating a seemingly endless party.

My heart was bursting with excitement when I finally collected my love at the airport at 2 p.m. on Hogmanay. It was a brief reunion, as I dropped him at my house, then headed to work for the ultimate celebration of the year. We could lie in bed all day tomorrow – the only day of the year that the club was closed.

At 11 p.m. that night, sixty minutes before the bells would ring in the new year, the foundations of Tiger Alley creaked under the strain of 4,000 revellers. The hours before had been relatively trouble free – two punch-ups and an inebriated man flashing his bum in the ladies' toilets.

As I stood at the door, I thought about how I would miss this. There's nothing like the chat-up lines of a drunken Scot: 'Yo, Ruby Lips, are we shagging?' (Not so as I had noticed).

Or the joy of separating the fights between grown men who thought that they were Rocky and Van Damme.

Or the inevitable cries of 'Do you know who I am?' when we refused entry to all males wearing white socks with black shoes.

I felt two arms circle my waist from behind and lift me into the air. Obviously a strong man. I was just about to give my assailant a reverse kick to the nether regions when a voice shouted, 'Holy shit, Cooper, you need to cut down on the Christmas puddings – I think I've slipped a disc.'

Mickey Quinn! One of my favourite people in Glasgow. Mickey owned the trendiest bars in the city and would invariably come to the club for a nightcap after his pubs had closed for the evening.

'Cooper, meet Jack McBurnie, one of my oldest mates. McBurnie, meet Carly Cooper, the best looking female nightclub manager I've ever met.'

'Mickey, I'm the *only* female nightclub manager you've ever met.' Gender equality hadn't quite reached the world I worked in yet.

'My point exactly,' he grinned, enveloping me in another bear hug.

I extricated myself and shook the stranger's hand.

'Excuse the deluded ramblings of this old man, Mr McBurnie. At his age, he gets very jealous of the younger generation.' Mickey clutched his heart in mock anguish as I continued, 'He'll be much happier when we get him in to a home with people of his own age.'

Jack McBurnie roared with laughter as I ushered them both to the VIP suite and sat them down with Kate, Carol, Jess and a bottle of Bollinger. Sarah wasn't with them – she was still living in Edinburgh, had moved in with her boyfriend there and hadn't been back since my first week at Tiger Alley, when she helped out behind the bar.

'Voluntary work for Help The Aged,' I informed them to more howls.

Across the room, I could see Tom laughing with Callum. My heart flipped. My fiancé was stunning.

He caught my eye and winked. I watched him for a few moments and realised how stupid I'd been. I realised I'd been neglecting him in my obsession with this club. No, I wouldn't let it get in the way of the best thing that ever happened to me any more, I decided. Okay, so life wouldn't be a roller coaster of excitement, but this was an artificial world I lived in.

That's it, I decided – I'd resign first thing tomorrow morning and by the end of January I'd be picking hay off my Jimmy Choo boots and having girls' nights out with Daisy and Ermentrude. I was heading for a new, stress-free, hassle-free, loving, happy life with the man I adored.

Ten, nine, eight...

The countdown continued.

I headed over to Tom, who pulled me in to his chest.

'I love you, Cooper,' he promised.

'I love you too, Tom McCallum,' I replied. And I did. At that moment, I really did.

I woke next afternoon with ringing in my ears. *Bloody tinnitus*, I thought.

Tom gave me a kick under the duvet and told me to answer

the phone. I scrambled for the receiver, knocking over a redundant alarm clock and a bottle of anti-wrinkle cream.

I groaned a hello in the general direction of the mouthpiece.

'Carly, hello. This is Jack McBurnie. We met last night.'

I struggled for some kind of memory to kick in.

'I was with Mickey Quinn.'

Ah! A vague but definite flashback was forming.

'I wonder if we could meet for a chat later today,' he continued.

'But it's New Year's Day.'

'I know, but I have to catch a flight later tonight and I really would like to speak with you before I go.'

Now I was intrigued. A flight? To where? The Christopher Columbus inside me woke up and sniffed a new adventure. I gave him directions to my house, trying desperately to remember what condition I'd left the lounge in when I'd come to bed.

An hour later, after I'd had just enough time to take Tom a cup of coffee in bed, evict Callum and four of his mates, shove a mountain of beer cans into bin bags and run a brush through my hair, the doorbell rang. I invited Jack in and offered him a coffee. While the kettle boiled, he filled in some of the blanks.

Jack McBurnie, it transpired, despite being born and brought up in Glasgow, was the Food and Beverage Director of the Windsor International Hotel (part of the extensive and prestigious global chain) in Shanghai. The hotel catered predominately for business people, which was why he'd taken the opportunity of a quiet Christmas season to return to Glasgow to visit his family and friends for the first time in five years.

A recent dilemma for him, he explained, was what to do with the hotel nightclub, Champagne, which was under his charge. It was old, shabby and run-down and, due to a lack of control, had become a magnet for criminals running prostitution rings.

Mickey Quinn had filled Jack in on my success at Tiger Alley and now Jack was offering me a position in Champagne.

Gobsmacked, I opened my mouth to explain to Jack that, much as I was flattered, I couldn't take him up on his offer, as I was about to get married, and run off to be a farmer's wife in Ireland, where there wouldn't be a nightclub or a vice crime in sight.

He looked at me expectantly.

Say no, Cooper, say no.

'Jack,' I began, taking a deep breath, 'I'm sorry, but there's a couple of things you should know.'

My mind was racing.

Say no, Cooper, say no.

But... what an adventure it would be. Tom could come with me and we'd be like explorers on one last voyage before settling down to domesticated bliss. It was completely reasonable in my ever changing, excitement seeking mind. If we were going to spend the rest of our lives in Ireland, one more year wouldn't make any difference. There must be farms in Shanghai. Tom could get a job and we'd have great stories to tell our grandchildren. It was a fantastic idea. He'd love it. I mean, how many times in life did you get an opportunity like this?

Christopher Columbus took over. I did a quick calculation in my mind and then reeled it off.

'I would only come for a year, I couldn't come until February, because I can't leave Ray in the lurch at the club. I need to give him time to replace me. Also, I'd need accommodation, full board, flights and all other expenses paid for my fiancé and I, and on top of that you'd have to pay me twenty grand a year after tax.' On top of expenses, I reckoned that was a forty or fifty grand package. There was no way he'd go for that.

He put out his hand and shook mine.

'Done,' he exclaimed.

Damn, I should have asked for twenty-five.

'My people will call you tomorrow with the details.'

He had people. And it seemed I was off to Shanghai to meet them.

I bit my bottom lip as I showed him to the door, before rejoining Tom in bed. He rolled over and cuddled me, as I lay willing him to wake up so that I could tell him our news.

It took about twenty minutes for the euphoria to wear off. What if he didn't want to go?

I shrugged the doubt off. This was Tom! My soulmate. Of course he'd want to go. He was a kindred spirit who loved adventure just as much as I did. Didn't he?

Apprehension set in. I switched on the radio, hoping that would wake him. Bad idea. Queen were belting out 'Another One Bites The Dust'.

'Who was that you were talking to earlier?' he asked sleepily.

'Er, it was, em, well, it was my new boss,' I stammered.

'Your what?' he asked groggily.

'My new boss. I think I just accepted a job in China.'

That woke him up. He sat bolt upright. 'Tell me you're joking?'

My optimism drained as his horrified expression told me this might be a harder sell than I'd hoped.

I tried to explain. It's only a year. Think of the money, the excitement, the people we'd meet. It would be a whole new chapter for us.

But no amount of pleading would win him over. He argued every point I made, and the more stubborn and angry he got, the more I dug my heels in.

It escalated from discussion, to debate to raging argument. That's when he got out of bed and pulled on his jeans.

'I don't believe you, Cooper. I just don't believe you. How

could you change our plans without even speaking to me?' he bellowed. He was furious and turning pink.

'I'm speaking to you now.'

'Yeah, AFTER you've accepted the job. You can't do this. Why would you even want to?'

'Why wouldn't I? It's a brilliant opportunity for both of us,' I countered, every bit as riled as him. If he wanted me to spend the rest of my life in wellies, then the least he could do was hear me out. I'd agreed to change my whole life for him, and he couldn't even consider making some temporary adjustments for me?

'But what if I don't want to go. Will you knock it back?'

That stunned me into silence. Would I?

The silence grew longer.

'I guess that tells me everything I need to know,' he said, pulling on a T-shirt. He grabbed his jacket and picked up his holdall from the floor. He'd only arrived yesterday, so he'd barely unpacked. Part of me wanted to ask him what he was doing, tell him to stop, use calm reason, but I was furious and I'd be damned if I was going to give in on our first full scale blazing row.

'You're definitely doing this?' he asked, one more time.

My fury and frustration were calling the shots as I nodded, then watched him turn and leave the room without another word.

His footsteps pounded down the stairs and then came the slam of the front door.

I raced to the window, to see his back as he stormed away, a black cloud hovering above his perfect head. Tears pricked my eyes and a gobstopper formed in the back of my throat.

He'll come back, I thought. *Surely he'll calm down and realise what a great idea it is.*

Luckily, I didn't hold my breath.

No, I never did see Tom McCallum again.

I'm sitting in Kate's kitchen, dropping cookie crumbs on her spotless tiled floor. We met here for breakfast this morning, but I've already scoffed my bacon roll and I'm on my third choccie biscuit and it's only ten o'clock.

'C'mon, Cooper, spill,' Kate urges as she does a dive to my feet with a shovel – admirable in her condition.

'Spill what?' I ask innocently.

Jess lifts her head from the *International Herald Tribune*. Since she started working for the government, her choice of reading material has gone seriously downhill.

Carol puts down her *OK!* Now that's more like it.

'Carly, you're totally distracted and you're inhaling Hobnobs.'

I sigh pathetically. 'Sorry, Kate. I guess I'm just having a bit of a panic.'

'About quitting your job?' Jess asks.

'No, not really.'

Kate pipes up, 'About leaving your flat?'

'No.'

Carol now. They're like a tag team. 'About spending every penny you have and ending up in a cardboard box in Leicester Square?'

This is getting too graphic. I pause while my overloaded grey matter struggles to formulate a sentence.

'It's just about the exes. What if they all hate me? I wouldn't blame them. I was a complete cow to most of them in the end.'

Kate smiles and gives me a hug. 'Carly, I've known you my whole life, and you always bounce back. That's what makes you. If this whole thing goes pear-shaped, which I have to say is an odds-on bet, then you'll have great stories to tell your best friends. Granted, we'll probably have to visit you in jail to hear them.'

My laughter interrupts her. I notice that the other two don't contradict her.

She goes on, 'They won't hate you, Carly. They might not love you to pieces, but they won't hate you.'

I hope she's right.

I don't know why I'm being so morose. It's obviously just a freak pre-menstrual moment.

That and having to say goodbye to so many people. It's only a week until I leave and I feel like I've spent the last twenty-one days explaining my departure to astonished faces. When I resigned, my boss's reaction was priceless: 'But, Carly, how can you contemplate leaving Quilties? You've got a great future here.' I couldn't believe it – after all, I have no emotional attachment to the world of toilet rolls. I only took the job all those years ago because after all the eardrum damage and sleep deprivation working in nightclubs, I decided I needed a normal Monday to Friday, nine to five job. Selling loo rolls was the only one I was offered that paid enough to keep me in life's essentials – rent, cigs and chocolate.

A lifetime of selling toilet rolls or a globe-trotting adventure that might just lead to happy ever after? I stuck with my plan.

I broke the news to my mother on the phone – not because I was being a total coward, but because since her divorce from Jack Daniel's she's taken to spending most of her life at a health farm, having her bits pummelled. I'm sure she's shagging an aerobics instructor. I called her at the spa to explain what I'd done. For once, she didn't take off like a space shuttle on a tirade of disapproval and recriminations.

She simply said, 'Well, darling, you only live once,' before whispering, 'I'm just coming, Ivan,' and hanging up. Ivan, the shagging aerobics instructor. It had to be true. I laughed as I replaced the receiver.

Callum and Michael were even easier to win round. Callum and I had persuaded Michael to come to London for a few days the week before, by telling him that if he didn't venture out in daylight at least once a month he'd develop scurvy and rickets.

I love that both my brothers are happy. Callum spends his life travelling for work, but his base is a London flat that he shares with a couple of other models. It works really well because they're never all there at the same time. And Michael has his own place in the West End of Glasgow, a few miles from the head office of the games software company he works for. He's always been the baby of the family, so I still can't get my head around the fact that he's a fully developed adult who has got his life together. Especially when I don't seem to have managed that.

When Michael arrived, we headed for Fashion Café. Callum loved it there because he could see himself strutting his stuff on the big screen and Michael liked it because it was near the Trocadero, home of more computer games than Japan.

We ate all the most fattening things on the menu, then I launched a pre-emptive strike before pudding.

'Guys, I have something to tell you and I want you to promise me that you'll still love me,' I announced sheepishly.

'Yes!' Callum exclaimed. 'I knew it.'

'What?' I replied, intrigued.

'You're gay,' he said.

'What?'

'That's why you're such a disaster with men. How cool, a gay sister,' he mused.

'No, I am not gay,' I replied laughing. 'At least not last time I checked.'

'You're pregnant?' That came from Michael.

'Nope, not pregnant.'

'Lottery win?' he countered hopefully.

I decided to put them out of their misery and blurted out the whole story. Tears formed in their eyes and I was so touched. *They're going to miss me so much*, I thought, feeling love and affection welling up inside me. Then I realised that they were tears of amusement as they tried to control outbursts of hilarity.

'Sis, I love you,' Callum said, melting my heart until he added, 'but you definitely got the crazy genes.'

Michael was muttering something about a trade descriptions act. He was twenty-five now, but with his cute curls and Michael J Fox face, he could pass for much younger.

'What are you on about?' I quizzed.

'I was just saying that older siblings are supposed to be an example to us younger and more innocent in the brood. Look what I ended up with,' he continued. 'Two serial shaggers with love lives that are epic carnage.' I'd be offended if it wasn't for the fact that he was right. Callum still opted for casual flings and I... well, clearly relationships weren't my area of expertise. Michael was still talking. 'Just promise me something. If it miraculously works out, then I want to dance with Kate's sister, Karen, at the wedding.'

This was nothing new. Michael had been in love with Karen since they were six and she belted him in the face with her clackers. His nose broke on impact and it's never been straight since.

'Michael, if it all works out, I'll pay for you to take her to Majorca for a week.'

'Even you could seduce a woman there,' Callum barbed, still smarting over the serial shagger comment. Michael took no notice. He was the first to admit that other than a couple of brief flings (the now-legendary 'Mikey-baby' girl being one of them), he wasn't a roaring success in the romance department.

Now, a week later, hanging out in Kate's kitchen, the sounds of her throwing up in the downstairs bathroom snap me back to reality. God must be a man to subject females to both periods and pregnancy.

I sit at the table and try to make a list of the tasks I still have to cover in the next seven days.

No 1 – Call gas, electricity and phone companies and have all disconnected.

No 2 – Give lava lamp to Mrs Smith next door (she's had her eye on it for ages).

No 3 – Find foster home for Fish and Chips (my goldfish).

No 4 – Pack up belongings and ship boxes to Kate's garage.

No 5 – Find new frock for my leaving party.

No 6 – Give credit cards a practice run by paying for party frock.

No 7 – Inform bank manager that due to me losing my mind, I may require a sudden overdraft.

I recruit Carol for the shopping trip and Jess for the organisation of the removals. I like to play to people's strengths.

Kate staggers back into the kitchen, looking pale and faint. I decide to go for it while her resistance is low.

'Kate, darling,' I ask, tentatively, 'how would Zoe, Cameron and the bun in your oven like to foster two goldfish?'

10

GOODNIGHT GIRL – WET WET WET

The week before I left for Shanghai, I decided to have a quiet night in for many reasons. I'd had five going-away parties the previous week and I now felt the need to tumble-dry my liver. My eyes needed serious attention after bawling them out every night over Tom. I wanted to spend yet another night on the phone, pleading with him to change his mind, in the vain hope that, unlike my previous twenty attempts, this time I'd be successful. And finally, Clive James was on the TV.

Now, much as Clive is gorgeous, funny and has a devilishly attractive twinkle in his eyes, I wouldn't normally make a special effort to catch his show. However, tonight's programme was entitled *Postcard From Shanghai* and I wanted to see exactly what I'd let myself in for. Since Jack had offered me the job, I'd read loads of books on China's second city. 'The Paris of the Orient', they called it. Despite my searing heartbreak, I was so excited to be going there. I could picture myself at grand balls, in taffeta and tiara, mingling with ambassadors and other windswept and interesting people.

As the programme started, I settled down on the sofa with a

coffee and a box of chocolate eclairs. The titles rolled and Clive was off investigating the glorious, cosmopolitan, elegant Asian city. Only it wasn't. It looked grey, dull, overcrowded, dirty, depressing and corrupt. My eyes widened in amazement as he proceeded to show Shanghai in a very different light to the glitter ball I'd imagined. Where were the windswept and interesting people? Where were the ambassadors laden down with trays of Ferrero Rocher?

I tried to calm down and think rationally. Television programme makers always exaggerated things, didn't they? Clive James should be ashamed of himself, focusing on one tiny negative aspect of the city and sensationalising it like that, omitting all the fabulous aspects of what I was sure was a vibrant and exciting place.

Optimism kicked in. It couldn't be that bad. It was just a one sided view. I would love it, I was sure I would. I had a good mind to write to the government and demand the return of my TV licence. In hindsight, I should have listened to Clive.

As for my fruitless phone call to Tom, I can't remember who slammed the phone down first, but there was a tidal wave in the North Sea caused by the resulting earth tremor. Once again, I thought about changing my mind and trading my one-way ticket to Shanghai for a Dublin shuttle, but why should I be the one to compromise? For the purposes of that argument, I conveniently forgot that it was me who had changed the plans in the first place.

Right up to the last minute, I thought he'd wander through the door, bag over his shoulder ready to go, but no. Flight ticket for one.

* * *

Jack McBurnie met me at the airport late in the evening. Or

should I say the collection of hangars in a big field which masqueraded as Shanghai International Airport. I was excited but apprehensive. I was twenty-three and other than Clive James' programme, all I knew of China was that I was a fan of the cuisine.

As we left the airport, a sign on some scaffolding caught my eye. 'SORRY TO BOTHER YOU. WE ARE A BUILDING.' Obviously the message had been lost in the translation. It suddenly warmed me. Maybe this wasn't going to be so bad after all.

We made our way to the hotel, my face pressed against the car window, looking for signs of life. But there were none. It seemed that the city was in almost total darkness. There were very few street lights. The roads were bumpy and seemed to collide in a haphazard fashion, and if the driver of our car didn't choose a side of the road to drive on soon, then that's exactly what we would be doing too. It was chaos. Thankfully, there were not many cars to be seen, but the ones that were there were driving with no lights, criss-crossing the roads like they'd drank the fuel instead of putting it in their vehicle. I feared for my life. Had I written my will?

I glanced at Jack, but he seemed calm and nonplussed by the whole experience. I decided he must be meditating to take his mind off his terror.

We arrived at the hotel. Based on the airport and the highway systems, I was now expecting a warehouse building containing bunk beds and a canteen, but as we drew up outside it, I gasped. It was stunning. The building rose like a kaleidoscopic palace from the very old and basic structures surrounding it. There were glass elevators going up and down the front of the marble exterior like lasers, stopping at a huge gold entranceway leading to the foyer. Inside, there were fountains and man-made rivers weaving around the reception area and lobby bar. The ceiling was a magnificent atrium, allowing a stunning view of the stars. It was exactly as I dreamt. All I needed now were the Ferrero Rocher.

I arranged to meet Jack back in the bar an hour later and accompanied the bellboy to my room. I felt a twinge of disappointment as I entered – obviously the staff rooms were the ones that previous guests had wrecked. The Rolling Stones must have stayed in mine because it looked like it had been ransacked. Still, I reasoned, once I'd unpacked my things and rearranged the furniture, it would be fine.

I tried to salvage my appearance. After travelling for two days, my eyes were swollen and my hair resembled a burst sofa. I slapped on some foundation, ran a brush through my unruly mane, changed my clothes and went to join Jack. As I entered the bar, I realised that I had a welcoming committee. The other nine expat managers in the hotel had come to view the new exhibit. Jack introduced me.

There were two Australians, Dan and Arnie, both food and beverage managers. Dan was in his fifties and looked like a happy soul, chuckling away at nothing in particular. Arnie was younger, maybe late thirties, and seemed nervous and twitchy, his fingers the colour of burnt toast as he smoked a Dunhill down to the tip.

Heinz was the Austrian head chef and he and his assistant, Hans, both had red hair, huge stomachs and talked in utterly endearing lilted tones.

There were two engineers, both American and somewhere around middle age. Chuck was tall, handsome and – obviously no stranger to the gym – he could have passed for Tom Cruise's dad. Linden was the complete opposite: short, rotund and chubby faced.

The General Manager was a distinguished, greying Englishman called Harry Southfield. As he pulled out a chair and beckoned me to sit, I immediately felt comfortable. But not for long.

Standing just apart from the others were two fierce looking women. Jack introduced them as Ritza and Olga, who were responsible for the maintenance and housekeeping in the hotel. One German and one Russian, I guessed they were probably both in their late forties and as they stood there with their arms folded, sneering in my general direction, they made me feel as welcome as a fart in a tent. I swear I heard them growl.

'Well, Jack,' Ritza snorted, her voice heavily accented, 'we can see now why you employed her.' With that, she grabbed Olga and they stormed off, furniture trembling as they swept past. Even the pot plants shook nervously. Somehow, I knew we weren't going to be best friends.

We had a few drinks to celebrate my arrival. As I studied my new colleagues, it suddenly struck me. They all – except Dan – looked exhausted and depressed, like school teachers at the end of term. I contemplated holding up an airline ticket to anywhere and seeing how high they would jump in desperation to flee this place. It couldn't be that bad, could it? At least there was Jack.

'C'mon, Carly, let me show you Champagne,' he suggested.

I followed him through a maze of corridors, each one less grand than the one before, until we reached an annexe at the back of the hotel, so far from the main reception that it must have been in the next town. Champagne, it transpired, had its own entrance at the back of the complex. As we entered, I gasped out loud. And not in a good way. The club was the biggest dump I had ever seen. I tripped over the holes in the carpet as we weaved between broken chairs and ring-marked tables. The walls were dark brown, the ceiling was dark brown and the furniture matched. There was not a glimmer of glamour or gorgeousness here.

I scanned the room. The staff were shoddily dressed in ancient, sequinned floor length brown dresses, all badly fitting and in need of repair. They lounged around, some smoking in the corner, none of them paying any attention to the customers. And no wonder. The room was packed with women wearing short, tight-fitting but tatty clothing. Some of them were beautiful, some just pretty, but they all had the same hardened, bored expressions under their expertly applied-with-a-trowel make-up. What had I let myself in for?

I examined the men in the club. Jack explained that they were a mixture of local entrepreneurs, Taiwanese and Japanese and Hong Kong businessmen, all of them smoking like trains. Some of them were with women, while others sat and leered at the dance floor where a few of the girls danced in groups with blank, numb, depressed expressions. This place didn't need a manager, it needed to be closed down

Jack spoke again, disturbing my thoughts.

'The girls are escorts and here they call them "chickens". The staff detest them as they're considered to be lowlifes. As for the men, well, let's just say that I'm glad that employees in China don't sue for sexual harassment or our customers would spend their lives in court.'

'Jack, this place is unbelievable. Peter Stringfellow couldn't make it work. How did it get into this state?'

He at least had the decency to look a tad embarrassed. He hadn't exactly given me a full picture of just how dilapidated this club was.

'There are only two nightclubs in Shanghai. This one was leased by the hotel to a Hong Kong businessman. He used it as a base for his operations when he was in China. We, in the hotel, just took the rental money every month and ignored this place.

It's only now that we've revoked his lease and resumed control of it that we've realised just how bad it's become.'

'What happened to the Hong Kong businessman?'

'Life imprisonment for drug smuggling.'

Not a surprise.

'Jack, I think I'll stay here for a while, if you don't mind. I'd like to watch what's going on and see what I can come up with.'

'Sure. Meet me in my office tomorrow morning at ten. Ask at reception, they'll show you the way.'

I sat in a corner for an hour, to strange looks from staff and customers alike. I looked for positives. The size of the room was good. Properly designed, it could easily hold two hundred people. There were plenty of staff, four behind the bar and about twenty waitresses, none of whom looked like they wanted to be there. The sound system was adequate, although obviously wasn't calibrated properly for the room. The most interesting thing, though, was the amount of money being spent. The customers all had bottles of brandy and whisky on their tables, and these were being replenished frequently. Only the single females were buying drinks by the glass.

The noise of a chair smashing down on to a table jolted me back. Six men in the opposite corner were brawling, arms and legs flailing. I looked around for a reaction. There was none. Six men killing each other and nobody gave them a second glance. It was obviously a common occurrence. The fight eventually blew itself out, the two losers staggering out, while the four victors ordered another bottle of brandy. The staff swept the broken glass and furniture further into the corner, with not so much as a raised eyebrow.

Next morning, bleary-eyed from jet lag and traumatised by my night at the club, I went to my meeting with Jack. What were my options? Throw in the towel, admit I'd made a mistake and go running home? Call Tom and beg him to take me back? Nope. Absolutely not. Whether it was pride, delusion or optimism, there was no way I was quitting.

Jack looked up sheepishly as I entered.

'Well, doctor, what's the diagnosis?' he asked.

'It's terminal, Jack. Amputation and a severe dose of radiation couldn't save that place. You're going to have to put it out of its misery. Give me a week to suss out the city and the people here and I'll have a proposal for you.'

He agreed. I set off, as Clive James had done before me, to explore the city. I staked out the hotels, the bars, the shops and the one other nightclub. It wasn't any different to ours – same dated interior and clientele. I wandered down the Bund, Shanghai's main street, in the early evenings to watch the tourists. I approached the embassies, all the Western companies with offices in the area and phoned the newspapers and tourist offices. I started to feel encouraged. The right people were here, we just had to get them into the club. I began to think that this just might be a mountain I could climb.

I outlined my plan to Jack. He sanctioned all of it except the changing of the staff, explaining that there were no procedures to fire staff in China. A job there was a job for life. I was going to have to work with the existing team. That evening, I went to speak to them. They eyed me suspiciously as Jack introduced me as the new manager. They didn't say a word as we informed them that we were closing the club for two months, but we would still expect them to come to work every day for training.

'Can they speak English?' I whispered to Jack, as yet another question I'd asked had gone unanswered.

'Of course. They just don't want to talk to you.'

Great. One week there and they already hated me. Had my mother and previous boyfriends tipped them off?

A week later, we closed the club, bringing in a team of builders, electricians, lighting engineers, sound engineers and decorators. Our budget was limited, but I was determined to make the most of the place. We stripped the club back to a shell and started from scratch. I wanted to create a very classy impression – lots of gold, mirrors, with rich animal-print fabrics, over-stuffed sofas and marble tables. We installed a lighting rig, modified the sound system and re-sited the DJ booth from a side cupboard to centre stage. The bar was re-covered with a mirrored front panel and top, bar stools positioned in front. Marble columns were sited to break up the room, each one with gold leaves entwining it.

To attract the expat crowd, the most important thing was an expat DJ. Jack recommended an entertainment agency in Singapore, so I contacted them and gave them the specification. Within a day, they had faxed over the CVs of three DJs (a Brit, an American and a French guy) who were available. I selected the one with the most credible experience and the best demo tape and enlisted his services. I was assured he would be there in time for the re-opening.

There were two major tasks left: the staff and marketing. I set the staff to task, helping the decorators and cleaners to keep them busy, while I concentrated on the PR. They still weren't bursting into song when they saw me coming, but I was too busy with my other priority to worry about that yet. I had fliers printed and circulated them round every expat office and embassy in the city. I wrote copy for the tourist magazine, the English newspaper and the hotel bedroom information booklets. I had posters in gold frames strategically placed in the hotel corridors and contacted all the airlines offering free tickets for their flight crews.

I now knew why the other expat managers in the hotel had all looked so knackered when I'd met them. Running a hotel of this size (1,000 bedrooms and 1,000 staff) was a mammoth task. Everyone worked flat out for fifteen hours a day and was on call for the other nine.

With three weeks to go, I turned my attention to the staff. I called a meeting and to say that they were frosty was an understatement.

I started by showing them their new uniforms. For the girls, stunning red silk dresses, high necked, floor length with splits at each side. Elegant and classy. For the barmen, red ties and waistcoats with a white evening shirt and black trousers. I waited for their reaction, but it wasn't a long pause. Their faces lit up and they dived on the fabrics, holding them up to the mirrors as they posed. Ray of hope, number one.

Then I told them of my plans for the club, emphasising how important they were to the success. One of the girls, Lily (they had all chosen English names when they joined the hotel) listened carefully. I had watched her over the previous few weeks, always working diligently and completing any task I set her. She was just over five foot tall, with waist length black hair and cheekbones that you could ski off. She was stunning. Her English was excellent and she seemed to garner respect from the other girls. I decided she would be the assistant manager. It had already been explained to me that all the hotel staff received the same salary, regardless of position, so the only reward for promotion was more responsibility, more hassle and more work. I hoped that Lily would embrace the challenge and was relieved when she did. Another beacon of optimism.

We allocated the duties in the outlet – hostesses, cashiers, waitresses – trying to meet everyone's preferences where we could. In the main, they seemed happy with their roles. Third little nugget of positivity!

I then set about training them in meeting, greeting, serving and attending to the guests. Gradually, they warmed to me as I tried to get to know them all individually. Every day I would separate them into two groups: one group role-playing as guests, the other serving them. They learned quickly and by two nights before the grand opening, when we had a small staff gathering to celebrate the completion of the refurbishment and thank them for all their work, we were ready.

I'd just served the first glass of non-alcoholic punch (the girls didn't drink alcohol) when an apparition filled the doorway. He was five foot ten, with blonde curly hair cut short at the sides and long at the back, wearing black leather trousers and a white vest over his skinny frame. He wore more jewellery than H. Samuels and his jaws chewed on gum as he swaggered towards me. He looked like the founder member of the Bee Gees fan club.

'I'm Zac Storm, babe,' he announced, taking my hand as he bowed to kissed it. 'DJ to the stars.'

Oh. Dear. God.

'Show me the decks and I'll get spinning.'

I'd rather have shown him the door and let him get walking. The staff looked on in barely concealed amazement. Zac mistook it for adoration.

'All right, goddessess?' he winked at them.

They nodded in bemused silence.

As he waltzed up to the DJ booth, carrying his record case, I gave the girls a weak smile.

Lily spoke up.

'Miss Carly, maybe I be wrong, but he looks like a... What is right word? Oh yes, he looks like a cockhead.'

I cackled with laughter and surprise. I'd never heard any of the girls swear. They were always impeccably mannered and reserved.

'A dickhead, Lily,' I corrected her through the giggles. 'And I think you could be right.'

Zac stopped the music and dimmed the lights. At least he knew his way around a mixing desk, I thought. There was prolonged silence. On second thoughts, maybe he didn't. I was just about to send him back and demand a refund under a law that prohibits impersonating a DJ, when the spotlights flashed onto the dance floor. There was a rumble from the speakers, then James Brown's 'I Feel Good', so loud it could wake every guest in the hotel. I raised an eyebrow. Maybe this guy wouldn't be such a disaster after all.

The next day, I joined the other managers at lunch for the first time. With the exception of Jack, who was taking a keen interest in the refurbishment, I'd had no time to hang out with them over the previous weeks, too busy with my opening preparations to think about socialising.

Chuck, Linden, Dan and Arnie had popped in every day for a quick chat and to see how I was doing and I looked forward to their visits. It was great to speak to anyone who understood what I said first time around. In saying that, my staff were showing distinct signs of Scottish accents. Only yesterday, I'd heard Lily call the painter a 'tosser'. She was a quick learner.

As I placed my napkin over my lap, I covered the noise of Olga's growling with an invitation to the opening the next night. I also took the guys up on their offer to take me out and show me the local sights. That night would be the last night off I'd have for the foreseeable future, so I happily accepted. It was time to sample the hidden delights of my new home.

* * *

Dan, Arnie, Chuck, Linden and Jack whisked me into a taxi.

'Where are we going? Somewhere glam, I hope.'

'Oh yes,' Linden replied. 'It's very glam.'

Twenty minutes later, we drew into a dingy back alley and they ushered me out. I looked up at a dilapidated sign over a blacked out shopfront. 'The Angel Bar'. It didn't look very heavenly to me. We went inside and I took an involuntary sharp intake of breath. It was a dive. It looked like a front room from the forties. Which was probably the last time it was decorated. I was rooted to the spot, but I wasn't sure if that was through shock or the fact that my feet were stuck to the floor. In a corner was a makeshift bar, with a wizened old Chinese woman behind it. The guys introduced me.

'This is Mama-San.'

This was obviously a test, I decided. Would I stay and drink in a total hovel? I suddenly realised that I hadn't had a drink for two months and I needed one now. Badly!

'I'll have a tequila please, Jack. Make it a double. And a straw, please,' I laughed as I received a standing ovation. I'd passed the test. I was now officially 'one of the boys'.

We slammed ourselves into a state of giddiness, the banter flying. The guys had me in stitches with their stories of working here and I returned the favour with tales of my disasters over the years.

By midnight, I was speaking fluent Chinese. Or Swahili. It was difficult to tell.

The next evening, I had a sore head and a cramping stomach, which at least took my mind off my worries that our opening night would be a total flop. I was in no mood for Zac's smarmy chat so I pushed him into the DJ booth and ordered him not to leave it until the end of the night.

The lights dimmed. James Brown was back with 'It's a Man's World', just as Jack stopped by.

'How's the head?' he asked.

'Feels like it's had a frontal lobotomy without an anaesthetic. I'm pretty sure that stuff we were drinking last night could fuel rockets. What about you?'

'Same. I want to take it off and wash it out with Alka-Seltzer.'

'Jack, tell me that tonight's going to be great. I need some positive reassurance.'

'Carly, it'll be okay. And even if tonight isn't too busy, you'll get there. Look at this place. You've done a great job. Once word gets out, you'll have them knocking down the doors to get in.'

I looked around. He was right, the club did look great. Now all I needed were the people to fill it. Jack went off on his rounds of all the other food and beverage outlets in the hotel, while I checked the staff were in position. The girls looked beautiful in their uniforms, with their black hair tied up and held in place with ornamental chopsticks, their make-up carefully applied. I beamed at them. I could see that they were all excited and nervous.

'You all look great. I'm really proud of you.' Oh bugger, I was getting emotional. This always happened when I was hung-over. *Get a grip, Cooper.*

Lily ran in.

'Miss Carly, Miss Carly, we have a big problem at the door.'

Oh shit. This I could do without. What was it? Were the tills jammed? Were the doors stuck? Had my new bouncers chickened out and fled for their lives?

'What's the problem, Lily?'

'It's the people. They're making a big noise. They say they want in now.'

I stumbled to the door, and then gasped as I saw the issue. People were queued for what seemed like miles outside. I suddenly felt giddy and it wasn't due to the hangover.

'Are you okey-dokey, Miss Carly?' Lily asked warily.

'I'm fine, Lily. Open the doors. Our customers are getting restless.'

* * *

The club took off. It was full every night of the week except Sundays, when we closed to allow me to sleep for twenty-four hours before starting all over again. It was exhausting, but I loved it, mainly because every night was different, the place was rocking and it all took my mind off Tom. We'd made so much progress. The staff were happy – the first sign of inappropriate behaviour towards them and the offender was swiftly shown the door. The criminal element was mostly gone and we had genuine revellers as opposed to a crowd that was just there for the hustle.

After ten months, I felt like I'd been hit by a bus. I'd had a couple of holidays – a week in Phuket and a week in Singapore – but I was exhausted and suffering from lack of daylight. Shanghai was such a polluted city that there was not much to encourage us to leave the hotel. As a result, I worked until 4 a.m., slept until early afternoon and then went straight back to work again. And because I was a glutton for punishment, Jack had managed to persuade me, with emotional blackmail and American dollars, to extend my contract for a further six months.

It struck me that I hadn't had sex (with another person) since I arrived in Shanghai. I didn't know whether to be proud of my career focus or horrified by the lack of fun.

One morning, I decided to make an effort and rise early enough to join the others for lunch. There was an air of excitement at the table.

'What's going on?' I asked.

Linden answered. 'Today's the big day, Carly. The film crew are arriving.'

Film crew? It was the first I'd heard of it.

They explained that ninety-six rooms had been booked for the next three months for an American film crew that was shooting on location in the city. *If there's a God, then Sylvester Stallone will be the star*, I thought. I could so do with a Rocky experience at the moment. But no, there were no big names – not a Sylvester or a Mel Gibson or a Kevin Costner in sight.

That night, I warned the girls that we might be even busier than normal and explained why. Their faces lit up, not because they hoped to be discovered and whisked off to a life in Hollywood, but because most of them saw marriage to an American as an opportunity for a prosperous, gilded life. There was a bang as twenty females (okay, twenty-one, I did it too) slapped their make-up bags, hair sprays and gels on the table. This called for serious preparation.

We waited in anticipation all evening, but it was just the normal assortment of expats, tourists and businessmen that crossed the threshold. By eleven o'clock, we were beginning to give up hope, when I spotted Lily coming in the door giving me the charades movie sign. I smiled and watched as a troupe of American guys wandered in and made straight for the bar.

I waltzed over and introduced myself, being the gregarious hostess with the mostest. As I worked my way around them, I spotted another bloke enter and join the crowd. He was a god.

'Who's that, Phil?' I asked the short dark-haired guy I'd been talking to for the last ten minutes.

He laughed. 'That's the star. Dirk Chain. Do you want me to introduce you?'

I tried to act cool, responding with a vague nod. 'Sure.'

'Dirk, over here,' Phil shouted. 'There's someone I want you to meet.'

Dirk swaggered over, flicking his long copper hair as he walked. Every inch of him was perfect: his wavy hair that gleamed, his deep blue eyes framed with the blackest of eyelashes, his gorgeous pouting lips that seemed to shine, beckoning me to attach myself to them. I looked him up and down, trying not to show that I was blatantly objectifying him.

Phil looked on, a grin of amusement overtaking his face.

'Hi, babe', Dirk drawled in a Texan accent. I'd seen *Dallas*, I knew these things.

Before I could even reply, someone interrupted us and pulled Dirk away.

Phil handed me a damp cloth from the bar.

'He has that effect on all the women,' he chuckled. 'Girls stampede over us to get to him.'

I realised how rude I was being. I snapped myself back from fantasy land.

'I'm sorry, Phil. Tell me what you'll be doing here.'

Phil Lowery told me about himself. He was twenty-five, and a cameraman from New York. Taurus. Two brothers and three sisters. Parents happily married for thirty years. Liked animals, sport. comedy shows and he had aspirations to give stand up a try. Single. Split up from five year fiancée six months ago. Had a soft spot for old movies and had been to Scotland twice and loved it.

I liked him already. He was funny, with a dry, sarcastic sense of humour that had me in creases. And he was genuinely interested in hearing about me, too. Phil Lowery was, I decided, one of the good guys. But where had Dirk gone? My radar kicked into action and as the music slowed down for the final songs of the evening, I spotted him heading back from the gents and cornered him.

'So, Dirk, there's a party in my room tonight and you're welcome to join us.' Shit, my mouth was talking crap before informing my brain again. What party?

He nodded. 'Sure, sweetcheeks. But I can't stay too long, need my beauty sleep. You know how it is.' He winked at me. How was it? Was he trying to tell me something? Okay, so I knew that my face looked like a well-slapped bum after months in this humid, daylight-free environment, but I didn't need beauty tips from a male Julia Roberts look-alike. I decided that I must have misinterpreted him.

I rushed back over to Phil and announced the party. He was delighted and quickly spread the word, rounding up a dozen others who were up for carrying on the revelry.

We all headed to my room, cranked up the stereo and emptied the minibar. I hoped the noise wouldn't disturb Ritza and Olga, in their rooms on either side of mine.

I made an effort to talk to everyone, always keeping one eye on Dirk. I must have looked like I had a sight impediment. He frequently caught me staring and smiled back lazily.

Phil kept the party going with jokes and anecdotes until 6 a.m., when the guys finally drifted away. Soon there was only him, me and Dirk. Phil gave me a kiss on the cheek.

'It's been great meeting you, Carly. I'll see you tomorrow for lunch.'

I forgot I'd suggested that. I chose not to point out that lunch was only six hours from now and I'd still had no sleep. I'd worry about that later. I showed Phil out and turned to face Dirk. Without saying a word, he stepped towards me and kissed me. What was that taste? Bloody strawberry lip gloss. So that's why he kept disappearing to the toilet – to reapply his lip gloss. I'd thought he just had a weak bladder.

I ran my fingers through his hair and nearly lost a thumb.

Hair extensions. Still, it didn't dent my libido, which – after almost a year in solitary - felt like it had been let out of jail. He pulled me over to the bed and laid me down.

'Just wait there, baby doll, I'll be right back.' He dived into the bathroom.

What was he doing, for God's sake? And what was I supposed to do in the meantime?

After several minutes, a voice came from the depths of the bathroom.

'Carly, pumpkin, have you got some moisturiser?'

What? Tell me he wanted the cream to lather it over my back and blow my mind with a sensuous massage. Somehow, I didn't think so.

I took some in to him and stopped in my tracks. The guy in front of the bathroom mirror looked different. I glanced down. On the sink top was a small white case with two blue contact lenses floating in it.

He took the moisturiser and applied it to his face, then took a tissue to remove his mascara.

I couldn't contain my giggles.

Dirk looked confused and slightly wounded.

'A man's got to take care of himself, you know,' he said defensively.

I struggled to compose myself, by this time feeling as turned-on as a TV in a power cut.

'I understand,' I promised, trying to assume a straight face. 'Listen, Dirk, I'm really sorry, but I've just had a call to say that there's some drama down in the lobby that I have to attend to, so if you don't mind...' I gestured to the door.

He couldn't hide his surprise. 'Eh, sure. Rain check?' he asked, as I pulled the handle and then stood back to let him past.

'Mmm, I'm not sure. Maybe the universe is trying to tell us

something here,' I replied, trying to force some regret into my voice.

Before he could respond, I closed the door, then leaned against it and laughed until my sides hurt. So much for my wild night of passion with a movie star. Just wait until I told the girls at home about this one. I'd kept in touch with occasional letters since I arrived in China. Kate and Jess wrote back, but I hadn't heard from Carol or Sarah. I wasn't surprised about my model pal, but I did wonder about Sarah. I hadn't seen her for almost two years now. Last I heard she was still living in Edinburgh, and was loved up and spending all her time with her boyfriend. I was happy for her, but I missed her. We all did. Before I went to sleep, I dashed off a quick note to each of them.

The following day, I dropped them in the postbox at reception on the way to meet Phil for lunch in the hotel's main restaurant. I'd only been to bed for a few hours, but I felt absolutely fine. Years of working nights had given me the ability to function on just snatches of interrupted sleep.

'Well, are we now besotted with our leading man?' he asked.

That set my giggles off again. I swore him to secrecy, then told him about the encounter. I know it was indiscreet, but I had a gut feeling that he was trustworthy and it wasn't often that I was wrong about people. Unless you count ex-boyfriends and actors. We were in hysterics the whole way through our meal, and afterwards, I reflected that it had been a long time since I'd had so much fun. I'd found a new mate.

Phil and I fell into the habit of meeting every afternoon when he wasn't filming, then he'd come to the club in the evenings.

After work, we'd go down to the all-night coffee shop on the ground floor, eat a disgusting concoction that masqueraded as the hotel's only brand of ice cream and talk until the sun came up. 'We should get danger money for eating this stuff,' I'd moan as I spooned another blob of creamy goo into my mouth. 'They're sucking the joy right out of my only pleasure here.'

I'm sure everyone thought that we were having a passionate affair (Dirk Chain fixed me with a wounded expression every time I met him), but it was purely platonic. I tried to set him up with a couple of my favourite new customers in the nightclub, two Australian beauties who loved to party, but he said it was too soon after his previous relationship and he was more interested in having conversation than romantic nights out. So that's where I'd been going wrong all these years – I thought the best way to get over someone was to plough into another debacle. You know – the 'get back on the horse' theory.

We talked about everything. No subjects were taboo and he treated me with the same brotherly affection as Callum and Michael did. He was protective of me and we were both happiest in each other's company. And oh, he made me laugh more than anyone I'd ever known. His one liners were brilliant, his timing was perfect and his satirical commentary on any subject made me howl. I implored him to swap to the other side of the camera and follow his stand up ambitions.

Every chance we got, we explored Shanghai. We shopped in the markets where we bartered over the prices with the vendors and wandered down the backstreets, talking to the locals with our hands because they spoke no English and our Mandarin was appalling. We tried eating chicken's feet, a local delicacy, and vowed to become vegetarians thereafter.

A month after he arrived, he called my room half an hour before we were due to meet. 'Cooper, hurry up. I can't wait any longer. I've got a surprise for you.'

I dashed downstairs and he ushered me in to a taxi. I couldn't contain myself and begged him for a clue as to where we were going, but he gave away nothing. Thirty minutes later, we pulled up at a new hotel on the opposite side of the city. He put his hands over my eyes and walked me inside, into an elevator, then along a corridor. Finally, he stopped.

'Are you ready?' he whispered.

I nodded.

He took his hands away and I blinked, trying to focus. I looked around in astonishment. There, in front of me, was a recreation of an American ice cream parlour.

'I knew that somewhere in this bloody city, there'd be decent ice cream,' he said. 'It just took me a while to find it.'

I blinked again, this time trying to fight back the tears. He'd spent a whole month looking for an ice cream parlour for me. It was the nicest thing anyone had ever done. If only I fancied him, and he fancied me, it would be perfect.

* * *

The film crew were running eight weeks behind schedule due to inclement weather, temperamental actors and government red tape. I was delighted because it meant that Phil had now been there for four months and still had at least another month to go.

One Sunday, over chocolate chip and maple walnut, we pondered how great life would be if we were physically and sexually attracted to each other. Phil was cute, same height as me with short dark hair, huge brown eyes and a slight frame. I could see that he was appealing to women, but somehow he just didn't have that effect on me. When he was around, the world was a better place, but my sex drive stayed firmly in the garage. Phil felt the same. He was drawn to the dark, petite, Asian girls with their beautiful eyes and shy smiles.

Nevertheless, we decided to put it to the test. That evening, after a bucket too many cocktails, we stumbled back into my room. We slumped onto the bed and cuddled up as we'd done on many nights before.

'Carly,' he slurred, using all the logic of a drunken man, 'maybe we're not into each other because we've never actually had sex. Maybe if we did, then we'd see each other in a whole new light.'

My logic was just as inebriated. I contemplated his suggestion.

'Are you saying you want to try?'

'Maybe. Do you?' he replied.

I didn't answer. In my usual shy, reserved and conservative manner, I just pulled off my top and pounced him.

Next morning, I woke up with a groan. I looked at Phil, still sleeping soundly. He was so adorable. I thought about the night before. Where on the Richter scale of fuck-ups did it register? I loved him, I thought, I really did, but the sexual chemistry still wasn't there.

He stirred and I turned to look at him.

'Good morning,' I smiled tentatively.

'Good morning.' He looked at me for a minute. Eventually he spoke again. 'We need to talk, don't we?'

I nodded as he sat up and gazed at me searchingly.

'The way I see it, we make amazing friends, Carly. I've never had a female mate that I've loved like this.'

I nodded again, biting my lip. It was my turn.

'I love you too, Phil.'

'But?'

'But I don't think we'd make an amazing couple. I'm a nightmare, Phil. It would only end in tears and you mean too much to me to let that happen.'

He thought for a moment, then grinned. 'Thank God. I was

worried that you'd be hopelessly besotted now and I'd have to fight you off.'

I hit him with a pillow, then paused. 'I've got a solution,' I suggested, laughing. I reached over to the bedside table and pulled the gold foil out of my cigarette packet. I rolled it up and tied the ends, making a circle. He looked on, intrigued. I slipped it over the third finger of his left hand. 'We'll wait till we're thirty,' I said. 'And if we haven't found the right person for us in that time, then we'll have another try.'

He nodded. 'I'll carry you up to my cave, where we'll settle for platonic togetherness. I'll even father your children if you bring a test tube and a turkey baster,' he offered.

I accepted.

'Friends?' I asked.

'Friends,' he agreed. He enveloped me in a cuddle, then suddenly pulled back and his eyes met mine. 'Carly, can I ask a favour?'

'Anything.'

'Before we go back to platonic world, could we do that blow job thing again?'

I yelped in outrage and smacked him again with the pillow. 'You should be a comedian, you know that?'

He flashed my favourite cheeky grin. 'I do. My best mate keeps telling me. Maybe one day I'll listen to her.'

Weeks passed and Phil and I continued to spend all our time together. I'd already been in Shanghai for over a year and I knew that despite the success of the club, I wanted to explore another city. I applied for a transfer to our Hong Kong hotel and waited impatiently for the answer.

The film crew finally completed the shoot, but Phil decided to quit and stay behind in Shanghai. He'd fallen in love with Asia.

He found a job with an independent production company, making corporate videos and tourist information films. When the crew left, he moved into my room, sharing my bed every night, but with not a penis in sight. We were both content with the arrangement.

One day, Jack called me in to his office. He put a piece of paper in front of me.

'What is it?' I asked.

'Your transfer to Hong Kong.'

I dived over the desk and hugged him, then kissed him on each cheek.

'We're going to miss you around here, Cooper.'

I blushed. 'Right back at you, boss.'

Two weeks later, I threw a party for the staff at the club. I had grown so attached to them, especially Lily, whose eyes were red as she hugged me. I was going to miss them all so much; even Zac the twat.

Next morning, Phil took me to the airport. I clung on to him, crying my eyes out.

'Keep in touch, Cooper. I love you.'

'I love you too, Phil,' I sniffled.

As I walked through passport control, I turned and waved. He gave me a bow.

It was the last time I ever saw Phil Lowery.

11

Two things struck me this morning. In all the excitement, trauma and panic of the last few weeks, I've somehow lost ten pounds in weight. The only problem is it all seems to have come off my boobs, which are stretching to the floor so badly that I'm throwing out my Wonderbras and looking for a Miraclebra.

I've also been sadly neglecting myself in the beauty stakes. I could lose small children in the hair on my legs and knit a jumper with my eyebrows. As for the bikini area, it looks like no man's land, which, let's face it, is exactly what it's been for far too long. My pores are blocked, my nails are chewed and my hair resembles straw hanging out of a bin.

I call Carol in a panic. Luckily she doesn't have an assignment today so she agrees to take me in hand and book us in for a complete overhaul at her favourite beauty salon. 'Complete Overhaul' were her words. Luckily, as well as excess hairy bits and a lack of grooming, I also have thick skin.

An hour later, a stunning blonde with a Claudia Schiffer figure takes my coat as I enter. She's like a walking advert for this place and I accept that no amount of work is going to make me look like her before I leave here. I immediately flatten down my hair, pull in my stomach and ram my hands into my pockets. Carol spots me eyeing up the distance back to the door as I plan my escape and intervenes.

'Cooper, you look like you've been living rough for a month,' she whispers impatiently. So much for friends being a boost to the confidence. 'Sit down and behave yourself. You're just going to have to suck it up and chew the bullet.'

I know she means bite the bullet but I don't correct her, realising her mixed metaphors might just be the brightest moment in my day. I decide capitulation is the only answer for now – I can always escape through the bathroom window later.

As I sit down, Chantal introduces herself as my personal consultant.

'Now,' she asks, 'what can we do for you today?'

'I need the works. Throw everything you've got at me. I want to look stunning by the time I leave here.'

I look at Carol for reassurance – she's grinning at me proudly.

However, the look on Chantal's face says that she thinks there's more chance of her conjuring up a loaf and five fishes, or walking across the local swimming pool carrying a cured leper, than there is of making me stunning.

We agree a plan. First, the body. She's going to remove everything with a follicle from my legs, bikini line and underarms, then she'll sandblast the rest to remove all dead skin. This will be followed by a body wrap to remove radical free toxins (nope, absolutely no idea what that means) from my dilapidated system, before using a tanning treatment to make me glow like a bronzed goddess.

As for the face, Chantal takes a deep breath before recommending a deep cleanse, a non-surgical facelift, eyebrow shape, eyelash tint, and yet more fake tan.

The hair is beyond even her considerable talents, so she calls for reinforcements. Jacques, who was probably born Bert, gushes that only a complete reshape with highlights, lowlights and floodlights will do.

I consider sending Carol home for my weekend bag because I'm obviously going to be here for days. But before I can say anything, they whisk me into a private room at the back of the salon, where I lie back and close my eyes as Chantal gets to work.

I run through my preparation checklist in my head. Fish and Chips have now been dispatched to their foster home and the lava lamp has pride of place in Mrs Smith's front room, next to her knitting box and her British Seaside Towns plate collection. It blends right in.

Arrrrrrggggghhhh! Chantal removes three layers of skin as well as the forest from my lower left leg.

Deep breath. Try not to cry. Focus on something else. Back to my list.

My flat is now bereft of personal belongings, as all my worldly goods are crammed on top of kids' bikes, a lawnmower and a fourteen piece luggage set in Kate's garage. All that's left are the essentials – clothes, toiletries, electric hair appliances – that will be coming with me on my adventure.

Arrrrrrggggghhhh!! She's moved on to the bikini line. It's so excruciatingly painful, I decide I might cancel my trip because there's no way another human being will ever be allowed to touch that area again. I know this girl's type. She's the kind of woman who dresses in PVC with a studded collar, spiked boots and a whip and reduces pathetic men to mincemeat by beating them into submission.

Anyway, back to my adventure. That's how I'm starting to see this whole idea now – it's just one great big adventure. Since my panic last week, I haven't had one moment's doubt that I'm doing the right thing. I know this makes me sound naive, but I'm just so sure that something great is going to happen. I mean, how bad can it be? So, suppose that I get rejection after rejection? I'll still have had a year off work, visiting some amazing places and having new experiences. And yes, I'll be in a chronic financial state at the end of it, but it's only money. Let's face it, if this whole thing is a huge flop, then I'll gladly work three jobs for the rest of my life just to get me out the house.

Armpits are done. Chantal's now digging out the sandpaper to give me a good rub-down.

Back to my ponderings. I've got my itinerary all worked out. If I survive today, then I'll return my keys to the landlord tomorrow morning and head to Kate's house, where Jess and Carol will meet us for lunch. We'll spend the afternoon eating, drinking and preparing ourselves for my final 'going-away' party at Paco's tomorrow night.

Poor Paco doesn't realise what's coming. We told him to expect fifty people, but somehow the numbers have escalated and we're up to eighty-five already. I'm sure I don't even know half of them. Let's hope either he overestimates the buffet or we get a stampede of weight-watchers.

Chantal has now lathered me with foul smelling sticky stuff (I'm not brave enough to ask what it is) and is wrapping me in bandages. I ask if that's to cover the waxing burns, but she assures me this is the body wrap.

Back to the plan. The morning after my party, supposing I can lift my head from the pillow, I'll leave for Scotland. Nick Russo came from St Andrew's, so I've decided to stop at my mum's for a couple of days, then head to the coast.

The bandages come off. Thank God. I was beginning to panic that there'd be a fire in the salon, I'd be unable to escape and they'd dig my body out already mummified. There would be an irony.

Anyway, where was I? Oh yes, St Andrews.

I'm hoping it'll take no more than a week to find Nick. St Andrews isn't a big place, so even supposing I have to stop every resident or knock on every door, I'm bound to get a lead from somewhere.

Chantal's pasting on the tanning cream now. I've been here for three hours and my body feels like it's been battered, abused and shrink-wrapped.

So what happens when I find Nick Russo? Will he rush into my arms like a scene from a bad movie, gushing that he's never loved another woman and has waited all these years for me to return? Unlikely. Will he look at me blankly and ask what I'm selling? Probably.

The tanning cream has taken effect. From the neck down, I'm a subtle shade of pepperoni. Miss Whiplash moves on to my face, massaging it with a cleansing cream. I tell her that she'd be quicker using bleach and a sink plunger, but she ignores me.

I haven't booked any flights yet because I can't put a timetable on events. I'll just have to play everything by ear. That's presuming I still have my ears after Chantal has finished with me.

It's less than nine months now until the millennium, and I reckon that's just about the right timescale. It'll take that long before the credit card companies realise that I'm robbing Mastercard to pay American Express and vice versa. As Kate never stops reminding me, there are other ways I could do this. It would probably be cheaper to hire a private investigator to track them down. Or I could even have a go at doing it from home, writing letters to last known addresses and phoning international directory enquiries to try to track down numbers. I could take a month off work to go and find them, or I could carry on working and just devote my weekends to the search. But all those ideas completely miss the point. I want this to be an epic, life changing adventure. I want to have the experience. I want to shake up my life and see where everything falls. And if I don't do it now, then I never will.

It goes quiet in the room and I tentatively open one eye. Oh, sweet Jesus. Chantal's coming at me with two probes attached to an electricity supply. Isn't electric shock treatment illegal? I can't believe I'm actually paying someone to do this to me.

I block that thought out by returning to the practicalities. I've added up the available credit on my cards. Twelve thousand pounds. All of them have the facility to withdraw cash, so when the bills come in, I can just take out money from one to pay another. I have a chilling thought. I wonder if this is illegal? I wonder if running up a huge bill on your credit card when you have absolutely no means of paying it back is a criminal offence? That's all I need – to be financially destitute and on Scotland Yard's most wanted list at the same time.

Chantal's plucking my eyebrows and my nerve endings are screaming with pain. This shouldn't be done without a general anaesthetic or a bottle of vodka.

I distract my brain with more thoughts about the trip.

I consider the best and worst case scenarios. Worst case is that I end up back in the UK in a year's time with nothing – no man, no money, no house, no job, no self-respect and a mountain of debt.

I'm desperate to blink, but the eyelash tint would splatter everywhere and I'd spend the next two months with black freckles on my cheekbones.

Best case scenario is that one of the guys turns out to be Mr Happy Ever After and I achieve a life of love, peace and contentment, where the only things I worry about are the guest list for my next dinner party and whether to dress the kids in Baby Gap or Baby Next.

The beauty tag team has made a substitution and Jacques is now fussing around me as Chantal goes off to sharpen her cleavers in readiness for her next victim. I look around for Carol, but apparently she's buggered off for lunch.

Jacques is applying tinting gel to sections of my hair, then wrapping them in tinfoil. He informs me that when he's done that, he'll put me under the dryer to speed up the process.

So, twelve thousand pounds, almost nine months, six guys and a bigger disaster potential than the deterioration of the ozone layer. This is the biggest gamble I've ever taken. Remind me to pack a rabbit's foot, a sprig of lucky white heather, a four leafed clover and a St Christopher's medal.

Jacques has removed the tinfoil, sheared my locks, dried them and applied enough hairspray to give my hair the flexibility of a motorcycle helmet. He stands back and admires his work, then dramatically sweeps me round to face the mirror.

Oh my God! I look like I've been marooned on a tropical island for six months. I'm weather-beaten and my hair looks like it's never seen a hairbrush in its life. There isn't a strand longer than an inch and it's going in more directions than the Labour Party. If you turned me upside down, you could use me to scrub floors.

But the shock renders me speechless, so without complaint, I pay and head for the nearest hat shop via the nearest pub, where a tipsy Carol is chatting up the barman. The look on her face as she bends over, clutching her sides, says it all. I'm about to remind her that it's all her fault, when I realise that there's no point – the damage is already done.

If this is an omen of things to come, then I'm in big trouble. Maybe I'd be better trying to track them down by phone after all.

12

When the plane landed at Kai Tak airport on a humid early August evening, my grin was beaming. I was twenty-five years old, felt forty-five and couldn't believe that I had actually survived eighteen months in Shanghai, still relatively sane and in one piece. This was my reward – a whole year in Hong Kong.

I fought my way through baggage and customs and exited into a sea of people. I looked around for the hotel representative who was supposed to meet me. How would I recognise them?

I tried to appear cosmopolitan and nonchalant as I scanned the signs being held aloft. Eventually I spotted it. 'Carvy Cooler'. It had to be me.

The driver ushered me to a waiting Daimler. I felt like royalty as we headed to the Central area of Hong Kong. The contrast between my arrival in Shanghai and this city couldn't have been greater. Hong Kong was a blaze of neon lights and a veritable hive of activity. But it was the cars that amazed me. There were more Rolls-Royces, Bentleys and Mercedes than you'd find in the car park at a state banquet. Hong Kong was built on money. And I was the very girl to spend it.

The hotel was one of the best on the island. It was a glittering testament to modern architecture, stretching forty floors high and with stunning views over the harbour to Kowloon. I couldn't believe my luck. What was a girl like me doing in a place like this?

As I unpacked, I wondered what the guys would have made of this. Nick Russo would be oblivious, as he'd be too busy looking for a beach to sunbathe, Joe would have dragged me off to the nearest dodgy bar to learn to talk dirty in Cantonese. Doug would have set up a car dealership on the first available plot and blown his savings in five minutes on luxury saloons. Tom, oh God, it still hurt to think about him, Tom would have taken me to a rooftop and danced with me in the moonlight.

And Phil? I'd have had the best time with Phil. I wished he were with me. We'd have hit the nearest bar, drunk cocktails until dawn, laughed until we ached, met loads of new people and then danced the tango all the way home.

That reminded me – I had promised to call him the moment I arrived to let him know that I was okay. I rummaged in my bag for my electronic organiser. It was my most essential piece of technology, a little digital contact book that stored the phone numbers and addresses for everyone I knew. Shit, where was it? I couldn't have lost it – I'd just mastered how to work the damn thing. I'd bought it at Heathrow on my way to Shanghai, forgot all about it, then found it again when I was packing up to leave. I'd spent the next day transferring all my contacts from my old Filofax – the same Filofax that I then shredded because I didn't have room for it in my case. My whole life was in that little black machine. I turned everything inside out to no avail.

Fuck, fuck, fuck. It was gone. I had no way of getting in touch with him. When he moved out of my room, he'd moved to another expat's flat in Shanghai, but I couldn't remember the number or the address. Not that the address would have been any use, as Shanghai didn't exactly have an efficient directory enquiries service. In fact, it didn't even have a directory enquiry service. Bugger it. I'd just have to go back on my first leave and track him down. Meantime, there was no point worrying about it because there was nothing I could do.

I spotted a letter on the dressing table with my name on the front. My heart leapt – it must be a message from Phil and if there was a God, it would have his phone number on it. I ripped it open. Leapt heart returned to original position. It wasn't from Phil. It was a letter from my new boss, an Australian called Peter Flynn, requesting an audience at nine o'clock the following morning for an 'induction' meeting.

I decided to go on a reconnaissance mission to my new club, 'Asia'. I dressed in what I hoped was still a trendy outfit – black mini dress with a gold zip going from breast to thigh, black stilettos, and hair piled high on top of my head in a messy bun. I consulted the mirror but had no idea whether I looked good or not. It was so long since I'd been out somewhere trendy and glam that I didn't know what was in and what was out.

I made my way to the basement, the strains of B52's 'Love Shack' guiding me in like a heat-seeking missile. At the door, the bouncers eyed me suspiciously. Was it the dress? Had the zip burst to reveal my wobbly bits to the world? I looked around, but the general public weren't panicking and fleeing for the exits in distress. No, the zip must still be in one piece.

'Can I help you?' one of the bouncers enquired.

I gave him the two second top-to-toe inspection. 6'2" tall. Hair, the colour of Dairy Milk, crew-cut. Brown eyes with eyelashes that you could stir tea with. Square jawline. Sun-tanned. White teeth, crowned and straight. Nose that had been broken. At least twice. Broad shoulders. Defined pecs. Washboard abs that I couldn't see, but I just knew they were there. Slim hips. This guy was an 'after' picture for a health food supplement advert. Could he help me? Let me count the ways.

I showed him my room key. 'I'm a guest in the hotel.'

He scrutinised it and hesitantly waved me in. What was his problem? Why was he looking at me as if I'd stolen the key and was entering under false pretences? I swept by, hoping that I looked aloof and superior, but probably just managing grumpy and irritated.

I ordered a gin and tonic and stood at the bar scanning the room. It was a huge square, with only pillars punctuating its vastness. The capacity was about three hundred people. In the centre was the dance floor, surrounded by chrome railings separating it from the raised seating areas. On three sides of it were rows of 'poser pod' tall tables, each with six bar stools around them. On the fourth side was the slumber area: leather sofas and padded stools with low glass tables. The bar stretched along the wall to the left of the door, providing both direct and waitress service. This was a massive step up in the glamour and style stakes from the club in Shanghai.

The joint was jumping. The clientele were obviously Hong Kong's beautiful people. Most of the guys were in suits (Boss and Armani), walking with limps due to the weight of their Tag Heuer watches and concentrating furiously on their bottles of Bud to ensure they didn't spill a drop on their Gucci shoes. I hoped the mirrors in the toilets were huge, otherwise I feared violence as they jostled for position to check their designer stubble and super-gelled hair.

So, lots of people, lots of money, lots of style. The place had great potential.

I checked out the predominantly Western staff: two bouncers inside, four on the door. The two internals were both holding court to groups of ladies, clearly turning on the charm. In my experience, it was a familiar scenario with door stewards. As soon as you gave them a black tie and a title, they walked like a cowboy and became irresistible to women.

My eyes strayed to the door, then locked on to Mr Adonis, who'd spoken to me when I entered. He was staring back with a look that combined disdain with mild amusement. Were my knickers showing? Was the fluorescent lighting making me look like I had dandruff?

The sound of glass smashing interrupted my thoughts. I swivelled round to see an obviously intoxicated guy looking extremely wet, picking maraschino cherries out of his hair and being yelled at by an outraged Sandra Bullock look-alike. What a waste of a good cocktail.

I watched as Mr Adonis swiftly interjected. He had crossed the room and was now calmly steering one confused drunk to the nearest exit. I was impressed.

Thirty seconds later, he was back and negotiating with the female. I could see her face snarling in anger, then gradually mellowing into a smile as he replaced her drink and calmed her down. Here we go, I thought, predator goes in for the kill – soon they'll be exchanging phone numbers and she'll be gazing into his eyes in adoration. But that didn't happen. He just made sure that she was happy and then returned to his post at the door. Smooth.

I glanced back to the two internal guys. Both were still engrossed with their groupies, oblivious to all that had occurred. There could have been an all-out riot and these guys wouldn't have noticed. Somehow I felt that their employment was about to come to an abrupt end.

I studied the bar staff for the next hour. It was a bigger scam than the Maxwell pension fund. There were eight waiting staff and nine bartenders. Three of the bar workers were under-pouring and under-ringing, pocketing the excess cash, and another two were drinking more than they were serving. It was a miracle that they were still standing.

The Commodores' 'Three Times A Lady' softened the mood. Those who'd already paired off were smooching on the dance floor, the guys surreptitiously checking between the gold, platinum and black credit cards in their wallets for change for the condom machine. The few remaining blokes were now approaching all single females, taking the view that if they asked enough women, eventually one would say yes.

I made for the door, relatively satisfied with my new place of employment – a couple of problems to iron out, but I was going to have a lot of fun.

I was just about to exit, when Mr Adonis filled the doorway.

'No business tonight, love?'

Pardon? I was confused for a second, then realisation dawned. You could almost see the light bulb flash on above my head. He thought I was a hooker!

I looked up at him and smiled. 'Not tonight. You see, I'm very, very expensive and I don't think any of that lot could afford me.'

I held my head up and squeezed past him. That's it, the dress was going in the bin.

* * *

I arrived promptly for my induction the next morning. Peter Flynn was the kind of guy that you woke up with after a party and immediately vowed to be teetotal for the rest of your life. About 5'8" tall, with brown, Brillo-pad hair, tiny darting eyes, and a sneering expression.

'Miss Cooper, delighted to have you on board. I've heard great things about you from Jack McBurnie.' He said the whole sentence without looking up or cracking a smile.

'Glad to be here.' I suddenly wasn't sure that I was.

'Now, down to business. "Asia" is open every night except Monday from 10 p.m. until 3 a.m.. You'll have complete autonomy to do whatever you want, as long as you stay within budget. You are fully responsible for all aspects of the operation. If you miss target sales in three consecutive months, we will immediately terminate your contract.'

He really needed to work on his motivational speeches.

'I expect you to start work tonight. You're not entitled to vacation time until you've completed four months' service. You may stay in the hotel for one month to allow you time to find suitable accommodation. Thereafter you will receive a 50 per cent discount on hotel facilities.'

Be still my heart. His compassion was overwhelming.

'Any questions?'

'Yes. I need the services of five bar staff from other areas of the hotel tomorrow night and I need to inform you that I'll be recruiting new stewards.'

He didn't even ask why. He picked up the phone and barked orders to some poor defenceless minion. He replaced the receiver.

'It's arranged. I'll meet you at the club at 8 p.m. tonight to introduce you to the staff and then you'll take over from there. Good luck, Miss Cooper.'

He handed me a folder of financial records and I was dismissed with a wave of the hand.

I spent the afternoon shopping like a woman possessed. I prayed that they didn't terminate me after three months, as I'd just spent six months' salary on new clothes. I was having an out-of-body experience. My brain was carefully calculating the costs and advising caution whilst my body was careering around stores with my credit cards.

That night, I took hours getting ready. My hair was styled to within an inch of its life, I donned more fake tan than a body-builder and I took ages applying about forty-seven make-up products in the hope of looking like a natural beauty.

I pondered what to wear before deciding on my favourite purchase of the day – a black crepe dinner jacket with silk lapels and trousers with a silk seam running down the side. Under-neath, I forced my lumps into a black satin bodysuit and slipped into black stilettos with heels so thin and high that they'd be handy for making kebabs.

I looked in the mirror, threw back my shoulders and smiled. Ready for battle.

Flynn met me outside the club and ushered me in. About thirty staff were congregated on one of the corner sofas, smoking, drinking and chatting. He banged on the bar as I stood in the background surveying the crowd.

'Attention, please. As you all know, we have been waiting for a replacement manager to join us from Shanghai. I'm glad to say that she's finally arrived.'

He turned to beckon me forward.

'Miss Carly Cooper.'

They all looked up with mild curiosity. Except Mr Adonis. He visibly groaned, then put his head in his hands. I struggled to suppress a grin.

I went round the room, letting each one of them introduce themselves. I learned that Mr Adonis was Sam Morton, London born and bred, ex-army, twenty-seven and couldn't look me in the eye. I gave them all the 'I'm glad to be here and I'm sure we'll make a great team' speech. Sam Morton's rueful grimace suggested that he wasn't too confident about that.

I spent the night exploring every area of the club, familiarising myself with the operation. In the office that was more suited to the role of cupboard, I dug deeper into the financial books, stock records, personnel files and cash systems.

I checked out the cellars, stores and back-of-house areas, before spending a couple of hours serving behind the bar to assess the layout and set up. Finally, I moved to the door for the busy period, watching the entering clientele and the cash desk. I avoided conversation with any of the staff, other than to ask questions relevant to their role or duties. Still no eye contact from Mr Adonis.

For the last couple of hours, I just stood in a corner of the DJ booth from where I could see every corner of the room. The DJ was a tall, breathtakingly handsome black guy with gleaming dreadlocks called 'G'. He was dressed in a black T-shirt and jeans and was the epitome of cool.

'What does "G" stand for?' I asked.

'Gorgeous and Great in bed,' he replied, with a cheeky grin.

I laughed. 'And there's me thinking it was Gerald or Gene.'

It should have stood for 'Genius on a mixing desk' as he hyped up the crowd, always knowing exactly what record to play next to keep the atmosphere just right. It was a classic combination of old Motown, seventies soul, R&B and hip-hop.

I surveyed the scene. The gigolo bouncers were at it again, spending more time chatting up girls than actually working. The bar staff were still doing their bit for organised crime and systematically draining the stock that they weren't selling, and I was glad I'd asked Peter for several new members of staff for the next day. It had been the right call. I was satisfied that I had a fairly good handle on the situation. Nothing here was incurable; after a couple of areas of minor treatment – nothing even close to the massive changes I'd made in previous clubs – it could be a fairly healthy specimen. The essentials were there – a busy crowd spending buckets of money, a great music policy, classy venue and other than the few undesirables, the rest of the employees were doing a decent job.

At the end of the evening, I asked the staff to wait behind and allowed them all a drink. They congregated again on the corner sofas and I sat at the bar on the opposite side of the room, in view, but out of earshot of normal conversation. I summoned the three fiddling bar staff first. They walked over, the weight of the cash in their pockets slowing them down. I handed each of them an envelope containing a week's wages, more than generous considering they'd probably scammed twice that amount tonight alone. When I informed them that their services were no longer required, one started to protest loudly. I stopped him, mid-yell.

'See that flashing light in the corner?' I pointed to the smoke detector in the ceiling at the end of the bar. 'That's a camera and we've got your whole performance tonight on tape. You pocketed at least 25 per cent of the cash you took and you underpoured half your drinks, I'm assuming to try to balance the stock levels. Now, you can either leave quietly or I call in the police and let them view the film. So, what's it to be?'

They were out before I'd finished the sentence, which was a good thing, because I was lying through my teeth about the camera.

Next were the two alcohol guzzlers. They staggered over, trying and failing miserably to walk in a straight line. I repeated the camera story, giving them their wages and the telephone number of Alcoholics Anonymous.

I called over the Viagra twins.

'Lads, if you want to chat up women all night, then I suggest you join a singles club.'

They looked shocked, then recovered admirably.

'C'mon, babe. It's all part of the attraction of this place. We've got the ladies flocking in. Tell you what, why don't you let us take you out for the night and show you our credentials,' one suggested leeringly.

'Interesting offer, but I'll pass. Now, why don't you take your credentials outside and stick to using them to pee out of.'

It took them a moment to process the refusal. I don't think they'd ever been rejected before.

It was ironic, I mused. Here I was, Miss In Control, Calm and Collected at work, yet the minute I had to deal with my personal life, all control and calm went out of the window.

I was contemplating how to get off the bar stool without breaking my neck, when Sam, the door steward, approached.

'I thought I'd save you the trouble of calling me over.'

Direct. Bold. I liked that in a man.

'That's very kind of you. And why, exactly, would I want to speak to you?'

He looked puzzled. 'Well, last night...'

'Sam, in that dress *I'd* have thought I was a hooker. I'm not going to fire you just because I decided to dress like an extra in a blue movie. It was my mistake, not yours. I'm just insulted that I got no offers.'

He paused, then flashed his pearlies. He could be an ambassador for Colgate.

'Now, come back over and join the others and help me convince them that I'm not about to cast them all into the nearest dole office.'

He visibly relaxed and followed me to the waiting crowd. I poured everyone drinks and gave a toast.

'To "Asia".'

'To "Asia",' they repeated, looking relieved and happy.

I caught Sam's eye and he winked.

Oh, shit, I thought, feeling a sensation that had been absent for a long time.

Hello, danger.

* * *

My first two weeks at 'Asia' were focused on understanding the operation, building rapport with the regulars and gaining the trust and respect of the staff. It was a fairly straightforward operation to manage. There was little trouble, the club filled to capacity most nights and after my initial clear-out, I had no further problems with the staff.

I recruited two new bouncers – a mad Australian surfer called Zeek, and Kenny, an unusually tall, kick-boxing, Hong Kong national. I stationed them on the door with Sam and Hugh, a cheeky Welshman who had a never-ending stream of really bad jokes.

I moved Derek and Jamie, two overdeveloped, bodybuilding Scotsmen inside, warning them that if they so much as swapped telephone numbers with a paying customer, I'd cut their wages for a month. That did the trick.

My only problem was finding somewhere to live. The rentals in Hong Kong were astronomical. It cost the same there to rent a claustrophobic one bedroom flat as it would to rent an estate with deer and a babbling brook at home. Even though the hotel was giving me a generous housing allowance, I still couldn't find anything that I liked.

I contemplated the problem one night as I stood at the door, watching the nightly exhibits in the 'Asia' catwalk enter.

Sam interrupted my thoughts. 'So, Carly, when are we going out?'

I wondered if I'd misheard him. 'Pardon?'

He repeated his question and I immediately grasped what he was asking. This presented me with a dilemma. You see, there is an unwritten law in man-management called the DEFTS code – Don't Ever Fuck The Staff. I had always adhered religiously to it, having seen too many casualties who had broken the code and ended up unemployed, lonely and bitter. It just wasn't worth it. As a result, although I tried to form congenial working relationships with my employees, I always kept my personal life completely separate.

'We're not going out, Sam. Why don't you concentrate on the door instead of on your love life?'

Succinct. Detached. But suddenly I was feeling ambidextrous. On the one hand, I was impressed with his boldness, the concept of a man – especially one who looked like Sam – taking charge was reducing me to a submissive, drooling teenager. On the other hand, I was outraged at his audacity. How dare he assume that his boss would just jump when he deigned to snap his fingers? Trouble was, I couldn't remember if I was left or right handed.

It didn't matter. My rebuff had zero effect.

'Look, Carly. We're going out together. It's inevitable. Just tell me when.'

'Forget it, Sam. It isn't going to happen.'

He was obviously a guy who bore up well under rejection. He bombarded me all night; every time I passed him, he repeated the question. What aspect of 'No' didn't he understand? I acted irritated, aloof and disdainful, but inside I was melting like lava. He was cute, funny, cheeky and bold, but he was also smart and quick-witted. I'd observed him over the previous nights, handling every potential situation with maturity, firmness and calm. He had the people management skills of a diplomat. If I ever developed musical talent and became a globe-trotting rock star, then this was the guy that I'd want to watch my back.

But no. A relationship with a bouncer was out of the question. Absolutely not. No way. Never.

At the end of the evening, desperate to put some space between us before I weakened and did something I'd regret, I achieved a new world record for the clear-out, clear-up and clean-down of a nightclub. I was back upstairs in my hotel room before the last drunken reveller had reached the end of the street.

I undressed and climbed into bed without even removing my make-up. I put a pillow over my head and groaned. God, this was like being a compulsive eater in a sweet shop, but knowing that if I took so much as a bite of a Yorkie, I'd explode into a big, fat trucker.

I tossed and turned; my body severely pissed off with my brain for rejecting an opportunity to rediscover my sex drive.

I gave up trying to sleep at 6 a.m. and dialled Kate's number in the UK. The international call would cost about a week's wages, but it was worth it. She answered sleepily.

'Kate, what are you doing in bed? It's only 10 p.m..'

'Cooper, come and take me away from all this. This baby has turned me in to a physical wreck.'

Kate's life had changed dramatically too – when I was in Shanghai, she'd had the opportunity to move to London and share a flat with Carol. She'd snatched the chance, and almost as soon as she arrived, she met Bruce, when he popped in for a trim. Within four months, they had a quickie, low-key wedding, and six months later, Cameron was born. At least I couldn't be accused of being the only spontaneous one in our group – Kate had moved to London, met Bruce, was married and became a mother all in the space of less than a year. It must have been something in our upbringing.

I explained the night's events.

'Let me get this straight. An intelligent bloke with the body of a Greek God is lusting after you and you're resisting because of some stupid rule that was probably made up by a hypocritical guy whilst he was banging his secretary. And let's face it, how many times in the last eighteen months have you had sex?'

'Once,' I murmured sheepishly. That was below the belt! And it wasn't the point! And God, I still missed Phil so much. Focus, Cooper. Focus.

'But, Kate, he's a *bouncer* for God's sake. They'd shag anything in a skirt.'

'Cooper, you're being so bloody judgemental. How many females has this guy copped off with since you met him?'

'None.'

'How many have you heard him chatting up?'

'None.'

'Well, stop being such a snob then. Just because he's a bouncer doesn't mean he's a slapper. What does he do as a day job?'

'He does personal training for yuppies to support himself. He's learning Cantonese and practising some karate thing. He wants to open a martial arts school for kids.'

The volume of her groan nearly made me drop the phone.

'Jesus, Carly. He sounds like a cross between Dolph Lundgren and Mother Teresa. Now take advice from an old married woman. After kids, the sex deteriorates to the occasional knackered fumble, so make the most of it while you can.'

This wasn't quite the pep talk I'd been hoping for.

A wave of homesickness drowned me. To make it worse, Kate brought me up to date with the latest gossip before hanging up. Carol had landed her first national TV commercial. She'd been the Glasgow Tourist Board's 'Flirt in a Skirt' in their last advert for tartan kilts, but this was the first television job she'd bagged since she moved to London.

'How long did you celebrate for?' I knew I was torturing myself, but I had to ask.

'Three days,' she answered, hesitantly.

My bottom lip began to quiver. I missed the girls at home like crazy.

'But we had lots of toasts in your memory,' she added quickly, trying to console me. It didn't work. It just made it sound like I had died.

Jess was next. She'd joined Carol and Kate in London and had a research post with Brixton Council. Only Sarah was still in Scotland. 'Since she moved in with that guy in Edinburgh she's fallen off the face of the earth. She's bailed on everything we've invited her to for ages now. Always says she's too busy. And the once or twice that I've managed to get her on the phone, she just says she's been way too busy to keep in touch. She says she's really happy though. I guess sometimes friendships just drift apart, but I wish she still had time for us,' Kate complained.

'Me too. She never replies to my letters.' I didn't mind. I was glad she was happy and I knew we'd catch up eventually. Although, I'd have to track down her address because the last one I had for her was lost when my personal organiser vanished.

'Don't take it personally,' Kate said. 'Just one of those things, but we miss her.'

I could hear Kate's voice getting sleepy.

'Be good, Cooper. And remember, if you can't be good, be—'

'I know, be careful.'

'I was going to say "outrageous",' she laughed. 'I know your limitations.'

I put the pillow back over my head. The sun had come up outside and I wasn't ready to face the day yet. There was a knock at the door.

'Room service.'

'I didn't order room service,' I replied. This was all I needed – a confused waiter with a continental breakfast.

Another knock.

'Room service,' he repeated.

Fuck! I stomped out of bed, grabbed a robe and threw open the door.

'I told you I didn't...' I stopped mid-sentence. Leaning against the door frame was Sam, looking tired and sweaty, in shorts and a T-shirt.

'I couldn't sleep, so I went for a run. Found myself here.' There was no sense of pushiness or grand gestures, just honesty.

'And?'

'You tell me,' he shrugged, his expression questioning.

Bugger the rules. I pulled him inside and wound my arms around his neck, kissing him until I could barely breathe.

'More?' he asked, when we eventually broke apart.

I knew what he was asking and I didn't hesitate before whispering, 'Yes.'

He picked me up and carried me to the bathroom. He turned on the shower and stripped off both his clothes and my robe before pulling me under the water jet. He took the soap and lathered me from head to toe, massaging every part of me. I returned the service, reaching for an extra bar of soap.

He pushed me under the water and lifted me up. Instinctively I wrapped my legs round his waist and closed my eyes tight. The fact that I could potentially drown under the shower didn't even cross my mind, but I was relieved when he switched off the water and carried me to the bed.

'You sure?' he whispered.

I nodded, reaching over to my bedside drawer for condoms. It was the same supply I'd had for months, and when I'd unpacked I'd put them there more out of habit than optimism.

Meanwhile, primal instinct took over. We made love on the bed, on the floor, against the window, on the desk, over the coffee table. Sam reciprocated, alternating between taking charge and letting me control him. If this was his usual early morning work-out, then no wonder he looked the way that he did. This was the kind of exercise I could definitely get on board with.

Finally, we came together, collapsing against a wall and sliding down it. He reached over to the bed and pulled the duvet off, wrapping it around us.

I was mentally checking my body for broken bones, torn muscles and bruises as he stroked my hair.

'So what now?' My powers of initiative and reason had deserted me.

'We're having a relationship,' he stated definitively, like it was already agreed.

'We are? Don't I have a say in this?' Not that there would be any arguments from me, but still, I couldn't let him away with that level of surety.

He laughed and pushed my hair back off my face, looking into my eyes. 'Why? Do you have any objections, boss?'

I rolled my eyes and grinned weakly. 'No.' I was pathetic, I thought. A few hours of admittedly earth-moving passion and my resolve crumbled.

We lay in bed until early afternoon when we realised we were starving.

'Let's go back to my place and I'll make you lunch.'

'I can't. I have to house hunt.'

'Or...' he paused, and I could see he was thinking. 'You could bring all your stuff over and move in with me until you find somewhere.'

I closed my eyes. Here we go again. Why did I never have a relationship that started with a gentle friendship, then a couple of years to get to know each other before the engagement announcement went into *The Times*? Then another couple of years of occasional illicit sexual encounters, before we walked up the aisle, pension plans and endowments in place. I'd seen porno movies that had lasted longer than my courtships. Whoever invented the phrase 'seize the day' must have known I was coming.

I suppose, I thought as I emptied my underwear drawer into my suitcase, I just didn't see the point of delaying the inevitable. I loved the spontaneity and excitement of the beginning of a relationship. Enthusiasm and optimism, they got me every time.

At least it solved my immediate accommodation problem, but it created another one. The hotel management would frown upon me becoming overfamiliar with the staff. I explained this to Sam.

'If we are going to do this, Sam, then nobody can ever find out about it. Promise me.'

'And here's me planning to announce it over the tannoy tonight,' he replied, looking mortally offended.

'I'm serious, Sam. Nobody, okay.'

'Whatever you say, boss.'

'And stop bloody calling me boss. From now on it's "babe", "darling", "sweetheart" and in moments of passion, "you gorgeous, amazing shag". Understood?'

'Yes, boss.' His smirk made me giggle. I had the feeling that this was going to be interesting. Irrational, eventful, unpredictable but definitely interesting.

I made Sam leave five minutes before me, carrying my suitcase, then met up with him outside. We caught the MTR to Causeway Bay, then climbed a million stairs to street level. Any man who could do that carrying my suitcase and not require oxygen at the top deserved a medal. We weaved in and out the crowded streets before reaching the entrance to a block of flats. We were about to enter when a voice called out.

'Mr Sam. *Lay Ho Ma*.' I'd already learned it was Cantonese for 'how are you?'

We turned around to see the source of the greeting. I was confused. The only people in sight were three old homeless men lying on camp beds under a flyover across the road. Sam beckoned me over to them and shook their hands, talking to them in Cantonese. He introduced me and they giggled, winking at Sam and patting his arm proudly.

'Carly, this is Huey, Dewy and Louie. They help me with my Cantonese in return for a case of beer and some food money every week.'

'What are their real names?'

'I don't know. I don't think even they remember. They told me someone once called them that and it stuck.'

'They live here?' I looked around at the pile of sleeping bags and the makeshift beds. It was hard to believe that the authorities let them live like this in the middle of one of the world's busiest cities. Sam nodded, as the other three began chatting to him.

'What are they saying?' I asked him.

'That you look like a woman with lots of, em, energy,' he laughed.

Impressed by their easy friendship, I smiled. Sam Morton was full of surprises.

We said goodbye and went upstairs. I was feeling nervous. What if his house was a disgusting bachelor pad? It struck me that I knew nothing about him. I know, any rational person would have had these misgivings long before they were standing in the hallway, next to their suitcase, about to enter their new home.

He swung open the door and as I edged inside, I sighed with relief.

The flat consisted of three rooms. The largest was open plan, about twenty-five feet square with white walls and wood flooring. In one corner was a double bed, made up with cushions scattered across the top. Piles of books stood to attention next to it. In the centre of the room were two cream sofas, parallel to each other with a pine coffee table in the middle. Against one wall was a hi-fi unit with a television, video and stereo, against another there was a row of wardrobes. In the opposite corner from the bed, there was a small pine dining table and two chairs.

I explored the other rooms. One was a shower room, with a spotlessly clean white bathroom suite and the other was a tiny kitchen, with only room for two cupboards, a fridge, a two-ring stove and a microwave.

Sam had obviously discovered the minimalist look long before it was fashionable. I could live here, I decided. It would be cosy, but it was clean and bright and comfortable and so much better than anything I'd looked at in my budget.

He pulled me to him and kissed me.

'Welcome home.'

I resisted his manoeuvres to christen our new abode and made for the kitchen. For once my stomach was overruling my libido. I opened the cupboards and searched for sustenance, while he made space for my things in his wardrobe.

I opened a couple of cans of soup and heated them on the stove, then found a stick of fresh bread in the cupboard. When it was ready, I called him over. As he pulled out a chair at the dining table, he watched, puzzled, as I passed him, carrying a large Pyrex dish on the way to the door.

'Where are you going?' he enquired, appearing concerned that I was about to flee the scene.

'I'll be back in a minute. I'm just taking some soup down to Huey, Dewy and Louie.'

His laughter followed me down the corridor. Somehow I knew I was going to like it here.

We fell into the comfortable rhythm of a match made in heaven. I would go into work every day at lunchtime to take care of the stock, accounts and prepare for opening.

Running a club that was attached to a hotel was so much easier than an independent, because the hotel took care of all the major cleaning and maintenance. Before we left at night, we cleared all the tables, washed all the glasses and made sure the bar was pristine and locked. But other than that, no matter what state the rest of the club was in when we left at 4 a.m., it was always pristine when I returned in the afternoon. I wish the same happened at home – it would be great to leave clothes strewn around, then return to find them washed, ironed and back in the drawers.

While I was at work, Sam would alternate between Cantonese classes (both official ones, and the informal ones with his friends under the flyover) and martial arts training. He was completely focused on his plans and supplemented his income by charging an obscene amount of money to overpaid expats for personal training sessions at a local gym every night between 5 p.m. and 7 p.m..

Afterwards, he'd meet me for dinner. He was the most interesting guy I'd ever met – a complete encyclopaedia on Asia, on history, on life – so much for the stereotypes about bouncers. Not only was he smart, but he was completely without vanity. He didn't even look in a mirror except to shave. Another theory blown out of the water.

But the best thing about the relationship was the easiness of it. There were no heavy emotional scenes. No declarations of undying love. No fights and tantrums. It was just simple, relaxed, comfortable and fun, with long conversations and sex that left you smiling for a week. Heaven. I was actually starting to think that I was getting this relationship thing right for once. Every evening, we'd return to the club, separately, of course. Our affair was still filed under the Official Secrets Act and Sam was the epitome of discretion. If anything, it was me who was in danger of blowing our cover. As the months passed, I found it increasingly difficult to stand by while gorgeous women threw themselves at him. One night as I stood at the door with Sam, Kenny, Zeek and Hugh, my patience was tested to the limit.

A stunning blonde who had obviously shared a womb with Kate Moss, sidled up to him.

'Hi,' she pouted.

Sam nodded and then turned back to the door.

She wasn't deterred by his indifference.

'I was wondering if you wanted to go for a drink when you finish work.'

'Thanks for the offer, but I don't think so.'

She curled her fingers through his hair. I wanted to snap them like a Kit Kat.

'Oh, come on. Just one little, bitsy drink.' Her fingers were tracing down the side of his face now. I wondered how she would pick things up after I'd removed her thumb.

'Look,' he said, detaching her hand from his neck, 'I'm married. The only person I go for a drink with is my wife, okay?'

The other guys raised their eyebrows. The 'married' excuse was one that they all used, but usually only when they were confronted with drunken women they didn't fancy, not ones who would look stunning on the pages of a magazine.

'She would never know,' supertramp continued, 'and it would definitely be a night to remember.'

That's it. I looked around for a cleaver to amputate her limbs. Then my mouth started moving before it had consulted my brain and I interjected, trying to act more amused than enraged.

'I'm afraid she would know. You see, she's standing here wondering why you're salivating all over her husband.'

A burst of laughter came from the guys. Sam looked at me, clearly enjoying my reaction.

Blondie staggered off, seeking a hole to crawl in to.

'Way to go, boss. Don't suppose you'd do that for me if that little chick who's been stalking me appears again tonight,' Hugh asked.

'Sure, Hugh. All part of the service.'

I glanced at Sam. His amusement had turned to smugness, but the tables soon turned. Zeek spoke up, very bravely as the others were within earshot.

'Boss, I was wondering if you'd like to grab some lunch with me tomorrow. Maybe go over to Lan Kwai Fong?'

Tempting. Lan Kwai Fong was my favourite area, a collection of streets packed with cool bars and restaurants. But there was a Sam-shaped problem with the idea.

'Sorry, Zeek. I've already got plans.'

He was just being friendly, I thought, nothing more.

Maybe not.

'How about dinner then?'

'Sorry, Zeek, I can't. I'm already seeing someone, you know that.'

I'd been telling them for months that I was seeing someone, but I was sure they thought he was a figment of my imagination.

'No offence, boss, but how can you be? You're here every day and night and he never comes to visit you. No guy would put up with that. C'mon, tell the truth. You just give us the boyfriend story to put us off. Come out with me tomorrow. You could do with a bit of fun.'

I could see Sam flushing and grinding his teeth. Mr Cool was looking decidedly lukewarm. I was starting to enjoy this.

'You're right, Zeek, I could do with a bit of fun.'

Sam coughed loudly.

'But I'll still skip tomorrow. Sorry.'

Zeek shrugged his shoulders. 'Let me know if you change your mind.'

That night, Sam made love to me like a man who wanted to make sure I'd never let him go.

By Christmas Eve, Sam was losing patience with the subterfuge. Apparently, the staff in the club were running a book to see which of them could persuade me out on a date first. He couldn't understand the need for secrecy. He brought it up again in the office that night just before opening time.

'Please, Sam, don't get upset. I just want to keep my personal life private. It's got nothing to do with anyone else. I don't want the people who work for me to know I'm living with one of the bouncers.'

'But why?' he yelled. 'What is it, Carly, are you embarrassed by me? Well, I tell you what, I'll just fuck off out of your way then.'

He stormed off to his position at the door. I was dumbstruck. I'd never heard him raise his voice before, never mind swear at me in anger. He avoided me for the rest of the evening.

As G counted down the minutes to the arrival of Christmas Day, the club was in uproar. I fought my way through the bar to the door. I looked at Sam pleadingly, but he just turned away.

Over the speakers, Noddy Holder was screaming something about Merry Christmas and everybody having fun.

I begged to differ.

The rest of the night passed in a cloud of gloom. When we cleared out the crowd, I told the staff to help themselves to drinks. I'd promised them a party to make up for having to work over Christmas and there was no point in everyone being pissed off just because I was having a bad day.

I finished my paperwork and joined them. Zeek accosted me with a sprig of mistletoe. I kissed him on the cheek.

'Is that all I get?' he moaned.

I laughed and gave him a peck on the lips. Out of the corner of my eye, I saw Sam get up and make for the exit. Shit, it was now or never. I grabbed the mistletoe from Zeek.

'Hey, Sam,' I shouted, just before he disappeared into the night. 'I do believe you have to kiss a lady when she's holding mistletoe.'

He turned slowly, as opposed to the thirty heads that swung like spectators at a tennis match, to see what was going on.

There was a sudden silence. You could have heard tinsel drop as Sam strolled over to me.

He kissed me on the cheek.

'Is that all I get?' I repeated Zeek's moan.

Thirty heads were now looking at each other in astonishment.

I put my arms round his neck and snogged him.

'But, Carly, what about the boyfriend?' Zeek shouted, his chin so near the ground that his designer stubble was sanding the floorboards.

I grinned, still looking at Sam.

'This is the boyfriend, Zeek. Always has been.'

'Merry Christmas,' I whispered in Sam's ear.

He lifted me up and swung me round. The sound of stamping feet and a standing ovation filled the room.

'Merry Christmas, babe,' he replied.

So the secret was out. The whole world knew that we were shacked up, cohabiting, living in sin, as my gran would say. Sam won the hundred dollar bet among the doormen for getting past first base, but he was disqualified because he was already fraternising with me when the bet was made. I don't think he minded. And yes, if the bosses at the hotel got wind of it, there would be questions, but the club was making more money than ever, so I was fairly sure I had some leverage.

The week between Christmas and New Year was quieter than usual, but at least it allowed us to catch our breath before the bedlam began again. It also allowed the staff to get the gossip out of their systems – our big story of the week was superseded by the rumour of a mass Christmas orgy at one of the regular customer's houses.

On Hogmanay, we were full by ten thirty and the crowd was in great spirits. I couldn't help comparing it with the same time two years before when I was at home and in Tiger Alley with the girls and Tom. I wondered what he was doing now, then pushed the thought from my mind. The way things ended with Tom would always be a regret, but I locked it back in its box. Tonight wasn't the night for sadness or looking back, especially as I was facing down an irrepressible wave of homesickness.

I checked my watch. 11.50. I missed the people I loved. What was I doing in a room full of strangers on the most important night of the year? I'd give a year's salary and chocolate for Callum, Michael and the girls to walk in now.

I looked around for Sam but couldn't see him anywhere. Suddenly, the music stopped. *Oh, fuck, don't tell me we've got a blowout now. Not on New Year's Eve.*

The lights went up. G blared over the microphone. 'Would Carly Cooper come to the dance floor, please.'

Was there a fight? Had somebody collapsed? Tonight was just getting better and better.

I rushed over, but there was no drama.

A spotlight focused on me. G spoke again.

'Now, posse,' he addressed the crowd, 'we all know *our fine* manager here, don't we?'

There was a roar from the crowd. I made a mental note to sack him.

'Well, I've got a message here for her that I thought you all might like to share.'

Another roar from the crowd. Remind me to sack him twice. Another spotlight. But this time it was on Sam, holding a cordless mike and walking towards me. Oh, bugger, remind me to sack him too.

Realisation hit me and my stomach lurched. *Don't do this, Sam. Don't, don't, don't.*

He stopped in front of me and took my hand.

'Cooper, I love you very much.' He paused. There was a chorus of 'Aaaaahs' from the crowd and 'Go, Sam' from the bar staff. 'Marry me.'

Complete silence. What could I say? I'd been ambushed. There were three hundred pairs of eyes on me, two of them bearing down into my soul.

A tear ran down my cheek. I don't know if it was from embarrassment or terror. How could this be happening to me? Again! What was I, some king of marriage target practice? Was I a red rag to every non-engaged man on the planet?

I forced myself to focus on this nightmare. Did I love him? I'd come to realise that my emotions couldn't be trusted. Did I want to marry him? Not this very minute, but I wouldn't mind another couple of years of deliberation.

But was I going to humiliate him in front of all these people? No. There was nothing else for it.

I nodded my head.

'Yes,' I whispered.

He slipped a gleaming diamond solitaire on to my finger. I didn't mention that years ago I'd had another one just like it.

The roar from the crowd would have raised the roof if it wasn't for the fact that we were in the basement and there were forty floors above us.

G cut in. 'Ten, nine, eight, seven, six, five, four, three, two, one. Happy New Year, everyone!!!!!!'

We were engulfed by sweaty bodies.

'Happy New Year, Mrs Morton.'

'Happy New Year, Sam.'

How was I going to get myself out of this one?

* * *

My cowardly tendencies kicked in over the next few months. Instead of telling Sam that I wasn't 100 per cent sure about the ever-after stuff, I spent my time getting used to the idea of spending the rest of my life with him.

Somehow I managed to completely convince myself that it would work. After all, I adored him and loved every moment that we spent together. Yep, it would work. Definitely. Absolutely.

So why did I keep fobbing him off when he pressed me for a wedding date?

One day in July, I was summoned by Peter Flynn. I approached his office tentatively. Somehow, I knew it wouldn't be good news. I was right.

'Miss Cooper, your next posting has come through.'

I was stunned. 'But I didn't apply for one. I was planning to stay here indefinitely.'

'I'm sorry, but that isn't possible. It is the policy of this hotel to change the nightclub manager every year. That way, the operation stays fresh. I do believe you knew that.'

'Well, yes, I did...' I vaguely remembered him telling me that when we first met, but I hadn't realised it was set in stone. '... but I thought you would speak to me before deciding my fate.'

He was unrepentant.

'Miss Cooper,' he shrilled, 'I am a very busy man. I have over thirty expats working in this building. If I spent my time considering all their feelings, I wouldn't have time to run a hotel.'

I didn't know how to answer that, especially as there was clearly no point in arguing with him.

'And where will my next posting be?'

'We have vacancies in London or Dubai. Both hotels are happy to accept you. It's your choice. You leave in four weeks.'

London. Dubai. Both of them a world away from Hong Kong. Dammit.

I thought about it for the rest of the day. Did I want to stay here? I loved Hong Kong, and could probably pick up another job here, but the thought of starting over again in another venue filled me with dread. 'Asia' was the best club on the island, with a great clientele. Sure, there were bigger ones, but they were full of teenagers in Wonderbras and Lycra, raving themselves into exhaustion. The very thought of it was enough to give me a migraine. No, that wasn't an option.

I could try working in another field, but managing nightclubs was all I knew. I wasn't qualified to do anything else. Nor would I want to. I loved every drunken, decadent, unpredictable minute I spent in a club. They were as much a part of me as breasts and cellulite. No, I'd be miserable working anywhere else.

Dubai sounded appealing. Sun, sea, sand and the kind of wealth that would make my job easy. But London. Carol, Jess and Kate were there. I longed for a good night out with the girls, to be able to talk to them all night without a time delay. Surely it must be fate? But how could I ask Sam to leave Hong Kong? His whole life was here. He had the next twenty years mapped out like a battle plan. He would have enough money to open his school in two years and that was his lifelong ambition. It was his dream. How could I stand in the way of that when I didn't know what I was going to be doing a week on Sunday?

Why did life have to be so bloody difficult?

Options raced through my mind.

Maybe Sam would want to come to London?

Who was I kidding?

What about having a long distance relationship for a year? At least that would test the strength of our commitment! Sam wasn't Tom – he would work with me on this.

Yes, that was it. Sam wouldn't like it, but surely he'd see that it was the best of a bad lot of options.

Wrong.

When I told Sam that night, his reaction was not the one that I'd expected. He flew into his second ever rage, smacking his fist through the wall. At least now we had a ventilation hole.

'They can't do that!'

'They can, Sam. It's just the way it works.'

'So leave. Tell them to shove their job. You'll get another one here, no problem.'

I said nothing. He stared at me.

After a couple of moments, absurdly, he laughed.

'Oh, I see. You want to take one of them, don't you? You've made up your fucking mind already. When were you planning to tell me, in a note after you'd left?'

As if I'd do a thing like that! Eh, had he been speaking to Joe?

I suddenly transformed into 'cliché woman'. Every well-worn platitude I could think of was trooped out.

'Sam, look, I want to go home for a while. I've been away for nearly three years. I think that maybe I want to take the one in London, but I don't want it to be the end of us. This has all been such a rush so far. Maybe some time apart will be good for us. It would only be for a year; then I'd come back here. Please, Sam. Think about it.'

'Carly, my life is here. How can you just pack up and take off? I don't want you in another country, I want you here.'

He had a point. But surely what I wanted to do was important too? Was this what it came down to, his way or my way? Not again.

I thought back to Tom. Hadn't that relationship bitten the dust because I was too stubborn to change my mind? Had I learned nothing? But then, why did it have to be so cut and dried? Why couldn't we both make the choices that made us happy and trust that it would work out and we'd survive a temporary separation? Couldn't he even try?

Apparently not.

Over the next four weeks, we alternated between tears and tantrums. He begged me not to go. I begged him to understand that it was just for a year, but he refused to accept that. As far as he was concerned, if I left him, then it was over. It was a no-win situation and neither of us triumphed. It had stopped being a battle of wills. Now it was just a battle.

On my final day, I made a last-ditch effort to change his mind, and Sam did the same.

'Please don't go, Cooper. I don't want to live without you. Don't leave.'

'Then wait for me, Sam. I promise I'll come back in twelve months.'

'But don't you see, if you really loved me, you wouldn't leave?'

That old chestnut. I sighed. There was nothing like dramatic emotional blackmail to get a girl running in the opposite direction.

'Sam, I'm going. I have to.' It was true. I felt an overwhelming need to go to London and reconnect with my old life, my family, my friends.

He looked at me and shook his head.

'Then go,' he murmured, voice thick with sadness. He got up, grabbed his jacket and left.

I slowly slipped off my engagement ring and placed it gently on his bedside table. My heart was breaking. I picked up my passport, tickets and suitcase and followed him out of the door. Downstairs, I gave Huey, Dewy and Louie all my remaining Hong Kong dollars, keeping only enough to get me to the airport, then I hailed a taxi, tears blinding me, mascara running down my face like black rain.

'Kai Tak airport, please.'

The driver looked at me quizzically. I knew what he was thinking. Crazy lady. Maybe he was right.

I never saw Sam Morton again.

PART II

13

It's the big day – Mission Manhunt starts here. Unfortunately it's also the first day after my 'Leaving London' party. The next time I decide to fly with a hangover, I'll remember this moment and stay in bed. My head feels like there's an illegal rave going on in it. Why do I do this to myself? If that stewardess doesn't get over here soon with the coffee, I'm going to cry. For the hundredth (maybe thousandth) time in my life, I vow to give up alcohol. Or at least drink in moderation. Okay, at least not drink on an empty stomach.

As we start our descent to Glasgow Airport, I ponder last night, or at least what I can remember of it. I know it was fantastic. Before I lost my powers of comprehension, I had counted over a hundred people. Paco looked like he was going to faint. There was loud music, even louder singing, and the waiters will never be the same again.

Last thing I remember was belting out 'Addicted To Love', with Kate, Jess and Carol doing backing vocals. One of these days, we're going to listen to people who tell us that we can't sing.

On the bright side, I'd managed to dampen down my orange

complexion to a case of mild sunburn with make-up, and after washing and restyling my hair, I somehow made it settle into a passable pixie cut, as opposed to Billy Idol circa 1982.

The night wasn't without its share of drama though. And from the most unexpected source. Carol finally buckled to our demands that she bring George, her latest bloke, so that we could give him a full inspection. Her relationship with Clive didn't survive the swanky holiday. She discovered that he took his teeth out at night, and it was all too much for her. She said goodbye the minute they touched down at Heathrow and we haven't been allowed to mention him since.

Not long after she got back, she met George at a photoshoot for his investment company. The first thing she did was check his dental habits and ensure his molars were the kind that stayed in his mouth. She's only known him for a month and already there'd been a weekend in Venice, a Chanel bag and a diamond bracelet with matching earrings. He passed physical inspection – tall, grey, early sixties, Savile Row suit, Armani shirt, Oxbridge accent and when he pulled out his wallet to buy a bottle of champagne, I spotted layers of gold cards. He looked decidedly uncomfortable in the midst of the mayhem though. Poor bloke. Metaphorically that is – he owns half of Mayfair.

All was going along according to plan – lots of drinkies, lots of going-away prezzies, lots of 'we'll miss you's (although a lot of these were from gatecrashers whom I'd never met before in my life, just trying to act like they belonged there).

Kate arrived, looking gorgeous in black leather hipsters and a white T-shirt, not showing so much as a hint of baby yet. How could she look that devastating after giving birth to two children and now being pregnant with her third?

Bruce gave me a huge cuddle. 'I feel like one of my kids is leaving home, Cooper,' he laughed.

'Don't worry, Bruce. The police will probably bring me back to your door in handcuffs any day soon.'

He thought I was joking. We'll see.

A voice rang out. 'Cooper, get over here and tell me you've changed your mind about this manic idea, you daft bint!'

It was Jess, for once ahead of us in the alcohol stakes. As I looked over her shoulder, I saw why. Dutch courage. Basil Asquith, MP for Infidelity, was standing behind her. This was unheard of. Basil was never seen in public without his wife and a *Hello!* photography team. Jess must have used every threat in the book to get him here. Go girl! She was always moaning about being apparently manless at every party, but I never thought she'd do anything about it.

Suddenly, from behind me, there was a loud, sharp intake of breath. I turned to see George, Carol's boyfriend, staring at Basil with undisguised fury.

Basil looked up just in time to see a hand grab his throat and push him with the force of a torpedo through the crowd and out of the front door. The rest of us gawped in amazement.

We ran after them and reached the front door in time to see George knock Basil to the ground with a right hook that would have done Frank Bruno proud. Basil tried to get back up, but his legs were obviously blancmange.

George straightened up, marched back inside and informed Carol that he was leaving. When she made no move to join him, he did an about turn and marched straight out to his chauffeur-driven limo, which then roared off.

Jess ran outside to apply emergency first aid. One of the benefits of being a mistress is that while the unfaithful tossers are maintaining appearances by doing their one night a week out with their wives, you get to sit in every Saturday night and watch *Casualty*.

Kate turned to Carol, who was still open mouthed and rooted to the spot. 'Do you think maybe he didn't like his tie?' she volunteered weakly.

There was more screeching of tyres outside. It was Basil fleeing the scene.

Jess wandered back in, looking dazed. We got her a seat and a brandy, whilst fanning her with napkins and shouting 'stand back, there's nothing to see here'.

'What happened? What was that all about?' Carol, who'd regained the power of speech, asked.

Jess looked up, still dazed, and shrugged her shoulders as she said lamely to Carol, 'How was I supposed to know that "George" was George Milford? You never mentioned his surname.'

'What's the problem with that?' Carol persisted.

Jess whispered something. We all stooped to hear.

'George is Basil's wife's brother.'

I had a feeling Jess's life was about to get as complicated as mine.

I arrive at Mum's flat and let myself in with the door key that's hidden under the mat. She's still a neighbourhood watch nightmare. It's so strange having no ties to my mother's home. She sold the family house when she divorced my dad and bought this two bedroom flat in the South Side of the city. She got an extra room for Michael, in case he came back after Uni, but he never did, moving in with his buddies initially, and then, when he landed a job, finding his own place in the West End. Dad lives a few miles away, but they don't have much contact. That ship has well and truly sailed and I honestly believe it's better for both of them – they were miserable together.

I shout a hello, but there's no answer. There's a note on the fridge.

Carly, darling,
>   *Have gone to the health farm.*
>   *Will be back in a week or so. Make yourself at home.*
>   *Love, Mum*
>   *PS. Please ask Mr Roberts at number 39 to clean the stairs.*
He only charges £5.

So much for my welcoming party. It's not that I expected banners in the street or anything, but a hello and a hug would have been nice. Still, at least if she's on Ivan's back – not an image I want in my mind – then she's not, metaphorically, on mine.

God knows what she thinks of my latest escapade. Or what she will think when I eventually pluck up the courage to tell her. All I've told her was that I was coming to Glasgow and that I'd need a bed for a couple of nights. I'm still a complete wimp when it comes to Maw Walton. I even bribed Callum and Michael with Boss ties not to turn me in. I wish beyond words that they were here, even if it does make me feel totally inadequate to see how they've both achieved so much and got exactly the lives they aspired to.

But there's still hope. I've got eight months until my target date of the millennium to sort my life out. Despite the odd moment of doubt, when I worry that I've completely lost the plot, I'm still absolutely sure that I'm doing the right thing. How many other women of my age have no house to clean, no kids to worry about, no job to get stressed over? I contemplate this for a moment, before the rational side of my brain adds, no money, no prospects, no future.

Anyway, for all I know I could be snogging Mr Right within

the week. Nick Russo is target number one and from what I remember, he has definite potential, even if he didn't keep his promise to track me down one day and whisk me off into the sunset. I can't believe that was more than a decade ago. He probably doesn't even remember *being* in Benidorm.

The familiar gurgle of excitement rises up from my stomach. Or it may just be a longing for a hangover bacon sandwich.

There's not so much as a pint of milk in the fridge, so I head off to Tesco. I can't help but be amused. Here was I setting off for the epic adventure of my life and on day one I'm in the dairy aisle at Tesco's. I hope this isn't an omen.

I'm so busy contemplating my predicament that I smash into a fellow shopper as I turn into frozen foods.

'I'm *so* sorry,' I bluster, 'I wasn't looking where I was go...' I stop suddenly. In front of me is a woman with long brunette hair scraped back into a ponytail. She's wearing no make-up and is standing with shoulders slumped in an almost defeated posture. Her thin frame is covered with a baggy grey sweatshirt and old jeans. She avoids eye contact. '*Sarah?*'

For the first time, she raises her gaze to meet mine and her face lights up like a sparkler.

'Cooper! Oh my God! What are you doing here?'

14

I rush to hug Sarah, forgetting that I am holding a basket and almost amputating my legs. I'm dumbfounded! It's only a few weeks since I was thinking about her and wondering what had happened to her. I make a mental note to wonder about next week's lottery numbers and see if that gets the same result.

My gin-soaked brain cells start to kick in. The last time we were together was just after I went to work in Tiger Alley. That was... I struggle to count, about eight years ago. Eight years! How had I let that happen?

After I'd left for Shanghai, I'd written to her a few times. At first she replied, then the letters had dried up. I remembered speaking to Kate about it when I was in Hong Kong, but by that time Kate, Carol and Jess were all living in London and Sarah either didn't return their calls or was offhand when she did. I've thought about her so many times over the years and now I wish I'd tried so much harder to track her down.

I realise I'm having a rush of blood to the head and reach out to grab the yoghurt counter to steady myself, putting three fingers through the foil of a pineapple Muller Light. Without thinking, I hastily wipe my fingers on my jeans, too shocked to care about the mess I've made.

'Where have you been? What are you doing now?' I gush. 'I mean apart from shopping. Are you in a rush?'

She laughs, shaking her head. I don't even give her a chance to speak. I grab her basket and deposit it on top of mine on the floor.

'C'mon, we're going for coffee.' I take her hand and drag her to the café at the front of the store. We're the only people in it under sixty – it looks like a welcome meeting on a Saga tour. I order two cappuccinos and two chocolate eclairs. She needs fattening up.

When I take them over to the table, she gives me another hug.

'It is so good to see you, Cooper.'

'And you. I can't believe it's been so long.' I resolve to be subtle and gently probe for answers, before blowing it completely by blurting out, 'What happened to you? Where have you been?'

She smiles wryly and I can see the sadness in her eyes. 'It's a long story.'

I push my chair back and get comfortable, although instinct tells me that I'm not going to like this.

'Well, all I was planning today was a long lie-down on the couch with a double episode of *Murder, She Wrote*, so I've got all day if you have. Start at the beginning.'

* * *

I was right about not liking it.

We spend the next two hours draining the store's coffee supplies while she tells me her story. Sometimes it's difficult to match this woman sitting across from me to the memory of the crazy, unpredictable, hilarious Sarah that I knew. This person is drained and defeated and almost, well, old – not so much in appearance but in manner. It's almost as if she's already lived two lifetimes.

It transpires that after we all went our separate ways, Sarah was doing her postgrad teaching course at university, when she'd met a guy on a night out.

'You remember Bill,' she says. 'Bill Davies. He was in school with us. I bumped into him when he was on a stag night in Edinburgh.'

I'm stunned. 'Wait a minute. You were going out with Bill Davies?' I remembered Bill from school: tall, attractive and a bit of a charmer, but he had a real mean streak and a quick temper. If I remember correctly, Mark Barwick once threatened him with serious injury for calling me an ugly-faced cow.

'Why didn't you tell any of us that you were with him?'

She shrugs, embarrassed. 'He asked me not to. Said you all hated him and he didn't want anyone to get between us.'

I hate him even more now and I haven't even heard the rest of the story.

She pushes a stray lock of hair back off her face. 'I know it sounds crazy, but I was totally besotted with him and I was pregnant within just a couple of months of meeting him. Please don't judge me. It was one night without a condom.'

'Trust me, I'm in no position to judge anyone about anything,' I reassure her, just as my brain rewinds and picks up the other shocking revelation in this story so far.

'And wait, you have a baby?' Oh my goodness. I immediately felt a wave of crushing guilt. We'd made such a fuss of Kate and her gorgeous children, and yet, all this time Sarah had a child too and we hadn't even known. We were shit friends.

She plays with her teaspoon on the table, as if focusing on that distracts her from the pain of the story. 'Two.' For the first time, I see a flash of joy as she says that, before going on, 'They're incredible and the very best thing about my life. But he wouldn't let me tell any of you that I was pregnant either. The girls called a few times but I blew them off, because it was hopeless – he'd listen in on the call, then sulk for hours after I spoke to them. He was sure we were conspiring against him.'

I feel physically sick and I reach over and take her hand. 'We thought you were just loved up and drifting away from us because you were so happy with your new life. I'm so sorry.'

'Please don't be,' she argues. 'I should have known then, when I still had the chance to get out, but it all happened so fast. I quit Uni, we got married and moved into his mum's house, and my life completely changed. You were all gone, and that became my world.'

I could understand how that could happen. Hadn't I gone from zero to fully loved up in record time with several relationships?

Sarah was still pouring her heart out. 'At first, he was great, Carly, so loving and caring.'

'So what happened?' I ask, my stomach knotting in dread.

'I don't know. He gradually became more and more moody and controlling, snapping at me constantly, criticising everything I did. No matter what I did to please him, nothing was good enough. He worked in a warehouse, and he didn't want me to work, so we couldn't afford our own place. We ended up staying with the in-laws for another four years.'

A big tear rolls down her cheek and lands in her coffee.

'Then he lost the plot altogether. He'd always been possessive,' she grimaces ruefully. 'At the start I quite liked it, because I was stupid enough to think it showed how much he cared. But his possessiveness became a complete obsession. He complained if I spoke to anyone or if I left the house on my own. He said that if I loved him then I didn't need anyone else. In the end, it was easier just to go along with it.'

'I'm so sorry, Sarah,' I say again. 'We should have done something to help.'

Where were we when Sarah needed us? Completely wrapped up in our own insignificant little dramas.

She shakes her head. 'It would only have made things worse. My family tried, but eventually I asked them to leave us alone too. Anything for a peaceful life. I just didn't want the children to see constant fighting, so I'd do anything to keep the peace.'

My blood is boiling. What a bastard!

Sarah bites her lip, then takes a breath, as if summoning her strength to carry on. 'Over the years, his temper got really out of control. He flew into a rage if I was ever late or if he saw me speaking to another guy, no matter how innocent it was. Looking back now, I can't believe I put up with it, Carly. I can see how it looks. I was pathetic.'

'Other people's shoes, Sarah. Who knows what any of us would have done in the same situation?' I answer, quoting a phrase my gran used to berate me with if she ever caught me being judgemental. I have to ask the obvious, though. 'Why didn't you leave?' I'm holding on to her hand so tightly that it's turning blue.

'How could I? I had two babies, no money, no home, no job. I was trapped but I couldn't see a way out.'

'I so wish you'd told us. We could have helped. We would have done anything.'

She shrugs her shoulders. 'I guess I didn't want to admit it to anyone. I didn't want the world to know that I had made a complete fuck-up of my life.'

The tea ladies run to the aisles for a box of Kleenex for the two blubbering wrecks in the corner. Two more coffees, six tissues and a medicinal Bakewell tart later, she is still recounting what happened and it doesn't get any better.

When they had finally managed to afford their own flat, Bill's behaviour had become even worse. He had a lock put on the phone so that she couldn't dial out and he called her ten times a day to check where she was. He was cold, abusive and violent.

It had all come to a head a year before when her grandmother had died. Bill had erupted when she said that she was going to the funeral and for once Sarah had fought back. It was the first time she'd seen her family in years, and she finally told them everything that had been going on. Horrified, they pooled their resources to help. Sarah and the kids were given her grandmother's house and the whole family chipped in to redecorate it and furnish it. Bill threatened all sorts, but that stopped abruptly after a visit from Sarah's two brothers. A mischievous grin crosses her face when it comes to that bit. I can tell she relishes the thought. As she tells it, she visibly straightens up and pushes back her shoulders, like a woman in control. Like she's determined to put it all in the past.

'So what now?' I ask.

She beams as she tells me that she's going back to teacher training college in September.

'And Bill?'

'I only see him when he collects the kids on a Friday and returns them on a Sunday. I hear he's living with someone else now, poor woman.'

I notice a clock on the wall and realise we've been sitting there for hours.

'Sarah, where are the kids now?' I ask in a panic, suddenly conscious that it's after four o'clock.

'It's Easter holidays. Bill took them to Butlin's last night for two weeks. That's why I was looking a bit miserable when I met you – I don't know what to do with myself now they're gone.'

We sit in comfortable silence for a few moments as I absorb what she's told me. An idea starts to form. It's the perfect solution! I scream with delight, making Sarah jump and splash her coffee over the remnants of her Bakewell tart.

'I know what you can do. You're coming to St Andrews with me.'

It makes perfect sense in Cooperland...

'What? Carly, I can't afford to do that. I'm a skint student again.'

'But I'll pay for both of us. Or, rather, American Express will.'

I fill her in on the plan and for the first time she cries with laughter instead of pain. She dries her eyes.

'Oh, Carly, you haven't changed. You're still a walking disaster.'

I nod my head gleefully. 'I know,' I agree. 'Does that mean you'll come?'

She thinks about it for all of three seconds. 'I suppose someone has to keep their eye on you.'

We go to Sarah's house, pack a suitcase and take it to my mum's. I call for a Chinese takeaway and open a bottle of wine. I dial Kate's number in London. If I'm not wrong, Carol and Jess will still be there, nursing their hangovers. Strange, but for me, last night's going away party already feels like a lifetime ago.

Kate answers almost immediately. 'Home for Drunks and Strays.'

'Kate, it's me. Are the girls still there?'

'Unfortunately, yes. I've had to warn Bruce not to light a

match, because with the fumes in here, the house would explode. I'm in the kitchen making the tenth coffee pot of the day.'

'Put me on loud speaker and tell them to come and listen into this call. I've got a surprise for you all.'

There's a yell, then a pause, before Carol speaks first. 'This had better be good, Cooper. I risked an aneurysm by getting off the couch.'

'I've got someone who wants to speak to you.'

'It had better be Richard Gere,' Jess moans.

I look over at Sarah, who's holding the cordless phone procured from my mother's bedroom and grinning from ear to ear. I motion to her to speak.

'I was just wondering which one of you lot borrowed my black sequinned boob tube about ten years ago. I think it's time you returned it.'

Another pause. I can almost hear the sound of their brains whirring.

Think of the noise in a stadium when the Scotland football team score a goal, then triple it. That comes close to the bedlam coming from the phone. They're all talking and screaming at once.

'STOP!' I yell. Silence. 'Now, one at a time. Jess, you go first.'

'Sarah, this is even better than Richard Gere. Where have you been?' There's not a hint of a rebuke in her voice, just sheer joy.

'In the frozen food aisle at Tesco's.' She laughs. 'It's a long story, Jess. We'll catch up next time I see you. God, I've missed you lot!' More tears are flowing.

Kate takes over. 'I can't believe it's you, Sarah. We've missed you too, babe. When can you come visit us?'

'Soon, I hope. But right now, I'm getting ready to go to St Andrews with our crazy friend here.'

I can hear them all simultaneously groan and clasp their hands to their foreheads.

'Don't let her get you into trouble, Sarah, there's every chance she'll end up in jail this time,' Carol jokes.

I protest loudly.

Two hours, three bottles of wine and a beef kung po later, we eventually hang up.

When my mum gets the phone bill, she'll hit the roof – probably with Ivan still attached.

Sarah looks completely different from the woman trudging round the supermarket this morning. Her face is glowing, her eyes are bright, she's chuckling incessantly and she looks five years younger. She flops out on one sofa, I do the same on the other one.

She raises her glass. 'To us, my friend. It's been a great day.'

In two minutes, she's fast asleep, still smiling.

* * *

Next morning, a knock on the door wakes me. I open my eyes and look around, trying to remember where I am. There are posters of monsters and robotic warriors on every wall. Michael's room. My mother brought Michael's teenage bedroom from our old house when she moved here. No wonder he never came back.

I stumble to the door and open it just wide enough for me to see who it is, but not to allow them to see that I'm wearing blue pyjamas with Terminator 2 blazoned across the front and woolly socks. I look like an overgrown cartoon character.

'Er, I have a hire car for a Miss Cooper?' He looks about fourteen. Surely he's not old enough to drive? God, I'm getting old.

Covering my pjs with a cardi, I get my driving licence and we complete the paperwork.

When he leaves, I wake Sarah by wafting a cup of Kenco's finest under her nose. She sits up, then clutches her head and lies back down.

'My head hurts,' she whines.

'That's because you're out of practice. Now, get your kit on and let's go. We've got a man to find.'

'Story of my life,' she answers.

An hour and two packets of Resolve later, we set off. It's like a Scottish version of *Thelma and Louise*. More 'Morag and Agnes'.

The drive to St Andrews is beautiful. We stop for a coffee and a doughnut at the services beside the Forth Road Bridge and admire the view. I suddenly come over all patriotic. I want to paint my face blue with a white cross in the middle and shag Mel Gibson in a kilt.

We detour to the petrol station for fuel and Pick'n'Mix, but as I pass the newspaper stand, a familiar sight is plastered across the front page of every tabloid. Sarah recognises the astonishment on my face.

'Carly, what is it?' She follows my eyeline to the picture on the newspapers. 'Who are they?' The photograph is a little grainy. It was obviously taken in the evening by an inexperienced photographer at an unfortunate angle. But there is no mistaking the situation. Or the main characters.

BAD BOY BASIL AND BROTHER-IN-LAW BRAWL
    MP DOWN AND KNOCKED OUT
    STREET CRIME RISES, BASIL FALLS

'Sarah, let me introduce you to Jess's boyfriend, Basil. This was taken at my leaving party.'

She looks at the papers and then slowly back to me. 'Basil Asquith? The MP?'

I nod.

'Bloody hell, Carly! What kind of lives have you lot been leading?'

We look at each other for a few seconds before our shoulders begin to shake. Our world is getting more absurd by the minute.

We rush to the payphone to call Jess, but there's no answer. We try Carol, but no one's there either. There's nothing else for it. I call Kate at work.

'Good afternoon, this is the Cutting Edge, Porsche speaking, how can I help you?'

'Can I speak to Kate, please?'

'I'm sorry, Kate is frightfully busy at the moment.' She whispers the last bit in a smug, superior tone, as always. This is like trying to get past the receptionists at my local doctors.

I assume the most superior voice I can muster. 'This is her gynaecologist and I must speak to her IMMEDIATELY about her recent STD test. It's a medical emergency.'

I can picture Porsche visibly paling at the thought of stirrups, spatulas and sexually transmitted infections. Kate is on the line in twenty seconds.

'Kate, it's me. I saw the papers! Oh, and don't hate me but the only way I could get past your receptionist was to tell her I was your gynaecologist and calling with your STD results.'

Porsche is obviously listening to Kate's side of the conversation, because she just groans, as opposed to threatening to kill me.

'You have the results then?' she answers wearily, playing along.

'No, I can't get through to Jess or Carol. Where are they?'

'Ah, gone into remission,' she stammers, as if repeating what I've said. This is hard work.

'Is Jess okay?' I persevere.

'Yes, fine.'

'And Basil?'

'It's definitely terminal.' I hear a thud in the background as Porsche hits the floor. At least there's never a dull moment.

* * *

We drown out Motown's Greatest Hits on the CD player. We're Dancing In the Street as we cross the bridge, giving Respect as we head up through Cupar, then getting soaked by a Rainy Night in Georgia as we approach the coast.

My twenty page guide to St Andrews bed and breakfasts is on my lap. After all, we're on a budget – albeit a fraudulently attained one.

The first thing we see as we enter St Andrews is the beach and the resplendent Old Course Hotel.

'That is stunning,' I gasp.

Sarah's eyes widen. 'Who stays in somewhere like that? It must cost a fortune!'

I take a deep breath and shake my head. Oh, no!

'Fuck it. We do.' I do a handbrake turn to the left and screech up the driveway.

Sarah splutters, spilling coffee down the front of her shirt. 'You're joking, aren't you? No, you're not! Oh, sweet Jesus.'

As Carol would say, 'May as well get hung for a sheep as a bird in the hand.'

We cross the marble floor of the reception area. In the middle is a table with a display of lilies that must have cost more than a small cottage.

'Excuse me, do you have a twin room available?'

Sarah's behind me, sniffing the lilies.

'For how long, madam?'

I haven't thought about that. How long will it take me to find him? I hope it's not long or my credit cards will be up to the limit before I even leave Scotland. I say that four nights will suffice. Even if I find him quickly, I know I'll want to stick around and get to know him again.

The receptionist checks her computer, then looks up and smiles. 'We do, madam. The rate will be—'

I hold up my hand. 'Stop! Please don't tell me, you'll give me indigestion. Just charge it to this, please.'

I hand over my Visa card. The last of my sensible brain cells give up and go into hibernation.

We find our room, giggling like two schoolgirls trying on their first bras, and throw open the door. For once in my life I'm speechless. The room is class, class and more class. In the centre are two stunningly dressed double beds. Cream fabric covers them, matching the drapes that are so perfect that I'm afraid to touch them. There are fresh flowers on the oak dressing table, lace cushions on the sofas and a selection of chocolates on the coffee table, which is probably just as well because I'll never be able to afford to eat again. But it's worth it for the look of sheer wonderment on Sarah's face.

We unpack, make a posh coffee using some swanky, high-tech machine, and stretch out on the sofas, contemplating the view of the golf course and the beach beyond it.

'Isn't that Michael Douglas down there?' Sarah asks.

I dive to the window and press my nose against the pane. She could be right. I've been besotted by him since *The Streets of San Francisco*.

Right, down to work before I capitulate to a life of luxury.

Plan A. I locate a phone book and search for 'Russo'. I mean, how many can there be in a town this size?

I search some more.

None. Zero. Zilch. He must be ex-directory.

I throw down the book in disgust.

'What's plan B?' Sarah asks.

'I don't know. I hadn't got past A.' I feel defeated.

'Right. C'mon, get your jacket,' she says assertively. That's the old Sarah.

'Where are we going?'

'Didn't your mother teach you anything? When all else fails, ask a policeman.'

She pulls me out of the door by the scruff of the neck. Ten minutes later, we're standing in the reception of the local cop shop. How do I explain this?

'I wonder if you can help me. I'm trying to find a guy who lives in this town. His name is Nick Russo.'

PC Plod looks at me like I've landed from another planet. 'Are you having me on?'

'I know it's a long shot. I guess I'm wasting your time. I'm sorry.'

'Follow me, lass.' He's coming round to the front of the desk. Is he going to arrest us for suspected chemical abuse? Or is he just going to kick our bums out onto the street?

I contemplate making a run for it but he reaches the door first. He opens it wide and signals for us to join him.

'I think that might give you a bit of a clue, lass.'

My eyes follow the direction of his finger and my face turns a ripe shade of tomato. Across the road, not twenty yards away, is what looks like a wine bar and bistro. Above it, in two foot high letters, is 'Russo's'. He guffaws. 'Do me a favour, love. Don't ever decide to become a detective.'

He's still laughing as Sarah and I dash across the road. Outside the bar, I grind to a halt. It's suddenly struck me that I'm about to meet the guy that I've thought about for the last twelve or so years. I'm panic-stricken. I clutch Sarah for reassurance as I enter.

I approach a barman who looks like the car hire guy's younger brother. Have they lowered the legal age to sell alcohol to twelve? I feel like my gran.

I try to speak, but the saliva in my mouth has turned to glue and my tongue can't move.

Sarah steps in. 'Excuse me. Does Nick Russo work here?'

'Naw, he disnae work here,' he replies.

My hopes plummet.

But the barman isn't finished. 'He owns the place.'

'Is he here?' Holy crap, have I actually found him? I can't believe it. Thank God Sarah is with me because I'd still be stumbling over my words.

The barman shakes his head. 'He won't be in till t'night.'

I finally regain the power of speech. 'Tell me, does his wife work here too?'

Sarah looks at me, proud of my astuteness.

'His wife? Naw, Nick's nae married, love.'

I exhale loudly. I hadn't even realised that I was holding my breath.

We thank him and leave. As soon as we're out of sight, we look at each other and shriek. Passers-by stop and stare as we hug, jumping up and down.

'Half an hour, Sarah, that's all it took. You're a genius. I love you, love you, love you.'

An old woman shakes her head and mutters, 'Oooh, there's two of those gay people, Martha. What do you call them? Has-beens?'

'*Lesbians*, Ethel, *lesbians*.'

We collapse in a heap. This beats normal life any day of the week.

* * *

At eight o'clock, we enter Russo's and ask for a table. I should be feeling calmer now that I've had all day to prepare, but the passing hours have had the opposite effect. My insides are churning and I'm smoking. Lots.

I'm wearing a white T-shirt, black boots and black leather trousers. Kate looked so good in the same outfit at the party that I've decided to copy her. It's a big mistake – from the back, I look like a two seater sofa and I'm sweating so much that it'll take a week to get them off. And my hair has rebelled against the product I'd used to flatten it down and now looks like I've travelled here on a motorbike – kind of Meg Ryan after electric shock treatment.

I scan the room, but there's nobody that even resembles Nick. What am I thinking? It's been a million years. I could win him in a raffle and I wouldn't recognise him.

We order two wines. Bottles, that is.

'Will you be eating, madam?' the waitress asks.

Sarah takes charge. 'We'll just have an Americano pizza to share, please.'

I say another prayer of thanks that Sarah is with me. I couldn't have done this without her. We check out every man in the room. Not one of them could be him.

The waitress returns with the pizza and I take my chance.

'I wonder if you could possibly get the owner for us. Tell him that we have a complaint.'

'But you haven't even tried your pizza yet,' she looks puzzled. 'Did it take too long?'

'No, it's nothing to do with the food or the service. I'd rather discuss it with the owner.'

She shrugs her shoulders and leaves, obviously thinking that we're neurotic tourists.

'What are you doing?' Sarah hisses.

'I can't wait any longer. My trousers are going to melt or shrink if I don't get this over with.'

Three minutes later (I count the seconds), a door opens behind the bar and the waitress points in our direction. She stands to one side and there he is. Nick Russo is walking towards us.

Please God, don't let me have a heart attack now – not until I've at least spoken to him.

I study him as he approaches. His hair is now flecked with grey, his face a little haggard. He's broader than he was back then, and dressed top to toe in black. He's still attractive, but no longer drop-dead gorgeous. He used to be David Ginola. Now he's more like a bloke that occasionally plays Sunday league.

He frowns as he stops at the table.

'Ladies, I'm Nick Russo, the owner here. I believe you have a complaint?'

That voice. I melt, before summoning all my strength to formulate words. *English, Cooper, English.*

'Yes, we do. We just think it's ridiculous that old friends aren't welcomed with a personal greeting.'

'Old friends? I'm sorry, do I...?' He stops, confused.

Please recognise me. If you don't, I'm going to go outside and crawl under a stone.

'Benidorm,' Sarah helps him.

He swings his head back round and stares at me.

'Carly? Fuck, Carly Cooper.' Well, at least he remembers that bit.

He sits down next to me and crushes me in a bear hug.

'Carly Cooper. What are you doing here?'

I disentangle myself.

'Well, I waited ten years for you to come for me and you didn't. Then I decided to give you the benefit of the doubt and waited another two, in case you had trouble tracking me down. Finally, I gave up and thought I'd come here and make it easy for you.'

'You're kidding.' He looks shocked and confused. And so do the entire staff of the establishment as they stare incredulously.

I laugh. 'Yes, of course I'm kidding. Sarah and I are up here for a break and we saw the bar and figured it must be you.'

I'll never pass a lie detector test.

He leans over and gives Sarah a kiss. He keeps shaking his head. 'I can't believe this – it's brilliant. Can you stay? Have dinner with me. Where are you staying? How long for?'

'Yes, okay. The Old Course Hotel and a couple of days.'

He orders a bottle of champagne and more food and we start to swap stories. Benidorm is first. Then we move on to fill in the gaps of the last twelve years.

Nick tells us that he married his childhood sweetheart when he was twenty-one and divorced when he was twenty-five. He has no children and has owned this place for five years, since his parents retired to their home town of Sorrento. It had been a quiet restaurant in the old days and he has transformed it into the 'in-place' in St Andrews. He had a few relationships over the years, but his marriage, or rather his divorce, has put him off wedding rings for life.

'What happened to your friend? Graham, wasn't it?' Sarah asks. Of course! When I was with Nick, Sarah had a fling with his pal.

'God, Graham. I haven't thought about him for years. He emigrated to Australia soon after we came back from Benidorm and we lost touch.'

I have a sudden pang of disappointment that Graham isn't around. Wouldn't that have been a brilliant twist? I bring her here to track down my ex, and she rekindles an old romance of her own? That would have been brilliant, but if Sarah is disappointed, she doesn't let it show.

Instead, we answer Nick's questions, giving him edited versions of our life stories, both of us leaving out the troubles and sticking to the good bits.

I suddenly realise that we're the only people in the room. I look at my watch. One o'clock. We must be in a time warp, I'm sure we just got here.

Nick stands up. 'Why don't we go for a wander along the beach?'

Sarah yawns. 'I'm really tired. Why don't you two go and I'll head back to the hotel.'

She'll never win an Oscar. That's the worst performance since Farrah Fawcett left *Charlie's Angels*.

We walk her back to the hotel, then head for the sands.

I feel awkward. What should I say to him?

He takes my hand. 'It really is good to see you, Cooper.'

'And you.' And it is. So how come I'm not being swept away on a wave of desire and longing? Maybe my libido drowned inside my leather trousers.

We walk for a mile in silence.

'Did you ever think about me over the years?' he asks.

'Yes. A lot. And you?'

'Sure. I tried to contact you once, but your mother said you'd gone to Paris, or Amsterdam or somewhere.'

'She never told me,' I reply honestly. Deep down, I know it wouldn't have made any difference. Back then, I wasn't ready for us to be anything more than what we were.

He shrugs. 'I figured that it was just a holiday romance and you'd have forgotten all about me.'

'Nick, you were the first guy I ever slept with. I'll never forget that.'

He kisses the top of my head. 'Likewise.'

I do a mental inventory of my body. No weak knees, no rushing blood. I think these trousers have destroyed all my nerve endings.

We make our way back to the hotel, chatting like old friends. At the door, we pause. It should be awkward, but it isn't. It's just, well, nice. In a non-lusty kind of way. I'm never wearing leather again.

'Will you join me for lunch tomorrow?' he asks.

I'm confused. My body obviously belongs to someone else or has died and failed to notify my brain. I'm feeling nothing from the neck down – except sweaty.

'Sure,' I agree and kiss him goodnight on the cheek. 'Lunch would be great.'

* * *

Sarah opens the door before I've even had a chance to knock.

'I was listening out for you. Well, what's the verdict?'

'He's lovely. Really lovely.'

'Carly, that's like saying that someone is *nice*. How come I fear that there's a "but" coming?'

How can I explain it? I know that I've only spent a few hours with him, but unlike the first time we met, there was no spark, no electricity. Okay, so I'm a spontaneous nightmare and I can't base every judgement in my life on an instant reaction, but surely if this man was going to father my children, then I should at least have a glimmer of attraction? I should be desperate to drink champagne and dance in the moonlight with him, not just order a cappuccino and talk about old times. Not once tonight had I had the urge to back him into a corner and snog his face off. What's more, I'm pretty sure that he felt the same about me, otherwise we'd probably be lying out on the beach just now, talking romantic nonsense about the stars and fate.

Sarah is still waiting for a reply.

'I don't know, Sarah. Maybe I've changed a lot since I was seventeen. Or maybe he has. Maybe I was expecting too much. Maybe I'm a hopeless case who should think seriously about joining a nunnery.'

'You don't fancy him.' It's a statement, not a question.

She is right.

* * *

I go to lunch the next day with an open mind. Okay, so last night he didn't light my candle, blow my socks off or set my knickers alight, but maybe it was just an off day. C'mon, hormones, feel free to kick in whenever you're ready.

Nick's waiting for us when we arrive at the restaurant. He's wearing blue jeans, a pale blue polo shirt and deck shoes. He's Ralph Lauren. As we attack our nachos, he tells us of his plans to open another three restaurants in nearby towns over the next four years. I can see the excitement in his eyes as he talks.

Okay, Cooper, weigh up the pros:

a. He's a good-looking guy who's funny, kind and sweet. And he drives a Jaguar.

b. He's successful, obviously wealthy and full of ambition. A top-of-the-range, black Jaguar.

c. He's open, interesting and passionate about life. Leather interior, CD system, Jaguar.

d. All in all he's a great catch. A Jaguar-driving catch.

And the cons?

a. I don't care about flash cars much.

'So, when are you leaving?' Nick cuts into my thoughts.

My mouth makes a split-second decision, way ahead of my brain. 'Em, we're leaving, em, tonight.'

His face falls and Sarah's trying her best not to look gobsmacked.

'That's a shame,' he frowns. 'It's been great seeing you again.'

'You too, but I'm going abroad tomorrow.'

'Anywhere nice?'

I look at Sarah. *It's no use*, I tell her telepathically, *he's not 'the one'.*

'Amsterdam.'

I can smell the tulips already. Joe Cain, I hope you're ready.

I hug Nick tightly as I kiss him goodbye.

'See you in another twelve years.'

'It's a date,' he laughs.

Sarah puts her arm through mine as we walk back to the hotel. 'Are you sad?'

'Nope. I guess it would have been too good to be true if Nick had been "it". Life's never that easy. And anyway, I've got my credit cards to think of – they're expecting a round-the-world trip. It would be terrible to disappoint them.'

'You're right. The Royal Society For the Prevention Of Cruelty to Credit Cards would have you shot. Still,' she adds, 'I'll be sad to leave here – I was just getting used to having room service and a shagpile carpet.'

I have a flash of inspiration. 'Come to Amsterdam with me,' I beg.

'I can't. I don't have a passport.'

My spirits crash, then I have an idea. 'Then stay here. Sarah,

I've paid for four days. Just because my mission has crashed and burned like a home-made rocket doesn't mean you have to leave too. Stay another couple of days, relax, spoil yourself, drink all those posh coffees in the room. You deserve it.'

She thinks about it. 'Are you sure? It would be amazing and I could just jump on the train home.'

'I insist. But only on one condition.'

'What's that?' I could hear the joy bubbling in her voice.

'You use the hotel stationery to send a letter to Bill and let him see that you're living it up and moving on to better things. There's nothing like rubbing salt in the wound. Or, as Carol would say, rubbing pepper in the cut.'

Her face creases with laughter. 'So she still gets her sayings mixed up?'

I nod. 'As sure as eggs are bacon and more often than always.'

She's still laughing as I wave her goodbye. In my rear view mirror, I can see her waving back, looking radiantly happy and contented with life.

This definitely wasn't such a waste of time after all.

Now, where are my clogs?

15

I do a mental review of the situation as I attack the aeroplane breakfast roll with a chisel. One down, five to go.

There's a tiny little bit of me that's disappointed about Nick, but, to be honest, I've now got a desperate curiosity about all of the guys. Don't get me wrong, the minute I meet 'him', then I'm going to seize the moment, but it would have been so pathetic to tell everyone who knew about this trip that I never got further than Scotland. Not exactly a grand voyage, is it? It would have been like Marco Polo stopping at the first ancient Little Chef for breakfast and deciding to just stay there.

The Schiphol Airport to Amsterdam city centre express train screeches into Centraal Station and I disembark with the hordes of tourists seeking either to experience the stunning views of the city's beautiful architecture, or the stunning architecture of the city's ladies.

I jump into a taxi.

'Damstraat, alstublieft.'

Big mistake. The driver now thinks I can speak Dutch and

launches into a fifteen minute dialogue as he drives. I just smile and nod my head in agreement when he pauses for breath. When he drops me at my destination, we're already best friends forever. He probably thinks I'm a great listener.

I enter the hotel and approach the gent at reception, who's engrossed in the morning newspaper behind the desk.

'Excuse me, I'd like a room, please.'

He grunts and opens his registration book without even looking up.

'Yes, I'd like a room with peeling paint, holes in the carpet, fungus in the bathroom and a grumpy old bastard knocking on the door every five minutes with cups of coffee that taste like diesel.'

René lifts his head. 'Oh, mon dieu.' He throws open his arms and reaches across the desk to envelop me in a bear hug 'Carly! You have come back to us. We thought you were dead!'

'Cheery as ever, René,' I laugh and return his squeeze. 'It's so good to see you.'

After many more hugs, exclamations and chat, he shows me to my old room, still a resplendent dump. I don't think it's been decorated since I left it and I would swear they're the same blankets on the bed.

I shake my head, laughing. 'My God, René, how do you get away with charging people to live in this squalor?'

'We charge for the friendly service and the wonderful staff,' he answers with a wink, as he backs out of the room. He's incorrigible. If he were forty years younger, I'd snap him up.

I throw open a window before my respiratory system collapses and then unpack, making sure that I line the drawer with a plastic bag before putting my clothes in it. I don't want my sweaters being eaten before I get the chance to wear them.

When I join René back downstairs, he has a cup of diesel ready and waiting. I can't stop grinning. I explain why I'm here, leaving out the fact that this is part of a master plan that will hopefully end in me wearing white satin and dancing up an aisle. I don't want René joining the long list of people who think I'm bonkers.

I ask him if he knows where I can find Joe and he ponders for a moment, rubbing his chin. 'Ma chère, it was so long ago. I'm an old man and the memory is not so good now.'

I'm surprised. The René I knew could remember the colour of a hooker's bra from 1962.

'You must know something, René. You're the Buddha of all knowledge,' I joke, rubbing his hugely expanded belly. 'Anything that would make this easier. I don't want to have to trawl the streets for days looking for him, only to find he fled the country two months after I left.'

'Would that be so bad, my chérie?' he asks.

I frown. Why's René being so coy about this? I have a growing suspicion that there's something he's not telling me.

'It would be terrible, René! Then I'll have to go to America to find his parents and track him down that way. I'm not giving up until I've found him.' Good grief, my resolve is even surprising me.

René sighs and pauses for a few seconds, before something shifts and he decides to elaborate. 'The Premier Club closed many years ago – about two years after you left.'

Oh, crap! I've only just got here and I've hit a dead end already.

But René continues, 'I did hear that your Joe still owns a club on the other side of town, though.'

My spirits soar. Or maybe that's just the aeroplane food having a strange effect.

'You know, my darling, there have been a lot of changes since you left here.' He seems apprehensive and I suspect again that I'm not hearing the full story.

I try to probe but he tells me nothing more.

I persuade him to join me for a walk along the canals, with the promise that we'll stop at a café so he can sample what real coffee is supposed to taste like.

'Why have you never married, René?'

He says nothing for a long time and then sighs.

'I was in love once with a beautiful girl from my home town. She was, how you say, spectacular. She was everything to me. But she left me for another man, an American.'

That would explain why he refused to sell Budweiser and bagels.

'After that, my heart was broken. You see, she was the only one for me. I believe that everyone has one person in the world who was made for them and she was mine.'

Oh, the romance of it.

I take his arm. 'So what if you never meet the person who's right for you? And how do you know when you have?'

'Ah, my petite chérie, that's where God comes in. He arranges the meeting and when it happens, you just know.'

I ponder this. So how come I've 'known' so many times? I think I might have been reading the signals wrong. Or maybe I haven't met the right guy at all. I have a scary thought. What if this is a completely futile mission fuelled by desperation and optimism and it's doomed to fail?

I'm consumed by gloom for a whole five seconds before I shake it off and give myself a talking to. Fuck it. I'm young-ish, healthy (if you excuse the lungs and the liver), mostly happy and I'm walking along the banks of a canal on a glorious day with a charming man. What is there to be miserable about?

Too much profound thought – my head is starting to hurt. We cross the Singel canal and head for a tiny French café opposite the beautiful copper-domed Koepel Church. The owner greets René with handshakes and a kiss on both cheeks.

'René, my old friend. It's been too long,' he roars. 'C'est formidable! And this,' he turns to me, 'this must be your daughter, no?'

Cheeky bugger. If he's an old friend, then he must know that René doesn't have children.

'Non, monsieur. René is not my father. How do you say it in French, René? He is my sugar daddy.'

René beams with pride. I think I just made an old man very happy. He's now been elevated to the status of 'babe-magnet' in his friend's eyes. This will be in the Dutch OAP's Gazette before the day is out.

After coffee, we stop at a shop so that I can buy disinfectant for the bath in my room.

I lie surrounded with bubbles until I look like a marinated prune. I eventually managed to wangle the name of Joe's club out of René, and now I'm trying to decide if I'm more excited, anxious or petrified at the prospect of meeting him again. Excitement wins, but it's a tight contest.

How do I introduce myself? 'Hello, Joe, did you get my note?' or 'Remember me? Carly Houdini?'

I blow some bubbles off my nipples. Optimism kicks in. Okay, guys, I tell them, brace yourselves, we're going out to play.

I pull on a pair of white Capri pants and a pale blue shirt. I look in the mirror. Nope, too casual. A red miniskirt with a black T-shirt? I'll never get to the club without being offered money for a quickie. I settle on black trousers and a black skinny-rib polo neck. Useful outfit for hiding in doorways and I can always plead a recent bereavement if I have to make a quick exit.

René hugs me like he'll never see me again as I leave. Given my track record, maybe he has a point, but he's acting as if he's casting me off to meet my doom. If I wasn't nervous before, then I am now.

'Just remember, ma chérie, keep an open mind.'

Again, I have the distinct feeling that there's something I'm missing here. Is the club a sadomasochistic whipping room? Knowing Joe, that wouldn't surprise me. Is it some other kind of illicit place where people live out their sexual fantasies? No great surprises there either.

I turn into the Rembrandtplein just after nine o'clock. Music is pouring out of every pub and club and there's a thronging, eclectic crowd. Cross-dressers, crazy dressers, no dressers – the whole street is Rio on a carnival day. I search for Joe's club, which René has reliably informed me is called 'J.C.'s Heaven'. I bet the Catholic Church isn't amused about that one. There are probably nuns picketing the door.

I spot a group of beautifully formed men entering what looks like a converted warehouse a few yards ahead of me. When they've passed, I see the bouncer standing on the door. Good God, doesn't anyone ever leave this place?

'Has anyone ever told you that you'll catch a cold standing out here?'

He stares down at me, ready to crush me like a cockroach until a flicker of recognition crosses his eyes. 'Holy shit! Carly Cooper. What the hell are you doin' here, girl?'

I seem to spend my life surprising people these days. I feel like Cilla Black.

'Just passing through, Chad. Thought I'd come and see if I could find my favourite pillar of the community.'

He booms with laughter and slaps me on the back. That'll be a fractured spine and two broken ribs.

'And I also came to see Joe. Is he here?'

He pauses. Am I being paranoid or does he look uncomfortable? What is it, is Joe's wife in there or something?

'Sure, baby. He's inside. I'll get someone to take you to him.'

He calls another bouncer, who is so tall he must have spent his childhood in a growbag. Leon, as he introduces himself, takes me through the crowd to a back staircase. As I climb up it, my legs are doing a good impersonation of strawberry jelly. Leon gestures to a blue door.

As I knock, my mind rewinds to the last time I knocked on Joe's door, straight out of Scotland and so naive. Joe listened and took a chance on me. I just hope he's as welcoming this time.

'Come in,' a voice calls out, but it's not Joe's.

I tentatively open the door and gasp. In front of me is a Nordic god: long blond hair, eyes like sapphires, cheekbones that could fell a tree. My libido flares and I mentally rein it in. Right reaction, wrong guy.

'Can I help you?' he asks in a thick Dutch accent.

I'm trying to think of a witty answer when I sense someone to my left. I turn to see Joe Cain, hands behind his head, feet up on the desk. He looks different – his head is completely shaven and he's wearing a black net T-shirt and skintight suede jeans. He's a cross between a Buddhist monk and a Tetley teabag. But he's still seriously, seriously attractive. In a Yul Brynner kind of way.

I can see he's stunned, but he recovers quickly. 'Well, well, well, if it isn't the prodigal girlfriend,' he laughs.

This is good – humour, no anger, no outrage, just a tiny touch of bitterness. I can deal with bitter. After all, I didn't expect a 'Welcome Home' banner and a marching band.

'Looking for another job?' he asks, a cheeky glint in his eyes now.

I'm desperately trying to come up with a witty reply when there's the sound of someone clearing his throat – I'd forgotten all about Hagar, the Norse god.

'Cooper, this is Claus, my partner. Claus, meet Carly Cooper, disappearing act extraordinaire.'

'Ah, Miss Cooper,' he says, as though everything is suddenly making sense. 'I've heard a lot about you.' I have the feeling that it wasn't glowing testimonies to my virtues as a human being.

'So what brings you here then?' Joe asks.

I'm still trying to play cool and collected. 'I was in the city and wanted to look you up. Can we go somewhere and talk?'

'I'm not sure. Every time you go to the toilet, I'll expect you not to return.'

'You can tie a piece of string to my ankle.'

He smiles. He seems to be defrosting. Maybe this isn't going to be so bad after all. I just need to make sure I keep him away from sharp objects.

I turn to say goodbye to Claus and he grunts a response. Is it my imagination or does he look like he wants to scratch my eyes out with a pickaxe?

* * *

We go to an Italian restaurant across the road from the club, where Joe orders two glasses of wine and some garlic bread. Obviously there'll be no snogging tonight then. There's an awkward silence as he stares at me. He's not going to make this easy.

I take a deep breath, hold my nose and jump in. 'I don't suppose "Sorry" will make a huge difference now?' I mumble hopefully.

He's quiet for a moment, then, 'No, but maybe an explanation will help.'

I was kidnapped and sold into white slavery? I bumped my head and suffered complete amnesia? There's a hint of sadness in his voice and it ramps my guilt up even further.

I go with the truth – I was confused and got cold feet, then bottled out like a heartless coward. That just about covered it.

'I came looking for you, you know,' he says.

Now I'm even more confused. 'What? When?'

'About six months later. I remembered the name of the area you came from, so I went there, asked around and discovered you were working in a nightclub.'

'Why didn't you contact me?' If a feather hits me, I'll be on the floor.

'I came to the club and I saw you there, but you were rushing around like crazy. At the end of the night, I came to talk to you, but you were in a tongue lock with a huge blond guy. I decided it would be a better idea to leave quietly.'

He looks so dejected. Oh, give me a bolt of lightning! I am the most horrible person to walk this earth. I've no right to be here. No right to be dragging all this up again. Haven't I done enough damage?

'Joe, I am so sorry. I'll get out of your way.' I get up to leave, to look for a sewer to crawl into. He grabs my arm and pulls me back down.

'You're not getting off that easily, Cooper. I want to know what you've been doing since then. I want to know everything that happened to stop you coming back to me.'

I see Carol in my head saying, 'In for a penny, in for two pounds fifty.'

'How long have you got?'

He looks at his watch. 'About, oh, a week. I've got a feeling I should make myself comfortable.'

I admit that for a split second I consider being economical with the truth. But what's the point? The look on his face says that he's not exactly over the moon, but I don't think he's ready to have me tortured and mutilated either. No, he deserves the truth, so I tell him everything that happened up until I quit my life in London. I feel like I'm in a confessional. 'Bless me, Father, for I have sinned, it's been seventeen years since my last confession and I'm a complete trollop.'

He interrupts me a couple of times for clarification, but otherwise just listens for the two hours it takes to spill all the gory details.

'Want me to leave now?' I ask when I'm done.

He shakes his gorgeous bald head. Then smiles, almost sadly. 'No. You see, in a fucked-up way I think it was meant to happen.'

That surprises me. 'What do you mean?'

'Well, after you left, I made huge changes in my life and they've worked out for me.'

'Don't tell me, you're married with six kids and spend Saturdays coaching the school soccer team.'

He laughs. 'Not quite, but you're close.'

I encourage him to tell me his story. Bad move.

'After you left, I waited for you to call or return. I was convinced you would come back. How could you not? I thought we'd been so happy. But when you didn't, then I began to worry that something terrible had happened to you, so I came looking.' He gives a derisive sneer. I deserve it. 'And of course, I see you with...'

'Doug,' I offer, completely unnecessarily.

'Yes, you were trying to remove his fillings with your tongue.'

Ouch.

'So, I returned to Amsterdam and I worked. I lived every minute of the day in the clubs. I worked day and night and I partied. I never slept, drank too much and then I decided that I wanted to experiment a little, so I did.'

Oh, bollocks! He was a druggie! So that's what René was avoiding telling me. I can't speak.

He continues. 'A year later, I met Claus and we opened a club together. We figured we'd capitalise on the growing gay scene and J.C's Heaven has been full since the day we opened the doors.' That didn't seem like such a drastic change. Or had we not got to that bit yet?

'And what about love? Don't tell me there's been nobody since me?' Bloody hell – had I turned him celibate?

'I've told you already.'

'When?' Had I missed something?

He looks puzzled. Not as puzzled as I do, though.

'When I introduced Claus as my partner, he's not just my business partner, Cooper, he's my *life partner*. That's what I meant by "experimenting". I experimented on the gay scene and discovered I belong there.'

'Oh.'

Holy fuck! I didn't see that one coming. Astonishment sends a rush of blood to the brain and I feel a need to put my head between my knees. It takes me a couple of minutes to recover my power of thought and run it through my mind again. Joe is gay. My first reaction is that I'm pleased he has found a life that makes him happy, but there's no getting away from the fact that this has blindsided me.

Had I ever suspected he was gay? No. In hindsight, were there any tell-tale signs? No. Do I want to cry because it means that I'm definitely no longer his type? Yes.

'Tell me, Joe, were you seeing guys when we were together?'

'How can you ask that? You know I was faithful to you. I'm not denying I'd been curious for a long time, but I didn't act on it until I met Claus.' He looks hurt and angry at my question.

I should have known better. Joe Cain is an honest man, he always was.

My voice mellows. 'Are you happy?'

'Very. What Claus and I have got is special.'

I reach over and touch his face. 'Then I'm happy for you, Joe. I really am. I'm just sorry I hurt you and that things didn't work out differently for us.'

'Me too, Cooper.'

We sit in silence, holding hands, for a few moments.

'So what are your plans now?'

I decide to tell him the rest of the story. The great ex-boyfriend manhunt. He thinks it's hilarious.

'Wait a minute, I was number two on the list? Can't believe I wasn't top,' he teased.

'I'm doing it in chronological order,' I explain, giggling.

Laughter is making his eyes crinkle in that way I always adored. 'Thank God, that would have been a crushing blow to my ego. Who is next then?'

'That big blond you saw me molesting in Glasgow.'

He's clutching his sides now. 'Fantastic. I'd have been pissed off if you'd dumped me then rode off into the sunset with him. Anyway, he was more my type than yours.'

I hit him with a garlic bread crust.

'Where does he live?'

'Manchester. I guess I'll head there next.'

'Don't leave yet, Carly. Amsterdam is beautiful this time of year. Have a bit of a holiday – you can stay with Claus and me.'

It's an interesting offer. I could do with a couple of weeks in the sun. Some time to relax and chill out. More importantly, I want to rekindle a relationship with Joe. If I can't have romance, then I'd really like friendship, and for him to be part of my life going forward.

'Won't Claus have a problem with that?'

'Don't worry about Claus, he's a very secure guy. Besides, he knows that my clog is now firmly on the other foot.'

It's a deal.

We return to J.C.'s Heaven and go up to the office. Claus looks relieved that we're back. I go over and give him a kiss on the cheek.

'Claus, since you've stolen my man, I think the least you can do is put me up for a couple of weeks and pamper me to death.'

He glances at Joe, who nods his head and then he smiles lazily.

'Okay, but only as long as you have our dinner on the table every night and clean the bathroom.'

I think I'm going to like him.

I sigh. 'What a waste. I'm in a room with two gorgeous men and they've only got eyes for each other. I think I'll have to take up knitting.'

* * *

My two week stay stretches to three. Every morning, I make the guys breakfast, then we spend the days wandering through Vondelpark and up and down the canal banks. In the evenings, we have dinner, then the boys go off to the club. Sometimes I join them, sometimes I have an early night with a good book. I could get used to this. I've never felt so mellow in my whole life. Claus is an absolute darling. I can see what Joe sees in him. He's strong and funny and caring and way too gifted in the looks department.

I'm not even remotely sad that things didn't work out with Joe, because the kind of love they've got gives me hope. My person is out there somewhere. And I've got a few more chances to find him.

Eventually, I summon the energy to leave and call Kate to tell her to make up a bed for me.

'Cooper! Well, what's the scores on the doors?'

'The ex-boyfriends two, Carly Cooper nil.'

'Sarah told me what happened with Nick. But what about Joe? The girls are running a sweepstake and my money was on him. You just cost me a tenner and a day at a health spa.'

'It's a long story, Kate. Dust down a bottle of your finest plonk and I'll fill you in at the weekend. I'm going to stay a couple of nights and then head to Manchester. How are Jess and Basil?'

'Well, his broken jaw healed in time for the latest *Hello!* edition. He and his wife are on six pages, explaining that it was all a huge misunderstanding and how it's brought them even closer together.'

'Shit, Jess must be spitting.'

'She's not chuffed.'

'And what about Carol?'

'George sent her a Tiffany cross to apologise, so she's got over it all in record time.'

I laugh. That's so Carol. There's no wound that diamonds can't heal.

'I'll see you on Sunday, Kate. Get the girls round too, the latest episode is priceless.' Obviously Sarah wouldn't be there because she was still in Glasgow, but we could phone her and fill her in on developments.

'It can't be too bad – you sound really happy.'

I glance over at Joe and Claus, lying cuddled up on the sofa, looking utterly contented. If nothing else, I tell myself again, it's restored my faith in love.

'I am happy. But I'm still a woman on a mission. Roll on number three.'

16

'You are joking!' Kate screams, crossing her legs to ensure that her hysteria doesn't bring on pregnancy incontinence. Her bump is definitely starting to show.

We're sitting in Kate's dining room on a sunny Sunday morning. Once again, the aeroplane food on my flight from Amsterdam this morning looked like a botulism breeding experiment, so I'm devouring last night's leftover apple crumble.

Bruce and the kids have been dispatched to the swimming baths to make room for Carol, Jess and Callum, who's dropped in to say his goodbyes before catching a flight to the States. He's going to do a three month stint as the face of the new Donna Karan range. He's got a tough life, my brother. Looking at him, it's hard to see the family resemblance. Callum is perfection and I still look like an exploding loo brush.

I've just got to the bit where Joe tells me he's gay. Jess has gone pink, Carol looks like she needs a loo, and Kate's yelling for a midwife. And I know they're laughing at me, not with me, but I don't blame them. My life is getting more like a bad sitcom every day.

'Honestly,' I continue, 'they are so happy together. I've never seen a more contented couple.'

'I think that one is a lost cause,' Jess breathlessly states the obvious. 'There's still hope though. Although, you might want to do something with that hair because that isn't winning anyone's heart.' They're all laughing again.

I decide to buy a wig first thing on Monday morning.

Carol pipes up. 'How is it that all the gorgeous, caring, sensitive, interesting men out there are gay? It's a tragedy. No wonder there're no men out there for us.'

Callum fires a wicker place mat in her direction. 'Not *all* of them. Last time I checked I was decidedly heterosexual.'

'You don't count, you're family,' she replies. 'And anyway, I like a bit of mystery in a man. You have zero mystery. None.'

That'll be my brother put firmly in his place then. Callum's petted lip reaches the floor. Jess gives him a cuddle.

'Ignore her, Callum. She's just pissed off because Clive cancelled her American Express card and George hasn't given her a new one yet.'

Carol yelps with indignation, but I'm saved from her ire, because Jess gets us back on track. 'So what's next, Miss Desperado?' I ignore the dig.

'Doug. Last I heard he was in Manchester, so I'm going to head up there tomorrow.'

'He's not in Manchester. He's here in London,' Callum throws in.

I turn to him, astounded. 'Since when is he in London? And how do you know?'

'No idea when he came here – I lost touch with him when he moved to Manchester. But I met his mum last time I was home and she told me he runs a Mercedes garage in Wimbledon.'

I can't believe it. All these years, he's been twenty miles away and I didn't know about it. I decide to put Callum up for adoption.

I suddenly get a good feeling. This one has started off so easy. I mean, no searching, no travelling, no fraudulent expenditure. This is too good to be true. And that can only mean one thing – it's meant to be. I have an overwhelming feeling that Doug is going to be *The One.*

* * *

Next morning, I dress with care. If I'm going to be a potential purchaser of a Mercedes, then I have to look the part. I settle on a charcoal grey trouser suit, black boots and a silver blouse. Chic, but not over the top. After relentless begging, grovelling and promises of a lifetime of favours, Carol allows me to borrow her black Prada bag. I don't know whether to wear it or frame it.

I call Joe before I leave and tell him that I feel like I'm about to play a championship match on centre court. My knees are like jelly and my mouth is drier than Kate's apple crumble.

'C'mon, Cooper. You'll be fine. Just knock him dead with your sparkling wit and charm,' he humours me.

'I'm more worried about him knocking me dead. The way he feels about me, I'm likely to be under the wheels of a new Mercedes within five minutes.'

'You'll be fine, sweetheart. Claus and I are right behind you.'

'Mmm. At a safe distance of hundreds of miles.'

Joe laughs and the irony of this situation isn't lost on me – my gay ex-boyfriend is trying to give me confidence to face the man I left him for in the first place. This could keep a therapist in fees for years.

I call Sarah on my mobile as the taxi heads for Wimbledon. I had to hand back my work phone when I left my job, so I invested in a brand new Nokia. I feel very high tech.

She sounds so bright and breezy, it's a huge relief. Maybe the break in St Andrews reset things for her and she's found her old optimism again. I hang up as I arrive at the garage.

Okay, deep breaths. I can do this. I can do this.

I'm so busy concentrating on my opening line that I forget to look where I'm going. Three seconds later, I'm lying sprawled on the floor after tripping over the welcome mat on the way in. I'm just glad I wore trousers, otherwise the world would have had a bird's eye view of my tartan knickers.

As I mentally check my limbs for broken bones, a hand takes my arm and pulls me up.

'Are you okay?' It's male, it's Scottish and before I even look up, I know it's him.

'I'm fine, I think, Doug. And you?'

He stares at me for what seems like an hour but is probably about three and a half seconds. I do the top-to-toe scan. The blond hair is now short and swept back, the eyes even greener than I remembered. His body still looks like a Calvin Klein mannequin. He's wearing a navy suit, the Versace buttons giving a clue to its origin and a gold tie over a white shirt. He is perfection. I don't know whether to talk to him or just stare for a while longer.

'You always did like to make a big entrance.'

'Yes, well, there's nothing like indoor gymnastics to get a girl noticed.'

He doesn't even smile and I feel a distinct frost forming around us.

'What can I do for you, Carly?'

'I'd, em, like a Mercedes.'

He folds his arms and raises his eyebrows. 'Really, what model?'

'Em, a kind of, well, one of those, em, blue ones.'

He raises an eyebrow and I crumble.

'Okay, Doug,' I confess, 'I don't want a sodding car. Callum told me you worked here and I came to talk to you.'

'Why? Running out of men to be unfaithful to?'

Point taken.

I turn to leave. There's only so much humiliation I can take in one morning and this can only go downhill from here. A swift exit seems like a better plan.

But, to my surprise, he puts out his arm to stop me.

'Okay, Carly, we'll go to the coffee bar across the road. You've got half an hour.' Maybe that's just how long it will take him to round up enough passers-by to witness my public flogging.

A few minutes later, he's sitting across the table, still staring at me. How do I start? Somehow, asking 'how have you been' seems totally insufficient.

'First of all, I'm so sorry about what happened, Doug. I know I've got no right to ask you to forgive me.' I am so crap at grovelling, but I keep it succinct. I know for sure there's no point in rehashing it all. "I'm sorry I slept with Mark Barwick behind your back and crushed our plans for the future," would just be twisting the knife.

'Correct.' At least he's speaking. This could be a breakthrough.

'Look, Doug, what else can I say? I was a pathetic, horrible cow and I don't blame you for hating me, but I am sorry.'

'Okay, so you're sorry. What do you want now?'

Since when was he so direct? This is the same guy who took five weeks to snog me. Has he been on an assertiveness course?

'I guess I just wanted to see you. It's been a long time.'

The look on his face tells me that it hasn't been long enough. Perhaps I should have waited another, oh, I don't know, fifty years?

* * *

'What happened next?' Kate interrogates me when she arrives back from work.

I tell her how it took half an hour before he would even utter a whole sentence, and then another half hour before he deigned to enter into a proper conversation. He finally returned to the garage two hours, eight coffees (ours), a chocolate fudge cake (mine) and two paracetamol (also mine) later.

'And?' she persists.

'And I'm meeting him tonight for dinner,' I squeal, doing an impersonation of a pogo stick. She's incredulous and I don't blame her. I could hardly believe the turnaround myself. To start with, he was absolutely hating me and then it was like a switch flicked and he suggested we carry on the conversation tonight at some trendy restaurant.

She bangs a drum roll on the kitchen counter. The kids flee for cover – Mummy and Auntie Carly have obviously had too much caffeine again.

That evening, I don my new Kookai dress, purchased on my return from Wimbledon. Yes, I know I've got the financial stability of a seesaw, but this could be one of the most important nights of my life. Anyway, I can always take it back for a refund tomorrow.

Doug takes me to Marco Pierre White's Titanic. Not exactly quiet and romantic, but definitely my kind of place – it's frantically busy, deafeningly noisy and unbelievably shallow and trendy. I catch sight of us in the mirrors behind the bar. We look good together. We could definitely be a couple.

We're seated at a relatively quiet table. For once I'm glad that a waiter called Tarquin takes twenty minutes telling us about the specials – it gives me time to regulate my heartbeat. I choose 'Steak à la McDonald', expecting a prime cut of meat draped in a sauce made of the finest Scotch whisky. Instead I get a hamburger. Marco has a strange sense of humour.

At first, conversation is awkward, so I go for the safe option. We swap tales of the events in our lives since our last meeting, me being somewhat economical with the truth. I've done this three times in the last two months now. I'm considering putting it on tape for any future reunions.

Doug tells me that he's never married but he lived with a girl-friend in Manchester for six years before deciding that it wasn't right. Now, *that* sounds like the Doug I knew.

We share a sticky toffee pudding. As I contemplate my ice cream, I do a quick mental review of the situation. I have to say there's been an incredible thaw in his attitude since this morning.

In fact, I hate to be too confident, but I actually think we're having a good time. The starter was a bit awkward, main course was decidedly warmer and by the time dessert came there was lots of laughing, accidental brushes of hands and long lingering looks.

I contemplate Doug and, to my eternal amazement, realise that he's being, well, just Doug again – he's charming, funny, sweet and comfortable. I spoke too soon – he's just gone silent.

'What are you thinking?' I ask, not sure that I want to hear the answer.

'I'm thinking that I want to take you home with me. What are you thinking?' he says, staring at me earnestly.

This is a bad idea. It is. A really bad idea. The worst idea I've ever heard. I just can't quite think why at the moment because my libido has assumed control of my faculties and absolutely, definitely wants to play.

'I'm thinking that I just might let you,' I reply, trying to smile seductively, but probably only managing inane and gormless.

We take a cab back to his house in Fulham. It's a three storey town house on a litter-free street, lined with BMWs, Porsches and Mercs.

Inside, Doug switches on a lamp to reveal a lounge straight out of *Good Housekeeping*. The walls are cream, with gold uplighters focused on prints of Monet, Michelangelo and Leonardo da Vinci's works of art. The flooring is stripped wood and there are two black leather sofas bordering a glass coffee table with an antique gold base. The television and hi-fi are neatly set in a glass unit on the far wall and there are brass statues on the two glass side tables. I'm terrified to touch anything in case I leave finger marks. How does he dust all this?

He presses a button on a remote control and the sounds of Quincy Jones flood the room. I cringe a little. This is paint-by-numbers seduction and, to my shame, not only are my hormones whisking up a frenzy, but the rest of me is enjoying it too.

Doug pours me a glass of champagne, then takes my hand and guides me through to the bedroom. He kisses me slowly, then urgently, pressing me against a wall.

I pull at his shirt, sending buttons ricocheting across the room. He tears at my dress and it dissolves into pieces before falling to the floor. Shit, there goes that refund. Still, at least I wore my black, lace, G-string and underwired, 'hold all your bits in place' body suit.

He pulls me up and over to the bed. He kneels above me and bends to kiss my lips, my neck... all the way down to my toes. If this goes on for much longer, then I'm going to come before he does. I remember his haste in the sexual department and realise that'll be a first.

He slides back up to kiss me on the lips, at the same time reaching into a bedside drawer, pulling out a condom, opening it and slipping it on with one hand. This boy's been practising.

'I love you, Cooper. I always have,' he whispers as he slips inside me. His words send my lust level into orbit. He still loves me. Wow.

He moves slowly back and forward, murmuring in my ear the whole time, telling me everything he's going to do to me. My legs are locked around his back just in case he thinks of escaping. There's no way I'm letting this one go.

He's relentless, moving my body into positions that I thought were only possible after years of intensive yoga. Every time I think he's going to climax, he controls himself and carries on. After multiple orgasms on my side, he finally lets go and comes, gasping and grinding to a halt. He collapses beside me.

I want to say something, but I can't. I'm in shock. This guy has developed serious skills. Oh, and he loves me. Or was that just something he blurted out in the moment?

He leans over and traces my face with his finger.

'I love you, Carly,' he tells me again. Not an accidental outburst then.

I smile back and lean over to kiss him. Nope, I'm not even going to go there. Too many times before, I've rushed into the whole 'love you' stuff and it's ended up in chaos. This is a new me. I'm going to take my time, be sure of how I feel before promising the earth and delivering disaster. I'm a reformed character. But I have to say, I'm feeling something here that's more than just lust.

'So what happens next, Mr Cook?'

'Carly, there's no way I'm letting you go again. Is that okay with you?' he smiles and pushes my hair back off my face.

'I think maybe I could get used to the idea.'

He holds me tight as he slips off to sleep. I've never felt so warm and safe in my life. How did I ever let this man slip through my fingers?

Doug starts to snore quietly, but I'm so excited that I'll be lucky to sleep again this year. I look at the clock – 2 a.m.. Who's likely to be awake at this time?

I pad through to the lounge and call Carol. She answers immediately.

'George, I told you to fuck off,' she yells, before slamming the phone down.

Okay, I've obviously missed an episode in her life. I thought her and George had kissed and made up? I try again. 'Carol, don't hang up, it's me. Are you okay?'

'No!' she cries.

Oh, shit. Trust me to walk right into the middle of a crisis. I knew today was too good to be true.

'I'll be right there,' I promise, slamming down the phone. I find my dress, but the only thing it can be used for now is dusters. Bugger it. I grab Doug's trousers and belt, then slip on his shirt and tie it in a knot. I pause to look at him before I leave the bedroom. He is truly beautiful. And he loves me! I would dance, only my legs are so sore they'd probably buckle.

In the lounge, I search for a pen and a piece of paper.

Doug,

Carol's had a crisis and I'm the only available emergency service. Last night was amazing. Please call me in the morning (mobile: 0911 234231). Can't wait to speak to you.

Luv,

Cooper.

I call a cab, then realise that I don't know where I am. I run outside, check the street name and house number and try again. How is it possible for a night to go so far down the toilet in such a short space of time? This is a record even for me.

Twenty minutes later, Carol lets me into her flat. She's still sniffling and her eyes look like burst plums.

'What's happened?' I ask as I give her a cuddle.

That does it – Niagara gushes down her face.

I pour her a large brandy, then an even larger one for me and order her to lie down on the sofa. I get a flannel from the bathroom, run it under the cold tap, then return to the lounge and put it over her face.

'Don't say anything for a moment,' I tell her.

After a few minutes, I remove the cloth. That's better – she only looks mildly disfigured now.

'Tell me what happened,' I urge again.

She's silent for a long time.

'George asked me to marry him.'

I'm confused. 'And that's bad, why?'

'Carly, look at me. How did I end up like this? I'm thirty-one years old and a guy who'll soon qualify for a bus pass is the closest I can get to a stable relationship.'

'But I thought that was the whole point. I thought that was what you wanted – older, rich guys that have their lives sorted.'

'I know, Carly, it was, but it just all seems so pointless now. I mean, how can I spend the rest of my life with men who take an afternoon nap. What have I been thinking?'

I'd forgotten about the golden rule of being female. It's our prerogative to change our minds at any given time, without warning and expect the rest of the world to understand and fall in line.

'So what do you want now?'

'I want a real relationship. One that's not based on bank balances and being a trophy girlfriend. I want children and a house and a life.'

Well, knock me over and call me Kate Moss.

'Carol, you can have all that. You're beautiful, you're successful, you're funny, you're intelligent and you're a good person. You could have any man you wanted.'

She wipes her nose on her sleeve. Remind me never to borrow that jumper.

She thinks for a moment. 'But look at you. You're all those things too and you still haven't found anyone.'

A stake through my heart.

'Yes, but that's because I'm officially hopeless.'

She laughs.

I take that as progress and press on. We talk until the sun comes up, until I have to sleep before my body collapses in a heap.

'Right, from now on, you will accept all offers of dates that you receive from any men under forty-five, regardless of their bank balance. You'll only be drawn to men who are younger than your dad and you'll stop socialising in the Help the Aged canteen. Okay?'

She smiles, then clutches her hand to her mouth. 'Oh, shit, Carly. I've been so busy talking about me that I forgot to ask how your date with Doug went.'

I wrinkle up my nose and grin like a deranged maniac. 'Well, we ended up in bed making *lurve.*'

She doesn't miss a beat. 'Okay, so that took care of five minutes, what about the rest of the night?'

Crisis over. Carol is definitely back to her wonderfully sarcastic self.

Friends. Who'd be without them?

* * *

I wait all day for Doug to call, but he doesn't. At four o'clock, I capitulate and call him.

'Doug, it's me. I'm really sorry about leaving last night, but it was an emergency, honest.'

He explodes. 'Carly, I don't want to hear it. You show up after all these years, I tell you how I feel about you, then you fucking disappear again. I'm not playing your stupid games any more.'

Do I detect a note of unhappiness? I pull on kneepads and grovel, offering every piece of mitigation I've ever seen on re-runs of *LA Law*. I finally resort to that old girl's favourite. 'Look, Doug, it was a gynaecological thing. You see what happened was...'

'Stop!' he bellows. It works every time. I've not yet met a guy who can bear to discuss anything to do with a woman's reproductive system. He finally concedes. 'Look, I can't see you tonight. I play football on Tuesdays, Thursdays and Fridays. But I'll pick you up tomorrow night at seven, okay?'

I feel like a cat who's just discovered that she's got ten lives.

I spend hours preparing for dinner the following night. Every surplus hair is electrocuted, every pore exfoliated, hard skin is sandblasted and three buckets of body lotion are applied.

As Doug walks up Kate's path, there's an earth tremor. No, that's just me trying to walk in Carol's four inch Gucci heels without tearing Jess's pink Voyage dress. I'm a living, almost breathing, almost walking, hand-me-down.

We go to Henry's, one of my favourite Richmond restaurants, and sit at a table on the balcony overlooking the Thames. Over dinner, my mind wanders back to that last morning, all those years ago, with Doug. I can't believe he's sitting here with me now. I look up at the sky. If this were a Danielle Steel novel, it would say that the stars were shining down on me.

I snap back to reality. Sod Danielle Steel. If I remember correctly, she helped me get into that mess in the first place.

I tell Doug about Carol and Jess and about meeting Sarah again. I warn him that I'm unemployed, in debt and homeless. He laughs and shakes his head at that bit. He might at least have the decency to look surprised. But before I have time to put my offended face on, he leans over and kisses me.

'Carly, who cares? This is more important than any of that.'

And he's right. Suddenly everything has been worth it. Maybe this was all meant to happen. We were supposed to break up, so that we could find each other again and this time we'd have no worries that we were too young or settling down too soon.

We go back to his house. After a few hours in bed, I'm desperate to ask him where he got his new techniques and stamina from, but I figure that's a boat I don't want to rock.

I wake in his arms the following morning.

'You're still here,' he nuzzles into my neck.

'Thought I'd wait around to see what you're like in the mornings.'

He pulls my hand under the covers and wraps it around his hard-on. 'Answer your question?'

'Definitely.'

Here we go again. At this rate, I'll have the toned body of an athlete before the week's out. Either that or chronic exhaustion.

* * *

It's girls' night at Paco's. We've changed it to the first Thursday of the month to accommodate Kate's antenatal classes. Paco loves us to pieces after the publicity generated by the Basil and George show. The restaurant has been fully booked ever since.

I can't believe it's July already. It's been over three months since I left my job and eight whole weeks since I rediscovered Doug.

'Cooper, will you stop grinning like that, it's nauseating and you're putting me off my nachos.' Jess is in a foul mood. There must be trouble in the world of politics again.

'I'm sorry. I forgot to practice my "miserable cow" face before I came out tonight. So anyway, what were you saying?'

Kate kicks me under the table for not paying attention.

Jess, it seems, has finally given the Right Honourable Basil Asquith MP an ultimatum – he either leaves his wife and moves in with her or it's over. The upstanding Mr Asquith buckled and begged her for more time, pleading that he had his children to think of and he must prepare them for such trauma. Given that his kids are thirty-two and thirty-four, I can understand why she's cynical.

'And this time I mean it. I'm not capitulating. No. Definitely not. I'm getting way too old for this mistress nonsense. No, I mean it. Absolutely. This is it.'

It's a reaffirmation thing Jess does when she's facing a challenge. You know, like the self-help books preach that you should look in the mirror every morning and say, 'You're beautiful, you're fulfilled, and all is right in your world.' I would try it, only I fear that my mirror would answer back and contradict me.

We move on to Kate's condition. She now looks like she's hiding a basketball up her shirt.

'Well, I think Bruce is a great name,' Carol is trying to convince her.

'I'm not bloody calling him after his father. You know what happens. He'll end up being known as "Wee Bruce". That's bordering on child abuse.'

'What about Douglas?' It's out of my mouth before I realise that I've said it.

Four heads spin round to face me.

'Cooper, you're obsessed. First sign of a decent shag and you lose control of your senses.'

'I know, isn't it great?' I agree.

'You're a nightmare.' Kate tries to introduce logic into the conversation, 'You've only been seeing him again for a few weeks and the whole sex thing has got you completely entranced.'

'It's not just the sex, Kate. Would I be that shallow?'

Even the people at the next table nod.

'It's not, honestly. He's, well, he's...' I struggle to find the words. 'He's *everything*. I am totally, completely falling in love with him again.'

Four groans. It sounds like the diners at this table have a bad case of indigestion.

'So the great manhunt is over?' Carol asks.

'Definitely. And at the cost of £1934.56, it was a bargain.' I'd finally opened my credit card statements that morning. Now I just have to take more money out of them to pay the bills. I need a job quickly.

'Jesus, Cooper, what did you buy in Scotland, a small island?'

'Don't even ask, but it was worth it.' Every time I talk to Sarah on the phone, she sounds like she's still smiling.

'Have you told him yet?' Kate asks.

'Who? What?'

'Focus, Carly, focus. Have you told Doug that he's the lucky winner in the potential husband competition?'

'Not yet. I'm just taking it slow and letting things take their natural course.'

More cynical looks in my direction. I ignore them.

Jess isn't letting it go. 'Natural course? Didn't you say that you weren't supposed to see him tonight but you're going over anyway?'

I ignore her, mostly because she has a fair point. He plays football on a Thursday night, so it was one of our nights apart. But after three glasses of Prosecco, I'd decided I was missing him and that it was a great idea to go and surprise him. 'Banoffee pie with ice cream, please,' I tell the waiter. 'And if you could tell my pals here to stop judging me, that would be lovely.'

I jump out of the cab at the end of Doug's street. Eleven o'clock. I'm not sure that he'll be home yet, but I'm happy to sit on the steps outside until he arrives. What does a case of piles matter when you're rediscovering a past love?

As I reach his doorway, I see that the lights are on. Yes!

I ring the doorbell once, then again after a couple of minutes. I'm just about to press it again when it opens. But it's not Doug. It's a stunning, tall, supermodel type, with raven black hair and a wide smile, and only a towel covering her dignity. If this is his cleaner, then she wears a highly unusual uniform and keeps strange hours.

'Can I help you?' she asks, smiling.

Silence. My teeth have fused together. Then I realise what's happened. In my state of catatonic bliss, I've rung the wrong doorbell.

'I'm sorry, I'm looking for Doug Cook. I must have the wrong house.'

'No, you haven't, he's upstairs. C'mon in.' She stands back to let me enter, then follows me.

When we reach the lounge, Doug is just coming out of the bedroom, wearing the 'his' version of their 'his & hers' matching towels. I want to vomit.

'Carly, this is a surprise. Saskia, this is Callum Cooper's sister, she's here to talk about his birthday party,' he smiles, oozing nonchalance.

What? But... I don't... Again, *what?* It takes me a moment before realisation dawns. The bastard! He doesn't even look shocked. He's so smooth you could fucking skateboard on him.

'Carly, this is Saskia.'

'Nice... nice to meet you.' I'm stammering, all signals from my brain to my gob being hijacked by sheer disbelief and total fucking fury.

'You too. I'm just gonna go throw some clothes on, babe,' she tells Doug, letting her fingers trail across his hips as she sashays past him. I wait until the door closes behind her.

'You bastard,' I spit, articulate as ever.

The smug smile on his face tells me that the insult hasn't even permeated his brain.

Oh, no. Suddenly, I have a flash of understanding.

'Tuesdays, Thursdays and Fridays, you don't play football at all, do you?'

'Nope. Saskia is an air hostess. Those are the nights she's in town. In saying that, after we're married, she's giving up her career. We're anxious to start a family.' He's enjoying every messed-up, tortuous minute of this.

I struggle to stay composed. I will not let this dickhead see me cry.

'So what was it, Doug? What was all the "love" crap and the "I'm not letting you go again" shit? Was it all some fucked-up game?'

Is there a world record for the number of times that you can swear in one minute? If so, I'm going for it.

He leans back against the wall, still with that lazy smug grin on his face. I want to wipe it off with a brick.

He laughs. 'What can I say, Carly? You didn't really believe me, did you? I thought that's the way people treat each other in your world – they promise everlasting love and affection while they're shagging someone else.'

So that was it. Good old-fashioned revenge. What's the penalty for manslaughter these days?

He's not worth it, though. I dig deep to try and find a shred of dignity. I hold my head up and stare at him. 'I feel sorry for you, Doug. You're a sad, sick, pathetic bastard.'

With that, I turn and walk to the door. Please God, don't let me trip over anything, not when I'm doing the dramatic departure bit. I slam the door for effect, but forget to check that my feet are clear first. Crack! I don't know if it's my toes or the door.

I limp to the end of the street (it was my toes) before disintegrating into a hysterical lump. This is all a bad dream.

I hail a taxi and the driver rolls his eyes as I climb in. Just what he needs – a distraught female. Bet he wishes he'd gone off shift early.

Twenty minutes later, I'm in Kate's kitchen, telling her everything.

Two hours and twenty minutes later, I'm talking gibberish after consuming two bottles of wine in record time, my whole life in the bin with the empty bottles.

When she finally puts me to bed, the combination of exhaustion, grief and half a vineyard has me sleeping in two minutes.

* * *

I wake with all the symptoms of a heart attack, and in the depths of my self-pity, I'm disappointed to see that it's only Cameron and Zoe bouncing on my chest.

'Auntie Carly, Auntie Carly, Mum says you've to get your sorry bum downstairs,' they giggle, finding the word 'bum' highly amusing. They take off squealing, one of them chasing the other along the landing and down the stairs.

I attempt to stand, but someone has put the planet at a ninety degree angle without telling me. I pull on my robe and stagger downstairs like a coma patient in *Awakenings*.

Kate throws a bacon sandwich in front of me.

'Right, Cooper, you're allowed one day of feeling sorry for yourself, then it's time to snap out of it. Any longer than that and you'll scare the children.'

I push away the sandwich. There's only one food for me in times of trauma. I search the freezer but come out empty-handed.

'Kate, why have you never got ice cream in this house?'

'Because I've got kids. The ice cream's devoured within ten minutes of leaving the supermarket car park.'

I settle for Ambrosia Devon Custard, straight from the tin. If I've only got one day of self-pity, then I'd better get started – there's still the whole dairy section at Sainsbury's to get through.

17

On Saturday night, I volunteer for babysitting duty and send Bruce and Kate to the pub. I adore Cameron and Zoe, and I've decided to spend more time with them from now on, as they're probably the closest I'm ever going to get to kids of my own. Another huge wave of despair washes over me.

When they finally go to bed, I pour a coffee and settle down with a packet of Jaffa Cakes. This is what it's come to. My big adventure has ended with me sitting in on a Saturday night with a packet of chocolate biscuits.

After several hours of contemplation and lots of crumbs, I realise that it's over. I haven't got the heart to go on with this stupid farce any more. I've already lost enough – my job, my house, a couple of thousand pounds, not to mention the not insignificant matter of pride. I feel totally defeated. I've cried so much in the last few days that Kate now has a man-made stream in her back garden. Well, no more. I'm going to find a job, some-where to live, beg the credit card companies for mercy and start again.

I call Sarah, the only other person I know who'll be sitting in on a Saturday night, but the phone rings out. Brilliant. The whole bloody world is out having a great time except me.

When Kate and Bruce return, I tell them that I'm giving up. Bruce pours us a nightcap, then disappears to bed. That man has the patience of a saint.

'Are you sure?' Kate asks.

'Positive. It's time I grew up and faced reality, Kate. I can't keep chasing pipe dreams for the rest of my life.'

She nods like an indulgent mother – a normal mother, that is, not one like mine, who's probably at this moment doing bedtime crunchies with Ivan. I choose not to dwell on the fact that my mother's love life is more successful than mine.

'Well, you can stay here until you get organised,' she offers.

What would I do without her?

* * *

At seven o'clock the next morning, there's an almighty banging on the door. On a Sunday! If this is a police raid, then they've got the wrong house. Unless they've come for me on behalf of Mastercard.

Kate, Bruce and I all reach the door at the same time. We let Bruce open it and hide behind him, brave to a fault.

'Jess!' he exclaims.

Kate and I peek over his shoulders. Jess is standing there looking like she hasn't slept for a week and has been dragged through a hedge backwards.

'When's your next trip, Carly?' she stammers.

'There isn't one. I've given up on the whole idea.' I can hardly speak for shock.

'No, you haven't, you're going. Where was the next one supposed to be?'

My mind's gone blank. No, it hasn't. Tom, Ireland.

'Em, Dublin, but I'm not…'

'YES YOU ARE,' she bellows at me.

My God, what is wrong with her? She's always the calmest and most composed of us all.

'Now, get your bags packed, quick,' Jess goes on.

Kate finally finds her voice. 'What's going on, Jess? Tell us what's happened.'

She rummages in her bag before pulling out a newspaper. She holds up the *News of the World*. The headline screams:

BASIL AND THE RANDY RESEARCHER.

'The press have got my flat surrounded. I'm leaving the country before they find me. Cooper, why are you still bloody standing there? Get a move on, I'm not keeping the taxi waiting all day.'

* * *

Oh, the excitement! Just when I thought things couldn't be any more bizarre, I'm now wearing dark glasses, on the run from the tabloid press and sharing an airline bottle of wine with a Randy Researcher. And I seem to have gone from giving up the search to being right back on it, and not of my own free will. This is a mercy mission, I tell myself. I'm only doing it for Jess. If it was down to me, I'd still be drowning in self-pity and wailing into Kate's biscuit tin. A few days in Ireland suddenly seems like a pretty good idea.

Jess is bearing up remarkably well. There was a brief moment of panic when a nervous looking girl at the ticket desk informed us that the next flight to Dublin was fully booked, but we salvaged the situation by flying business class. Isn't this what all fugitives do – flee the country while drinking champagne and eating smoked salmon sandwiches?

Dodging anyone who looks even remotely like they could be carrying a press badge, we keep our heads down as we stride through Dublin Airport and over to the nearest car hire desk.

'I'm sorry, madam, but the only car we have available today is a Fiat Uno.'

Is she serious? I'm 5'8" and Jess is three inches taller. One of us is going to have to travel on the roof rack and since I was the only one who remembered to bring her driving licence, it would have to be Jess. She looks less than amused.

In the end, by using Vaseline, yoga and removing several layers of clothing, we manage to fit in. Lord knows how we're going to get out again. We'll need a harness and a crane.

As we hit the motorway for our drive south, I marvel at Jess's composure. She hasn't shed a tear. If this were Kate, Carol, Sarah or me, we'd be on our third box of tissues, wailing and beating our chests by now. But not Jess – she's always been the strongest of the five of us. I can honestly say that I haven't seen her cry since she was fourteen and she got drunk on illicit cider smuggled into a school disco. She had been inconsolable because the DJ refused to play 'Stand and Deliver', by Adam Ant. It was a very emotional time, fuelled by hormones and Strongbow.

As I drive, she starts to relax, as much as she can in an Uno. I still can't believe I'm here, although now that I am, I'm feeling a strange mix of excitement and apprehension. I'm not sure I'm ready to fall on my face again, so if I decide to bail out at any point, then I'm going to give myself permission to do so. Although, I might just tell Jess in a note, because right now, I'm mildly terrified of her reaction.

I decide to try to assess the lay of the land.

'What are you going to do?' I ask her.

Her feet are on the dashboard and she still can't straighten her legs. 'Nothing. I'll stay out of sight for a couple of weeks, then go back and ignore the stares and sniggers. If nothing else, at least it now forces his lordship to make a decision.'

'Don't you think he's more likely to come to you if you're in the same country? You know, that out-of-sight, out-of-mind thing?'

She laughs. 'Carol used to say, "out of mind, out of earshot". Anyway, I've had enough of trying to second-guess what he's going to do. If he's waiting for me when I get back, then great, if not, then I'll live. I've had enough of being his bit on the side – I deserve better.'

I give her a round of applause, then panic as the car veers off the road.

'Besides,' she adds, 'if all else fails, then I can always sell my side of the story to the News of the Screws. "Randy Researcher Rights the Wrongs". I'd make a fortune.'

I nod, going with her thought process. 'Then there's the book deal, of course, and the obligatory weekly column in a trashy tabloid. Jess, this could open up a whole new world for you,' I joke. 'Just don't forget your friends when you're famous. The dosh from that lot would keep us in facials for years.'

I switch on the radio, right in the middle of 'What Becomes of the Broken-Hearted'.

We burst into fits of giggles, then join in with the song.

By the time we reach the nearest village to Tom's farm, it's lunchtime and we're hungry and hoarse. I'm still not sure I'm going to go through with facing him, but maybe I can at least get some info on where he is and what he's doing. That way, if he has six kids and a devoted wife, I can back away without causing any damage to his life or my heart.

I push Jess out of the car, then she grabs my arms and pulls. Two dislocated shoulders and a slipped disc later, we're standing outside the village pub. I bang on the locked doors. After a few moments, an elderly gent with wild grey hair, wearing a woolly jumper and old farming trousers, opens it a few inches.

'Sorry to bother you. I was wondering if you had a room for a few nights?'

'Sorry, lass. We don't open on a Sunday.'

I assume my most crestfallen face. 'Look, please, we don't know this area very well and we want to visit friends here, the McCallums at Blue Peacock farm.'

He ponders for a few moments, then opens the door wider. 'I can't promise you any food, mind, as I say, we're closed on a Sunday.'

The door is open wide enough now for us to pass through. As we step into the main body of the pub, we're stunned to see about sixty faces looking at us. The whole population of the village is in here and they're all sitting in complete silence.

'It's all right, now,' he announces, 'these lasses are friends of the McCallums.'

They look us up and down, obviously double-checking that we're not from the Trading Standards Authority, then immediately start chattering again, presumably continuing with the conversations that they were having before we rudely interrupted them by banging on the door.

I turn to the landlord. 'I thought you said you were closed,' I say with a grin.

'Aye, lass, that we are. Except for regulars, of course.'

Within ten minutes, Jess and I have two pints of Guinness and two geriatric companions. By late afternoon, we're on first-name terms with everyone in the bar and six different families have invited us to their homes for dinner. When the whole pub breaks into a chorus of 'The Wild Rover', I astound them by standing on a chair and singing the third verse on my own. As I climb down to rapturous applause, Jess laughs in wonder.

'Where the hell did you learn that?' she cries.

'My gran used to sing it to me when I was a kid, after she'd given me a nip of whisky to help me sleep.'

'Cooper, suddenly it's all become clear. Now I know the seeds of your delinquency were sown in childhood.'

I give her a hug. It's great to see her laughing and after the day she's had, she deserves a bit of fun. I call Kate on Jess's mobile to let her know we're okay. Mine doesn't allow international calls but hers is government issue and on an extortionate price plan that covers calls to anywhere in the world.

'Carly, I can hardly hear you, what's all that noise in the background?'

'That's our new friends and Jess singing "Danny Boy" out of tune,' I shout.

'I'm sorry I asked, and even sorrier that I'm not there with you. It sounds like a riot.'

'Oh, God, hold on, Kate.'

I throw the mobile down and go and rescue Jess, who's fallen off her bar stool.

I pick the phone back up. 'Sorry, Kate, what were you saying?'

'I have a message for you from Carol. She has to go to Tokyo for a three day shoot tomorrow, but she's got three weeks off after that. She says she'll meet you in Shanghai if you're still going.'

'That all depends on how it works out here. For all I know, I could be Mrs McCallum by the end of the week.' Ten drinks ago I was still contemplating backing out, so I realise that this new sense of deluded confidence is the alcohol talking.

'Nothing would surprise me, Cooper. Just give me enough time to buy a floppy hat.'

* * *

At eleven o'clock, having consumed a keg of Guinness, four packets of cheese and onion crisps and two packets of peanuts, the landlord, whom we now know is Seamus, married to Nula, with eight kids and a collie, gives us a room key.

I wake the next morning on a single bed, with Jess's feet in my face.

Getting her up requires brute strength and violent threats, but eventually I succeed and we stumble downstairs. Seamus is waiting with two cups of tea that could unblock drains.

'Thanks, Seamus, you're a star,' Jess mumbles.

'Seamus, where can I buy some chocolates and flowers to take to Mrs McCallum?'

I have a feeling I'll need all the bribes I can muster. Tom's mother never liked me, and given that I broke her son's heart, she probably prays for my damnation at mass every Sunday.

'There wouldn't be much point in doing that, m'dear. She passed away about six years ago. Heart attack, if I'm not wrong.'

I feel like someone has just kicked me in the stomach. Poor woman. And there was me thinking evil thoughts about her. Oh, the shame.

'And Mr McCallum?' I ask.

'Aye, him too. Keeled right over one morning when he was milking the cows. 'Bout four years back.'

'No!' I exclaim. It can't be true. Oh God, poor Tom. He's got nobody now. 'And Tom, please tell me he's okay?'

'Well, I wouldn't be knowing about that, now. He sold up and left, right after his old dad died.'

He wasn't even here! It might have been handy if Seamus had shared that little nugget of information before now.

'Do you know where he went, Seamus?'

'Nay, lass, not a word been heard from him since he packed his bags. Last I heard, he was going off to Canada, but I don't know how long he was heading there for. I would have told ye all this when ye arrived yesterday, but I hate to give bad news on the Lord's day.'

A phone rings and Seamus picks up the receiver, barking into it for two minutes before he realises that the ringing hasn't stopped.

'Ooops, sorry,' Jess mumbles as she fishes her mobile out of her pocket and moves to the other side of the room to answer it.

I sit in silence, trying to absorb the news. How would I ever find him now?

Jess rejoins us and I ask who called.

'It was Carol. I told her you'll meet her on Wednesday in Shanghai.'

'But I can't leave now, I need to find Tom,' I argue half-heartedly. Or maybe I should just forget this and go back home.

'Look, Carly, you haven't got the time to chase all over the place looking for him. He could be anywhere and it could take months. I'm going to stay away from London for a couple of weeks. You go and meet Carol and I'll try to track down Tom. I need something to keep my mind occupied. Don't worry, Seamus here will keep me company.'

Seamus's face beams. It's probably the best offer he's had this decade.

I ponder Jess's suggestion. 'But how will you find him?'

'Cooper, it may have escaped your notice, but as this weekend's headlines pointed out, I'm an expert researcher. Apparently I'm also a nymphomaniac home wrecker, but we'll overlook those bits. Trust me, I'll find him. Now, you're going to Shanghai and no arguing.'

I love it when she gets assertive and bossy. I know she's right.

Compared to the elusive Mr McCallum, Phil and Sam should be relatively easy to find.

I borrow her phone again and, with the help of Directory Enquiries, I start to call airlines. My credit cards tremble with fear as I give the numbers over for flights and hotels.

Next day, I'm back at Dublin Airport, and as I board the plane to Bangkok on the first leg of a complicated route to Shanghai, I look back to see Jess waving furiously from the viewing deck. I blow her a kiss. For a woman who's being hunted by most of the British press, she looks remarkably calm and happy.

That reminds me, I never did ask her who leaked the story of her affair to the tabloids. I bet it was a jealous colleague of Basil's – they must be salivating at the mouth over a woman like Jess. Or maybe the jealous wife? No, that would put an end to her five page spreads in *House & Garden*.

A sudden thought strikes me. No, surely not! Not Jess! She wouldn't have... Would she?

The man in the next seat looks at me with true concern as I laugh and raise my can of Guinness – 'To Jess, a woman who has taken her destiny into her own hands. A woman after my own heart.'

18

BABY ONE MORE TIME – BRITNEY SPEARS

I think I've left the plane at the wrong destination. After brief stops in Bangkok and Hong Kong, I arrive at Shanghai's international airport and discover it is now sleek, modern, spotless and completely unrecognisable.

In the five years since I left here so much has changed. Maybe Phil has too. Technically speaking, he isn't an ex, however, I adored him with all my heart and we did make a pact to hook up again if I wasn't married by the time I was thirty, so it's only right that I track him down to see if it's time to keep our promise.

Outside the terminal it's about a gazillion degrees, so I jump into the first taxi I see and dredge my memory for the floppy disc labelled 'Conversational Mandarin – use only in cases of emergency'. When I ask the taxi driver in his native tongue to take me to Shanghai's Windsor Hotel, he looks at me quizzically. Oh, hell, I must have my words mixed up again. I've probably asked him to take me to the nearest fried egg sandwich.

'Do you mean the Windsor Hotel, lady?' he asks in English that's better than mine.

I smile ruefully and nod. How times change. When I was last here, I never once encountered an English-speaking taxi driver.

I check in, dump my gear in my room and decide to hit the coffee shop on the ground floor of the hotel, for a double expresso. I want to be awake when Carol arrives tonight, but the way I'm feeling, it's doubtful. I've had a grand total of three hours' sleep in the last two days. It's not that the planes were uncomfortable, it's just that there were so many movies that I wanted to see and I hate to miss anything. I'm regretting it now, though.

The coffee shop is almost deserted when I enter. The whole coffee trend hasn't quite caught on here yet. If it were a tea shop, it would be standing room only. I'm about to sit down when I notice a Western man sitting on his own in the corner, immersed in paperwork. I recognise that face! No, it's not Phil Lowery, that would be too simple, but it's close. It's my second favourite person in China: Jack McBurnie, the Food and Beverage Director and the man who offered me the job here in the first place.

'Hey, mister, fifty bucks and I'm yours for the night. I'll show you a good time,' I offer.

He simultaneously raises his head and reaches for his walkie-talkie to call security.

I sit down, grinning. 'Or, alternatively, you could buy me a coffee and I'll give you a freebie.'

His mouth is open, but nothing is coming out, then he laughs so loudly that the staff stop to stare.

'Carly, what the hell are you doing here?'

'Don't even ask, Jack, you wouldn't believe it. Anyway, what about you? It must be over fifteen years you've been here now. Jesus, you get less than that for murder.'

'I know, I know, but this place grows on you. Shame you didn't stick around long enough to find that out,' he teases.

I finally get my coffee, with a double thick doughnut to keep it company. I tell myself I'm comfort eating to soothe the pain of recent traumas. In truth, I'm just desperate to indulge in a pastry that I know will have come out of the oven only a few hours ago.

Jack brings me up to date with the events since I left. None of the original management team remain except him. Heinz and Hans now run an Austrian restaurant in the centre of the city. Dan and Arnie returned to Australia shortly after I left, and Chuck and Linden work in the same hotel in Hong Kong that I had transferred to.

'And what about Ritza and Olga?'

'Last I heard they opened a private nursing home in Berlin.'

I feel an immediate wave of sympathy for the elderly.

We chat for a while longer, every bit as comfortable as we were the day I left. After my second coffee, I check my watch. Six o'clock. If the shoot finished on time, and Carol made her flight, then she'd land around nine.

'Jack, can you do me a favour?'

'Anything.'

'I've got a friend arriving on the nine o'clock from Tokyo. Could you send the flashiest, most over-the-top, fuck-off car that you've got for her?'

'Is she as superficial as you?'

'Maybe even more,' I answer proudly.

He grins. 'Then it would be a pleasure.'

I'm waiting in the lobby bar when Carol rushes in, face flushed with what could be excitement, embarrassment or a desperate longing for the loo. The head of every man in the bar turns to stare in awe. With her chocolate hair in tendrils reaching down to her waist, brown eyes the size of hazelnuts and a figure that looks seriously deprived of a good pudding, she's every man's fantasy.

'A gold Rolls-Royce! A bloody Rolls-Royce! Cooper, I don't know what you did to get that car, but it was worth it.'

'I sold my body. Twice.'

'Well, sell it again – I want that car for a week.'

That's why I love Carol – she makes me look deep.

We take a bottle of champagne up to the room to drink while we change. Yes, I know it's a superfluous overindulgence, but how often does one of your best mates fly from another country to support you in a ridiculous mission? And besides, after the journey in the Rolls, I can hardly bring her crashing back down to earth with a vodka and diet coke.

'Thanks for doing this, Carol. For coming all this way. After Doug, I don't think I could have done this on my own.'

'Don't mention it, my love. You're always there for me.'

'What happened with George? Is it over?'

She nods. 'I have no idea what I was doing with him. Or any of the others for that matter. Don't get me started again – we can only have one midlife crisis at a time. Anyway, I'm here, so every cloud has a silver cover.'

She's totally bemused as to why I've collapsed in a fit of giggles on the bed.

We polish off the bubbles and head for Champagne, the nightclub that I managed when I worked here. Only, when we get there, it's not called Champagne any more. It's now the 'Downtown Karaoke Club'. Inside, it has been redecorated, but still in the same colours and fabrics. Even now, it doesn't look dated.

'Right then, ladies and gentlemen, next up is Johnny Woo, singing "That'll Be the Day". C'mon up here, Johnny.'

There aren't enough exclamation marks in the English language to describe my hysteria. Up on the stage, still with the

Bee Gees haircut and a gold medallion that's sure to leave him with osteoporosis in later years, is the DJ, Zac. I catch his eye and he bounds over, Johnny Woo now murdering his chosen song.

'Hey, Carly, baby. You're still the ravishing sex bomb you always were.'

'Yes, Zac, and you're still a twat,' I laugh.

'All part of the service, baby.' He gives a bow and we swap small talk before he checks out my ring finger and gets to the important stuff. 'So, not married? Never meet anyone that could match up to the Zac machine?' he asks, so over the top that I lose it again.

'Zac, you put me off men for life. I'm a nun now. Sister Carly.'

He doesn't know if I'm serious or joking. He never was the brightest light in the disco.

'So where is everyone? Where's Lily, Lila, Mimi and Cora?'

When they'd chosen their Western monikers, I was pretty sure they'd come from the *English Four Letter Christian Names Book.*

'All gone. All married Westerners and went abroad.'

I'm glad for them – it was what they always wanted.

'And you?' I ask, positive that no one would be crazy enough to take him on.

'I married Susie. Remember her?'

Only too well. She was a regular who was often seen on the arm of wealthy customers. Seems like both Zac and Susie found love – or whatever it was – in the end.

Johnny Woo is screeching to a conclusion, so Zac races back to the stage.

By the end of the night, after outstanding renditions of 'Crazy', 'I Will Survive', 'Summer Loving' and the 'Shoop Shoop Song', we're propping up the bar and being hit on by two very flash Frenchmen.

'Tell me something,' Carol slurs to hers. 'Are you rich?'

'Mais oui, we are very rich.' The Rolex on each wrist gives it away.

'Are you over forty?'

I can tell he's trying to decide whether or not to lie. He decides against it.

'Maybe by one or two years.'

'Then I'm sorry, I can't possibly be seen with you. I have a rule, you see. I only date poor men who were born in the same decade as me, sorry.'

She turns and grabs my arm as she floats out the door, leaving two very bemused males.

'Don't worry, mate,' I hear Zac whisper to them in a moment of male bonding. 'They're nuns.'

* * *

The following morning, our first stop is at the production company Phil started working at before I left Shanghai. With a bit of luck, he still works for them and they can tell me where he is.

The girls behind the desk stare at me blankly – they've never heard of Phil Lowery and no Westerner works for them now, it's local photographers only. Progress can be a pain in the arse sometimes.

We need a plan. We buy a map of the city and split it into six areas. I'm counting on the fact that the expat community in Shanghai is still relatively small and very incestuous – everyone knows someone who knows someone. We circle every hotel in the area, then I recruit Zac to pinpoint all the bars and restaurants regularly frequented by expats.

Next day, we set off for the furthest away zone and start scouring the streets. Initially, we're too embarrassed to just walk into a bar and ask every Westerner if they know Phil Lowery, so we try to be as low-key as you can possibly be when you're trailing round Shanghai with a Cindy Crawford look-alike. We order a drink and then casually enter into conversation with the bar staff and customers. By early evening, we've reached three conclusions:

1. This will take us a year to complete;

2. We'll be pissed every day by lunchtime;

3. Cagney and Lacey never had these problems.

On day three, we try a different approach – it's time to be ruthless. We go in and out of establishments like an SAS hit squad, leaving a trail of curious faces in our wake. Not one person shows even a flicker of recognition. I'm beginning to think I imagined him.

Four days later, we're down and we're out. There's only one area left to try and my optimism has deserted me. Carol and I sit on the edge of the bath, our feet soaking in six inches of water.

'How did I ever get involved in this?' Carol wails.

'Because you're a loyal and loving friend,' I remind her.

'Cooper, I do love you, but I don't love you this much. My feet are disfigured for life. No more Dr Scholl commercials for me.'

I take her to the bar for a consolation drink and Jack finds us there two hours later. Carol has adored him ever since I introduced them and explained that he sent the Rolls. However, to her credit, it's been purely in a platonic fashion.

'You two look like ladies who need cheering up.'

'Jack, the only things that will cheer us up are a foot massage and another cocktail,' Carol answers. 'Which one are you offering?'

'I'll stick with the cocktail, since we're in a public place,' he chuckles. 'So, should I take it that the hunt's not going well?'

'It's right up there with Betamax videos and the Middle East peace agreement,' I reply.

'Have you tried the American Embassy?' Jack asks. 'He must have been registered there.'

I need to go back to detective school, I hadn't thought of that. In saying that, there's no way they would divulge that kind of information unless it was an international emergency.

Jack smiles and picks up the phone. In two minutes he's through to a contact there, then gets put on hold.

'I haven't been in Shanghai all this time without making a few friends,' he says.

A few minutes later, he's listening intently. He frowns and replaces the receiver. 'Sorry, Cooper, but it seems Phil Lowery returned to New York eight years ago.'

There's a silence for a few minutes, then Carol finally speaks. 'So, let me get this straight. We've come all the way to Shanghai, we've walked more miles than a nomadic tribe, been in more bars than an alcoholic, our feet look like they've been sanded by a floor buffer and you manage to find out he's not here with a ten minute phone call... Jack, I think you owe us another few cocktails.'

* * *

The next day we have a choice – either head to New York on Phil Lowery's trail, or stop off in Hong Kong to search for Sam Morton. Jess has called to say that she hasn't found Tom yet, so there's no lead to chase up there. The decision is made by the fact that Callum is already in New York, so we'll have a free place to stay and some very welcome time with my crazy busy brother.

I'm sad to leave Jack when I hug him before heading off for

our flight the following afternoon. It's been worth coming back just to see him again.

As our plane soars into the skies, the stewardess offers us a drink. Carol looks at her watch.

'I do believe it's happy hour,' she exclaims.

'Carol, it's only two o'clock.'

'Well, I'm happy and two o'clock is as good an hour as any. Two gin and tonics, please,' she replies. Who am I to argue? I'm too busy being delighted that I've got a buddy to share this trip with.

Callum meets us at JFK Airport, the result of a frantic call before we left Shanghai. This was turning into a regular family and friends outing. He smuggles us into his room at the Plaza.

'I see you're slumming it then,' Carol observes.

We bring him up to date with the latest instalments, then crash out on one of the two queen-size beds and sleep for the rest of the day. At seven o'clock, he wakes us.

'I've got to go to a premiere tonight of the new Tom Cruise movie. Do you want to come?'

The fact that we're up, showered, made-up and dressed in five and a half minutes gives him his answer.

Downstairs, a limousine the size of Newcastle is waiting for us.

'Sorry about this, ladies,' he actually looks embarrassed. 'I know it's naff, but my agent insists on it. It's all part of the image thing.'

Naff? Doesn't he realise that Carol and I *do* naff in a big way? I think we invented it.

Flashbulbs pop like fireworks as we walk along the red carpet and into the cinema. Fame at last. I just wish I'd lost ten pounds and had my nails done.

There are so many stars here, I can hardly watch the movie.

Sylvester's in the front row with Jennifer. Arnie's sitting just behind him with Maria. Jack and his harem are in the row in front of us. Sitting at the back are Tom and Nicole.

Carol nudges me. 'Don't suppose we can get popcorn and a hot dog, I'm starving.'

Someone who looks very like Richard Gere turns around and chides us for giggling.

The after-show party is at the Four Seasons, which makes the hotel in St Andrews look like a Travel Inn.

'What do we do now?' I whisper to Callum.

'Mingle. Be a social butterfly,' he jokes. 'Smile and nod a lot.'

A woman who is clearly no stranger to a plastic surgeon corners him. 'Callum, dahling, such a delight to see you.' Her air kisses are laughably wide from each side of his face. 'And who are your lovely companions?'

Callum introduces us.

'This is Delphine Di Angelo, agent to New York's finest.'

'*Divine* dress, dahling,' she tells me. 'Is it Dior?'

'Debenhams,' I reply.

Callum and Carol choke on their drinks, but Delphine is undaunted. She obviously thinks it's a *fahbulous* new designer that she hasn't discovered yet. She whisks Callum away.

'Don't worry, dahlings, I'll bring him back to you undamaged,' she reassures us, slipping her arm around Callum's shoulders.

He looks back at us and rolls his eyes. I'm so proud of him. I still can't believe that's my little brother over there. And he was so ugly as a child.

I turn to speak to Carol, but her eyes are following Callum. Oh, no. I've seen that look before, usually in the presence of a chequebook and an American Express card.

'Carol, I know what you're thinking. Stop it right now before I send you home to bed without any dinner.'

'It's your fault. You set the criteria for my next man.'

'But I didn't mean my brother. Carol, he's not equipped to deal with women like us.'

'Oh, I don't know. He looks pretty well equipped from where I'm standing.'

Her voice has gone all that husky, sexy way, so I slap her with a celery stick, but she continues.

'Look, Carly, he is under forty.'

'Mmmm.'

'And he's not *really* rich, not in the same league as my usual type.'

'Granted.'

'And he's so gorgeous that he doesn't need a trophy girlfriend.'

'True.'

'And I've known him all my life and I've always loved him to bits.'

'Okay.'

'And now I'm getting a stirring in my loins every time he looks at me. I first noticed it a couple of months ago in Kate's kitchen.'

'ENOUGH. Don't you dare give me a mental image of my gorgeous little brother having sex. You'll put me off my Bloody Mary.'

The more I think about it, though, the more it makes sense. They'd be great together. They are both in the same line of work, so they'd understand each other's schedules and pressures. They do know each other better than anyone, excluding family, and they're from identical backgrounds.

But then there are the potential down sides. If they lived together, they'd have to have separate bathrooms with huge mirrors, otherwise they'd never get out of the house in the mornings. They'd end up in the bankruptcy courts, having spent all their money in Harvey Nicks. And if they split up, I wouldn't know whose side to take.

How could I agree with, 'He's a complete bastard and he's ruined my life', when the subject was someone from the same womb? I can feel a crisis coming on. At least, for once, it doesn't involve my sex life.

I'm still deliberating on the dilemma when it's time to leave. We go to a late-night coffee house for decaf and toast. Within an hour, Carol and Callum are trying desperately not to gaze longingly into each other's eyes. I put my head in my hands. Both their lives will be ruined and it's all my fault.

We finally crash into bed at 2 a.m. – Carol and I in one bed and Callum in the other. I'm still wide awake, so I read the guest services manual cover to cover.

Carol is on the side nearest Callum and as I reach up to switch the light off, I see that they're holding hands across the space in the middle. I'm about to demand a change of positions, when I realise that they're both smiling in their sleep. They look so happy. I feel a lump in my throat. And it isn't the Toblerone from the minibar.

* * *

Callum leaves early for a shoot the next morning and Carol and I decide to treat ourselves to breakfast in bed. As we hoover up our scrambled egg, we discuss tactics and come up with a plan. We're going to call all the Lowerys in the phone book and then all film and video production companies listed in the Yellow Pages, not forgetting to try directory enquiries too.

Carol takes the room phone and I use her mobile after promising to pay the bill for it. Before I even start, I have a feeling that it's a lost cause. What are the chances of Phil even living in this city, never mind having a phone registered to his name?

Six hours later, I realise my premonition was correct.

I've had eight porno film companies, twenty-six offers to video my next wedding, christening or funeral and forty-seven bemused receptionists claiming that there are no employees of that name in their companies.

Carol has had eight potential leads, which, after relentless pursuit, turned out to be dead ends, one elderly man who pretended to be Phil just to have someone talk to and three accusations of being a stalker.

Directory enquiries were no use either – they didn't have any listings that weren't already in the book.

I try desperately to stay positive – I didn't come all this way to give up. But by the time Callum gets back, I'm considering hiring a plane with one of those banners flying behind it, saying PHIL LOWERY, CALL THE PLAZA, ROOM 202.

'Come on, ladies, I'm starving. We've got a table booked downstairs at seven.'

I look from Carol's face to Callum's and decide to pass, pleading nervous exhaustion. Let Romeo and Juliet have a night out on their own. Neither of them look too disappointed that I'm crying off.

Carol goes into the bathroom and emerges an hour later, looking like she just walked off the front cover of *Vogue*. As they leave together, I can't help hoping that they get it together. I'm over the shock of last night now and I know they would make each other happy.

I started this looking for a happy ever after, but I've realised it might not be mine.

* * *

I spend the night with a fruit basket and a remote control. I love American TV, but I'm going to give myself a migraine if I don't stop flicking from channel to channel. How does anyone ever decide what to watch?

Just after eleven, I hear footsteps in the corridor outside and quickly switch off the TV and lights.

Barbie and Ken burst in, giggling like kids.

Carol switches the light back on.

'Stop pretending to be asleep, Cooper. We went for a walk after dinner and got you *pizza*.'

Rumbled. I sit up as she fires the pizza box over to me like a frisbee.

Callum follows behind it and gives me a huge kiss.

'What's that for?' I ask him.

'Just for being you.'

'You mean pathetic, lonely and doomed to a life of misery?'

He laughs as he flicks the TV back on. David Letterman is warming up the crowd.

'So what's on the schedule for Cagney and Lacey tomorrow then?' he asks.

'I don't know, Callum. I've run out of ideas.'

Carol starts to make suggestions, but my attention is drawn back to the television.

'Now, ladies and gentlemen, straight from a record breaking national tour,' his voice raises in anticipation, 'Emmy award winning comedian,' the tension mounts, 'Mister PHIL LOWERY.'

Callum and Carol stop talking and turn slowly to face the screen. Pepperoni slides out of my open mouth and down my chin.

Callum finally speaks. '*That's* him? I recognise that guy. I spoke to him at a party last week, but I didn't catch his name. Hold on a minute.'

He reaches for the phone.

I'm still staring, transfixed. This can't be happening. This is all a dream. It's like when Pamela Ewing died in *Dallas* and then came back in the next series. I'm going to wake up tomorrow in my flat in Richmond and think of another excuse to phone in sick to work.

Callum replaces the receiver. 'Get up, quick and get dressed. Hurry up.'

'Where are we going?'

'Carly, this show is broadcast two hours before it goes out and afterwards they all head to the Rainbow Room for drinks. Now, move your bum.'

Twenty minutes later, we're outside the Rainbow Room. There's a very serious looking bouncer at the door.

'Sorry, folks we're fu— Oh, it's you, Mr Cooper, go right on in.'

I'm impressed. If only he wasn't my brother.

As we rise in the elevator, my heart is thundering. I still can't believe this is actually happening. It's one of those freak, once in a lifetime coincidences that you read about in magazines or see at the end of a rom com. Back in Shanghai Phil had said he wanted to try stand up and I'd told him time and time again he should do it. Looks like he'd made it in a big way. Huge.

Carol holds my hand until the sweat on my palms threatens to glue us together for life. I jump as the doors ping open.

We enter the crowded room, eyes squinting to adjust to the light. I search every corner, but he's not here.

Carol pulls at my sleeve. 'Isn't that him? The guy over at the bar, talking to the barman?'

My eyes follow hers, and in seconds I'm striding in his direction. I stand behind him.

'Gin and tonic, please, and a maple walnut chocolate chip to go.'

There's a pause, then he spins round. Before I know it, I'm in a bear hug and gasping for breath.

'I can't believe it's you! I thought I'd never see you again!' he blurts, causing the bemused barman to knock over a vodka bottle.

Over his shoulders, I can see Callum and Carol watching with huge, perfect, pearly white smiles.

'I missed you too, Phil. I lost your number and I had no way of finding you.'

'Never mind, babe, never mind. We've got all the time in the world to make up for it.'

Now this is a welcome. Maybe this time…

The tears are streaming down my face. I wipe them away and disentangle myself to introduce him to Callum and Carol.

I hear a scream from a nearby table, then a chair falling over. I turn to see an exquisite, dark-haired beauty running towards us.

'Miss Carly, Miss Carly!'

'LILY!'

I'm stunned, speechless and stuck to the floor. Beautiful, sweet Lily, my assistant manager at the club in Shanghai.

As she reaches us, Phil puts his arm around her and beams at me. 'Cooper, I'd like you to meet my wife.'

* * *

'You're joking!' Kate yells down the phone. 'Carly, I swear to God, if this baby is premature, it'll be your fault. There are only so many shocks I can take. So what happened next?'

'We went back to their apartment in Soho and sat up till dawn catching up. Turns out that Phil went to Champagne after I left Shanghai to see if I'd been in touch, got speaking to Lily and they were married and back in the States three months later.'

'And then?'

'Then he was working as the cameraman on a late night comedy show, decided to try it for himself and hit the big time. Fabulous career, fabulous wife and fabulous family. They've got two gorgeous kids and a Rottweiler called Cooper. Do you think I should be offended?'

'Definitely not. So what are you going to do now?'

'Well, I'm going to stay here with Phil and Lily for a while. It really is great seeing them again and I want to spend some time with them. They've said that I can have their spare room and it's just as well because if I don't get out of the Plaza soon and let Callum and Carol have sex, they're going to combust.'

There is a pregnant pause. Literally.

'Hold on, I have to sit down. What did you say?'

'Don't worry, Carol's going to call you later and give you a news update. Make sure that you're in a comfortable position, your legs are well crossed and the maternity ward is primed for your arrival – this one really is going to induce labour.'

'Mother of God, I can feel the contractions starting already. By the way, Jess hasn't found Tom yet, but she's still working on it.'

'Tell her I said thanks. I intend to head back to Hong Kong in a few weeks, but I can change my plan if she finds anything. I have to go, Kate. Can you let Jess and Sarah know the latest, and tell them I'll be in touch? Take care of yourself and give the kids a kiss for me.'

'I will. And, Cooper, don't be disheartened. There's still Sam and Tom. It's not over till the fat lady sings.'

I launch into a chorus of 'You Are My Sunshine'. She's still chuckling as she hangs up.

I hope she's right.

19

HEARTBREAKER – MARIAH CAREY

I crane my neck to see the neon jungle below us as we pass over Kowloon, then descend to land at Chek Lap Kok, Hong Kong's new state-of-the-art airport. Today is the twenty-eighth of October 1999 and I have renewed optimism that by the new millennium my life will be back on course. I feel totally relaxed after spending most of the month with Phil and Lily and good old positivity has kicked back in. This is it! I can feel it in my bones. Sam Morton is down there somewhere, waiting for me with open arms. The very thought of it makes my breath deepen and my face flush. I think I'm running a temperature.

When we land, I reach for my mobile phone to call Callum and let him know that I've arrived safely. I upgraded to an international calls package while I was in New York, thanks to my Visa card, in the hope I'd hear good news from Jess about Tom, but there's been nothing. I rummage through my bag, then abandon the subtle approach and tip out all the contents in the arrivals hall. A passing gent stares incredulously as two packets of condoms go flying across the floor. That'll be the optimism again.

Back to the phone. Where the hell is it? I'm sure I packed it last night. Bollocks. I must have left it at Phil's.

I find a payphone that takes credit cards and call the New York Plaza.

'Callum, it's me. I'm here and I'm in one piece.'

He's out of breath and sounds flustered. I don't want to contemplate why.

'Great. Listen, Phil stopped by with your...'

'Phone,' I finish the sentence for him. 'Hang on to it for me and whatever you do, don't let Carol near it, she'd bankrupt me.'

'Carly, you're already bankrupt,' he laughs.

'Thanks for the reality check. I'm still hoping the Y2K bug everyone is talking about will wipe out my credit card debt.' I hang up. He may find it funny now, but just wait until I'm calling him from jail to borrow bail money.

I call the Hong Kong Windsor to reserve a room, then jump in one of the taxis that's queued outside the terminal – no gold Rolls-Royces for me. I look around as I check in and decide not to even ask the room rate. I'm in Hong Kong, I'm surrounded by marble and chandeliers, there are several seriously wealthy looking people mingling around and I no longer get a staff discount here. This is another of those occasions where oblivion is bliss.

I consider asking if my old boss, the swivel-eyed misery, still works here, but frankly, I'd rather chew my own shoe than ask him for a discount on the room rate, so I hand over my credit card and take the hit.

Upstairs, I unpack for what I hope will be the last time. I never thought I'd say this, but travelling the globe is starting to wear me down. I wake up every morning and have to look out of the window to check what city I'm in.

Hell, I'm grumpy. Undefeated though, I shower, throw on a

red shift dress, and head down to 'Asia'. It would be too good to be true if Sam was still standing on the door and I found him with no searching whatsoever.

Indeed. Too good to be true. 'Asia' was gone and in its place was an incredibly chic seafood restaurant that, according to the menu, charged the price of a Mini Metro for something that was swimming in the ocean just a few days before.

Dejected, I decide to have a long bath and an early night. The world will be a sunnier place in the morning.

I'm wide awake at 4 a.m.. Obviously, I left my body clock somewhere over the ocean. I've counted sheep, recited the alphabet backwards and counted to ten thousand, all to no avail. I consider calling the manager, but I don't think talking to insomniac guests is in the *Guest Services Directory*.

I give up and call Jess from my bedside phone. She's back in London and going to work again, opting for public denial and hoping the whole scandal will fade sometime soon.

'How's things with Basil?'

'He's in therapy and publicly blaming the stress of work for his episode of diminished responsibility. His wife kicked him out and she was last seen dancing in Stringfellows with a French rugby player. I'm still playing hard to get. Let him grovel.'

'Why don't you come over here and join me? I could do with some company.'

'Thanks, Carly, but I've taken enough time off lately, what with fleeing the country. They're docking my wages for that already.'

'Docking your wages! They should have been paying you a bonus for shagging Basil. It wasn't in your contract.'

'I'll contact the government with your suggestion,' she jokes. 'Anyway, I've had no luck yet finding Tom. I traced his friends in

Canada, but they told me that he'd returned to Ireland. I think I'm going to have to call in Interpol.'

Given her connections, that wasn't completely outlandish, so I hoped she was joking.

'Thanks, Jess. You'll get your reward for all this eventually. I'll leave you my engagement rings in my will.'

'You gave them all back.'

'Ah, yep, I did. Will you settle for my shoe collection and custody of my goldfish?'

'It's a deal.'

Despite our exchange making me smile, I hang up feeling more than a little dejected. So far, Mission Manhunt sucks. I've met four of my potential partners and so far there's been one with no sexual chemistry, one is gay, one is a twisted cheat and the other is a lovely pal who's happily married. Maybe my claims of joining a nunnery weren't too far-fetched. Two more disappointments and I'd happily volunteer to be Sister Carly.

After four more sleepless hours, I searched for the old address book I'd bought years ago to replace the personal organiser I lost last time I was here. I found Sam's home number and called it. Disconnected. The way my luck is going, he's probably back in London, living round the corner from my old flat, and in a polygamous relationship with half the street. Nothing would surprise me.

Next, I try all the martial arts academies listed in the book. Nope, no Sam Morton.

I throw on a pair of jeans and a T-shirt and decide to try his old apartment. Maybe he's still there and has just changed his number.

I take the MTR to Causeway Bay. When I alight, I'm astounded by the changes. In front of me is a huge new shopping mall called Times Square. For a few moments I'm torn between looking for Sam or wandering round the designer shops. My credit cards start to tremble in my bag.

Stay focused.

I put my head down and charge past the mall. Get thee behind me, Satan.

As I turn into Sam's street, I spot a familiar face having an afternoon siesta. Huey, one of the lovely old guys who lived under the flyover, is still there. Good grief, he must be about 106.

He smiles as I approach. Either he recognises me or I look like a sure thing for a couple of dollars.

'Huey, lay ho ma?' I greet him with the only Cantonese I can remember.

His eyes light up and I know for sure he remembers me. He starts speaking rapidly and I look around in panic. I don't understand a word. I spot a jewellery shop across the road and dash over. Inside, I enlist the services of an assistant and drag him over to Huey's penthouse. Huey eyes him with suspicion and clams up.

'Please ask him if he remembers Sam, the Englishman who used to live in that building,' I ask, pointing to Sam's block.

He chatters to Huey and my hopes rise as Huey nods his head.

'Ask him if he still lives there.'

Another Cantonese monologue, but this time my elevator of optimism crashes back to the ground floor as Huey shakes his head. He still hasn't uttered a sound to the stranger.

'Ask him if he knows where he lives now.'

This time, Huey responds by shrugging his shoulders. This isn't going well. I ask the shop assistant to say 'Thanks', and turn to walk away. I haven't got more than ten feet when Huey shouts something.

'What did he say?' I ask the jeweller, who is now thoroughly fed up with this game and just wants to get back to his shop.

'He says that for fifty dollars he can tell you how to find the man you're looking for.'

I'm aghast. 'That's extortion! Shame on you, Huey.' But my money is already out of my purse and in his hand.

He talks to the translating gem dealer.

'He says that he still comes here every Friday evening to bring him beer.'

Friday! That's tonight.

'What time?' I realise that of course Huey doesn't wear a watch. 'Early evening. Or late?"

More chat.

'Early. Before the sun goes down. Just after rush hour.'

It's all I can do not to punch the air. Instead, I thank them both profusely, using lots of thumbs up to Huey. I slip him another fifty dollars and resolve to bring him some food when I come back later. I wonder what happened to his friends, but I think it's probably obvious. I reckoned they were both in their eighties when I was last here.

I head back to the MTR station to return to the hotel, thinking about the fact that Sam still looks out for the old man. I wonder if that kind of loyalty extends to ex-girlfriends who ran out on him too.

Back at the hotel, I spend the rest of the day preparing myself for the big reunion. I can't decide what to wear. Bearing in mind that I'll probably have to stand on a street corner waiting for Sam to arrive, I don't think that a black leather miniskirt is a wise choice. Not unless I want passers-by to throw money at me. Although, given my VISA bill, that wouldn't be the worst thing in the world.

In the end, I opt for the 'recent death in the family' look. Black three inch stiletto boots, black jeans and a shirt to match.

I take a taxi back to Causeway Bay; there's no way these boots will get me up and down the steps of the subway without danger to life. I arrive at exactly six o'clock and take up residence on the steps of Sam's old building. I wave across to Huey and he waves back, then shrugs his shoulders. I take that to mean that Sam hasn't come yet.

My legs are starting to shake, but I don't know if it's nervous excitement or because my jeans are too tight. The time drags by. Six thirty. Seven o'clock. Seven thirty. Eight fifteen.

He's not coming. He's heard I'm in town and he's gone into hiding.

I'm trying to decide how long I can sit here before getting arrested for vagrancy – twenty years, if Huey is anything to go by – when a silver Porsche turns in to the street. Flash git. People shouldn't be allowed to buy cars like that; it just makes the rest of us mere mortals feel inadequate.

Huey jumps up and the car stops beside him. He leans into the driver's window. So that's it. Huey has a drug habit and this is his dealer.

Suddenly, the driver's door flies open and Sam is running towards me. My chin bone drops to the pavement. God, I'd forgotten how magnificent he looked. His brown hair is still short and no stranger to styling gel, he's tanned and exquisitely muscular. He's a work of art. Someone should cast him in bronze and open him to the public. What had ever possessed me to leave this man?

'What did you do, Sam, rob a bank?' I splutter.

'Cooper! What the hell are you doing here?' How many times have men asked me that in recent months?

'I forgot my keys. I came back five years ago and you weren't in, so I've been sitting here ever since.'

His face cracks into a huge smile as he hugs me.

'No, really, why are you here?'

I can think of a thousand bullshit reasons but I'm tired of all the subterfuge and nonsense, so I go for compete honesty.

'I came to see you. It's a long story.'

I can see this catches him off guard, but he doesn't look horrified, so that's a bonus.

'Where are you staying?'

'At the Windsor.'

'That place is extortionate!'

'I know. My credit card cried when I checked in.'

'Look, that's crazy. Come and stay with me.'

I thought he'd never ask. I'm about to thank him when a flicker of something crosses his face, turning his grin to a frown. 'Shit, there's a slight problem.'

Here we go, I think, running through my past experiences. Which one is it? You're gay, you're married, you hate me, or you have to disappear to Canada. As for the question of whether there's still a sexual attraction, that was answered the moment I saw him.

'I need to go to work for a while tonight. Tell you what, I'll take you back to the Windsor and you can grab your stuff and head over to my place. I'll get back as soon as I can.'

I breathe a sigh of relief, sending the butterflies in my stomach into overdrive again. This could be good. It could be really, really good.

He drops me at the Windsor, gives me his new address and a set of keys, and I promise that I'll be waiting there for him tonight.

I pack my bags, check out and take a taxi to his apartment,

giddy with excitement. I scold myself. Have all my experiences so far taught me nothing? Be calm. Be wary. Take it easy. My optimism gene hears the warnings and decides to ignore them all.

When the taxi driver stops, I'm sure he's got the address wrong. Sam did rob a bank. The flat is on the Peak, the most expensive area on the island. It's in an ultra-modern block, with a red carpet under the awning leading to the entrance. There are two doormen in uniform waiting to open the doors for me. I can visualise myself living here. I am *SO* destined to end up in a place like this. When I say who I'm here to see, they immediately summon the lift.

'Welcome. Mr Morton called and said we should expect you.'

I flush. Giddy optimism is in charge yet again.

As I open the door to the flat, it just gets better and better. The floor is a light cream marble, the walls a pale shade of gold. Three of the walls have white leather sofas curving round them and in the centre is a low marble table big enough to throw a blanket on and sleep four. There are church candles on every surface and a chandelier that could illuminate Blackpool is suspended from the ceiling.

I move through to the dining area. The colour scheme is the same and I can't stop staring at the dining table. This wouldn't be out of place in a royal residence. There are twelve Chippendale chairs placed around a twelve foot mahogany table that I can see my reflection in. In the middle is a two foot tall bronze piece of art – a perfectly formed nude male body. I wonder if it's Sam's.

The surprises keep coming. I wander through to the master bedroom and gasp out loud. On one wall, there are three doors; one leading to a dressing room that's larger than the gents' department in Harrods, one leading to a sauna and the other to a marble bathroom with a bath you could swim laps in. On another wall is a multimedia centre, with television, hi-fi, video and laser disc. The bed is king size and covered in white silk. But it's the other side of the room that takes my breath away. There's a floor-to-ceiling window spanning the whole length of the room, with a view of Hong Kong that's normally reserved for postcards. This is a palace.

I don't know what to do with myself, what gadget to play with first. I decide on the sauna and Jacuzzi, then choose an Otis Reading CD from the collection of hundreds. By the time I've worked out how to switch the hi-fi on, the sauna is too hot and the Jacuzzi is too cold.

The telephone rings, then clicks on to the answering machine. I hear Sam's voice first. Just hearing his voice makes me hug myself in happiness.

'Hi, this is Sam Morton.' His voice is oh so sexy. 'Please leave your name, number and message after the tone and I'll call you back as soon as possible. Thank you.'

A female voice cuts in.

'Hi, Sam, this is Vivian.'

Who the fuck is Vivian?

'I know it's short notice, but I wonder if you're free on Saturday night?' she purrs. 'Call me.'

Call her? I'll kill her. Doesn't she know yet that he's officially off the market? Okay, so I've only been back for an hour and a half, but I'm already choosing hymns and planning the honeymoon.

Twenty minutes later, I'm blowing bubbles in the Jacuzzi when the phone rings again. If it's Vivian, then we have to have a serious chat.

'Sam, baby, this is Estelle,' her voice is husky, like a telephone sex line. 'I need you. Now. Call me back soon.'

I want to tear the phone out of the wall. But what did I expect? Sam is a gorgeous man; of course he's going to have women falling at his feet. In fact, I tell myself, it's probably a good thing that there's more than one because it means that he's not serious about either of them. That leaves plenty of room for little old me to step in and sweep him off to a life of bliss.

I'm lathering on enough body lotion to moisturise a small horse when the phone rings again. I groan inside. Please let it be his mother calling to ask if he wants her to send over sweaters for the winter.

'Hello, Sam, long time no see. This is Caroline. I'm in town for a couple of days and I'd simply love it if you could fit me in. Call me at the Sheraton.'

Okay, the joke's over. Is this Sam getting all the female bar staff at whatever pub he works in now to call up in some crazy attempt to make me jealous? Well, if so, it's working. Or did he finally start his martial arts school and these are all clients? Yep, that must be it. Makes total sense.

I take a book out of the bookcase and lie back on the bed – the very bed that, with a bit of luck, I'll be lying in with Sam tonight and every night from now on. This is finally it, I muse. All these months of blood, sweat and heartache have finally paid off. I know he won't have changed – he'll still be the sensitive, funny, intelligent guy that I fell in love with before. And I'm ready for it now. I'm ready for the whole marriage and ever-after bit. All the others were just trial and error to get me back to where I belong, here with Sam. I just hope he still feels the same. Then I remember the look on his face when he saw me sitting on the steps. He still loves me, I know he does.

I brush out my hair, reapply my make-up, then slip on a huge white robe that's hanging on the back of the bedroom door. I check my appearance in the mirror, practising my most seductive 'come over here and bite me' looks. I light the candles. Okay, lights, sounds and looks are taken care of. I'm ready.

* * *

At midnight I hear the now familiar ringing.

'Sam, this is Diane. I've had a good day today; I closed a deal that's made both my bank manager and me very happy indeed, so I've decided to treat myself to a night with my favourite escort. How about Monday? Let me know, darling.'

My coffee mug smashes to the floor. What did she say?

My heart starts to race. I frantically press every button on the answering machine and finally manage to play the message back. *'ESCORT'*. What was she talking about? She can't have had the wrong number, because she referred to Sam by name. Maybe she meant 'escort' in the old-fashioned sense, like my gran does when she talks about her courting days.

But then I look around and realisation dawns. My stomach does a spin cycle. Who am I trying to kid? The Porsche, the millionaire's row apartment...

I close my eyes. I am so stupid. My head is spinning and I want to throw up and I suddenly feel very sorry for myself. I need fresh air and a brandy, so I pour one and go out on to the balcony. I slump to the floor and cry until there isn't a drop of fluid left in my head. I'm exhausted. I'm gutted. And I've absolutely had enough of this ridiculous bloody quest. How insane had I been to actually think it could work?

Sam finds me there an hour later.

'Carly?'

I don't answer him, just stare into the skyline. There's a long pause. Then a groan.

'How did you find out?' He sounds terrified, devastated. Good.

'You mean that you're a hooker?' I say, and the challenge in my voice makes him recoil. Another pause.

'I prefer "escort",' he whispers.

'I bet you fucking do. How did this happen?' I ask, my words tight and stilted. 'You were the most moralistic person I'd ever met.'

But he's gone. I sit outside until my teeth start to chatter. This never happens in the movies. The heroines gaze into the darkness, looking serene and poignant, they never get swollen eyes and snot that refuses to stop.

I go back into the lounge. He's sitting in the candlelight, looking defeated and weary. For a moment I can't speak. In some crazy way, I feel like I've never loved him more. He senses that I'm there and starts to speak slowly, in a low, quiet voice.

'After you left, I couldn't bear it. I didn't know what to do with myself. Everything hurt so much and I was so angry. I would go to work every night and watch all the couples, all looking so happy, and I couldn't believe that it wasn't us. One night, one of the women that I trained asked me to go to a company dinner with her. It was a "partners" function and she didn't want to go on her own. I felt sorry for her, so I went. And afterwards, she insisted on paying me for my time, said it was just like a personal training session.

'The next week, she called again. Then her friends started calling and, before I knew it, I was booked out every night. Gradually I charged more and more, but the business just kept coming in. Soon after, I gave up everything else. I was making more money than I could ever have dreamt of. And it was so easy.'

His devastated expression makes guilt and sorrow seep from my pores.

'So you never opened the martial arts school?'

'No,' he answers, and there is more sadness and regret in that one word than I can bear.

My silence prompts him to continue.

'At first, it was just dinner and conversation, then somewhere along the line it became... more. I didn't care. They were buying my time, I was already selling myself, so what did it matter? I was convinced I'd never fall in love again and that part turned out to be true...'

A knife twists in my chest.

'... So now this is who I am. And it works for me. No strings, no emotion, no hurt. In a few years' time, when I don't look so good, I'll take the money and run. I'll retire and I'll never work again. Things happen, Carly. We don't always end up how we'd imagined in life.'

Don't I know it, I think sadly.

He gets up and walks past me to the bedroom.

'I understand that you want to leave. You can sleep in the spare room tonight. I'll take you back to the hotel in the morning.'

I sit down on the sofa and think for a long time. The rage has dissipated now and I just feel empty. What right do I have to judge him? He's not a bad person. He doesn't hurt anyone. It's not his fault that my dreams have just been shattered; it's not as if he promised me anything or was unfaithful to me. If anything I should be drowning in guilt because running out on him led him to this life. It was his choice, but my actions played a part. And as for the way I'm feeling right now, I've brought all this upon myself with some crazy idea that I'll probably regret for the rest of my life. I'm no better than him – we've both fucked things up.

What do I do now? Go home and face the music, I suppose. What else is there?

I get up and head towards the spare room, but as I pass Sam's room, I can see him lying in bed, staring at the ceiling. I change my direction and slip in beside him. More than anything else in the world right now, I want to feel him close to me.

He looks at me in surprise.

'The spare room is next door,' he murmurs.

'Yes, well, my sense of direction always was crap.'

He squeezes me like he never wants to let me go. After a few minutes, I feel his hand move slowly down my back. I can't believe I'm in the same bed as him.

'Carly,' he whispers, 'does this mean...?'

'Don't take this personally, Sam. I love you, but I wouldn't touch your privates without rubber gloves and a surgical mask.'

He's still laughing when I slip off to sleep.

The next morning over breakfast, I tell him my story; every last detail. He alternates between laughter, shock, outrage, concern and sadness.

'So, you see, now it's over and I've got a choice – I can either disappear, change my name and go and do missionary work in deepest Mongolia for the rest of my life, or I can go home and start again. Mongolia's tempting, but I'd miss my pals, so I guess I'll go home.'

He thinks for a moment. 'Or you could stay here.'

'And do what, be your pimp? I haven't got a white suit or a gold medallion.'

'Cooper, I'm serious. Stay here. You could help me, really. I need someone to organise me and do stuff like pay the bills, take my calls and sort out my finances. C'mon, Carly, think about it. It would be great.'

I consider the idea. Could I live in the same house as him? After last night's revelations, my libido is now a 'no-fly zone', so that wouldn't be a problem. Could I handle seeing him coming home every night, knowing that he'd just had sex with a paying customer? I think I'd just refuse to think about that. And then there are the living arrangements. The choice is either sleeping on a camp bed in Kate's junk room in the British winter or living in the sunshine in a luxury Hong Kong penthouse. Mmmm. Give me two and a half seconds to contemplate that one.

'Tell you what, I'll stay until Christmas. I need to go home then to spend it with my friends. Kate's baby is due around then and if all goes to plan we're having a very swish, extremely elegant millennium party in her back garden that I wouldn't miss for anything. But I'll stay until then, okay?'

He reaches over and cuddles me, spilling my coffee and squashing my croissant in the process. Well, it's probably a good day to start a diet anyway.

I call Kate to tell her what's happening.

'Well, what's the latest? Should I order a maternity brides-maid's dress?' she asks.

'Sorry, Kate, that's one treat that you're going to have to miss. Listen, I won't tell you what's happened over the phone because your waters will break, but it's safe to say that Sam and I won't be marching up the aisle in this lifetime.'

'Oh, babe, I'm so sorry. Are you okay?'

'I am, honestly. I'll put it all in a letter to you. But I am going to stay with Sam for a while longer. Have you got a pen and I'll give you his number? Oh, never mind, I'll put that in the letter too. Have you got any news on your due date?'

'Still Christmas Eve,' she says, groaning. 'Although I'm the size of a small planet, so I wouldn't mind going early.'

'Don't you dare. I promise I'll be back by then so just keep your legs crossed, ok?'

'Ok.'

'Good. Now go and lie down and tell my new niece or nephew that I love it and it's never allowed to follow in my footsteps in any way.'

Her chuckle makes me smile. 'Oh, we covered that one a long time ago,' she teases. When she hangs up, I sit down to write the letter I promised her, but then get distracted by a flurry of calls for Sam and I never do get it written. Instead I settle for sending postcards over the next couple of weeks, hastily bought in tourist shops as Sam and I explore Hong Kong together again. That's the great thing about being an escort – no daytime work. He cuts down his evening shifts to four nights a week to give us even more time for fun.

We must look like the perfect couple as we wander around, laughing and joking, often with his arm slung casually over my shoulder. Four different people ask us if we're on our honeymoon. If only they knew. I spend half my time giving Sam messages like 'Daphne wants to book you for tomorrow night and she says can you wear the black leather thong.'

Two weeks later, I'm feeling happier than ever. Sam's great company. He's everything I remember and more. He makes me laugh (except when he forces me to go on mid-morning jogs that leave me requiring oxygen), he never stops and he's full of ideas about what we're going to do next. Life's just one big adventure again.

I do have the occasional pang of regret that things didn't work out differently. But then, knowing me, I'd have messed it up somehow anyway. Let's face it, this quest has proved that I am to relationships what China is to human rights. When I get home, I'm going to stick with my new lifestyle choice and continue with a celibate existence... until the next man comes along.

That night, Sam cooks me dinner and puts an envelope in front of me. I open it to find two tickets to Thailand. I stare at him open mouthed.

'Don't worry, Carly, no strings. I haven't had a holiday for years and I thought I'd take advantage of you being here to kidnap you for a few weeks. Call it an early Christmas present.'

For a split second I consider saying no. But what's the harm? I am his personal assistant now – I have to be there to rub suntan lotion on his back.

I call Kate to report in, but there's no answer. I try Carol: no answer. I dial Jess's number: same result. It must be a girl's night out in London. I call Sarah in Glasgow. No answer there either. Michael picks up and we have a quick chat, but I can hear lots of explosions in the background so I can tell he's distracted by whatever video game he's using to conquer a universe. I feel a pang of homesickness. I miss him. I miss Callum. I miss my pals. If only they were here.

I call Kate again and leave a message on her machine. 'Kate, it's me. Hope your bun is baking nicely. Listen, I was just calling to catch up, so tell all the girls I send my love and I'm missing you all madly. Sam and I are going to Thailand for a few weeks, so don't worry if you don't hear from me for a while – I'll be on a beach getting sand on my arse. And no, I'm not going to be a "kept woman" – I've got a couple of grand left on my Amex card so I'm going to blow that. I promise that when I get back, I'm going to be a reformed character!'

I get a mental picture of Kate's face as she dismisses that one out of hand.

* * *

Thailand is bliss. We start in Bangkok, before travelling up north to Chiang Mai and then south to Koh Samui and Phuket. We spend long lazy days by the beach, with only windsurfing and waterskiing to rouse us from our sunloungers. At night, we hit the bars before stopping for food and then walking for miles.

The irony of this situation strikes me – here I am in the land of more brothels than bakers, with a male hooker for company. The Mighty Romano couldn't have predicted this one.

Sometimes I catch myself looking at Sam and wondering if we could make it work, but I know we couldn't. It's not that I'm being judgemental, but somewhere along the line, all physical attraction to him has vanished. His line of work extinguished that fire and it refuses to relight.

Sam is true to his word – there are no big seductions, no innuendo and no quick gropes when he thinks I'm sleeping. I guess his tastes run more to high-powered career women these days. No, it's definitely purely platonic. But does he really have to wear those tiny swimming trunks?

I wake up one morning and realise that it's the third week of December. Where has the time gone? The last few weeks have flown by.

I know it's time to do some serious thinking. I briefly consider postponing the use of my brain until I've had another day in the sun – a kind of mental avoidance strategy – but I can't put it off any longer.

The notion of staying in Hong Kong with Sam is tempting, but ultimately crazy. Apart from the fabulous surroundings, it's no different from selling bog rolls for a living – only the product has a lot better packaging.

My stomach tightens like a drum as I realise that I have to accept that my adventure is over. I've failed. Crashed and burned. So what now? I guess it's back to the UK to eat enough humble pie to make me clinically obese.

But do I regret it? I consider this for a few moments, then a smile overtakes my face as I decide that I don't. Okay, so I'm skint. And yes, I've achieved nothing except a bad haircut (when will this bloody grow out????), a suntan and a decidedly bruised arse from landing on it with such frequency. But at least I tried. A wave of consolation sweeps over me. At least I'm not still sitting in my kitchen in an ancient dressing gown, wondering about what might have happened if only I'd given it one last shot.

Let's face it – apart from money, I haven't lost anything except a job that I didn't like anyway, a flat that was the size of a garden shed and my friends' confidence in my judgement and maturity. That was always shaky anyway.

I weigh up the gains. We found Sarah again – this whole escapade was worth it just for that alone. Carol had sex with a man under fifty – another major breakthrough – although I still refuse to think too deeply about that because the man in question is my brother. Jess has made progress in forcing Basil to make a definite decision (no mean feat when we're talking about politicians) and Kate has had something to take her mind off the fact that she's now bigger than a fully grown hippo.

So do I regret it? Not one insane, traumatic, tear-shedding, fantastic moment of it. Now I just need a recovery plan.

The sun is now streaming in through the window and I'm starting to sweat, so I head for the shower and turn the cold water on full blast. Priorities. From now on, men will be the least of my worries. There're one or two small issues like gainful employment, a roof over my head and a payback plan to the credit card companies to sort out first.

January is taken care of. I'll spend it with Kate, helping to take care of the baby while I lick my wounds and try to avoid anyone who'll be curious to know about the results of my mission. I'm not quite ready for a full public humiliation yet.

I'll apply to prospective employers and I'll explain my travels by saying I was on a retreat to 'find myself'. That's so trendy that it's bound to get me a job in the City. With the job taken care of, I'll promise to donate every penny to my debts (except for food, drink and shoes money – that's completely reasonable). Eventually, I'll find a flatshare with at least two single guys who belong to football and rugby teams and hold regular parties. I may have failed miserably, but that doesn't mean life is over.

'Sam, it's time for me to go home,' I tell him that morning over breakfast.

He looks forlorn. 'I was wondering when we'd get around to that. I was hoping you'd changed your mind. We could just hide out here for ever.'

Tempting. So tempting.

But I know I've got to go back, I've got more battles to fight. Most of them with credit card companies and the small claims court.

* * *

The first thing I do when we land in Hong Kong is call Kate to let her know I'm booking my flight home.

The phone rings for an age before a groggy voice finally answers. Shit. I forgot about the time difference.

'Kate, it's me.'

She springs to life. 'Cooper, where the hell have you been? We've all been bloody frantic and we had no way of getting in touch with you – you didn't send us your number and then we got the message to say you were in sodding Thailand.'

'Okay, I'm down on my knees and begging forgiveness. I'm really sorry, Kate. Don't be mad, it's bad for a woman in your condition. Anyway, what's all the panic about? You know I'll be back for Christmas.'

'Yes, but I didn't think you were leaving it to the last minute!'

Didn't she know me at all?

'This baby could come early and I want you here when it's born. I'll need someone to help with the ironing.'

'That rules me out. I wouldn't even know how to switch an iron on.'

'Also, Joe Cain called yesterday, looking for you.'

'I forgot to tell you I gave him your number,' I say apologetically, but she is already firing on.

'He said there's been a big mistake and he has to see you. I told him you'd be back for Christmas, so he's on his way over here.'

'Why?'

'Who knows? Carly, he's never met me in his life, he's hardly going to give me all the gory details. And, most importantly of all, we're going to a wedding on the 21st. Or at least, you're definitely going, and I'll be there as long as this little babe comes either really early or bang on time.'

'There's no way we're going to a wedding three days before your due date,' I tell her, surprised she'd be up for something so ridiculous.

'Eh, refusal isn't an option.'

'Why? Whose wedding is it?'

There's a pause.

'Callum and Carol's. They're getting married in Scotland, at Loch Lomond'

'WHAT?!!'

'Callum's been going crazy trying to find you. There was a cancellation at the hotel they wanted. Carol was going to knock it back because it was so close to my date, but I wouldn't let her, so they snapped it up but Callum says he's postponing it if you're not here. And Carol's at her wits' end – you're the chief bridesmaid.'

'Oh my God. Kate, I'll be there. If I have to hijack a Cessna, I'll be there. Tell them both I'm over the moon for them and I'm sorry I've caused all this hassle and I'm on my way. Kate, I have to go. I have to phone the airport. Just hang on till I get there.'

Oh. My. God. Carol and my brother were getting married. This was amazing. Incredible. The best thing I'd ever heard.

I dial the airport and speak to every airline that flies to the

UK. If one more person tells me in a patronising voice that they're fully booked because this is the busiest time of the year, I'll go down there and slap them. Don't they realise that with the money I've spent on flights over the last six months, I could have bought a small airline?

I finally manage to reserve a seat on Air Bangladesh. I didn't even know Bangladesh had an airline. Presuming the plane doesn't run out of fuel mid-air, get hit by storms over the ocean, or have to divert due to a new war in Eastern Europe, I'll arrive in London at 6 a.m. on the 21st. A connecting flight to Glasgow will see me back on Scottish soil by 9 a.m.. Plenty of time for the 3 p.m. wedding.

I call Kate back and give her the details. 'Cutting it fine, but it could work. We're all heading up by car the day before the wedding, so we'll see you there. We'll bring Joe with us. And, Coop—'

'Yep?'

'Don't balls this up.'

I thank her for the warning as I hang up the phone. I turn to see Sam looking sad and I do the mature, adult thing and burst into tears.

He asks me what's wrong, concern written all over his face. How can I explain it? I'm going back to a wedding and, much as I'm ecstatic for Callum and Carol, I'd hoped that the next wedding I'd be going to would be mine. Instead, I'll have to go back and tell the whole world on the first day that I arrive that I've been an abject failure. And not only have I not found the man of my dreams, but I'll be the only pathetic person at the wedding who hasn't even got a partner. I'll be publicly humiliated.

Sam tries to comfort me, but I'm inconsolable. Until I have an idea.

'Sam, come with me, please. Be my boyfriend for the day. Just get me through the wedding without having to suffer the indignity of having to explain that my grand plan was a big fat failure. Please, Sam, please come.'

He's shocked. I can tell by the way his mouth is open, but someone's pressed the mute button. After a few moments, he finally speaks.

'You're joking, Carly. How could I do that? You seriously want me to come back with you and spend the whole day pretending to be your boyfriend. It's insane.'

'Sam, I hate to point out the obvious, but last time I checked, you *were* an escort. Look on me as a client – I'm enlisting your services and we don't even have to do the nudity stuff.'

He laughs and shrugs his shoulders. 'I knew there had to be a catch.'

20

LIVIN LA VIDA LOCA – RICKY MARTIN

We reach the airport with three hours to spare – a result of my paranoia that we'll miss the plane due to getting a taxi driver with no sense of direction, the taxi breaking down, or a freak monsoon that will flood the road to the airport. Stranger things have happened to me.

We check in and head for the departure lounge, which has a stunning Christmas tree that twinkles from floor to ceiling. Christmas! I've barely given it a second thought. It suddenly strikes me that I won't have time to buy presents when I get home, so I send Sam to the bar and embark on a trolley dash that leaves skid marks on the floor.

I hit Gucci first. Ties for Callum and Bruce and a T-shirt for Michael. That's the men taken care of. The women aren't so easy. Carol is a nightmare to buy for – what do you get the woman who has everything, other than a lifetime membership to Shopaholics Anonymous? I spot a beautiful gold bracelet in the jewellery section of the duty-free, next to a tray of gold initials. I buy two C's, for Callum and Carol, and have them added to the bracelet, thinking that at least I'm getting to flex my romantic side, even if it's for someone else.

I search frantically for something for Kate, Sarah and Jess, but nothing appeals to me. Sod it, back to the jewellers. Three gold bracelets later, I reach for my credit card to pay. The assistant runs it through the machine, then looks up, embarrassed. My Visa card has been rejected. Oh, the indignity. I turn a mild shade of purple and hand her my Mastercard. Same result – no authorisation for payment. I look around to check that nobody in the store is watching me and that the manager isn't on the phone to the fraud squad. I'm so mortified that I stare at the floor as I hand her my Diners Card. I look like I need to pee because I've got my fingers, my arms *and* my legs crossed. The machine spits my card out like a fish bone. My panic is reaching hysteria. I curse myself for spending my teenage years in school, instead of in Marks & Spencer's learning to shoplift.

It's my last hope. My hand trembles as I pass over my American Express card. Even the shop assistant is willing it to work; such is her pity for this desperate woman in front of her. I close my eyes. I can't look, it's too painful. Kerching! The machine kicks into life and starts to print the receipt. YES! A cheer goes up from behind the counter and I open my eyes to see four shop assistants, all with their hands raised in triumph.

I decide to push my luck.

American Express card in hand, I buy a brooch for Maw Walton, and a case of Jack Daniel's for Paw. Almost done. Over to the toy section. I find a Barbie and Martial Arts Ken for Zoe and a two foot wide model of the Starship Enterprise for Cameron. Auntie Carly's credit card holds out and I stagger to the bar, laden down like a packhorse. Sam rolls his eyes in amazement as I slump down beside him.

'Sam, I'll love you for ever if a gin and tonic appears in front of me in the next ten seconds.'

Bing-bong. The PA system interrupts us.

'Air Bangladesh regrets that the 10.45 p.m. flight to London Heathrow is now subject to a three hour delay. We do apologise for this inconvenience, which was caused by the late arrival of the incoming flight.'

NO! Don't do this to me, I can't bear it. My life is over. If I'm late, my friends will hate me and my family will disown me. Mongolia suddenly seems like a good option.

I look up at Sam. 'Better make that a double.'

Three hours later, I'm wobbling in my seat and singing 'I'm Getting Married in the Morning.' Sam's doing backing vocals.

Bing-bong. 'Would the final remaining passengers, Miss Cooper and Mr Morton, flying to London Heathrow on Air Bangladesh flight BG2234, please make their way to Gate 41 as the flight is about to depart.'

Fuck! Where's gate 41?

We spring up, grab the bags and start running. Two minutes later, my legs hurt, my head is pounding, sweat is running down my back and we're still only at gate five. I spot an airport worker in an electronic buggy.

'STOP,' I scream as I jump on, followed immediately by Sam. 'It's a matter of life and death! Gate 41 and step on it!'

We stagger onto the plane, hot, sweaty and bedraggled. The stewardess eyes all my packages and I know she's about to tell me that I've got too much hand luggage. I stare at her, daggers shooting from my eyes and pinning her against the wall. *Don't even go there*, I telepathically tell her, *I'm a woman on the edge*.

She picks up the telepathic signal and lets me past.

We stow our luggage with some help from three flight attendants and find our seats. I snuggle down into Sam's shoulder.

He whispers in my ear. 'Carly, don't go to sleep, I want to talk to you.'

I straighten up to face him as he fumbles in his pocket. He pulls out a tiny black box and opens it. My hand flies to my mouth. Nestled in velvet in the centre of the box is my engagement ring, the one I left on his bedside table all those years ago. My eyes fill up.

'Sam, I can't...'

'Don't say a word, Carly. I've got a speech all prepared and I need you to listen.'

I bite my bottom lip and nod.

'I want you to have this back. You deserve it. The last few weeks have been the best of my life and I want you to know that. This is just to say thanks. Nothing's changed, Carly. I still love you more than I could ever tell you. I'd marry you tomorrow if you'd let me.' He pauses and swallows.

The flight attendant stares in amazement at the couple huddled over an engagement ring, both crying their eyes out.

Sam slips the ring on my finger and continues. 'But I know that's not going to happen. I know that everything that's happened over the years has made that impossible. But I want you to have this anyway, just in case you ever change your mind.'

I pull him over and hug him tightly, then kiss away his tears, my stomach in knots.

What do I do? I know I love him. I know that we could be so happy together. But I just can't do it, can I? I think for a few moments. Maybe I could. Why not? Maybe I could just forget what's happened and we could start afresh, somewhere that rich females don't automatically look for their chequebook and Filofax when they see him coming.

I look down at the ring. I'm not ready to decide on this.

'I'm sorry, Sam, I think you're right. I don't think it could ever happen. But can I have a few days to think about it?'

He nods his head and pulls me into his arms.

The air hostess flies over. 'Excuse me, I couldn't help noticing. Congratulations! Oh, it's so romantic. Can I bring you some champagne with our compliments to help you celebrate?'

Who am I to dispel her excitement? Champagne is exactly what I could do with right now. I can taste it already. I smile at her and nod.

'That would be lovely, thank you.'

* * *

Twelve hours later, we touch down at Heathrow. Sam and I steamroller our way through to the transit area. I collapse, breathless, over the British Airways desk.

'Cooper and Morton,' I gasp. 'We were booked on the 7 a.m. to Glasgow this morning, but our flight from Hong Kong was delayed. I need two seats on the next available flight.'

'I'm sorry, Miss Cooper, but there's a problem—'

'I DON'T CARE IF THE FLIGHTS ARE FULL,' I yell.

Everyone in the lounge stops to stare.

I take a deep breath and try to bring my heart rate down from a level that will induce a coronary. I try again, this time in a semblance of a reasonable voice.

'Look, I'm sorry, but this really is an emergency. I need to get to Scotland this morning, so I don't care if I have to pay double, just please get me on the flight.'

'Miss Cooper, you don't understand. It's not that the flights are full. Glasgow Airport is fogbound, so no planes can land. We do anticipate it clearing in the next couple of hours, though, so I can book you on to the first available flight. I just can't tell you when it will leave.'

A couple of hours? My head bangs down on to the desk. A couple of hours? Callum and Carol will be back from their honeymoon before I get there.

All I can do is pray to the weather gods.

We take our boarding passes and sit under an information screen, willing it to flash that the flight is cleared for departure. I sit. I stand. I pace the floor. I rip up tissues. I pick up a newspaper. Can't concentrate. I put it back down. I look at the clock – surely it must be wrong; it's moving far too slowly. I pace again. Hurry up. Hurry up.

At twelve o'clock, I call Kate's mobile.

'Kate, I'm stuck in London. Glasgow Airport is fucking fogbound,' I wail. 'I don't know if I'll make it. Where's the ceremony?'

'It's at the Lomond Manor Hotel. We're there already – we're in the hairdressing salon just now. Hold on, Carol wants to speak to you.'

'Cooper, if you want to stay attached to your limbs, you'd better get here. Callum's going ballistic and your mother is hyperventilating. I can't believe I'm joining this family, I must be nuts. Now, get here and make it faster than a speeding bloody arrow.' It's on the tip of my tongue to correct her, but I don't have the heart.

Instead I hang up and slump down the wall, staring into space. This is the worst day of my life.

Twenty minutes later, Sam rushes over and pulls me to my feet, telling me that the flight is taking off. I raise my eyes to heaven in thanks, then run after him.

At 1.40 p.m., we start our descent to Glasgow. I pull out my make-up mirror and check my appearance. Oh, good grief. My hair is standing on end due to four hours of trying to pull it out. I scrape it back, attempting and failing to look like one of the goddesses in Robert Palmer's 'Addicted To Love' video. The face, however, is irreparable. The combination of alcohol, fluid retention and outbursts of sobbing have left my eyes puffed up like marshmallows. There's only one thing for it. Dark glasses. I slip them on. I'm now like a rock star trying to be inconspicuous and standing out like a sore thumb. There isn't much call for sunglasses in Glasgow in December.

We gather up our collection of plastic bags, dash through to the reclaim area for our cases, then charge through customs. Don't even think about stopping us! But there's nobody there. They're obviously all away at their Christmas party.

We run to the front of the taxi queue and jump into the first cab, to indignant shouts from those waiting in line. I shrug apologetically, but carry on regardless.

I tell the driver that there's fifty quid for him if he can get us to Loch Lomond by two-thirty. Twenty-five minutes. It's been done before, but only by Concorde.

* * *

At exactly two thirty five, we race down the driveway of the Lomond Manor Hotel and screech to a halt at the front door. He missed it by five minutes, but I throw fifty quid at the driver for his effort.

I lunge out the door to see Callum pacing up and down. He screams, throws his arms out, and comes rushing towards me, forgetting to apply the brakes as he reaches me. We sprawl across the ground and he lands on top of me – yet another moment of indignity. After hugs, kisses, and vows of 'I knew you would make it', I throw him off, spit the gravel out of my mouth and jump up. I ask Callum to take care of Sam.

'Pleased to meet you, mate,' says Callum, pumping Sam's hand. 'Er, who are you?'

'Sam Morton. I'm Carly's, em, well, I'm her boyfriend.'

Callum gives me the girls' room number and I bound upstairs. When I reach the room, I throw the door open, giving Jess, who was standing behind it, concussion.

'I believe you're missing a bridesmaid.'

A collective shriek shakes the foundations of the building as we converge into a team hug.

Eventually, I disentangle myself and take a step back to survey the sight before me. Carol, mascara now smudged, is just the most beautiful bride I've ever seen. She's wearing an ivory silk sheath that is strapless and fans out into a train at the bottom. The edges are trimmed with pearls, as are her long silk gloves. Her hair is loose, in glossy dark tendrils that cascade down her back. On the top of her head is a magnificent pearl and diamond tiara and she's holding a massive bouquet of white lilies. She's breathtaking.

I turn to the girls. Jess and Sarah are wearing deep sapphire blue, sleeveless silk dresses, which fall from a high neckline in a slim-fitting column to their calves. They're both stunning and all traces of the sad, exhausted Sarah I'd met back in April are gone. She's bright eyed, gorgeous and radiating such happiness my heart swells. Kate also looks glorious, in an identical dress, but hers is punctuated in the front with what looks like a spacehopper.

'Good grief, Kate, you look like you've got the groom under there.'

She throws a hairbrush in my general direction. Still, at least she's got somewhere to rest her flowers if she tires of carrying them.

Carol pulls out a hanger with another bridesmaid's dress on it and thrusts it at me, ordering me to change at once. She's getting bossier now that we're almost sisters.

I quickly throw it on, grab a bouquet of bluebells from the windowsill and announce that I'm ready.

The others stand and we converge in the middle of the room for one last hug.

I kiss Carol. 'I'm so glad you're marrying Callum. Welcome to the family.'

Oh no, more mascara adjustments required all round.

As we finally move towards the door, Kate nudges me. 'Cooper, I think you should remove the sunglasses now, you look like a bodyguard.'

I'd forgotten all about them. I take them off and chuck them behind me.

Kate takes another look at my face.

'On second thoughts, maybe you looked better with them on,' she laughs.

* * *

We make our way downstairs and pause at the doorway of the ballroom while someone runs to tell the organist to start the music. I look at the backs of two hundred heads. There's Mum in the corner, wearing a hat that looks like a frisbee. The kids will be playing with that before the night is out. Who's that sitting next to her? On her left is a blond hulk of a man with Slavic features. Ivan, I suspect. On her right is Sam, now changed into a tuxedo and easily tying with Callum for the award of 'Best Looking Man in the Room'. Mum's obviously beside herself, because her head is whirling from side to side. I think she's overcome by the close proximity to that much testosterone.

I spot my dad. He's easy to find because he's the only one slumped at an angle on his chair. Obviously, his partner for the night is Jack Daniel's. Luckily, Michael, looking gorgeous, is sitting on his left in what must be the best man's seat, so at least he's propping Dad up. I can't wait to see what will happen when the music starts and Michael stands up.

Right on cue, the first bars of 'Here Comes The Bride' resound through the room. Michael jumps to his feet and a bewildered Dad lands in a heap on the floor, much to the amusement of the congregation and the disgust of my mum. No change there, then.

I'm just about to take the first step, when I hear Jess take a sharp intake of breath. I turn around to see her looking panic-stricken.

'What's up?' I whisper.

'I forgot to tell you, I found Tom McCallum. I invited him over 'cause I figured you'd want to see him. He's here somewhere.'

My thumping heart drowns out the music. Where is he? As we walk up the aisle, I maniacally search the faces of the people in each row.

Oh, no. NO. What the hell is going on? There's Joe Cain, sitting in the back row, looking pleadingly at me. And shit! In front of him is Doug Cook. This can't be happening. I turn my head to the other side and the first thing I see is Phil Lowery's smiling face. This is a conspiracy! My heart is now pumping so fast that blood is gushing through my body like a burst dam. This can't be happening to me.

I can see Sam playing the worried fiancé, watching me with a face full of concern because it must be obvious that I'm about to have a heart attack. Then, just when I think it can't possibly be any worse, life takes another nose dive. Nick Russo is sitting next to my gran. What the *hell* is he doing here? Somebody find a gun and shoot me, please.

Then I spot him. I think. It's hard to tell; I hardly recognise him. Yes, it is him. Sitting two rows from the front, looking at least seventy pounds heavier than he was the last time I saw him, is Tom McCallum. We make eye contact and he grins warmly, and I hope he realises that my panicked expression isn't down to him. It's down to all of them.

So this is what it's come to. What if... all my ex-boyfriends turned up at the same place, at the same time? What if... I made a sharp exit through the nearest window and hitch-hiked to Mongolia in a blue bridesmaid's dress?

I'm sweating so much that I'm in danger of making damp patches on my dress. Luckily, it's a dark colour, so it might not be too obvious. I could have bathed in Sure Extra Dry and I'd still be sweating.

The ceremony passes in a blur. All I can feel is six pairs of eyes boring into my back. Six pairs of eyes that belong to guys who either want to talk to me, kidnap me, marry me or kill me. I feel faint.

Please don't let me pass out in the middle of Callum and Carol's wedding. They'd never forgive me.

* * *

'I, Carol Sweeney, take Callum Elvis Cooper (yes, I know it's ridiculous, but he was apparently conceived during a rendition of 'Love Me Tender'), to be my lawfully wedded husband, to have and to hold, in sickness and in health, for richer and poorer, to the exclusion of all others, for as long as I live.'

She had her fingers crossed at the 'poorer' bit.

Callum repeats the vow, looking at Carol with such raw adoration that I suddenly have goosebumps. This is what it should be like. This is the kind of love that you need to spend the rest of your life with someone.

A jolt runs though me. What had I been thinking? If I had felt this before with any of the guys, then I'd never have left them in the first place. If they had been right for me, then I'd still be with them, not hunting them down in some sad attempt to recreate a feeling that never existed. Or had it? Oh God, I'm so confused. And it's not helped by the fact that I've been naked with at least six of the men in this room.

'I now pronounce you man and wife. Callum, you may kiss your bride.'

But Carol beats him to it.

A high-decibel cheer, accompanied by whoops, whistles and stamping feet fills the room.

We finally prise them apart and they dance back down the aisle. I follow closely behind them and, as soon as we're clear of the room, make a bolt for the nearest loo. I lunge into a cubicle, slam the door and sit on the closed lid.

I stay here for what seems like hours. I'm completely numb and thoughts are crashing around in my head. So what should I do? Should I marry Sam? Should I find out what Joe's 'big mistake' is and hope that he's come back for me? Should I go and find Tom and try to give our relationship another go? Should I punch Doug Cook in the mouth? And why are Nick and Phil here? And where can I find a black wig and glasses that will disguise me enough to get me out of this hotel without facing any of them? It's official. My life sucks.

There's a bang on the door.

'Cooper, are you in there?' It's Jess.

'No.'

'Cooper, come on. You can't stay in there all night. Okay, so I know it's a bit claustrophobic in there, a bit crowded with guys who've played with your wobbly bits, but you have to come out sometime.'

'I don't.'

'Yes, you do. C'mon, Carly, you've never shied away from anything in your life.'

Does she have a short memory?

'Yes, I have. I'm a born coward.'

'Look, Carly, just come out. Carol is looking for you for the photographs and if she has to come in here, she'll take the door off its hinges. Don't let her down.'

That does it. Reluctantly, I open the door.

Jess hands me a brush and a make-up bag. An ice pack and a brown paper bag would have been a better option.

* * *

The first face I see is Doug Cook's. I swing round to avoid him, but he moves like Road Runner and is in front of me before I can escape.

'I need to talk to you, Carly.'

'Why? Want me to return the knives that you used to stab me in the back?' Cutting.

He's silent for a moment.

'I deserved that. And more. Look, I wanted to say sorry. Me and Callum have sorted stuff out and he was good enough to invite me today. I'd like to sort things with you too. I know it won't mean much to you, but I really am sorry. I was a complete prick.'

No arguments there. But then I haven't exactly treated him well either. What's the point? What's the point of staying pissed off with someone for the rest of my life? Especially someone who is my brother's mate.

'Okay, Doug. Let's just forget the whole thing; call it quits.'

He smiles.

'Carly, I've been looking for you everywhere,' says a voice from behind me.

Sam! I introduce him to Doug. Sam stares at him and then growls in his face. Subtle.

Doug runs for his life.

'Sam, I need to talk to you.'

'I know.'

'I love you, but I can't marry you. You were right; too much has happened. I'm so sorry.'

'I know.' He nods his head in resignation.

I look at him in surprise. Has he developed psychic powers?

'I'll always love you, Carly.'

I smile and kiss him.

'Tell me,' he asks, 'do I still have to pretend to be your boyfriend? Only there's a rich woman in there who owns some model agency. Says she's on her own and looking for some company.'

I choke with laughter. 'Go for it, Sam. Knock yourself out.'

There's a tap on my shoulder.

Shit, who's next? Why don't they just form a fucking queue? If I had any emotions left, they'd be draining out of me and forming a puddle on the floor.

I turn to face Tom McCallum. Sandwich in one hand and a woman in the other.

'Carly, thanks for inviting me. It's been great seeing everyone again.'

I didn't want to spoil the moment by explaining that I didn't actually extend the invitation.

'No problem, Tom. I was sorry to hear about your mum and dad.'

He looks surprised. Join the club.

'How did you hear about them?'

'It's a long story.' He clearly didn't know we'd been to Ireland to look for him then. It was probably just as well. Who's this?' I ask, holding out my hand to the female by his side.

'Shit, sorry, this is my wife, Ellen. Ellen, this is Carly Cooper.'

That explains the weight, good old home cooking.

She shakes my hand. 'It's good to meet you. I've heard a lot about you.'

Wish I could say the same – I'd have saved myself a bloody fortune.

'It's good to meet you too. I hope we'll have a chance to chat later. Right now I have to go and have my photo taken. It's been great seeing you both.'

I turn on my heel. I'd rather be having a kidney removed without anaesthetic than subjecting myself to much more of this. I head for the door – apparently the photographs are being taken in the garden outside – but Joe is blocking it.

'Carly, I need to talk to you. Everything's gone wrong with Claus and you're the only person who'll understand.'

Oh, yes. I am the oracle of all knowledge when it comes to life and relationships.

'What's wrong, Joe? What's happened?'

He tells me that he and Claus are finished. Apparently, due to some temporary aberration of the brain, Joe had allowed himself to be chatted up and taken for a drink by a guy he'd met in the club. Just as he leaned over to kiss the guy goodbye, he got stuck in a headlock and ended up in a full-scale snog. He's obviously got the same kind of luck as me, because at that very moment Claus walked by and saw him. That night when he got home, the locks had been changed and his clothes were in a wheelie bin. Now he needs a plan to get Claus back and wants my advice and help.

'Joe, I hate to point out the obvious, but there is nobody on the planet with a sadder love life than me. I've systematically worked my way around half the men in this room and I'm still bloody single. So no, I'm not going to give you any advice. If I did, you'd probably be doomed to a life of bitter loneliness, but I am here if you need a shoulder to cry on.'

May as well make the offer. By the looks of things, it's the closest I'm ever going to get to physical intimacy for the rest of my life.

He leans over to give me a hug. Over his shoulder, I can see Callum waving frantically at me. The photographer must be getting impatient. I'm just about to extricate myself when I see a taxi thundering up the driveway. Oh no. Who is it now? It can't be any of my guys – they're all inside stuffing their faces with vol-au-vents and chipolatas.

It halts and the passenger flies out. I let go of Joe and turn him round. The look on his face as he sees Claus running towards him is almost enough to make me smile. Bearing in mind the day I've had, that's right up there with raising the dead.

* * *

I pose for an hour with a benign smile on my face while an assortment of guests are dragged out of the hotel and placed around us. There can't be anyone left to snap – I'm sure that last lot were the maintenance staff.

'Right, I want a photo of just me and the girls,' Carol announces.

The rest of the crowd stands to one side as Carol, Jess, Sarah and I try to squeeze into the frame with Kate and her bump.

'Okay, my lovely ladies, say cheese,' the photographer shouts.

'Urgh, he's smarmy,' Jess whispers and the five of us scream with laughter.

I want to frame this one and put it on my wall. That is, if I ever have a wall again.

'Okay, now I want one with the girls and their partners.'

Bollocks! What do I do? Why can't he have said 'past partners', then I'd have a multiple choice.

Kate reaches for Bruce and Jess grabs Basil. I think she just wants photographic evidence of their affair. The tabloids will pay a fortune for that.

Never mind, Sarah doesn't have a partner either, so she can be mine. I look around for her. Where has she gone? Then I spot her – heading back to the hotel with Nick Russo.

'Kate,' I whisper, pointing in their direction, 'What's Sarah doing with Nick?'

'Oh shit, I forgot to tell you. They're engaged. They've been seeing each other since you left St Andrews. He proposed to her last night on a boat out on the loch. It was so romantic.'

Great. Bloody, sodding, pissing great.

There's nothing else for it. I run into the hotel and grab Sam, much to the annoyance of the middle-aged, overdone, over-jewelled woman he's nestled in the corner with.

'Sam, I need you to perform one last task in your capacity as my fake fiancé.'

I frogmarch him outside and we grin for the camera. Another crisis averted.

Raindrops start to fall, so we all rush back inside for cover. I can't take much more of this. I want to go home. Slight problem. I wouldn't know where to go. Where is the nearest homeless shelter?

My mum appears from nowhere, startling me. 'Carly, darling, you look terrible.'

'Hi Mum, nice to see you too.'

'Where's that lovely boyfriend of yours? I was sitting next to him during the service. He was charming, darling.'

'He's not my boyfriend any more, Mum.'

'My goodness, that was over quick. Mind you, I'm not surprised; you never seem to hang on to anyone for very long, do you, dear?'

That's it! My nerves snap and I ceremoniously and very publicly lose control of any sense of dignity I ever had.

'He is not my boyfriend now, Mum, because he's an escort whom I asked to come with me today and pretend to be my boyfriend so that I wouldn't have to explain to people like you why I'm thirty, single, unemployed, homeless...' I can't stop. I'm a runaway train doing a hundred miles an hour and heading for a brick wall '... And so far into debt that I'm fucking drowning. It's not a man I need, Mum, it's a good lawyer and legal bloody aid.'

The whole room is now silent; two hundred open mouths in the middle of two hundred startled faces, all staring at me.

I turn and rush back outside, running through the rain until I can't run any more. I slump down on the banks of the loch and put my head in my hands. I sob until I can't even remember which part of my disaster of a life I'm crying about. How could I have been so stupid? What possessed me to gamble with everything I ever had? I should have played it safe, bided my time and just waited for things to happen. How could I honestly have believed that I could go charging around the world, meet Mr Right and live happily ever after? I'm a fool. A sad, pathetic fool.

'I hear you need the services of a good lawyer.'

A sad, pathetic fool who's now hearing voices in her head. At least now I can plead insanity in the bankruptcy courts.

'Thought maybe I'd offer my services.'

My head snaps up. I recognise that voice!

'Mark?'

Mark Barwick is leaning against a tree five feet behind me, a smile on his face, his wavy brown hair still flopping into his eyes, his underpants still on over his trousers. I might be making that last bit up.

'What are you doing here?' I stammer. 'I didn't see you inside.'

'I'm Callum's lawyer. We've kept in touch since school. I couldn't make it earlier because I was wrapping up a big case. I just arrived in time to hear your farewell speech. Quite a story.'

I close my eyes. Mark. First love, first fumble, first naked breast Mark. Slept with him behind Doug's back, Mark. Don't tell me he's come out here to gloat.

'Yeah, well you've had your laughs now.'

'It's not laughs I was looking for.'

I hear him approach me. He reaches down and takes my hands, pulling me up to face him.

'Although, I'd take that as part of the package.'

He kisses me. Slowly, gently. Oh my God, I'd forgotten how good he was at that.

Suddenly, I pull back.

'Mark, I need to ask you something first.'

'What?' he replies, puzzled.

'Are you married or gay? Have you ever been prone to psychotic acts of vengeance? And have you ever been paid for sex?'

He throws his head back and roars with laughter. He eventually composes himself enough to speak.

'Not that I know of.'

I smile and curl my fingers through his hair.

'Good. Permission to proceed granted.'

I almost got another snog. Almost.

'CARLY!!!!' It's a hysterical Sarah.

'Over here,' I yell.

She runs towards us, gasping for breath.

'It's Kate. Her waters have broken and they've called an ambulance. She's screaming for you; wants you to go with her.'

Panic! 'I have to go, it's an emergency!' I say as I kiss Mark, then start to run after Sarah.

I'm ten feet away when he shouts, 'Cooper, is your life always like this – one drama after another?'

'Always,' I reply, grinning.

'Well, I suppose I'd better get used to it, then.'

And as I watch him laugh and shake his head, I think...

What if... there's a happy ending after all?

EPILOGUE

ONE YEAR LATER

I've been Mrs Barwick for six months now. Mark always jokes about two things: one is that he's spent his life saving my ass and the other is that he always had money in the bank until he met me. His wedding present to me was to pay off my credit cards, much to the relief of the financial institutions involved. My present to him was to throw three packets of contraceptive pills, two diaphragms and a family size box of condoms (you can never be too careful) down the loo and start trying for his much-wanted brood. Unfortunately, my contraceptive armoury wasn't biodegradable; we kept our local plumber in business for a week. We decided to settle in London and he transferred to his company's office here. I don't want to be nauseatingly sentimental, but God, I love him. He's everything. We fit perfectly and I still can't believe that the right guy for me was there all along, and I didn't see it.

Our future kids will have two gorgeous cousins to play with as Carol and Callum are expecting twins next month. Carol is delighted about it now, but it took her six months to get over the shock of losing her figure. She's covered up every mirror in the house. They can't decide on names for the babies. We suggested 'American' and 'Express'; at least then she'll bond with them immediately.

Michael finally danced with Kate's sister, Karen, at the wedding and they've been together ever since. Or so we think. They went into Michael's bedroom twelve months ago and they've yet to come out.

Sarah and Nick also got married this year. Sarah is still studying and hopes to be a qualified teacher by next summer. Nick treats her like a princess. They were made for each other.

Basil is a thing of the past. Jess tipped an ice bucket over him at Kate's millennium party and he was last seen heading back to his wife, his tail firmly between his legs. We read in the papers the next week that she'd rejected him, though. Seems she's shacked up in Brisbane with the French rugby player; she told the *Sun* that she'd never realised what a real orgasm could feel like. Jess is now awash with passion for the very journalist who exposed her affair to the nation. It brings a whole new meaning to having press contacts.

My mum and dad are talking about reconciling. My mum has ditched Ivan and my dad's on some twelve step recovery process, having finally admitted that he drinks too much. Trouble is, he can't seem to get past the step where he has to walk by a pub without entering it. Mum is ever hopeful though. In some crazy way, I think she missed having someone to nag.

We see a lot of Joe and Claus. They decided to make 'J.C.'s Heaven' an international chain and opened their second one in London last month. Claus now doesn't let Joe out of his sight. I don't think Joe minds.

Phil and Lily came to the opening too, as did Tom and Ellen. They all stayed at our house for a week and I was sad to see them go. Still, we'll see them again at American and Express's christening. Carol couldn't decide who to pick as godparents, so they've ended up with twelve. It'll be like the Last Supper at the top table.

Doug Cook won't be there. He's gone into hibernation since Saskia left him. She was 'spotted' by a film producer who was on one of her flights and she's now in LA, testing for *Baywatch*.

She'll probably meet Sam there. He's been signed up to play the lead role in the movie based on his screenplay, *The Gigolo*. I believe he did all his own research for the part.

And Kate? Well, Kate's been fired from her job for threatening a diva client with a hot-brush. It's probably for the best. Since Bruce won the award of 'UK Architect of the Year', she's been frantically busy moving house, hiring nannies and cleaners, shopping and socialising. Now *she's* the one having her hair done every week. We live next door to each other now so we see each other every day. Bruce and Mark joke that we should get a bridge built between the two houses to save us from getting wet when it rains. We took their idea literally – the builders are coming to give us a quote tomorrow.

I sometimes wonder if I made a mistake by chasing my rainbow, but I know I didn't. I've found everything I ever wanted. From now on, there'll be no more 'what ifs...?' No more uncertainty. We've all got life sussed out.

'Sometimes I can't believe we all managed to settle down and sort out our lives,' Kate says one Sunday morning as we sit around her kitchen table eating brunch. 'Especially you, Cooper,' she adds, to the amusement of the others.

'I know. It's miraculous,' I tell her, breaking off a chunk of cinnamon bagel from the pile on the plate in front of me. 'We're like fully formed grown-ups.'

'You know what I was thinking about the other day though?' Carol asks, then waits for an answer, as if we could genuinely read her thoughts. Eventually she realises that no one is going to take a guess and she carries on. 'What will we all be like when we're fifty? Because you know what they say, with age comes maturity. And bunions, but we can get them lasered off.'

There were giggles and groans all round.

'I reckon we'll be drama-free and enjoying quiet, peaceful lives,' Jess offers.

'Really?' asks Sarah, one eyebrow raised in cynicism, and I catch her glancing at me.

'I agree with Jess,' I say indignantly. 'Look, I've already had enough dramas and disasters to last a lifetime. There's no way I'm messing up my life again.'

The others nod in agreement and I sit back, satisfied, happy and positive that from now on I'm in for a smooth ride.

But what if… what if I couldn't be more wrong?

ACKNOWLEDGMENT

Twenty-one years ago, I was working as a sales manager and had been married for five years to a bloke I got engaged to a week after I met him. I was a bit spontaneous like that.

And despite having a good job, a nice flat and a first name relationship with our local travel agent, I was in the midst of a premature mid-life crisis on two fronts. I'd been trying to get pregnant for years but my ovaries weren't obliging, and I'd harboured a dream to be an author ever since I was a teenager who, like Carly Cooper, secretly read eighties bonkbusters using the light on my electric blanket so I wouldn't get caught.

'I just want to be a writer,' I'd wail at my husband. Eventually, the poor man snapped. 'Well, maybe it would help if you actually wrote something,' he suggested gently.

Despite being knee deep in a self-indulgent whirlpool of woes, I had to admit he had a point. The problem was, I had no idea where to start. I'd never written a word of fiction, or been part of a creative writing group, or studied at college or university, so I had absolutely no idea how to pen a book.

However, I had a story floating about in my head, so I decided to try. For the next fortnight, I wrote every night after work and then sent my first ever 10,000 words off to agents and publishers.

On a chilly afternoon in March, I got a phone call to offer me a book deal. Twenty minutes later I discovered I was pregnant. A parade, a brass band and a Red Arrow flyover wouldn't even have come close to our feelings of celebration.

In November 2000, my first son was born and in January 2001, my first novel, What If? was released.

Two decades, two sons and twenty-six novels later, I've been lucky enough to have made a career out of writing. There have been many high points and some awful lows, disappointments and jubilations, skint panics and sales peaks, but I'm still here and happier than ever to have found a home with the brilliant team at Boldwood Books.

A few months ago, my first novel came up in a chat, and it set off a thought in my mind. Where would those characters be now, twenty years later? Would they still be friends? Would their dreams have come true? Would they have had happy lives?

I was desperate to answer the questions, so for the last few months I've been locked away writing the sequel to What If?. It's called What Now?, and it will be released in January 2021, twenty years after these characters first made it to the book shelves. I'm loving spending my days with them again.

The 20th Anniversary of my first book also feels like a great time to thank the people I'm eternally grateful to.

I first worked with Amanda Ridout and Caroline Ridding over a decade ago and I'm so happy to have joined them, the wonderful Nia Beynon and the rest of the fantastic team when they set up Boldwood Books in 2019. Ladies, thank you for your endless encouragement and for being the finest publishers I've ever worked with. Caroline, you deserve extra points for being my brilliant editor, a force of nature who inspires me and always has faith that we'll get there, even when it's all going wrong. Which it often is!

Thanks to the copy editors and proof readers, and to all the reviewers, bloggers and book sellers who have supported me so faithfully with every new release. I appreciate every one of you.

Thank you to the incredible women in my life, the pals who sit round my kitchen table, the far-away friends who are always on the other end of the phone, the aunts, cousins, sisters-in-law, nieces and grandmothers who have cheered me on.

Thanks to my husband, John, my sons, Callan and Brad, and my stepdaughter, Gemma, for the love, the laughs, and for twenty years of bringing me tea while I thump the keys on my laptop.

And finally, thank you, thank you, thank you, to all of you have read my books over the years. You've changed my life and I couldn't ask for more.

Except maybe that parade, a brass band and a Red Arrow flyover...

Much love,

Shari xx

PS – As always, I'd love to know what you think – I'm on facebook, twitter, Instagram and my website is at www.sharilow.com

What Now?, the next chapter in the life of Carly Cooper, will be published by Boldwood Books in January 2021.

MORE FROM SHARI LOW

We hope you enjoyed reading *What If?*. If you did, please leave a review.

If you'd like to gift a copy, this book is also available as an ebook, digital audio download and audiobook CD.

Sign up to Shari Low's mailing list for news, competitions and updates on future books.

http://bit.ly/ShariLowNewsletter

My One Month Marriage, another warm and insightful novel from Shari Low, is available to buy now.

ABOUT THE AUTHOR

Shari Low is the #1 bestselling author of over 20 novels, including *My One Month Marriage* and *One Day In Winter,* and a collection of parenthood memories called *Because Mummy Said So.* She lives near Glasgow.

Visit Shari's website: www.sharilow.com

Follow Shari on social media:

facebook.com/sharilowbooks

twitter.com/sharilow

instagram.com/sharilowbooks

bookbub.com/authors/shari-low

ABOUT BOLDWOOD BOOKS

Boldwood Books is a fiction publishing company seeking out the best stories from around the world.

Find out more at www.boldwoodbooks.com

Sign up to the Book and Tonic newsletter for news, offers and competitions from Boldwood Books!

http://www.bit.ly/bookandtonic

We'd love to hear from you, follow us on social media:

facebook.com/BookandTonic

twitter.com/BoldwoodBooks

instagram.com/BookandTonic

Milton Keynes UK
Ingram Content Group UK Ltd.
UKHW021319240823
427425UK00022B/716